D0209274

THE
OTHER
CHILD

Lucy Atkins is an award-winning features journalist and author, as well as a *Sunday (London) Times* book critic. She has written for many newspapers, including the *Guardian*, the *Times*, the *Sunday Times*, and the *Telegraph*, as well as for magazines such as *Psychologies, Red, Woman & Home,* and *Grazia*. She lives in Oxford, England.

THE
OTHER
CHILD

LUCY ATKINS

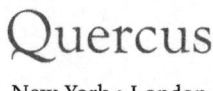

New York • London

Quercus

New York • London

Any member of educational institutions wishing to photocopy part or all of the work
for classroom use or anthology should send inquiries to permissions@quercus.com.

ISBN 978-1-62365-908-0

Library of Congress Control Number: 2015956645

Distributed in the United States and Canada by
Hachette Book Group
1290 Avenue of the Americas
New York, NY 10104

Manufactured in the United States

10 9 8 7 6 5 4 3 2 1

www.quercus.com

For my dad, Peter, and for beautiful Izzie—
never the other child, always my first

Tell all the truth but tell it slant—

—Emily Dickinson (poem 1263)

CHAPTER ONE

Greg had warned her that Boston summers were hot, but he never said it would be like this, sweltering and humid—like Bangkok, like suffocation. Joe will boil if she leaves him for long, even with the car doors open. A silvery line of drool trails from the corner of his mouth—a babyish touch on his nine-year-old face—but Tess resists the urge to wipe it away. She has to look at the house more closely before he wakes up. She has to prepare herself for whatever lies behind its astonishingly unattractive mock Tudor facade so that she can convey confidence and optimism, show her son that this move is a great adventure, not a reckless mistake.

The house is on a corner plot on a wide, deserted street. Its front yard curves around one side of the property, with a wooden swing set and a driveway leading down to a garage under the back of the house. Greg described the street as "almost a cul-de-sac," but it is not a cul-de-sac, really; it is a curved residential road that joins two other residential roads that lead to more residential roads. She recognizes it all from Greg's grainy Skype tour, but in the flesh everything looks broader, taller, heftier.

She had imagined them renting a picturesque white clapboard New England home with a wooden porch—a porch swing, perhaps—an apple tree, and a mailbox with a little red flag. This house has none of those features. It has a porch, but it is red brick with a pitched roof that dominates the front. The upper half of the building is stucco, hatched with Tudor-style timbers. Tall, dense, prickly-looking trees, possibly leylandii, separate it from the house next door. Greg was very clear that this place is "a find." Family-size rentals, he says, are a rarity in a suburb where people buy and stay.

Tess touches her belly, resting her fingers on its new slopes. This will be their baby's first home, and when she and Greg are old, they will look back at photos of them all standing on this porch, frozen forever against these dark red bricks.

"It's perfect," he'd said when he called from Boston to tell her that he'd given the realtor a massive deposit without consulting her, without even emailing her a picture. His face had blurred in and out of focus on her phone screen; he was in a public place, probably the cafeteria at Children's Hospital. She could see people in the background carrying trays or coffee cups, many wearing scrubs. "You're going to love it, Tess. I know you will. There's a great elementary school, a big park, a cute little main street with a couple of cafés, a bar, an artisan bakery, a market, a yoga studio. It's all very green and pleasant, absolutely no crime, and only twenty minutes from downtown on the highway. It's the perfect little town."

"I thought it was a suburb."

"We call suburbs towns."

She noted the "we." After fifteen years in London, Greg had seemed to feel no affinity with his homeland. His only remaining American traits were his accent, his handwriting, and an ongoing despair at British customer service. But now, suddenly, it was "we."

"You weren't answering your mobile, and I had to grab it." A baby wailed somewhere near him, an abnormal, plaintive sound, disturbingly thin and off-key. "Three other families were due to view the place after me this morning; it was going to go. But you'll love it, honey, I promise. It's not too far from Children's—maybe a fifteen-, twenty-minute commute max. There's three bedrooms, three baths, a big yard for Joe. A ton more space than we have now—"

"Three *baths*?"

He grimaced, his eyes half shut, and it took her a moment to realize that the connection had failed, leaving his handsome face frozen in a sinister, pixelated rictus, halfway to a smile.

She had always thought Greg liked her tall house on the outskirts of town, with the cornfield behind it and views of the Downs, improbably green in springtime, lightening to biscuit through summer, and, as autumn wore on, darkening and thickening into wintry browns. When he moved in, he had been charmed by the sloping floors and the wood-burning stove, her own photographs hanging next to her father's paintings, shelves crammed with books, old Polaroids tucked behind ceramics, Joe's drawings peeling off the fridge, things balancing on other things, and the light pouring in. He had said he did not want to change a thing.

Upon his leasing the American house, her chest had tightened at the thought of everything she'd be leaving behind.

"Greg? Are you still there? Greg?" But he didn't respond: FaceTime had definitely ended.

She is sweating already as she walks up the path. The effort of moving oxygen into her lungs feels overwhelming, as if a hot hand has closed over her mouth and nose. Close-up, the brickwork looks haphazard, with some bricks sticking out at angles and some larger than others. She remembers Greg zooming in on this feature in his after-the-fact Skype tour, saying that the mortar technique was fashionable in the 1920s, when the house was built. It looks to her like a structural defect, but he will have read about Massachusetts architecture somewhere, probably when he was at medical school here, and stored this fact away in his massive mental database.

She is going to have to trust him that this house is a find. Perhaps he is picking up cultural nuances that she can't. The front door looks like something out of a fairy tale: oversize, its dark wood studded with brass. She rifles through her bag for the keys. Somewhere behind her a bird rasps a repetitive *ha-ha, ha-ha,* and a mower hums. She feels as if she is hovering above herself, bewildered at how she can possibly be standing here, on the brink of this new life.

The speed of it all has been dizzying. In just a few months she has gone from the secure routines of Joe's school runs, his playdates and Saturday football, and her own photographic assignments and projects, to estate agents and house movers, flight bookings, new schools, visa forms, pediatricians, "ob/gyns," as they call them here, health insurance, American bank accounts, rental agreements. And now it is done. They are here.

Joe's school place has been taken by a child from Somerset; a Dutch family will move into their house today; her studio in the collective has been taken by a feminist conceptual artist who fills handbags with lard; and her old Ford is now owned by a math teacher. This is what death must be like: your space in the world simply closing over, like a pool of water when you lift out your hand. A wave of nausea rises through her: morning sickness, heat, jet lag—perhaps all three.

She really can't find the keys. She straightens, her head spinning, and looks back at the rental car. It squats like a silver insect, wings spread as if it is about to buzz and hum and take off with Joe inside. Behind it, on the other side of the road, a heavy brick house sits on a plot hacked out of the hillside. Steps zigzag up a steep rock garden to the front door. She imagines the building creaking, heaving, sliding off its foundations, and cruising over to flatten the car, the fence, the mock Tudor house, before moving inexorably down the slope, through the leafy streets beyond.

She bends back to her bag, digging deeper. Her T-shirt is sticking between her shoulder blades now, and her jeans have shrink-wrapped themselves to her thighs, the waistband already too tight, even worn low this way, under her belly. At eighteen weeks she is already much bigger than she was at this stage with Joe. She should have traveled in something cooler, but it was raining when they left

England, the kind of August day that makes British people dream of emigrating.

Nell was there to wave them off in the taxi—they both knew an airport good-bye would be too hard. "Look after yourself." Nell's voice had quavered. "And Joe—and this baby. I can't believe I'm not going to be there when it's born."

"Just come visit soon, OK?"

"I will." Nell pulled back, swiping at tears. "And if it doesn't work out, if for any reason it doesn't work out, just remember you can always come home. Nothing's irreversible." She stopped herself and tried to smile, pushing back her dark, curly hair, the dimples on either side of her mouth deepening. "But of course, you know, it's going to work out just fine! It'll be great!"

It was the first time that Nell had let any doubts show. Over the past few months she had made a phenomenal effort to be a supportive friend. But from the outside, this whole venture must seem reckless and impulsive.

When she'd agreed to marry Greg, she had not even known him a full four seasons.

For a moment this small fact yawns up at her, exposing the lunacy of standing here, alone and keyless, thousands of miles from home, while he is at a conference in San Diego, California.

She has been waking at dawn every day lately, her head crowded with doubts about the wisdom of moving Joe, leaving all her work contacts, giving birth in a foreign medical system, in a country in which 90 percent of the population owns a gun. And as Greg slept next to her, she would try to calm herself by going back over the reasons she had chosen to do this—other than loving Greg.

With her ex, David, posted to New York, it made sense for Joe to be in the same country as his dad. And it was surely good for any child to experience a different culture. She would build up new photography contacts in America, the hospital had world-class obstetricians, and Greg was right: this suburb was officially one of the safest places to live in the whole United States. But despite this list, in those early-morning hours, there seemed to be so many possible fracture points, so many things that could go wrong.

She shoves objects around in the bottom of her bag. She can picture the key envelope on the kitchen counter as she did her final walk-through that morning. Greg is not flying into Boston until tomorrow. She straightens her shoulders. If she has left the keys at home, then she'll just have to deal with it. She has a credit card. This is civilization. She imagines getting back into the rental car and driving Joe around, looking for a hotel, motel, or B and B, trying to make it all seem like fun.

She glances at her watch. It is midafternoon in California. Right now, Greg will be in a room full of cardiac surgeons, and he will not hear his phone even if it is on. She squats and tips her bag upside down. Tissues and cereal bars spill out onto the doormat, a Simpsons comic, her paperback, her scarf, receipts, lipstick, hairbrush, hair ties, hand cream. And then there it is, the smooth envelope. It must have been lying flat in the base of her bag.

KEYS. Greg's assertive capitals on the front feel somehow accusatory. Get. A. Grip. Tess.

She scrapes everything back into her bag, straightens up, and fits the bigger of the two keys into the lock. The mechanism is stiff, and she has to wiggle the key around.

She pushes open the front door. The harsh scent of antiseptic—some kind of cleaning product—instantly hits her throat, and she is thrown straight back in time. It is the smell of her childhood, of clinics, of institutions; she can feel her father's warm hand around hers, hear their shoes squeaking as they walk down too-quiet corridors. For a second she stands very still, waiting for these feelings to subside. It has been a long time since this happened. She shuts her eyes.

Then opens them. The foyer is cool and dim, with white tiles, white walls, a steep wooden staircase ahead, a vast parquet-floored room on her right with a wide brass fireplace, another room—a dining room—on her left, and a tiled corridor leading past the stairs to the back of the house, presumably to the kitchen. Hot air is seeping in behind her. Joe really will boil in the car. She has to get him out.

She turns and steps back through the porch and out again into the heat, blinking under the white sun. She hurries back down the path away from the silent, waiting house with all the empty, disinfected rooms that she has yet to enter.

CHAPTER TWO

Greg calls from San Diego as she is brushing her teeth in the pink and gray en suite. His voice is pumped with conference adrenaline, fast and staccato. "Hey! Honey! You made it. You found the house OK? The directions worked? What do you think?"

"It's . . . I don't know . . . It feels very weird right now, all empty and echo-y. It's so big—it's enormous, Greg." She looks at herself in the mirror: ghostly, shadow-eyed, lips white from toothpaste, hair scraped back, neck crooked to the phone.

"I know, right? Space at last!"

"It just feels a bit odd here without you."

"Of course it does—it's bound to. I miss you so much, Tess. I should be there with you—first night, no furniture, no me. I don't like to think of you and Joe alone there like that. I really wish you'd checked into a hotel."

"I know. I kind of wish I had now, too. You were right. So, how's the American Heart Association?"

"Fine—full on. Shit, dammit, sorry—someone's . . ."

She hears a woman's voice but can't make out any words. "Greg?"

His voice is now muffled. She pictures him standing in a conference center lobby, tall and handsome in a dark suit, next to yucca plants or a little marble fountain—and then he is back. "Sorry, sorry. I have to go. Someone's here that I have to talk to . . . I love you, OK? I love you so much—I'll be there first thing tomorrow. Sleep tight. See you tomorrow. Stay safe."

"Wait. I can't remember what time your flight—"

But he is gone.

There are no blinds or curtains anywhere on the top floor, and even though she knows that nobody can see her as she climbs onto the inflatable mattress with the lights off, she can't quite shake the feeling of exposure.

The cloying heat envelops her body. Cicadas tick rapidly in the trees outside, like the mechanism of a wind-up toy—she wasn't expecting cicadas in the suburbs—and somewhere in the distance she hears an anguished yipping, yowling sound. Shadows spread from the corners of the room, swelling from the walk-in closet and the en suite, as if her loneliness has burst out of her to fill the room with its dark, inappropriate blooms.

Something is rustling below the window, somewhere in the trees and shrubs that separate this house from its neighbor. Whatever it is, it sounds big. She sits up, unsteadily. The rustling stops, and the rattle of the cicadas rises up again.

It feels wrong to have Joe across the landing in his own room on this first night in America, but he'd insisted, showing a new streak of independence that she had not expected in such a strange situation. Perhaps he is instinctively distancing himself to make room for the baby. If so, she is not ready for that. He is only nine years old. He is still her baby, really.

They waited until after the twelve-week ultrasound to tell him of her pregnancy, and his reaction was thoughtful, if slightly concerned, as if they had announced that a distant relative was coming to stay.

"Is it a boy?" He didn't even look up from his LEGOs.

"We don't know yet, love."

"When will it be born?" He pressed a brick back into his LEGO ambulance.

"In the middle of January, after Christmas, when we're in America."

"Will it have to share my new room?"

"No, buddy," Greg said. "You're going to have your very own room, way bigger than your room here."

"But, then, where will the baby sleep?"

"Well, at first it will be in with me and Greg." She reached out and stroked his hair off his forehead. "Like you, when you were little. And then it'll go in its own cot in a bedroom of its own, next to yours."

He had not wanted to talk about the baby since then. Whenever she mentioned it, he looked politely uninterested and changed the subject. Sometimes she wonders if he is picking up on Greg's feelings, their deep, subconscious, male brains siding against this tiny interloper.

When she told Greg she was pregnant, he was bending down to pull on a sock, and it was as if someone had pressed a Pause button. She watched the smooth strips of muscle across his back quiver as he lowered his foot, then turned to face her. His dark hair, still wet from the shower, was swept back from his forehead, giving his face a looming severity.

She held up the pregnancy-test stick.

"Jesus. How is this possible?" he said. "You're on the pill."

"You're the doctor—you tell me." She tried to laugh, but it didn't quite work. She was expecting shock, but not this—not accusation. Suddenly she felt as if she was teetering above a dark space, knowing she must fall but not knowing how far.

Greg sat down, heavily, on the bed next to her, staring straight ahead. "Wow," he said in an odd, flat voice. "Tess. I mean . . . Shit."

"I didn't plan this," she said. "I have no idea how this has happened."

He took her hand then, as if realizing how unfair he was being. "God, no—I know. I know, but . . . Jesus, Tess. What do you want to do?"

She pulled her hand away. "What do you mean, what do I want to do?"

"Well, it's early, right? We have options."

"Are you talking about an *abortion*?"

"Termination is one choice."

She felt the anger rise inside her and got off the bed, standing in her pajamas, staring down at him. "How could that be your first thought?"

"But we were both very clear," he said. "We weren't going to have a baby."

"I didn't plan this, Greg!"

"No, I know you didn't."

"Then . . ."

He looked at his watch suddenly. "Fuck, Tess—if I don't go now, I'm going to miss the train." He stood up, facing her, reaching out his hand, his voice rising. It was not his fault. She had chosen a very bad moment to tell him. Fifty miles away, in London, sick children were waiting for him. He could not miss the London train that morning, even for this.

He yanked on a shirt. "Listen, we'll talk about this later. I love you. I'm sorry—this is shock, that's all; you must be in shock, too . . . This is not . . . We didn't . . . Look, I'll call you later, when I'm done, OK? I love you." He leaned down and kissed her on the mouth, looking into her eyes for a second before pulling away. His fingers moved swiftly down the buttons of his shirt. "We'll figure this out," he said, almost to himself. "We'll talk tonight."

But they didn't talk properly that night, because when he came home, he had been contacted about the Boston job, and he was elated, towering. It was an honor, an astounding opportunity. He had never planned to go back to the States, but Boston Children's Hospital had one of the best pediatric cardiology programs in the world, and a faculty position at Harvard Medical School—he'd be insane not to at least consider this, to fly over there and meet with them.

And now, just three months later, the job is secured, the move has happened, but the existence of this baby still feels subtly fraught. They don't seem to be able to talk about how they feel. Instead, they talk about practicalities: setting up prenatal care, the obstetrician—whom Greg knew at medical school, the choice of maternity care, the dates of all the checkups and scans, her physical sensations. What they never discuss is the actual baby—their child—who will be born in less than five months, changing their lives forever.

There is the sound again below the window—the rustling noise. She stiffens. The Boston Marathon bombers were gunned down in a leafy street just a couple of miles away. One was found bleeding in a boat in someone's backyard only fifteen minutes' drive from this house. She imagines what Greg's reaction would be if she were to admit that she was worried about fugitives in the shrubbery. When you spend your days treating gravely ill children, this sort of fear must seem point-lessly self-indulgent. She hears the yipping, yowling again—a dog? a coyote?—and the distant hum of traffic, the neutral buzz of lives stretching out for miles in all directions.

"Fuck you!"

She jumps.

"No. I mean it, really, fuck *you!*" It is a man's voice, close by. He spits each word. She sits up, the mattress swaying beneath her.

"I am not going to take this manipulative shit from you. Not again."

He sounds as if he is standing below her window, but, of course, he must be in the house next door.

"Wait—are you *laughing* at me now? Are you actually *laughing?* Seriously? I know what you're doing, and I'm not going to take this again. I mean it—no fucking way, not again."

Then she hears a woman's voice. She can't make out the words, just a low, persistent monotone. A door slams then, and she hears footsteps on a path, a car door, an engine, tires on pavement, passing the front of the house, growling around the corner, and vanishing into the streets beyond.

If Greg were next to her on the inflatable mattress, they'd prob-ably grab each other and laugh. She kneels up and peers over the window ledge. The neighbors' house is shielded by the jagged trees, but through the network of branches she can just see into their kitchen: hanging copper pots and wooden cabinets, green mosaic tiles, shelves of cookbooks, a stainless-steel blender, pictures on the fridge door—there are children in the house. She hopes that they are sleeping.

And then a figure appears at the kitchen window: a woman's face, round and pale, lit from above, features blurred, eyes like coals, hair massed on her shoulders. She stares out as if she is looking for something, or someone, in the trees—or perhaps into her next-door neighbors' downstairs rooms.

Tess lies back on the mattress and pulls the sheet over herself, even though she is too hot. Greg was right: it was a spectacularly bad idea to spend the first night here without him. It had seemed silly to pay extra for a hotel when they had this huge expensive house just sitting empty, but now she can see that this is not a good start. When his conference date changed, she should have booked herself and Joe into a hotel. The three of them should be starting this life together.

She feels a sudden wave of longing for him, to feel her husband's arms around her, his body weighing down the mattress next to her. She is used to his absences and, before she met him—not so long ago, really—to being alone with Joe. Usually when Greg is away, she misses his company, his conversation, his laughter, his touch, but a part of her expands contentedly into the space that he has left. Tonight feels different. Right now the longing is uncomfortable and uneasy, a metallic taste in the mouth, an ache behind the breastbone. She recognizes this feeling from long ago: a crumpled letter from childhood shoved beneath the door.

She glances at the clock. She has now been awake for almost twenty-four hours. No wonder she is feeling insecure. The man next door sounded positively demented. It occurs to her that she and Greg have never had a full-blown argument like that. Greg saves his passion for sex, and she certainly has no taste for hysterics. Nell and Ken, married for eighteen years, yell at each other openly, shamelessly, even in front of her sometimes, but they forget about it moments later, and while outrage and frustration might tinge their voices, there is never menace or hatred.

She hears the metallic clang of a window closing. All couples fight: fighting is normal. She and Greg will fight one day, too, and when he does unleash his anger, it will be impressive—she is sure of that.

She knows the darker side to Greg. The damage from what happened to him as a teenager manifests itself sometimes in introverted silences or the need to exert control. But this is what drew her to him in the first place. She had felt a vulnerability in him the first time they met, when she looked at him through the camera lens and, beyond the handsome architecture of his face, caught something haunted and pent up. She fell in love with him because of it. Maybe the fragile part of her recognized something similar inside him. She felt as if she knew his secrets.

The mattress undulates as she shifts onto her side. She closes her eyes, feeling nauseated again—travel-sick, homesick, heartsick, morning-sick, night-sick. The only thing to do is sleep, but sleep will not come, even though in England it is now dawn. She turns over and feels the baby flutter like a moth deep in the velvet darkness of her womb.

She wakes to the same repetitive bird she heard the evening before, a rasping, rhythmic sound like mocking laughter. Sunlight, diffused by the leaves outside the window, throws watery shapes across the hardwood floor. She is staring at a ceiling fan that somehow—God only knows how—she failed to notice the night before. She could have had it turning all night; instead, she'd sweltered on the rubbery mattress. Her sheets are tangled and damp. She is thirsty, queasy, and her head aches. She gulps lukewarm water from the glass next to the bed. She urgently needs to pee.

"Joey?" Her voice echoes off the ceiling as she wobbles up off the mattress. She pulls a pair of drawstring linen pants out of her suitcase, along with some underwear and one of the expensive T-shirts that Greg bought her before they came. He'd brought them back from Boston in a Nordstrom bag, four, in different colors, tissue-paper thin.

"You're going to need lightweight things," he said. He seemed to have forgotten the reality of her changing body. Already the T-shirts are almost indecent over her swelling breasts, and in just few weeks they will be riding up on her belly, unwearable. But she pulls on the white one, glad, for now, of its lightness against her hot skin.

"Joey? Where are you?"

"I'm here." His voice is high and echo-y, coming, she thinks, from the kitchen.

The en suite bathroom is so cramped, you can almost touch the sink from the toilet. As she pees, she notices a dark crack in the porcelain basin. She peers closer, but it is not a crack; it is a single hair, very long—nothing like her own fine, wavy, shoulder-length blond hair. She holds it up between her finger and thumb, then drops it into the sink, turning on the tap. It clings to the shining side. She gets off the toilet and swirls the water so that the hair is sucked down the drain.

The empty stairwell amplifies the slap of her flip-flops. She tries to ignore the smell of antiseptic cleanser. She will wash the floors herself today to dilute the odor before the moving truck arrives.

Joe is at the breakfast bar with the iPad. Greg must have fixed up Wi-Fi on one of his preparatory visits. Her son looks solid and definite, and her chest unclenches at the sight of him. She kisses the top of his head, but he doesn't look up. At home it would have depressed her to see him plugged in like this with the sun shining outside, but today any predictability feels welcome. You could take him to the top of the Empire State Building or dangle him over Niagara Falls, and he would still pull out a screen.

"What time did you wake up, love?"

"I don't have a clock." His tawny hair sticks up in waves and hillocks, his T-shirt is inside out, his hazel eyes wide and accusatory. "You didn't pack my alarm clock."

"No, I did—it's in your bag . . ." She stops herself. There is no point in arguing with a displaced and jet-lagged nine-year-old. "You know all our stuff is arriving this afternoon, don't you?"

She needs to walk around and decide where everything will go. She can already see that their furniture will not fill even half the space in this house. "It's coming in a huge container, all our furniture and your clothes and toys and all our books. Everything we packed up six weeks ago in England has traveled all the way across the Atlantic Ocean to here."

Joe still doesn't look up from his screen. He is a small, round-faced version of David, and when he is concentrating this way, he not only looks like his dad—even-featured, solidly built—he feels like him, self-contained and absorbed in something to which she has no access.

"Maybe we should call your dad and tell him you've arrived?"

"Is Dad coming?" He looks up. "Today?"

"Oh, no, love, not today, no. He's away working—remember, he told you? But he's going to come the moment he's back—in about three weeks, he thinks. I know he can't wait to see you. He wishes he could come sooner."

Joe's face falls. She shouldn't have said anything. Just because David is now based in New York does not mean that he is actually there. He will still spend most of his time traveling. She can't even remember where he said he was going this time—Kigali? Mogadishu? Baghdad?

"Greg's plane gets in soon, though," she says. But Joe is engrossed in his game again and does not even look up.

Greg has decided not to be pushy with Joe, but she sometimes wonders if he is any different with Joe than he is with his patients. He is genial, kind, and approachable but always slightly detached. But perhaps that's unfair—it's early days, and Greg has been away so much lately, crisscrossing the Atlantic, setting things up, finishing things off at Great Ormond Street Hospital. It is too much to expect him to have bonded with Joe. But surely this baby will change that. This baby is their shared biological tie. When it is born, it will knit them all together.

A trilling sound fills the kitchen, making them both jump and look at each other, big-eyed. She spots a cordless phone next to the fridge. She didn't know it was connected—Greg didn't say, and she doesn't even know their number here. She picks it up. "Hello?"

She hears only a hollow buzz.

"Hello?" She waits. "Hello?" The back of her neck begins to tingle. She can feel someone there, behind the white noise, listening but saying nothing.

"Greg?" she says. "Greg? Is that you?"

There is a click, and the line goes dead. She replaces the handset.

"Who was it?" Joe asks.

"Oh, nothing, nobody." She tries to sound breezy. "Just a wrong number."

"Can I have something to eat? I'm hungry."

"OK, I know. Me, too. Breakfast!"

She shakes herself into action, opening the cupboard above a shining Gaggia espresso machine that still has its tags on. The cupboard contains two plates, two cups, two glasses, a pouch of disposable cutlery, and a new, serrated kitchen knife. A Post-it has fallen off the door—she picks it up.

Bagels, butter, milk, and jam in fridge.

His writing is not a doctor's scrawl; it is clear and neat, with each line, angle, and curl thoughtfully spaced. There are no kisses or "love you"s, but that doesn't matter. He has thought of everything they'll need for their first morning, until their belongings arrive. A small part of her love for him, she knows, is rooted in his no-nonsense practicality, his efficiency—perhaps in simple gratitude that he is so unlike David.

David was useless in practical terms but prone to expansive, romantic gestures. Once, when Joe was eight months old, he showed up after six weeks in the Sudan with tickets to the opera in Verona. They couldn't afford the flight. Before Joe was born, she would take this sort of thing in her stride, but at home with a new baby, she felt the finances and practicalities throttle the romance, and David's absences began to feel willful and irresponsible. Nell has teased her about choosing another man whose profession takes him away a lot, and perhaps unconsciously that is what she's done. But Greg's way of loving—generous, fiercely organized, protective—never feels careless, and his absences are usually brief.

Sunlight pours through the French casement windows and doors, making the steel appliances gleam. She opens a few cupboards. There are, of course, no supplies yet—no herbs or spices, flour, baking powder, salt or pepper or cling wrap or paper towels or sponges. Without this domestic infrastructure, the kitchen feels precarious, like a film set that could be dismantled at any moment.

The shippers are due to call with their estimated arrival time. It will feel better once their things are here. In the end, almost all the packing and organization had fallen to her, because Greg was going back and forth between London and Boston, trying to sort out the job and the house. Other than the paperwork—which was substantial—his main contribution to packing had been to bring his four sealed boxes down from the attic and stack them in the hall.

The boxes were not labeled, but she recognized them from when he had moved in. They contained his old university things, some visa paperwork and essential documents such as his birth certificate. They were closed with masking tape, and it was clear that he did not want them opened, so she got the movers to put them in crates marked BASEMENT STORAGE. If Greg wanted to carry four sealed boxes wherever he went, that was his business.

She slices bagels and slides them into the toaster. Then she texts Nell:

We are here! All very odd. Huge, empty house. CICADAS. Wild foxes/ coyotes/dogs. Fridge you could live in. Shouting neighbors in the night. What on earth have I done? Xx

Alongside the kitchen is a wooden deck. It is painted white, peeling in places, shaded by the towering cypress trees that separate the property from the neighbors'. She fiddles with the locks and hauls the French doors open. A mesh screen stays in place. She drags this back, too, and it wobbles on its tracks. The air smells of cut grass and summer vacation. It is warm and muggy, even this early in the morning. She peers through the branches into the neighbors' backyard. It is modest for such a large house, mostly paved, with shrubs and wood chips but no flower beds.

She can see a low wooden building at the back with floor-to-ceiling windows. She is leaning over the railing to get a better look, when her eye catches a movement by the main house. It takes a moment for her to understand what she is looking at.

A woman is leaning against the side wall, camouflaged by shadows. Her long hair is loose, and she is wearing a vest top and yoga pants, her arms folded, holding a mug. She is staring over at Tess, but her round face is unsmiling.

Tess feels a tiny shiver pass across her skin and turns, walking to the farthest end of the deck, gripping the railing and looking down over the driveway at the back of the house. A basketball hoop hangs above it.

Maybe she should have waved or called out hello, but something in the woman's stillness had suggested an almost targeted hostility. She remembers her face at the kitchen window in the middle of the night, unnaturally still, as if watching for movement in her neighbors' downstairs rooms. She takes in a lungful of humid air. The neighbors' marital problems have nothing to do with her.

She looks at the branches of the trees. The house doesn't feel like part of a massive suburban sprawl, with the cut-grass smell, the birdsong, the whispering leaves all around. She tries to imagine Joe playing basketball in this driveway with new friends. And then, tentatively, as if biting into a potentially unripe fruit, she imagines sitting here, on this deck, with her new baby. She can feel the weight of its dense little body, tiny fingers curled around hers, hair so soft that it seems imaginary, and that new-baby smell—of green shoots, sweet dough. But, of course, when this baby is born, she won't be sitting out here, because it will be January, the dead of winter. And Boston winters, Greg has warned her, are brutal.

She feels a faint flickering in her belly and closes both hands over it. She is beginning to feel the baby, even at eighteen weeks, but perhaps it is unfair to expect Greg to connect with it yet. He was adamant from the start that he didn't want to be a father. He even mentioned it the first time he told her he loved her, as if the two statements were inseparable.

They were on the late train back from London, maybe a month after they had met; the car was empty, and he'd held her chin and looked into her eyes. "I'm completely in love with you," he said. And it hadn't seemed ridiculous, because she felt it, too. They fit together beneath the surface; she already knew that she belonged with him and nobody else. Then he said, gently but firmly, "I'm happy to have Joe in my life, but I don't want another child. Is that going to be a problem for you?"

She'd kissed him and reassured him that she was happy just with Joe, too. When Joe was smaller, she'd wanted another baby—she felt guilty that her son didn't have a sibling; she didn't want him to feel the sort of loneliness or responsibility for a parent that she had felt as a child—but then David had left, and gradually that longing had passed, and then they'd been content, just the two of them. But sometimes, now, she wonders what would have happened on the train if, instead of kissing Greg, she had pulled away, shaken her head, said that she did want another baby, that she longed for one—that she wanted his baby. Would he have pulled away, too? Changed his mind? Stopped loving her?

She thinks of the twelve-week ultrasound, when they held hands while the technician picked out a hand with tiny, identifiable fingers, the tight braid of a spine, a jawbone, a nose, two sharp leg-bones, and then, in the darkness, the squeezing knot of a heart. As she watched the map of their baby take shape on the screen, all her doubts evaporated, and she felt a rush of pure love—of joy. But Greg said nothing. She wanted to believe that he was overwhelmed, too, feeling the same things, but she wasn't sure. When the technician zoomed in on the baby's heart again, clicking, taking stills and measurements, Greg stepped closer, scrutinizing the images for abnormalities.

He will come around when he holds this baby in his arms for the first time. He has held thousands of infants but never his own—he has no idea how powerful it is to look down at your baby's face for the first time. She hears her phone beep in the kitchen. A text—Nell, probably. Joe will be waiting for a bagel. She walks back down the deck, keeping her eyes fixed forward. Her neck tingles as she steps inside. She knows she is being watched.

After breakfast, she goes onto the front porch. Greg said there were other families on their street, but it is the end of summer vacation, past eight in the morning, and the lawns are empty and silent except for the whirr and hiss of sprinklers. There are no flower beds, only shrubs and rock gardens and mown grass. Theirs, she realizes, is the only house with a fence.

A lawn mower buzzes nearby, and sunlight bounces off the windowpanes. She lifts a hand to shield her eyes. Perhaps the neighbors are looking out at her right now, but it is impossible to tell. She walks over to the fence and peers back at the house next door. It is a proper New England Arts and Crafts home with wooden clapboards painted a subtle green, a full-length porch, and—yes—a porch swing. Just the sort of house she'd imagined living in. All the blinds are drawn.

Then the front door bursts open. She shrinks back so that she is almost inside a tall shrub, then parts the branches and peers through. A man is on the porch, with a satchel, cropped brown hair. "Girls!" he yells over his shoulder. "Now!" His voice is unmistakable from last night, but it is more impatient than angry today. She watches him hop down the steps, pulling out a cell phone and scrolling through messages as he beeps open the locks of a car she can't see. He is wearing a pressed blue shirt and khakis, no tie. He is average size, attractive, clean-cut. She wonders what time he came back last night and where he went after yelling at his wife.

He glances up, as if he has sensed her, and she shrinks back. The leaves are prickly, a branch is digging into her rib cage, and pollen coats her lips and eyelids. She moves her leg, and a twig catches her ankle; then something trails across her face. She swipes up a hand

and pulls something sticky off her cheek—a big, brown, flickering spider drops down the front of her T-shirt. She jerks away, yanking herself off the branch, hearing the fabric rip; pieces of bark fall out as she flaps her shirt. A silver van is reversing out of the next-door driveway, and she finds herself standing by its open passenger window.

"Hey." The man leans over the passenger seat, grinning. "Everything OK?"

"I was . . . I was just . . ." She brushes herself off, unable to think of a reasonable explanation for hiding in a shrub. "We just moved in."

"Oh, you're English! I think I've seen your husband coming and going a few times—at least, I assume he's your husband. Tall, dark hair?"

"Yes, that's Greg. He's been here before, setting things up."

His smile stiffens. "My wife's met him."

Greg talked about signing the lease, getting keys, doing inventories with the realtor, blowing up mattresses, but he never mentioned meeting the neighbors.

"Well, I'm Josh."

"Tess."

"Nice to meet you, Tess. Welcome to the neighborhood. And now I have to get my girls to music camp."

She steps back, and he reverses fully into the street, yelling to "his girls" through his open window.

She walks over to the swing set and perches on it. There is now a triangular rip in the expensive white fabric of her T-shirt, and it is smeared with sap. She rocks, anchored by her toes, turning her face to the sky. Her ankle stings where the twig scratched it. This does not feel like a good start. A cloud floats across the sun, and small dark birds swoop to and fro as if lost.

"Hello, beautiful!"

She opens her eyes. Greg is striding across the lawn, his shirt a broad white sail against the sea of grass. She leaps off the swing, and he drops his bags, catching her in his arms, pulling her against him. She smells the staleness of airports on him, feels the warmth of his chest beneath the crisp cotton, and presses her nose into the crook of his neck, where he only smells of himself. He pulls back, they look at each other at arm's length, holding hands in the sunlight, and everything feels energized again, full and round and back in its rightful place.

CHAPTER THREE

It has only been four weeks, but already this is the time of day she dreads the most. The women gather in subgroups, holding travel mugs, wearing Lycra and Nikes, khakis and loafers, embracing, calling out to one another across the playground, making arrangements, sharing frustrations, information, and stories as their eyes skim over her.

She has never enjoyed the school gate, even at home. Nell, a member of the PTA, used to try to co-opt her into organizing cake stalls, quiz nights, and promises auctions, but even she gave up eventually. "You're just not a joiner," she'd said, "are you? You're a lone wolf."

But this level of discomfort is something else entirely. It is like being a gate-crasher at a party you never wanted to attend. The only other person standing alone is a woman in an ice-blue shift dress, on the edge of the playground. Tess squints through the sun and realizes it is the next-door neighbor, Helena.

She looks more groomed than she did at five-thirty this morning, when she was outside their house, talking to Greg.

Tess had woken up much earlier than usual, starving, with not a trace of nausea. She got up and rolled up the new blinds in the bedroom to find the street below bathed in rosy dawn light—and there was Greg, in running gear, talking with this woman. Her thick hair was in a ponytail, her body curved but athletic, and as the two of them talked, she raised her chin and ran both hands over her hair in a gesture that lifted her breasts in their Lycra vest. Greg glanced at them, then looked away.

When she heard the front door open, she went downstairs.

"Hey—what are you doing up?" Greg said. "It's not even six."

"I don't know, but I woke up starving. Was that our next-door neighbor?"

"Out there? Yeah."

"Did you run together?"

"What? No." He kicked off his sneakers.

"Is she nice?"

"You haven't met her yet?"

"Well, I've seen her a few times, but we haven't actually spoken."

He turned away to put his sneakers in the hall closet. "You should go say hi—she's pretty friendly. Her name's Helena, she's a doctor, and her kids go to Joe's school." He kissed her briefly on the mouth, then slipped past her, up the stairs, to the shower.

She tries to make eye contact across the playground, but Helena is typing into her phone, tapping one heel, leaning her shoulder on the knee of the sinister Humpty Dumpty statue at the side of the school building. It is a vast, bulbous, stone figure, the sort of thing first-graders must have nightmares about. Its gray eyes follow Tess as she crosses the playground.

She is almost there, when a chubby girl, around seven years old, runs past her—Helena's youngest. Helena looks up, says something sharply to her daughter, puts away her phone, and strides toward her silver Prius with the little girl trailing behind, dragging a Hello Kitty backpack. As she reaches the car, Helena looks back at Tess. Their eyes meet, and Tess raises a hand, but Helena gives no sign of recognition. She gets into the car and slams the door.

Tess turns back to the school, feeling her face flare. The snub was so obvious, she can feel the other mothers staring openly now. More children are pouring out the double doors, and she tries to collect herself, because Joe is going to emerge at any moment, pale and wild-eyed. A couple of times lately he has thrown his backpack at her feet and taken off across the nearby park toward the house.

And here he is, with a face as white as the puff of cloud above the redbrick building. She lifts a hand, and although she knows that he has seen her, he doesn't wave back; he just skims past, face closed, neck tight. She follows him across the road and into the park. Other children scamper in the sunshine, shouting, throwing baseballs and footballs, but Joe marches away. His arms are stiff by his sides; his backpack humps against his spine; he looks very small. She wants to run after him and fold her arms around him and hold him tightly, protect him against this unhappiness and stress, but she knows that if she tries to catch up, he'll only go faster. Two women glance at her, smile glassily, and murmur to each other she passes.

When she gets to the house, she can't see Joe, but a woman with a peroxide ponytail is standing on the porch, holding a huge plate of cookies. Her athletic legs, in cutoffs, are tanned, with veins creeping up the calves like vines.

"Hey! I'm Sandra Schechter. I live right across the street." She shows large, well-organized teeth, nodding at the tall house opposite. "I feel so bad for not coming over before. I've been traveling for work—you know how it is—but I brought you a little belated 'welcome to the neighborhood' gift."

"Oh, thank you. This is so kind." Tess takes the plate. It is decorated with stars and stripes and contains enough cookies to feed forty people.

"It's nothing!" Sandra's eyes are kind. "I'm just sorry it's taken me so long to come over and say hi. How're you guys settling in?"

Inside the house, the phone starts to ring. It does this at around the same time every day. Greg, Nell, and the obstetrician are the only people who have their home number, and when she picks up, the line is invariably dead.

"You're from England, right? Oh, my goodness, we just love England! We were in London last year for my niece's wedding . . ."

Then she remembers the phone ringing late last night, when she was almost asleep. Down in the kitchen she heard Greg answer it and say something in a low voice, then hang up. When he came upstairs, she'd surfaced from her half sleep to ask who was calling.

"Nobody. Wrong number." He pulled his T-shirt off over his head, obscuring his face. "Go back to sleep."

The answering machine clicks in now; she hears the distant burr of her own voice asking the caller to leave a message.

"I have to go get Kevin from the after-school program in a few minutes," Sandra is saying, "and drive him to his therapist, but I just wanted to, you know, stop by, say hi, let you know that I'm usually around on Fridays if you need anything. It must be a little lonely as a stay-at-home mom in a new place, huh? Or are you working?"

"Well, sort of, yes. I'm a photographer. I'm trying to finish a book."

"Oh, wow! A book? What's it about?"

"It's for a charity back in Britain. It's part of a campaign to support organ donation."

"Organ transplants?" Sandra's smile drops. "You're photographing transplants?"

"No, no, well, not the actual surgeries. I've taken pictures of hands—the hands of everyone involved in the donor process: doctors, nurses, the donor families, the recipients. The book's called *Hand in Hand*. It's to raise awareness and get people to sign up to the donor register."

Sandra nods, looking slightly queasy.

"I need to get it finished before my baby's born."

"Oh!" The smile lights back up. "I did wonder if you were . . . but you know what it's like: I didn't want to say anything, just in case! You never know, right? When's it due?"

"Mid-January." She hears Joe's backpack snagging on the brick-work somewhere behind the shrubs.

"You play tennis, Tess?"

"Tennis? Sorry, no, I don't."

"Oh, that's a shame. You could have joined us—me and some other moms play every Friday morning at the Y. I played right through my pregnancies—even with the twins." Sandra glances around the front yard. "I guess your son's in the after-school program, too?"

"Oh, no, actually, Joe's here somewhere. He just . . . he likes to run ahead."

"He does? What grade is he in?"

"Fourth."

"Well, that's great. Kevin's in third grade, and our twins, Parker and Dane, are in middle school; they're fourteen. You've probably seen them around."

"I'm not sure. I've seen your husband in his car once or twice, though, and a young woman dropping Kevin off at school."

"Oh, sure, that's Delia, our nanny. Mike would have come by himself to say hi, but you know how it is. He's in finance—he works long hours."

"Don't worry. Greg's the same."

"Oh, yes, your husband. I've seen him out running with Helena a few times. They go super-early, don't they? Doctors' hours."

The late-September sun suddenly feels as if it is burning her scalp. Her mouth has gone dry, and her armpits feel slippery, her hairline damp.

"What kind of a doctor is Greg?"

"He's a pediatric heart surgeon."

"A baby heart doctor? Oh, my! Wow. That's amazing!" Sandra becomes more focused, and she steps closer. "Listen, let's get you over to our house, introduce you to some of the neighbors. Soon—OK?"

"That'd be lovely."

"It's a plan, then!" Sandra steps back, as if it is. "Right now, I'll be late if I don't go. Nice talking to you, Tess."

Joe slips out of the shrubbery as soon as Sandra is gone: a small feral creature with leaves in his hair.

"Look!" Tess lowers the plate. "Cookies!"

He grabs one but doesn't follow her to the door. She has to force herself not to try to hug him or kiss his freckled face. He won't let her do that yet. He can't be rushed or chivvied after school—he needs to decompress.

"How about some milk to go with that?" She heads inside, leaving the door open for him to follow.

She puts her bag on the dining room table, shoving aside a stack of Greg's files to make room for the cookie plate, but the papers topple and slide off the edge, scattering across the parquet, knocking over a small recycling bin.

She puts the plate down and gets onto her knees, scraping up the papers, stretching under the table to scoop the recycling back into the bin. Greg is normally meticulous about his paperwork, but he is working ridiculous hours—no wonder he has let things slip. She reaches for a stray sheet of paper and smooths it out, not sure if it was meant for a file or for recycling.

There are just three short sentences, in tight, looping handwriting, unsigned.

I saw your picture.
Years have passed, but I'd recognize your face anywhere.
I STILL SEE YOU IN MY NIGHTMARES.

CHAPTER FOUR

The next morning when she goes downstairs, Greg is at the kitchen sink, rinsing out a bowl. He hears her and turns; his face is drawn but alert, as if he's been waiting for her. Through the window behind him she sees a gust of wind fling small orange leaves at the mottled sky.

She goes to him and kisses him. "When did you get home last night? I waited and waited, but I must have fallen asleep; I didn't even hear you come in." She rubs her eyes and glances at the kitchen clock. "Wait—it's seven-thirty; why are you still here?"

Usually, by this time, he'd have had his run, his shower, and been at the hospital for an hour, preparing for the weekly conference, going through the procedures he has scheduled for that day, catching up on paperwork. But he is still in pajama bottoms and a gray T-shirt.

"I'm going in a little later today." His eyes look sunken, and his face is rumpled, his olive skin unusually pallid. She wonders if he has slept at all.

"Are you OK?" she asks.

"What?" He places the bowl carefully on the draining board. "No, no, I'm fine."

She remembers the note then and goes to get it from the wire tray by the toaster. She unfolds it and slides it across the countertop. "Look. This is why I was waiting up for you—didn't you get my voice mail yesterday? I found this with your recycling. What on earth is it?"

He turns, drying his hands on a tea towel, and looks down at the paper.

"I almost threw it out." She waits for him to pick up the note, but he carries on rubbing his hands. She can sense the thoughts traveling fast behind his calm face.

"*I still see you in my nightmares?* What does that mean, Greg? Who sent this to you?"

He tosses the towel onto the counter, takes the paper, and crunches it in his fist. "I wish you wouldn't touch my papers; they're all in order."

"Don't be ridiculous. What is this, Greg?"

"It's nothing, really, just some crazy who's seen the announcement of my appointment, or maybe the prize."

"'Some crazy'? What's that supposed to mean?"

He throws the ball of paper into the wastebasket. "It means that the world is full of unstable individuals. Especially the medical world."

"Have you had this sort of letter before and not told me?"

"Of course I haven't."

"But you were throwing it away—weren't you even going to tell me?"

"It's nothing."

"It's not nothing. Who would recognize your face? Who sees you in their nightmares? Greg?"

He turns back to the sink. "I have no idea, Tess. My guess is that it's a mentally ill person who has seen my picture on the hospital website. The news about my appointment and the surgical prize is all over it. The prize has been reported in other places, too. I really don't know who wrote it, and right now I have far more pressing things to worry about."

He opens a bag of coffee beans, tips them into the grinder, and turns it on, cutting off further conversation.

She waits until he switches it off. "Aren't you going for your run today?"

"Not today, no. I have a bit of a hamstring strain; I thought I'd take it easy for a few days."

She reaches past him for the muesli. "Your new running mate's going to be disappointed, then."

"My what?"

"Our neighbor?"

"What neighbor?" He scrapes the coffee into the basket of the espresso machine and, with a jerk of his wrist, slots the basket back in.

"The woman next door—Helena. Haven't you two been running together?"

"What? I already told you we haven't. Why would I want a running mate?" He switches the machine on, and the kitchen fills with a whirring sound as it forces thick coffee into the cup.

Sandra must have seen him talking to Helena in the street and made assumptions. She realizes how paranoid she sounds. The espresso machine cuts out.

"Did you get back really late, then, last night?" she asks.

"Yeah." He nods and pours milk into a mug, slotting it under the steamer. Once again, the noise makes talking impossible. When the steamer stops, he says, "Past midnight. You were sleeping, and I had a whole load of paperwork, so I worked down here for a bit, then grabbed a couple of hours in the spare room. I didn't want to wake you."

"You look totally exhausted."

"I'm fine, really."

"You don't seem fine."

"I just have a lot on my mind right now." He takes the mug to the breakfast bar and sits on a stool, stirring the brew.

"What's on your mind?"

"Oh, lots of stuff. This case . . . a four-year-old . . . some complications . . ."

She can't remember Greg ever admitting that he is worried about a patient. She wonders if he has been waiting for her because he needs to talk about this.

"Is that what you were working on last night?"

He nods.

"What sort of complications?"

"You wouldn't . . . It's extremely technical." He hands her the mug he's been stirring. "Anyway, here, look, I made you a latte."

She takes it. Now would not be the time to remind him that she's trying to avoid caffeine.

"But I want to know. Can't you try to explain it to me?"

"It would be a bit like trying to introduce you to the rules of baseball, in Mandarin."

She feels a prickle of irritation. "You should have married a cardiologist."

"I did date an interventional cardiologist once. It lasted about three weeks. Two type A egomaniacs who are always right about everything. It was a bloodbath." He grins at her, looking more like himself.

"Still, if I was a doctor, at least I'd be able to help with your complicated four-year-old. You'd be able to run things by me, and I could help you come up with a brilliant solution." The image of Greg and Helena jogging side by side through the woods, sharing medical opinions, enters her head. She shuts it down.

"No, you wouldn't," he says.

"Why? Because nobody could possibly match your genius?"

"No. Because the boy is dead."

She puts the coffee down. "Oh, no. God, that's awful."

He shrugs, but his jaw is tense.

"What—how? In the OR? With you?"

He nods.

"Oh, shit. I'm so sorry, love. So that's why you're . . ."

"Yeah, well, listen, you know, it happens." He straightens his shoulders. "There was nothing I or anyone else could have done about it. There's actually no one better in the States—if not the world—right now for the particular condition this child had. If I couldn't save him, no one could." He looks bigger suddenly, more confident and healthy, as if reaffirming his expertise, even in the context of this poor, dead child, has boosted his blood flow. "The parents are angry, but the truth is, they should be grateful it was me, not someone else."

"Grateful?"

He gives his head an irritable shake. "You know what I mean. At some point they're going to realize that their son had the best shot possible with me—that there's no one better at this—and ultimately that will help them."

He may well be the leading specialist when it comes to this particular defect of a child's heart, but he seems to forget that he is also dealing with raw, parental grief. She understands why he has to protect himself, but sometimes his ability to cut off all emotion feels chilling.

As she sips the strong, milky coffee, she remembers the first time she saw this defense mechanism kick in. It was soon after they met—only their third date—and they were walking through central London on the way to the theater, when he took a call from a junior colleague. They talked for a few minutes—something about a patient, a young girl who was in a bad way. "Listen, I've told the ICU guys, she's not an operative candidate," he growled. Then she heard him say something about "withdrawal of care." And then he grew even more irritable. "Listen, if I'm not operating, I don't see why I need to come in and talk to the damned family. I really haven't got time for a weeping mother right now." He glanced at Tess, as if realizing what he must sound like, and then he slowed, turned away, and lowered his voice. "The ICU needs to handle the withdrawal of support and sort out the family. Yeah. Right. OK. Sure . . ."

As they pushed through the revolving doors into the lobby of the theater, she wanted to get away from him—jump on the train, go home, hold on to Joe. The space between them was suddenly fraught. Greg paid for the program in silence, but then, as they took their seats, he reached for her hand and looked into her eyes. "If we didn't detach from the emotions sometimes," he said, "we'd go insane. It's a defense mechanism, Tess, that's all. I know it sounds tasteless, but it's just a way to cope. If I didn't distance myself from my emotions sometimes, then I'd have to ask *why*: why are gorgeous children born with holes in the heart, arteries switched, obstructed valves? Why do babies' hearts fail before they can even take a breath?" He closed his eyes briefly. "It might seem disrespectful to talk this way about a dying child, but if I didn't, sometimes, then all the unanswerable questions would close in on me. I wouldn't be able to do my job." He squeezed her hand, then smiled. "If it's any consolation for you, the suicide rate among surgeons is five times that of the general population." Before she could answer, the theater lights dimmed, the audience fell silent, and the curtain rose to reveal the actors standing on the bright stage.

She takes another sip of the latte. It tastes harsh and slightly gritty. Greg is staring out the kitchen window now, no doubt thinking about the small boy whose heart he could not mend.

"I wish you'd talk to me more. You've had all this going on, and you haven't even mentioned it."

"It only happened last week."

"A week is ages, Greg. This is terrible. I feel like, since we got here, we hardly ever talk," she says. "I miss you."

"I know. I miss you, too. This is all pretty intense—we knew it would be, but I feel bad that you're so alone right now. I should be here for you and Joe. I feel like I'm letting you down all the time. Are you OK? Are you feeling OK, physically?"

"I'm fine—a bit bloated, sore boobs, and my ankles are starting to swell rather attractively." She glances down at her bare feet. "We have the anomaly ultrasound on Friday."

He nods. "OK. Actually, that's what I wanted to talk to you about. The parents of this boy . . . there's a meeting about it Friday, and I can't miss it. I can't get it changed, because there are so many people involved. The whole hospital machine has to kick in when something like this happens. I'm so sorry, Tess."

"You can't come to the scan?"

"If I could, I would, but these parents, they're . . . They've kind of lost it, and a lot of people are involved now. Could we reschedule the scan?"

"No," she says, "we can't. It has to be done before twenty-three weeks, and I'm twenty-three weeks this Saturday." This, she realizes, is the reason he is still at home. This is what he wanted to tell her.

He might not even have mentioned the little boy's death if it wasn't for this.

"I wish it wasn't like this," he says. "I really do."

She says nothing.

"I'd like to be there when we find out the sex." He sounds sad.

"But I don't want to find out ahead of time—do you?"

He widens his eyes, then nods. "Actually, you know what? I'd probably rather not know the sex yet, either. I just assumed you'd want to. But a surprise would be much better."

She wonders whether his reason for not wanting to know the sex is quite the same as hers. But he takes her hands. "Listen, I was thinking, how about we fix up a weekend away, just me and you, when things have settled down a little? I'd like to take you up the coast; it's beautiful up there in the fall. We could do it one weekend in November when David has Joe."

"OK." She nods. "Which one?"

"How about Thanksgiving weekend? Late November—that's not so far away, really. You could ask David if he can do that weekend."

Time has slowed down, she realizes, because right now even a week feels like a huge stretch to wait. But for Greg a month or two will pass in a blink.

"You working on the book today?" he asks. "How's that going?"

"Well, it's been harder than I thought, actually, to select and balance everything, to make all the images work together."

"It's a very valuable thing you're doing. You know that, right?"

"I know. I've been enjoying it. I'm glad you heard about it; it's turned out to be a great project for me, with the move and everything."

"I knew it would be. They were lucky to get you."

Sometimes it's like being married to two people: the godlike surgeon, fearsome and focused, decisive, uncommunicative, ruthless—and then this warm and beautiful man, full of love, rooting for her, respecting her work, supporting her.

"You know you can take a break, don't you?" he says. "When you finish the book, when the baby's born, you could just stop for a bit—if you wanted to. We can afford it, if that's what you want to do."

She leans against the doorframe. This is the first time he has engaged in the reality of this baby, and it feels like progress. She has always worked; she can't imagine not taking pictures. But maybe this time she won't try to take commissions with a newborn. It would be good not to have to rely on unreliable sitters, do rush jobs, worry all the time, and produce shoddy work. And the truth is that it is unrealistic to think that she will be able to build up a whole new set of contacts while caring for Joe and a new baby. When Joe was tiny, she'd had no choice but to work—and it had been an ordeal. She recalled one particularly painful shoot, when a babysitter didn't show up, and she had to take Joe, at about three months old, to the Holland Park home of a Tory politician. Joe wouldn't stop wailing, and the politician, rigid in his salmon-pink shirt, lost patience and stalked off to his gazebo, like a sulking flamingo.

She wants to talk about her work with Greg—how she will manage her career and the baby—but is almost eight now, and she has to get Joe going. "Can we talk about this tonight?"

"I'm going to Chicago tonight," he says. "The big event tomorrow— remember?"

"Oh, my God, your prize!" She feels something deflate inside her but tries not to show it, smiling wildly. "Shit! You've barely mentioned it, Greg. We have to celebrate when you get back."

"Sure."

"Aren't you excited?"

"Of course, I'm glad of it—it's great to be noticed. And it's going to help enormously with research funding."

"I should be coming with you."

"Don't be silly. We talked about this. You can't leave Joe, and you certainly can't bring him. Anyway, it's not a family thing. You can watch it online if you want to, though."

"Will there be lots of doctors there?"

He nods. "Several hundred, probably—my speech is going to be streamed live."

"Brilliant. I can watch it, then." She reaches up and kisses him. "You are a genius."

She goes to the bottom of the stairs, then, with one hand on her belly, calls, "Joey? Breakfast!"

The prize event is on the calendar; she shouldn't have forgotten. She can't possibly resent Greg for going away this time. This is a big deal for him. It is odd that he doesn't seem more excited. But perhaps the situation with the child who died is overshadowing some of the glory. She wonders, suddenly, whether he might have made a surgical mistake, misjudged something, perhaps tried a risky technique.

"Joey? Come on—you're going to be late for school."

Joe appears at the top of the landing and comes downstairs very slowly, one step at a time. His face is as white as the walls.

"Hey, what's up, love?"

"I'm sick."

"Oh, dear. Poor darling. What's wrong?" She reaches out and feels his forehead. It is perfectly cool.

"I have a bad fever."

"I don't think you do, lovey, or you'd be hot."

"I am hot. I have a bad tummy ache, too."

"Do you?"

"And a headache." He puts both hands up to the sides of his head, as if pressing on an invisible force field. "And I might be going to throw up."

"OK, well, luckily, we happen to have one of the world's top children's doctors in our kitchen right now. He can take a look and see what's wrong with you."

A look of panic flits across Joe's face.

"Greg." She smiles at her son. "It's only Greg."

"Actually, I might just be hungry," Joe says.

He looks small and sacrificial as he walks away down the narrow corridor and through the arch into the kitchen, where Greg is packing up his papers.

"Hey, buddy," she hears Greg say in a cheerful voice. "How's it going?"

"Fine," says Joe.

"You want me to make French toast? I have exactly fifteen minutes—that's just about time to rustle up the house specialty with extra maple syrup."

"OK."

"Good man."

Whatever Greg feels about the death of the four-year-old, or about strangers sending him notes, he is doing a good job of masking it. And then she remembers something he once told her. "Every surgeon has a graveyard in his brain," he said. "You forget the names of the ones who live, but the names of the ones who die are engraved on your mind forever."

Perhaps it works the other way around, too. She wonders how many grieving parents are walking around out there with Greg's name etched onto their brains.

CHAPTER FIVE

All morning, since she drank the latte Greg made her, she has had a lurching on-and-off queasiness, and the ground is no longer steady beneath her feet. Deep in her pelvis she can feel little stabbing sensations, as if the baby has grown spines. Perhaps the milk was off.

After she'd gotten Joe off to school and Greg had left for the hospital, the doorbell rang. Sandra Schechter was on the porch in tennis whites.

"Hey, Tess! How's it going? Listen, I'm in kind of a hurry right now, but we're having a potluck in October, and I wanted to ask if you and Greg and Joe could join us. We'd love to have you over and introduce you to some of the other neighbors."

Another wave of queasiness spread through her, and she swallowed, pressing her hands on her belly. "That sounds great, thanks." She had no idea what a potluck was.

"Well, fabulous!" Sandra started to move off down the path, calling over her shoulder, "I'll send you an evite!"

The nausea continued as she went to the supermarket and shopped. Usually she found it uncomfortable to stand around doing nothing while the cashier put the groceries into paper bags, but today she was glad it worked that way, because her limbs felt weak, her hands clammy, and there was a possibility that she was actually going to throw up.

Now, as she grabs the brown-paper grocery bags from the trunk, she wishes the supermarket person's job extended to carrying the shopping home and unloading it into kitchen cupboards. The late-September leaves are turning golden, but the air feels too close and warm. The mailman appears, a middle-aged Chinese-American man who is dressed like a schoolboy in a baseball cap, blue shorts, and pressed shirt with a canvas USPS bag over one shoulder. He flips up the neighbors' mailbox flag, raises a hand to her in greeting, and walks past the car. She wonders whether she could ask him to help her carry in the flat-packed bedside table she's bought for Joe. But she isn't yet at the obvious stage of pregnancy, and he might be upset to be asked.

Since the mock Tudor house has no mailbox, the postman always tosses letters onto the porch. As she bends to pick them up, her head spins. There is a Crate and Barrel catalog addressed to a former tenant; a letter from the IRS, addressed to Dr. G. Gallo; a coupon booklet; a couple of letters from Citizens Bank; and a large padded envelope for Greg, which rattles. She hesitates, and then she rips it open. Four large pill bottles tumble onto the doormat. Each has a tiny orange-flame logo and a name:

Dr. Vaus Energizing Complex
Dr. Vaus Biohacker Mix
Dr. Vaus Corsitol Balance
Dr. Vaus Tissue Repair

She peers into the envelope and pulls out a card.

Tissue repair for that hamstring—the others for your sanity and success.

Dr. V x

The handwriting is large and definite. She reads it again, her eyes lingering on the kiss. A colleague? An old friend from medical school?

Greg hasn't mentioned any old friends, and he would never order vitamins. He considers most dietary supplements to be snake oil.

She puts the bottles back into the envelope and goes back out to the car. At the far end of the street she sees a figure hurrying away—a slight and androgynous body, in dark clothes, moving fast, as if falling forward, hooded head bent. She sees a flash of dark red—a scarf? hair?—as the figure turns the corner and vanishes onto the bigger road. She shields her eyes against the sun, but the running person has gone.

Back at the car, leaning into the trunk for more shopping bags, she notices that Helena and Josh's garage door is open. Both their cars are gone. She can see recycling bins, bikes, a tub of footballs, scooters, ski boots on a shelf, a stack of flattened cardboard boxes. Maybe a burglar overrode the electronic mechanism and winched the door open. She peers down the driveway.

She should probably go and close the door—or at least call them to tell them it was open. But it has been over a month now, and she still hasn't actually spoken to Helena, let alone exchanged phone numbers.

A team of gardeners is trimming shrubs in a front yard down the way, but other than that, as always the street is empty. The mailman has vanished. She thinks about the thin figure hurrying away. It is possible that he or she came from the garage. But calling the police might be excessive. Josh might have just forgotten to shut the door.

If she can get their surnames, she can google them and perhaps call one of them at work. She crosses the lawn to their mailbox. The hatch creaks as she eases the letters out: the same Crate and Barrel catalog and one for a clothing company called Athleta, with a muscular woman in sports gear on the cover. She slides them back into the mailbox and looks at the remaining envelopes.

Dr. Joshua Feldman.

So he's a doctor, too.

She flips to a couple of white envelopes. Both are addressed to Dr. H. Vaus-Feldman.

She stares at the name. *Dr. Vaus.*

So it is Helena who sent Greg the vitamins. Helena is Dr. V. But the vitamin bottles were mailed and not dropped off. Perhaps she didn't want to knock on the door and hand over her little gift for Greg.

She shoves the mail back into the box and goes back to the Volvo, seizing the bedside table and hauling it out of the trunk. It isn't too heavy, but she hasn't quite got the weight balanced evenly, and she feels the strain down one side of her body. She lugs it to and drops it on the porch. She is sweating and breathing fast. She feels a wave of sickness, and her head spins.

She thinks about Greg's response when she asked him this morning about running with Helena. He didn't look at her—he was fiddling around with his coffee machine. She feels another wave of nausea and has to hold on to the doorframe to steady herself.

Back at the car, as she reaches into the trunk, she sees movement on the neighbors' porch—and there is Helena herself, coming out of her front door. The fabric of her forest-green dress swirls around her tanned legs as she hops off the bottom step. Her hair is in loose waves, and for a mad second Tess wishes she had her Leica so that she could capture this movement and color—the swing of caramel hair, the dress against the moss-green woodwork. But Helena is bending into her mailbox now, pulling out the letters. Obviously this is not a coincidence: she must have seen everything.

She straightens, then begins to walk over. Her hips sway. She is in no hurry.

"Hey." She gives a tight smile. "Tess, right?" Her eyes are the same murky green as her dress.

"Yes," Tess nods. "Hello."

"I'm Helena."

"Yes, I know."

"Hmm, I guess you do." The green eyes hold steady. "Were you looking for something particular in my mailbox?"

Tess feels her face grow hot, but she doesn't allow herself to look away. She raises her chin. "Actually, your garage door is open. Your cars aren't there, so I thought maybe someone had broken in—in fact, I saw this hooded person hurrying off down the street just now, looking a bit suspicious. But I didn't have your number or even know your surname, so that's why I was looking—I was going to try to call you."

The chilly gaze falters. This is obviously not the answer Helena was expecting. She glances down her driveway. "Oh, right. Well, thanks, yeah, my car's having work done today. I guess I forgot to close the garage door."

Her almond-shaped eyes are enhanced by a flick of eyeliner along the top lids. She is definitely beautiful but not in a conventional sense. She is in her mid-forties, probably, dewy-skinned with rounded features, fine lines by her mouth and eyes, a slightly upturned nose, and cheekbones rising like hillocks.

"Well, anyway, look, Tess, I'd love to talk more," she says, "but I'm about to go on a conference call. We should grab a coffee sometime, though, OK?"

Helena hops back across the front lawn onto her porch. She looks back before she closes the door, but she does not smile or raise a hand.

In the kitchen Tess gulps two glasses of water. A bluebottle butts the window, a small, desperate, thudding sound. She is, she realizes, being paranoid. If Helena is Dr. Vaus—and she must be—she probably routinely gives away her vitamin products to influential doctors. And as for the kiss, that could just be a friendly gesture, nothing more.

The nausea is intensifying now, and the uncomfortable prickling sensations are back, low in her belly. She cannot contemplate lunch. She will put in a load of laundry, then go upstairs and lie down, calm down, maybe sleep for a bit before she has to go deal with an unhappy Joe.

The clammy air in the basement folds itself over her skin as she goes downstairs. It smells mildewed, mushroom-y. The stairs are steep, and there is no banister; you could easily lose your balance and topple to the concrete below. She steadies herself with one hand on the wall. The bricks feel reptilian, with small slimy bumps beneath the cold paint.

Two industrial-size machines loom in the laundry room, near a wall of shelves where she has stacked Greg's four boxes, a crate of coats, and a big box of winter boots. The square mouth of the stainless-steel laundry chute gapes in one corner. She initially thought the door on the first-floor landing led to a storage space, until Joe opened it and shouted, "Mum! It's a tunnel!" It took her a moment to work out that it was in fact a steel laundry chute, plummeting through the house like a wide esophagus. The clothes she has thrown down it are piled on the floor now, along with some LEGO bricks and a few soft toys that Joe has shot down.

As she begins to gather up these things, her nausea rises until suddenly she knows that she is going to be sick. She presses her hand over her lips, but there is no time—there is no wastebasket here, nothing to be sick into—and she has to squat as her stomach heaves and hotness surges up her throat, bulging out of her, splattering onto the laundry.

Afterward she curls up on the floor. Her eyelids are heavy, her limbs and torso ache, and her throat feels flayed. The vomit stench is vile, but she cannot open her eyes or move. Everything feels far off. Somewhere in the distance she is aware of a scratching, scrambling sound. She slips into a flat, dead sleep.

There is knocking inside her head. She opens her eyes. Her left arm is numb, her throat sore, her brain throbs against her forehead, and the stink is appalling. She gets up, shakily, and scrapes everything into a pile, wiping the concrete with dirty clothing. She peels off her dress and adds it to the pile, then heaves it all into the drum of the washer. She wipes herself down with a pillowcase. Then she feels something sticky between her legs. She looks down and sees a dark smear on the pale skin of her inner thigh. She grabs a towel and wipes herself—more smears.

Very slowly, she walks upstairs, trying not to jerk or go too fast. She goes into the en suite and sits on the toilet, her heart beating cold and fast inside her chest. The pink and gray tiles sway. She doesn't seem to be bleeding anymore. She puts both hands on her belly. "Don't go," she whispers. "Stay. I want you to stay. I want you." The baby gives a delicate, answering kick. She closes her eyes, feeling the tightness in her chest release, just a little.

There is a precarious feeling in her belly, as if, were she to move too suddenly, something would unhook, causing everything to cascade out of her. She gets off the toilet and goes through to the bedroom, walking slowly, like a stiff princess. She gets dressed, using a pad, then calls Greg. Miraculously, he answers on the first ring.

Twenty minutes later she is curled on the sofa with a cup of tea, waiting for his car to pull up to the house. She stares at the framed photos on the side table. One has fallen facedown. She picks it up—it is the one of Greg's parents. She found it with the contents of his desk when she was unpacking the boxes, got it out, put it in a frame, and put it here with the others—of Joe as a baby, a toddler, of her and Greg on one of Brighton's beaches, of her and Greg and Joe in the garden. It is possible that Greg hasn't even noticed the photo of his parents. He so rarely even sits on the sofa these days. She reaches over and picks it up. The couple is arm in arm facing the camera: a tall, forbidding-looking Italian man with an angular face, wearing a slightly flared suit, and an equally solemn woman in a dress with a Peter Pan collar. There is a definite look of Greg about them—in the father particularly. These people are the flesh and blood of her flesh and blood; their genes are growing inside her. And yet she knows almost nothing about them.

She hears Greg's car pull up, puts the photo back on the table, and gets up, not too fast, crossing the room and peering through the diamond-shaped windowpanes. She sees Greg slam the car door and pause, straightening his shoulders. He is still wearing his green scrubs. He looks determined, granite-faced, as if bracing himself for what he might find when he turns the key.

"Tess?"

She steps into the hallway to meet him. The sight of him, so big and healthy and broad in his scrubs, so concerned, makes her throat tighten. "You didn't have to come home."

"Oh, my darling, my poor love." He folds his arms around her. She smells hospital soap and fabric bleach. "Of course I did."

"I'm really all right now, I think."

"So, how much did you bleed?"

"It was just spotting, just some smears, and it's stopped now."

"And you can feel the baby moving?"

She nods. "I just felt it kick again." She puts a hand on her belly. It occurs to her that if she is losing this baby, then a part of Greg will feel relieved—but she cannot allow herself to think like that, not right now. She sweeps the thought aside and looks back up at him again. His expression is kind, but she can feel his anxiety.

"I've left a message for An," he says.

"Who?"

"An—the ob/gyn. She'll probably want you to have a quick scan to check it out, but if it was just spotting, and if that's stopped now, and the baby's moving, then I'm sure everything's going to be just fine."

She does not want to go and see the ob/gyn, a tiny Chinese-American woman with a shining bob and a clipped, emotionless voice who makes her think of emergency rooms and surgical instruments.

"An's the best—she has a waiting list years long," Greg had said when he got her on the patient list. "People sign up with her the day they get pregnant. If something goes wrong, An's the one I'd want opening up your uterus."

"Jesus, Greg! Nobody's going to be opening my uterus." It shocked her how easily he could switch to seeing her body as an object that might malfunction.

"Come on," he says now. "Come and sit back down."

"What about the throwing up?" She follows him to the sofa. "I was pretty sick."

"That's probably unrelated. It might be just a virus. You're being exposed to a whole range of viruses here, probably for the first time, so you're likely to get sick more than usual at first, until you build up immunity." He tucks a pillow under her back.

"Do you think I'm miscarrying, Greg? I need you to tell me the truth."

"Blood spotting happens, even in the second trimester. It's probably nothing, really. We'll get you checked out, just to be one hundred percent sure. You should lie down now, put your feet up for the rest of the day. You look pale." He smooths a strand of hair behind her ear. "Everything's going to be OK."

"But I have to go and pick up Joe in half an hour. When's your flight to Chicago?"

"If I'm going to catch it and make the dinner tonight, I'll have to go in about"—he grimaces—"ten minutes."

She does not want him to get on a plane, not even to receive an important prize. She wants him to sit down on the sofa with her, put his arms around her, and stay.

"The moment the ceremony is done tomorrow, I'm going to turn around and fly straight home," he says. "I can be back here by midafternoon."

"I'll be fine, honestly." She feels herself retreat inside, curl back into herself. She stares at the parquet floor, at little nicks and scratches caused by all the feet and furniture that have passed through this house over the years. She thinks about the domestic dramas and the hurts, the misunderstandings and betrayals, that have likely taken place right here, on this floor.

"I wish to God I could cancel." He squeezes her hand. "But it would be—it's an annual national meeting; there's a plenary session just for me to give a talk, then get the prize; there are several hundred people coming. It would be . . . almost unforgivable not to show up . . ."

"You absolutely have to go."

"But I don't want to. This is horrible. I want to stay here with you— you know that, don't you? This is not what I want at all." He squeezes her hand again, and she makes herself look up at him. His mouth is grim. "I hate this," he says.

"It's OK." She feels as if she is pushing herself up through layers of heavy earth. "You can't possibly miss getting your prize. It's just bad timing, that's all. You have to go. I'll be totally fine. Don't worry, OK? You said yourself, it's just spotting. The baby's moving. And you'll be back tomorrow."

There is a long pause. He keeps his eyes fixed on her face. "No," he says, finally. "You know what? I can't. I'm just not going to leave you here. Fuck it. Fuck the whole thing. I just can't do this."

"But you have to go!"

"No, I don't. You're more important. I can't leave you on your own when you're feeling like this." His face is set. "I'm not going."

She takes his hand. "This is ridiculous, Greg; there is no way I'm letting you stay. There are hundreds of people expecting you, it's a massive deal, and I'm fine. I just felt the baby move again, just now. I've got a stupid virus, that's all. You'll be away less than twenty-four hours. You'll be back before we know it."

He is shaking his head.

"Greg," she says. "Really, honestly, this is silly. I'm not letting you stay."

"But—"

"No. Go and do your talk, get your prize. Then come back as soon as you can."

There is another long pause. Then he gives a slow nod. "I will turn around and come right back if . . . if anything . . . anything at all."

"I know you will."

"I'll have my phone switched on the whole time." He leans closer, kissing her on the forehead.

"I'm going to be OK."

"OK." He sighs and glances at his watch. "Shit, Tess."

"Go."

"I have to change my clothes; then I'll sort Joe out. I don't want you walking down to the school today."

"I'll do it—"

"No. No. I'm doing it. You're going to rest."

"All I have to do is call Sandra; she's home on Fridays. I'm sure she wouldn't mind picking him up; she's very nice."

"Really?"

"Really."

"I'm going to organize a babysitter for him tomorrow, so you can stay in bed."

"No, it's OK. David's coming tomorrow, remember?"

"Oh—right, sure. I'd forgotten he was finally showing up." He leans over and kisses her on the lips. "Good timing, for once. OK, now, you go upstairs, and you lie down. You rest. An's office will call soon—she'll probably be able to give you a quick scan later today if you can make it in." He holds her chin. "I love you. Everything's going to be just fine. OK? I promise."

He can't promise, and they both know it, but she nods anyway. He thunders upstairs, and she hears him opening and closing their chest of drawers.

When he has gone, she picks up her phone and calls Nell.

"Oh, Tess, you poor thing, that's horrid—you must be really worried. Are you resting? Are your feet up? I wish I was there to look after you and make you some soup."

"Soup?"

"You know what I mean."

"I wish you were here, too."

"Is Greg there?"

"He was. He came home, but then he had to go again. He's being awarded a big prize tomorrow morning in Chicago; it's a huge honor. He had to leave this afternoon."

"No way! He's flying to Chicago? He's leaving you alone there?"

"It's not like that at all. He wanted to stay, but I actually made him go in the end. The prize is important, and hundreds of surgeons are coming from all over just to see him get it—he has to give a speech, the media will be there, everything. He can't not show up just because I threw up."

"And had a bleed."

"It really was just spotting, and it's stopped now. I just felt the baby wriggle again."

"OK, I know, the baby's going to be fine, and you'll be fine. I just wish you weren't on your own right now."

"I'm not. I'll have Joe here in half an hour. And anyway, it's me—I like being alone."

"Actually, I remember I had some blood spotting early on with the twins—I'm googling it now. I think it's quite common. There you go: blood spotting in the second trimester . . ."

"Don't google!"

There is a pause. "OK, yes, you're right—bad idea. I'm shutting it down now."

"I'm a bit worried about caffeine. Caffeine can cause miscarriage, can't it?"

"What?"

"Greg made me this really strong latte this morning, and it wasn't long after that that I started feeling sick. I don't know if it was the caffeine, or maybe something was wrong with the milk—it was very milky. I don't know. But my body knew it was the wrong thing to drink. I had to almost force it down. I should have left it."

"I'm pretty sure the caffeine effects are only if you drink more than twenty-five cups a day, or something, for several months. One latte—even the strength Greg makes them—isn't going to make you miscarry. But I can google caffeine, too. if you want . . ."

"No, please don't." She remembers the bedside table for Joe. "Oh, God, I just remembered. I carried a nightstand out of the car today."

"OK, listen, stop. All around the world pregnant women are lifting heavy things—toddlers, farming equipment, factory machinery. The female body is tough and resilient; we're brilliantly designed. And if you were miscarrying, the blood wouldn't stop, would it? It would be getting worse. Didn't Greg say that? It would surely be getting worse, with cramps and things. And you wouldn't be feeling the baby move."

"I know, you're right; that's what Greg said, too. I'm probably going in for a scan later, just to be sure."

"Did Greg seem worried?"

"I don't know. He said he wasn't, but I think he was, really."

"If he thought you were miscarrying, even Greg wouldn't bugger off to Chicago."

Tess swallows a mouthful of the tea Greg had brought her before he left.

"Would he?" Nell's voice has a slight echo.

"Of course he wouldn't. It's not like that. It's just . . . I know it's silly, but I can't help wondering if he might be slightly relieved if I did lose this baby."

"Oh, Tess, has he still not come around? I thought he had."

"I don't know. He isn't saying anything obviously negative, but I honestly don't know how he feels, because we've barely talked about it—or anything else, really—since we got here."

"Has he ever actually explained to you why he was so adamant about not wanting a child?"

"He doesn't have time to cope with a newborn."

"But plenty of people work long hours and have babies. Anyway, presumably you'd be the one at home with the newborn, not him. Surgeons do have children, don't they? I have to say, I don't really buy that as an argument."

"No, nor do I. I'm sure it goes deeper than that."

"Could it be to do with his job? I mean, I suppose he's seeing the worst-case scenarios every day. Maybe he's scared something might go wrong with the baby. He's sort of seen the dark side of parenthood, hasn't he?"

"Maybe, but he sees the good side, too—the love, the recovery."

"I think you should talk to him, Tess, properly, before this baby's born. It's really not good to think that your husband might be relieved if you miscarried."

"I know, but it's pretty much impossible to talk to him at the moment. He's at the hospital all the time, or he's traveling, and even when he is here, he's exhausted. Sometimes I feel almost like Joe and I have moved to this place on our own. To be honest, this whole thing sometimes feels a bit insane."

"I know. But it's not, though, is it? You had lots of really good reasons for doing this, apart from loving Greg and wanting to be with him, obviously. Joe's nearer David there, and you're having an adventure; I mean, who knows what it might do for your photography—and it's an amazing thing for Greg's career. Don't lose sight of all that. I wish I could come and live in Boston. I'm telling you, it's incredibly dull here; nothing ever changes. I'd leap at the chance to live in America for a few years."

"I know, I'm lucky, I know. We just have to adjust, that's all."

"It was always going to be tough at first."

"Greg's doing his best—he really is. I'm just feeling a bit sorry for myself right now. And I'm sure he'll fall in love with our baby the moment he holds it—"

"Holy crap!" Nell gives a wild laugh.

"What?"

"No. You do not want to know."

"*What?*"

"Well, OK, so I was listening to you, I promise, but I was also googling caffeine and milky drinks and miscarriage at the same time, and I found this news story about a married obstetrician who slipped drugs into his pregnant mistress's tea to make her miscarry his unborn child. Good grief."

"Nell," she howls. "Stop googling, for Christ's sake!"

"No. It's OK. It all turned out all right in the end—well, kind of. The mistress spotted this yellow powder at the bottom of her tea mug and realized he was drugging her. It says here she put the tea mug in a plastic bag and took it to the police. It was all OK in the end—she gave birth to a healthy boy, and the doctor went to prison."

CHAPTER SIX

She hears the mail thud onto the porch and goes to the door. As she opens it, she sees Helena's silver Prius pulling up by the fence. The passenger window glides down, and a hand waves. Tess pushes back her hair and tightens her cardigan over her belly, wishing she had at least put on some mascara or brushed her hair. The sickness has passed overnight, but she still feels peaky. The ultrasound showed that the baby was fine, and she'd heard its heartbeat, a distant, rapid swoosh and thud, like tiny footsteps running across snow. Over the phone from Chicago, Greg had sounded relieved but not surprised. Everything was going to be fine.

She gets to the window of Helena's Prius.

"Hey, Tess." Helena is leaning on the passenger seat, her wrist laden with beaded leather bracelets. "How's it going?" She is in dark jeans, wearing subtle lipstick; her skin looks luminous.

"OK, thanks." Tess tucks her hair behind her ears.

"Wonderful! So, listen, Josh and I were wondering . . ." Helena pauses, then smiles, opening her eyes a little wider. "Could you park your Volvo somewhere else? Maybe in your garage? It's just that when you leave it out front like this, backing out of our driveway can be a little tricky."

Tess tries to keep the smile going.

"OK, great! Well, I have to go now—I'm on my way to the airport—but you have a great day, OK?" The window slides back up, and Helena pulls away, skirting the Volvo in an exaggerated arc.

Overhead, the branches of the oak tree knock together, a hollow, lonely sound. Tess looks at the Volvo. The street is three times as wide as her road in England—you could get a tractor-trailer past it. When she goes to the supermarket, parking out front is the fastest way to unload the shopping; the alternative is to carry heavy bags up the basement steps. Helena's request is nonsense, really, purely territorial, designed to make Tess feel like an outsider. It is as if Helena wants to make her as uncomfortable as possible. She leaves the Volvo where it is and goes back into the house.

She experiences a surge of relief when she opens the door an hour later to find David filling the porch, tanned and battered-looking, in the leather jacket he's owned since they were together. His messed-up curls are receding now, silvery at the sides, and there is the smile she used to find irresistible, his bottom jaw jutting slightly sideways. She hugs him tightly, and if he is surprised by her affection, he doesn't show it.

After some overexcited wrestling with his dad, Joe thunders upstairs to pack up some toys. She makes David an espresso, and, as they sit at the breakfast bar with the doors to the deck open, he talks about his new job defending human-rights campaigners in conflict zones. She doesn't ask too many questions. Over the years she has realized that it is best to avoid the specifics of the perilous situations David puts himself in. Nor does she ask why it has taken him a month get to Boston; it would only sound querulous, and Joe is delighted that he is here—she must not spoil that. They have always managed to be kind to each other in front of Joe, and that feels especially important now, with all the disruption Joe is going through.

"If you don't mind my saying so, Tess, you look knackered." He takes a gulp of espresso. "Everything OK?"

"Everything's fine, thanks."

He glances at her belly. "Are you as sick with this one as you were with Joe?"

"I really wasn't that sick with Joe." It feels too intimate to talk to David about the pregnancy. She doesn't want him to have a connection to her body anymore.

"You just look a bit pallid and pasty, sort of Bride of Frankenstein, in your own blond, beautiful way."

"Thanks." She scrapes her hair off her face and ties it at the base of her neck with a band from her wrist. "I'm just a bit tired, that's all."

"Why?"

It really isn't his fault. How would David know what it feels like to be five months pregnant in a new country with a dispossessed child, to make a blinding leap across the Atlantic after someone who is away so much that at times he feels almost imaginary? David travels with a passport, a carryall, and a multi-pocket vest stuffed with gadgets and dollars. He spends his time being tear-gassed and shot at. He is black-listed in China and banned from Bahrain and will—nominally—be living in a fully furnished apartment somewhere in Brooklyn with a stack of takeaway menus, a fridge containing microbrewery beer, and not a single cushion.

David puts down his empty cup. "Nice coffee."

"Gourmet beans. Greg's a bit of a coffee snob."

"Is he around?" He looks behind him, as if Greg might pop out of one of the kitchen cabinets making jazz hands.

"No." Their eyes meet, and she suddenly feels disloyal, as if she is siding with David against Greg. "He's away right now. He's receiving an award—I'm about to watch it streaming live from Chicago. He'll be back this afternoon."

"Blimey, Tess, that man travels almost as much as I do." She hears the tension in his voice. He has had so little time to get used to Greg. He handled the announcement of the marriage and move with equanimity because it meant that he would be on the same continent as Joe. He has been civil to Greg whenever they've met, but they have nothing in common, and it can't be easy to see another man step into Joe's life in this way. It helps that David is an optimist, unfazed by change, that he thrives on the unexpected and believes, unfailingly, that everything will work out for the best. Despite his flaws, she is lucky that David is Joe's father and not someone more conventional or sensible—or someone with more time on his hands.

"Are you ready, Joey?" She gets up and calls through the archway. "Don't forget to do your teeth, OK?"

The phone is ringing. She glances over at it. The stack of paperwork that is usually in the wire tray—bills, leaflets, and Greg's unopened mail—has been lifted onto the marble countertop and placed by the phone. She is sure that the previous evening, when she tidied the kitchen before she went to bed, it was in the tray. She tries to think whether she touched it this morning, but she can't remember. Maybe Joe was looking for something.

"You want me to get that for you?" David raises his eyebrows at the phone.

"Oh? No, no, don't bother. Nobody's ever there. Greg thinks it's an automated marketing thing. I keep forgetting to call the phone company and sort it out." The answering machine kicks in; there is her voice, the pause, then the flat burr as the call cuts out.

"You can dial star, six, nine to find out who's calling."

"I know. I tried that, but it just says 'number unavailable.'"

David looks around the kitchen. "It's all very *American Beauty* here, isn't it?"

"Is it?"

"Well, it's spookily quiet. Like Armageddon's happened, and nobody's told us."

"People work long hours here, that's all."

"It's Saturday, Tess."

"Well, they're at their children's sports games, then. They take kids' sports really seriously here—it's great, actually; they have proper facilities, semiprofessional coaches."

"What they have," David says, "is money." He looks around at the marble countertops and the Bosch appliances and runs a hand over his chin. "You've come up in the world, Ms. Harding. Remember Camberwell?"

They catch each other's eye and smile, and for a moment they are back there—idealistic twenty-somethings eating baked beans in a freezing efficiency flat. She looks away first.

"I know it's posh here, but the people are nice, the school seems good, and it's very handy for Greg to get to the hospital."

"But it's not really you, is it?" he says. "Suburban life in a mock Tudor?"

"It's an experience, David. It's also very pleasant and safe here. This is the fifth safest place to live in the whole country—it used to be the first, but someone got shot a few years ago on the border between this suburb and the next, so it was knocked down the league table a bit."

"Yeah, well, safety's overrated."

"Not when you have a child."

"I thought the police shoot-out with the marathon bombers happened just—"

"That was the next suburb along, David."

He leans back, sticks his legs out, and crosses them at the ankle, his eyes lively.

"What time do you have to get going?" She gets off her stool.

He holds up both hands. "It's OK, calm down. I'm just winding you up. I'm sure it's delightful here and outrageously safe."

"The biggest crime here last week was someone calling the police to report a severed foot inside a sock, bobbing in the lake."

David grimaces. "That doesn't sound particularly minor."

"When the police fished the sock out, there was no foot inside it."

"Are you working at the moment, Tess?" He laughs. "Or are you spending long days poring over the local paper's crime pages?"

She stops laughing. "I'm finishing a book project, actually."

"Good." He doesn't ask for details. "Because you'd go mad here before long without taking pictures."

She raises her eyebrows. He has never taken her photography seriously, despite the fact that it has largely fed and clothed his son for nine years. Perhaps if she'd been a war photographer or had pictures of Peruvian hill tribes published in *National Geographic*, he'd have respected her work more. But her career can never rival the hands-on, dirty, dangerous work that David does. Her photographs don't save lives.

Joe comes into the kitchen carrying a backpack stuffed with LEGOs and remote-controlled helicopters.

"Well done, love." She smiles at him, suddenly not wanting him to go with David. "You're all packed up."

"How's school going, big man?" David ruffles Joe's hair.

Her anxiety fades. When he is physically with Joe, David is an excellent father. He might be financially unreliable and hard to pin down, but he loves his son and is good at showing it.

"Made any new mates since we talked?" David keeps his hand on Joe's head.

"Two." She watches Joe inflate. This is the first time he has admitted to any successful social interactions. She tries not to look surprised.

"Which one do you like best?"

"Maybe Forrest, he's OK. He's into football—soccer."

"Ah, yes, it's soccer now, isn't it?" David sits, legs apart, on the stool, as if this is his kitchen, his house. "Vital to learn the lingo. Blend in with the enemy."

"OK. So. What's the plan?" Tess takes David's coffee cup to the sink.

"Guess what? I got us Red Sox tickets." David produces them from his inside pocket.

Joe's face lights up. After so much anxiety, the sight of his smile makes her almost dizzy with relief. She realizes she has not actually seen Joe smile properly since they crossed the threshold of this house.

She considers taking David's arm, pulling him aside, and warning him that Joe is more fragile than he seems—that he sobs at bedtime and begs her to take him home, that he daren't speak in class because of his accent and that he can't remember the Pledge of

Allegiance, that nobody sits next to him at lunch. Her chest tightens at the thought of Joe, small, alone, and sad at the end of a long canteen—cafeteria—table.

"Right." David slaps his thighs. "So, listen, Tess, I'll have him back here around midday tomorrow. My flight's at two. Sorry—a bit earlier than I said. I have to catch the red-eye to Amsterdam."

She comes out to the porch and watches David's rental car pull away with Joe waving through the passenger window, even smaller, suddenly, his face excited but uncertain, too, about leaving her, vulnerable, even with his dad. She has a sudden image of her mother's pallid face pressed against a car window, the pleading eyes and palms pressed flat against the glass, as she mouthed, "Take me home!" And then they are gone, and the street is empty again.

She drops her hand, and birdsong fills the air, a subtly aggressive, dominating sound. She feels the back of her neck prickle, and suddenly she is sure that if she turns, she will see someone standing in the shrubs between this house and Helena's. She forces herself to look. The garden is empty. She pulls out her phone and calls Nell. It goes straight to voice mail. She leaves a brief message as she walks back down the path and steps into the shadows of the porch.

Later, she watches Greg receive his award, standing on a Chicago podium in a dark suit. He is authoritative, deep-voiced, witty, self-assured—a persona that she has glimpsed but never fully seen in action. She feels her heart fill up and suddenly wishes she was there, clapping with all those hundreds of doctors, showing him how proud she is of what he has achieved.

She has just stepped into the shower when she hears a dull thud downstairs by the front door. It is less distinct than a knock, more like the palm of a hand slamming onto the mahogany panel.

She washes quickly, towels her hair, wraps herself in a bathrobe, and goes downstairs. Before she opens the door, she pauses, barefoot, on the cool white tiles and listens, but all she can hear are the water pipes gurgling and the repetitive, *ha-ha* birdsong. She opens the door a crack. The porch is empty, but something by her feet catches her eye: a thin envelope on the doormat. It is grubby, a little crumpled, addressed to Dr. Greg Gallo in tight, scratchy-looking handwriting.

She picks it up, steps back inside, and rips it open, unfolding a single sheet of paper.

How can you look at yourself in the mirror every day?

It is unsigned.

She steps out onto the porch again, holding her bathrobe shut, scanning the bright street. Nobody is there.

She goes back inside and double-locks the front door. Then she walks quickly through to the dining room and peers out. A woman with white curly hair, a floral shirt, and a small dog is walking briskly past.

She goes back across the hall and into the living room, looking through the side window, past the swing set toward the corner of the street and the square brick house opposite. She has seen the family getting in and out of their van: parents and three small children, all of them red-haired. But their driveway is empty today.

She goes into the kitchen, half expecting to find a face pressed against the French doors. But the deck is empty, too. A leaf flutters down like a tiny gold butterfly.

She checks the locks, then hurries upstairs and shuts the bedroom door behind her. Her phone is on the bed. She calls Greg's number, but it goes straight to voice mail, despite his promise to have his phone on all the time. Right now he will be surrounded by surgeons and medical reporters. She tries Nell again, but that goes to voice mail, too.

She needs to stay calm. Whoever left the note has gone. It is nothing, just a question, just a scattering of words on a page. She wonders if she should take it to the police—but presumably they will tell her that it is not a crime to ask a question.

It has to be the same person who wrote to Greg before. It seems unlikely now that this is someone with no connection to him, since whoever it is has gone to the effort of finding out his home address and delivering the note by hand. It is likely, surely, to be a grieving relative—someone who lost a child long ago and blames Greg. He has never told her much about his time as a medical student or about his life as young doctor here in Boston. The note-writer could have surfaced from those shadowy years, drawn out by the news of his return.

It is not surprising. Greg's working life takes place on the outermost edges of human experience; he sees and does things every day that take him across an indefinable border and back again. There must be times when a loved one crosses over with him—a parent, an aunt or uncle or grandparent—and can't get back the way he can; she or he doesn't know how; the pain is too deep, the loss overwhelming.

She pulls underwear out of the chest of drawers, shrugging off the bathrobe and glancing at her belly. New, red-penciled claw marks have appeared up her sides. As she tugs on a pair of underpants and a sports bra, she notices that her jewelry box is open. Her nicest earrings—the delicate aquamarine stones on thin gold hoops that Greg gave her for her birthday—are sitting on the bureau next to the box. She nestles them back into their velvet cushion. She is sure that she didn't take them out this morning. Maybe Greg moved them while he was looking for cufflinks yesterday. Or perhaps he got them out deliberately, wondering why she so rarely wears them. She should reassure him that she doesn't wear them every day because she loves them too much, not too little. But surely, if Greg got them out yesterday, she would have noticed them before now.

She pulls on drawstring pants and a clean T-shirt and, as an afterthought, slips the hoops into her ears. The quiet house folds itself around her again, the creak of an expanding floorboard, drops from the shower head plinking onto the damp porcelain. She has always craved solitude, but right now it feels cavernous and threatening. She crosses the room to the side window. A scarlet bird with a black face swoops from a branch of the cypress, spreading its wings, feathers splayed into sharp points, making her jump back. Then she sees movement in the next-door yard.

Helena is walking toward her garden office, talking on her cell phone, and as she steps into a patch of sunlight, the caramel streaks in her dark hair are illuminated like long threads of fire. She slows, still talking on her phone, and turns her head to stare through the shrubs at Tess's deck, perhaps all the way through the French doors and into the kitchen. For the second time Tess has the urge to photograph the woman—to capture the sunlight on her hair, the trees all around her. But then Helena moves on, vanishing into her office.

Tess slides onto the bed and picks up her laptop. Resting it on her knee, she googles "Dr. Vaus." Several links spring up, each one containing the word *toxic*. She clicks on drvaus.com, and a photo of Helena unfurls: pond-green eyes in sharp focus, the rest of the face softened. Dr. Helena Vaus, a "Harvard-trained physician," author of a *New York Times*–best-selling book, *The Green Doctor: Detox Your Life with Energy and Joy.*

The head shot has definitely been doctored. Helena's teeth look as if they have only ever bitten into almonds or apples, the fine lines around her eyes and mouth have been erased, her eyeballs whitened, any shadows removed, her skin tone evened, her nose slimmed, strategic highlights added to sharpen her jawline.

She skims through an excerpt from the book's introduction.

. . . After I gave birth to my first child, I was a mess. I couldn't shift the thirty pounds of baby weight, no matter how far I ran on my treadmill or how restrictive my diet. I was working all hours, stressed out and depleted— emotionally, physically, spiritually, sexually. So what did I do? I "leaned in," of course—worked harder, sucked it up. I was determined to succeed, as a physician, wife, mother, even if it killed me. I was in Toxic Meltdown.

There follows a long description of how Helena turned her life around with organic food and meditation.

I still run my Women's Clinic, but I now have a brilliant co-director. I have trained as a yoga teacher; I pick up my daughters from school, attend their soccer and track meets and recitals; I have a powerful sex drive; I sleep like a baby; I no longer fly into rages or take mood-regulating medications; my marriage has never been better . . .

She scrolls through more beatific images of Helena, in a Lotus pose, drinking a green smoothie, jogging through a dappled wood. There is a blog, too, with posts about diet and exercise, mala-beads meditation, toxin-free makeup, natural tampons, the benefits of a daily orgasm, "cortisol-lowering" green shakes. There is a Dr. Vaus Facebook community—a huge following—and links to YouTube videos. Helena is some kind of modern-day guru.

She clicks on "Dr. Vaus supplements," and there is a photo of the little pill bottles with their orange-flame logos—$159 for a month's supply of probiotics, omega-threes, vitamins, and herbal anti-stress remedies.

She pushes the laptop aside. It all feels like an elaborate lie. Helena is not picking up her girls every day from school—they are in the after-school program—and other than that one time at the school playground, it has always been Josh who takes and fetches their daughters. Their marriage, what's more, is clearly not problem free. But at least the vitamin gift makes sense now. It was not flirtation—it was promotion.

She should feel relieved, but somehow she doesn't. Perhaps a small part of her was hoping that Helena would turn out to be nicer than she seems, and they would become friends. This, now, feels out of the question.

CHAPTER SEVEN

Greg was supposed to be back from Chicago hours ago. It is almost seven now, and he is still not home. They spoke as he waited for his flight: she told him how proud she was, and he sounded tired but elated. He was due to touch down at around four, but now he is not answering his phone. There will be a simple explanation—his flight was delayed, or he has stopped by the hospital and become involved in something—but she is beginning to feel anxious. She just wants him home.

Darkness is creeping around the house. She has spent the afternoon working, rather unproductively, on *Hand in Hand*. There has been no more bleeding, the sickness has vanished, and the baby is active inside her, but after the last twenty-four hours her body still feels precarious.

She gets the ingredients for a stir-fry out of the fridge and begins chopping red peppers, trying not to slice into her fingers with the Japanese knife. She closes the blinds. She wants to call David and speak to Joe, but she knows she mustn't—she must leave them alone this weekend. It is important to do that.

She hears a noise—a shifting sound, a scramble, followed by a small thud—and stops chopping.

"Greg?" She holds the knife suspended. "Is that you?" She can't see into the hall from where she is standing. But there is it again: a shuffle, a little thud. "Who's there?" Her voice comes out high and unexpectedly loud. Someone is in the basement.

With the knife in one hand, its blade pink from the peppers, she steps toward the archway, peering into the pallid hallway. She hears it again. It is definitely coming from the basement. She lurches toward it and bolts the door.

Her head feels bright; her heart pumps against her ribs. "I'm calling the police!" She reaches for her phone, but then she hears a tiny tapping sound—rapidly receding claws, definitely claws, heading back down the basement steps.

If it is a rat, it is a huge one. Perhaps a dog—or a coyote—has found its way in through the garage. She presses her ear against the door. The tapping has stopped.

She dials Greg again and leaves him a message: "Where are you? I think there's an animal in the basement. Where the hell are you, Greg?" She wishes she could pour herself a massive glass of wine. Inside her, the baby turns, dreamily, as if she has woken it.

Back in the kitchen, she fries strips of tofu in ginger and garlic and cooks the noodles, leaving them to cool in a bowl like little entrails. The evening is still again; the cicadas are silent. She didn't notice when they stopped, but now that they have gone, everything feels eerily quiet.

She remembers a conversation she and Greg had about the cicadas, soon after arriving here. They were lying in bed, listening to the rasping, ticking sound.

"They're so loud, it's like they're inside your head," she said. "There must be hundreds of them, but you never even see one."

"It could be just a couple," he said. "A single male cicada can make a phenomenal racket when it's calling for a mate." He pulled her closer, and she rested her head on his chest, hearing the faint thumping of his heart and the comforting rumble of his voice deep in his rib cage. "There's this one type of cicada in Massachusetts that spends seventeen years buried underground feeding on roots," he says, "Then one day, all at the same time, they claw their way to the surface, split their skin, and sprout wings."

She lifted her head and looked up at him. "Seventeen years?"

"Uh-huh. Once every seventeen years cicada experts in Massachusetts get really excited. It's called a 'periodical brood.'"

She laughed. "What must it be like inside your brain, Greg? How on earth do you know this stuff?"

"At college I had a roommate who was studying the periodical brood. They're kind of scary-looking—black bodies, spooky red eyes, bright-orange legs—but they have very beautiful wings, iridescent, like fairies." He ran a hand through her hair, stroking it gently off her face.

She goes through to the dining room and lays the table now, using cloth napkins and their best glasses, wanting to make things special to dispel the feeling that everything is subtly off-kilter. She tries not to think about the fat black bodies that are out there deep in the soil, buried in the roots of the shrubs and the trees, biding their time.

Before she closes the blinds, she peers through the crisscrossed windows at the front yard. Dusk is closing in; the lights from the Schechters' front room casts a shallow yellow pool on the road. Just for a second she thinks she catches movement in the shadows by the Schechters' garage. She presses her nose to the glass, but it fogs up. She wipes the condensation away and peers out again, holding her breath. The street is empty.

She feels the baby swivel, then hiccup. It is definitely alive—its movements feel stronger, as if it wavered but has now committed itself to being here. She thinks about the little heart on the ultrasound, squeezing faithfully. She remembers, just a few weeks ago, hearing Greg telling Joe about a lecture he was going to, given by some doctors from California who put tiny balloons inside the hearts of babies while they were still in the womb.

The two of them were in the kitchen, and she was in the dining room next door, but she could hear everything they said.

"Inside its mom, the baby's heart is just the size of a little grape," Greg said. "Imagine trying to thread a needle into exactly the right spot inside a moving grape! The doctors practice using a grape in Jell-O, because it wobbles around like the heart would inside a tiny baby."

"Is our baby's heart the size of a grape?"

"Yes, right now it is, but it will get a lot bigger before it's born."

Her phone buzzes in her back pocket, making her jump. She yanks it out: a text from Greg.

hope you got msg? Just out of the OR—home in under an hour—
SORRY!

Before she can reply, the phone begins to buzz, and Nell's name appears.

"Tess? I only just got your messages—I had that massive engagement party today."

"Oh, sorry—I totally forgot. How did it go?"

"Fine, fine—I emailed you a picture of the cake I made; it's three tiers with a blue VW van as the top tier. Everyone loved it, thank God. But, look, are you all right? You sounded really rattled."

Tess glances at her watch. "God, Nell, what time is it there? It must be one in the morning—what are you doing calling me? Why are you even up? Go to sleep. We can talk tomorrow."

"No, no, I can't sleep; that's why I'm calling you. I need to wind down. What's happening? Did you have any more bleeding?"

"No, I'm fine. The baby's fine."

"You sound odd."

"No, I'm not. I'm just . . . well, something slightly creepy happened today." She goes through to the sofa and folds her legs underneath herself as she tells Nell about the note on the doormat. There is a long pause.

"What?" Tess says.

"*How can you look in the mirror*? I don't know, it just . . ." Nell is speaking quietly, presumably so she won't wake Ken. "It sounds a bit like something an angry lover might say."

"Does it?"

"Well, could it be?" Nell says. "I mean, I know Greg's a compartmentalizer and doesn't like to talk about the past and all that, but I do think it's odd how little he's told you about his life before he got to England. Could there be some rabid ex hanging around out there?"

"From his student days?"

"Maybe. Has he told you anything at all about Harvard?"

"Of course he has. But there's not much to tell—all he did was work. He graduated top of his class, which is freakish, really. He did have girlfriends, but they always split up because he basically didn't have time for them. I'm sure there was nothing big to tell, or he'd have told me."

"Would he?" Nell yawns, and her voice stretches with tiredness. "Well, I think you should ask him anyway."

As Tess hangs up, she realizes that this isn't the first time Nell has questioned Greg's past. Just before the movers came, the two of them were in Nell's kitchen, with the boys thudding around upstairs, excited about a sleepover, making the ceiling shudder. Nell was at the stove, in jeans and a striped top, her hair scooped up messily, some of the dark curls loose, and she turned, one hand on the teapot. "Has Greg *really* never been married before?"

They hadn't even been talking about Greg. There was no preamble. The question had obviously been on Nell's mind for a while.

"You know he hasn't."

"I know, but it's just . . . I can't stop wondering, why not? I mean, look at him: he's a brilliant surgeon, gorgeous, caring, solvent, and—what—forty-seven? It's just odd, that's all—isn't it?—that he wouldn't have been married at least once. Don't you find it odd?"

"I haven't been married before either."

"Yes, well, I suppose you're tolerably pretty and definitely not stupid, but you're only thirty-nine, and you and David might as well have been married—you were together for six years."

"OK, well, thanks for that, but you can stop worrying. He's had plenty of relationships. A few of them were quite serious—he was with one woman for almost four years."

"Why didn't he marry her?"

"Oh, my God, Nell, what is your problem? He didn't love her enough."

In fact, she knew, because Greg had told her, that his relationship with this particular woman, an academic at UCL, had ended because she wanted a baby and he did not. He'd told her that most of his serious relationships had ended for this reason. She is not sure, now, why she couldn't admit this small fact to Nell.

It is really late by the time she hears the electronic doors buzz and Greg's car roll into the garage beneath the house. She isn't hungry anymore; she is heavy-limbed and headachy, ready for sleep. She hauls herself off the sofa, but before she can get to the basement door, he is thumping on it.

"Tess?"

She slides the bolt back.

"Good idea to lock it." He kisses her. He seems to fill the hallway, taller and broader and darker than he should be. As he hugs her, she catches a whiff of coffee on his breath, a hint of soap on his skin, and something else—an odd, unfamiliar smell that makes her pull away.

"I am so sorry," he says. "I got the emergency call just as I touched down at Logan. It was a newborn, hypoplastic left heart syndrome . . . They sent a car for me. But just look at you, you poor thing—you're so pale. Have you managed to get some rest since yesterday? Did you? Are you OK? God, I hated leaving you like that."

"I didn't know where you were."

"But surely you got the call. It was critical."

"I didn't get any call. I was expecting you hours and hours ago. How on earth did you end up in surgery? I thought you were coming straight home from the airport." She closes the basement door behind him and bolts it, suddenly furious.

"I couldn't call you. I was on the phone from the moment the plane touched down all the way to the hospital, then I had to scrub in the minute I got there, but I asked the circulating nurse to let you know what was happening—didn't she call you?"

She dimly remembers hearing the phone ringing while she was cooking and ignoring it, assuming it would be another silent call.

"I didn't get a message." She glances across the kitchen to the answering machine. It is blinking.

"Oh, you poor thing." He reaches for her. "You must have felt completely abandoned."

There is no way, now, no possible way to be angry with him, because, of course, a newborn with a hypoplastic left heart, whatever that might be, outweighs everything else.

"Is the baby all right?"

"Well, she's stable right now, so she's probably going to be OK." He runs a hand through his hair and blinks. She recognizes this look. It is not just physical fatigue; it is more complicated than that. Greg has done things tonight that no human being is supposed to do, and he needs to transition back to domesticity, to home, to her. There is no point blaming him for not being here.

They walk into the kitchen together.

"I loved watching you get your prize." She pushes aside her resentment. "You were great. And there were so many people there. Have you come back down to earth yet?"

"There's nothing like emergency surgery for that." He steps toward her, reaching for her from behind and pulling her to his chest. "Are you OK, really?" he says. "No more bleeding? Is the baby moving?"

"I'm fine, apart from angry letters. Did you get my message about that?" she asks. "Someone dropped off an envelope here while I was in the shower."

"I only picked up your message about that just now. I called you from the car, but you were on the phone."

"I was talking to Nell." She moves away from him, picks up the letter from the countertop, turns, and hands it to him.

He takes it, and she watches his face as he reads it, but his expression remains blank. Then he turns away and hangs his jacket on the doorknob.

"This person knows our address," she says. "I think we should take it to the police."

"The police? There's no point in that." He runs a hand through his hair. "We'd only get embroiled in pointless police bureaucracy. You know how little the police in this town have to do? They'll tie us up for hours, if not days, but they won't do anything. What could they do? It's not even a threat; it's just a question. It's nothing. There's no law in Massachusetts or anywhere else that forbids asking a question."

"But it *is* a threat. Leaving an anonymous and hostile note on someone's doorstep is a threat. And we've got Joe to think about—we can't just ignore this. It's obviously the same person who sent you the other note. What if they're dangerous?"

He moves past her and reaches for a bottle of red wine. "Look, I'm not worried, OK? I'm really not. I know other surgeons who've had similar experiences. Just leave it with me, OK? I'll work out who it is."

"What similar experiences? So you *do* think it's an angry former patient or family member?"

"Maybe. I don't know. There's a couple of people it could be. I'm looking into it. I'll put a stop to it, OK?"

Under the kitchen lights the skin around his eyes looks jaundiced, as if he hasn't slept properly in weeks. But she can't just leave it there. "Who might it be?" she asks. "Who?"

"OK, well, off the top of my head I can think of one case—every doctor can. This person isn't dangerous; she just lost a baby, that's all."

"That's *all*?"

"Come on, Tess, you know what I mean."

"So you think it's a woman, then? Who is she?"

"Listen, there's not really any point speculating. And there's patient confidentiality to think about. I'll work this out, Tess. I promise. It's just someone who wants to be heard, that's all."

She wonders if it is less threatening—or more—to imagine that the person who wrote this note is female. She isn't sure. Then she remembers Nell's theory. "Is it possible that it's not about a medical case at all? What if it's an old girlfriend—you know, maybe someone who was once hurt by you and hasn't forgotten it?"

"No." He jerks his elbow and, with a deep pop, uncorks the wine. "There's no one like that—you know there isn't. Listen, just let me deal with this. Whoever sent it, it's me they're upset with, not you. Nothing's going to happen to you or to Joe." He puts down the corkscrew and rubs a hand over his head.

"You can't say that for sure."

"OK, honey, I get why you're unsettled by this, I really do, but I've been in the OR, and I need a shower, wine, and food—I haven't eaten anything since the flight." He peers through the archway at the table she has laid with napkins and glasses and a bowl of white roses. "Hey, wow. That looks nice."

"I wanted us to celebrate your award."

"Well, that sounds perfect. Let me just take a quick shower." He pours his glass of wine and takes a swig.

"Do you have to? It's so late."

"Two minutes. I'll be two minutes." He holds up two fingers, then vanishes through the archway. She hears him take the stairs two at a time.

She wishes she could pour herself a glass of wine, put her feet up, and just let go. Tension like this cannot be good for the baby. Perhaps she needs to trust Greg that it is not unusual for a surgeon to be badgered by people who can't move on and need someone to blame. If she and Joe were in any danger, he would be worried, but he seems almost casual. Perhaps this isn't as alarming as it seems.

She thinks about the bitter question in the note. Tonight Greg saved a baby's life. He used skills, honed through years and years of exhausting work and study, to reshape, graft, repair, and reconstruct a tiny malformed heart. Nobody has the right to ask Greg how he can look in the mirror. His whole life is devoted to saving others. She remembers a card she once saw on the wall of his Great Ormond Street office, sent by the father of one of his patients: "You," the man had written, "are the Hands of God."

The Thai tofu has the texture of memory foam. As they chew, she tells him about the scratching noise. "I thought it was an intruder—I almost called the police—then I realized it had claws. Big claws."

"Aha, yes, I got that message, too, in the car—it could be an opossum."

"A what?" She gives her head a little shake.

"An opossum—they sometimes find their way into basements. I'll call animal control tomorrow—they just come and catch them and take them away. It's nothing to worry about."

"It sounded worrying."

"Well, they aren't small, but they probably won't hurt you. In fact, when they're threatened, they often just lie down and pretend to be dead. It's a weird sight." He pulls a face. "They stick their tongues out like that and roll their eyes back and don't move even if you poke them. It's where that saying comes from, you know, 'to play possum.'"

He asks about *Hand in Hand* then, and she tells him how she is trying to choose images that will reflect the surgical miracle of transplants, as well as the hope, the fear, the urgency, the miraculous skill of it all.

"I can't imagine what it must feel like to have someone else's heart beating inside your chest, can you?" She puts down her fork. "I mean, you'd surely feel as if your identity had changed in some fundamental way, wouldn't you?"

"When it comes to transplants, I think the identity issue is often more complicated for the donor family than it is for the recipient. They can feel as if person they love is still alive, and then it's hard to let go. There's an anthropologist in New York who studies this stuff." He takes a sip of wine. "She calls it 'biosentimentality.'"

She tries to imagine how she would feel if Greg's heart, or Joe's, was beating inside a stranger. She, too, would want to be close to that person. *Sentimentality* of any kind seems a harsh word for what must be a profound longing.

"When I was photographing the man who got that heart, I wanted to ask him if he felt his identity had changed, but I didn't in the end."

"Why not?"

"It seemed intrusive."

"That's why you're such a talented photographer, you know," he says. "You don't intrude on people—you don't force your personality on anyone. Your subjects almost forget you're there, and they let their guard down, so then you capture something more in them than they might otherwise show."

"I wish I did."

"But you do—you did with me." He sits back and looks at her, his brown eyes fixed on her face. "You know what? You look amazing, Tess," he says. "I've been thinking that ever since I walked in, but I haven't actually said it."

"I was trying to make an effort tonight." She touches an earring. "I'm wearing the earrings you gave me."

He squints. "Hey. So you are."

"I got the hint. You're right: I should wear them more."

He frowns. "What hint?"

"Didn't you get them out of my jewelry box, before you left? They were out on the bureau."

"No—at least, I don't think so, not deliberately."

She suddenly thinks about the letters, lying next to the wire basket in the kitchen when she was sure she had tidied them away. "Did you see the vitamins?" she asks. "Helena's vitamins?"

"Helena's what?"

"The woman next door? She sent you some vitamins—they're in your pile of letters over there." She glances into the kitchen. "In the tray."

"I haven't touched my mail in days."

Perhaps she is going crazy—taking things out, moving objects, and forgetting she has done it. Pregnancy brain, hormones. But she hasn't noticed herself doing anything particularly absentminded. Maybe it was Joe.

"Did David and Joe get off OK?" Greg asks. "I bet Joe was happy to see him after all this time."

"Yes, he really was. David took him to a Red Sox game this afternoon, and he was so delighted. It was lovely to see him properly happy—I feel like I've hardly seen him smile since we got here."

"He'll adjust, you know. You just have to give him time. I know it's hard to see him miserable, but he'll be OK."

"I'm not sure. He's really deeply unsettled. I've been wondering if there might be something more going on—I know kids can be hostile to a new kid, can't they? I've asked the teacher, but he hasn't noticed anything. But I might go back in next week."

"I'm sure it's fine, Tess. It's normal. He'll be fine—stop worrying."

This is, no doubt, what happens when you spend your days with desperately ill children: you lose tolerance for more ordinary forms of distress in a child. "He's not fine," she says.

"But he will be, and he'll be able look back on this one day and know he survived, and that's a good thing for a child. It's the sort of thing that builds emotional resilience."

"Really? Do you feel like that about your own childhood? I'm not sure I do."

"I don't think we can compare what Joe's going through right now with what I went through—or you, for that matter, with your mentally ill mother. Joe has a stable home, and that counts for an awful lot."

"Do you feel stronger for what happened to you as a child?"

"What? I don't know, Tess." He frowns, looking down at his plate. "It's not like there's a control me somewhere, being raised without a family tragedy."

She can practically hear his internal doors swinging shut. But she is not going to back off, not this time. "What about when you moved to London? Didn't you feel homesick and lonely then?"

He refills his wineglass. "I didn't have time to feel anything at all. Plus, I was working with Kemi, so if I did feel anything, it was profound gratitude to be in that privileged position." He swigs the wine, puts down his glass, picks up his knife, and slices into a piece of tofu.

"You know, I was thinking, maybe we could take a trip to Pennsylvania one day. I'd love to see where you grew up, and we could—"

He stabs the tofu with his fork. "I don't want to go back there, Tess. You know that."

"But—"

"Look, I know what you're trying to do, but trust me, no part of me whatsoever wants to revisit my childhood." He puts the tofu into his mouth and chews. His eyes reflect the candles, two tiny yellow flames flickering in his black pupils.

"But surely—"

"Tess," he says, "do you think we could *not* do this right now? I've had a long and intense day today. I know you want me to talk about my childhood, but right now I just can't."

"OK. Fine. I know; but this is also the problem, isn't it?" She grips the edge of the table. "There is never a time when we can actually talk about anything. There's nothing left of you by the time you're with me."

"I know it's been tough lately. It won't always been this intense."

"It's not just intense. It's extreme. I bleed, and you make it back for five minutes; someone drops a creepy letter on our porch, and you don't even call me back. Sometimes I wonder what I'm doing here!"

"I know. I know—I'm sorry. I know I've just not been around for you. And you must be missing Nell, too. You need friends here."

"This is not about friends. I'll make friends. I don't care about that. And I do miss Nell, but that's not it either. It's about me and you—it's about you being completely absent."

"But I'm here right now." He reaches out a hand, a conciliatory gesture, but she doesn't move hers to meet it.

"It's not just this move. Ever since I got pregnant, I feel like there's this space that's opened up between us, and I don't like it. I wasn't expecting it to be like this."

"OK." His voice hardens. "What were you expecting, Tess? I can't be home for dinner at six every night. This position is phenomenal, and it comes with phenomenal responsibilities and phenomenal demands. I have no option but to do what I'm doing right now. I can't do anything else. It won't always be this bad, but you know what? This is exactly why a baby is such a—" He clamps his mouth shut and looks away.

"Such a *what*?" She grips the table harder, as if it might rise up and spin off into the air, scattering glasses, roses, wine, and candles across the parquet floor. "Go on—a *what*?"

"Such a complicated thing."

"You were going to say 'mistake.'"

He doesn't answer.

"Why can't you be honest?"

"What do you want from me, Tess?"

"I want you to be honest! When I called to say I was bleeding, a part of you was relieved, wasn't it?"

"No."

"I don't believe you."

"Look, if you'd wanted a termination, I would have supported that decision. I was always clear with you that I didn't want a child, so, yes, you're right, in a way, that I am struggling a little to adjust, but none of that—*none of it*—is the same as wanting the fetus to die inside you at twenty-three weeks. How could you think that?"

It is only one word, but it says everything.

"Baby," he says, reading her mind. "It's just terminology, Tess. I'm a bloody surgeon, and I'm exhausted."

"What I don't understand," she says, "is, why is it so awful for us to have a baby? What's so disastrous?"

"I just told you."

"No, you didn't. You really didn't. It's not time pressure; plenty of surgeons have families. So what is it, really? Is it something to do with your own childhood? Is it about your fears that something will go wrong with the baby's heart? What aren't you telling me?"

His jaw tightens, but he doesn't answer.

"You have to make me understand, Greg."

There is a long pause.

"I can't," he says at last. "I just can't."

"Why not?" She throws up her hands, fingers splayed.

He thrusts back his chair and looms up on the other side of the table, his jaw lit from below, his torso inflated, his nostrils flared, and she feels herself recoil, but then he reaches out a hand.

"I can't do this right now. I'm going to do the washing up." His voice is calm. "And then I am going to bed."

She shoves her plate at him and turns her head away. She hears him walk through the arch into the kitchen and dump the plates into the sink. Water splatters against a pan. She looks back at the table, at the trembling wineglasses and the flickering candles. She knows it is unfair to expect anything of him tonight. He has had a ridiculously intense day, even by his standards. But there is something he is not telling her—she can feel it sitting there, like a lump beneath the skin. Instinct made her push him because he is weaker tonight and she wanted him to crack, open himself up, show her the truth. But he will never crack. She hears steel wool begin to scrape against a metal surface, furious and rapid. She pictures his powerful shoulder jerking to and fro as the steel filaments score into the nonstick surface, damaging, scarring, ruining it forever.

CHAPTER EIGHT

Autumn has arrived with almost no lead-in, and the mid-October trees are in crisis, shedding leaves in great, panicky flurries. The temperature has dropped, and as Tess steps onto the porch, she shivers and wraps her scarf around her neck. It is nearly dark already, and a cold drizzle is falling. Joe is furious to be wrenched from the Disney Channel and is putting on his sneakers with exaggerated slowness. She glances at her watch, trying not to bark at him to hurry up.

Greg went into the hospital for a couple of hours to get some paperwork done. He was supposed to be home by six; it is nearly seven now, and he has called twice to say he has been held up but is coming as soon as he possibly can.

The day after their row over dinner, he arranged for animal control to remove the opossum—it turned out that a nest of them was tucked beneath the deck. And since then, for the last few weeks, he has been full of love and concern—calling or texting during the day to check how she is doing, bringing home big bunches of flowers wrapped in brown paper and raffia, calling to see if he can pick up food on his way home, rubbing her feet at night on the sofa, and running her bubble baths, telling her how beautiful she is, how much he loves her. He even canceled a conference in Denver that he said he didn't strictly need to go to. No more threatening notes have appeared on the doorstep, and once or twice Joe has even spoken to her on the way home from school. Everything is edging toward stability.

She has put on mascara and lipstick and is wearing her pregnancy jeans and a dusky pink cardigan over a silk top that is definitely now too tight. Her breasts are at least a cup-size larger, if not two, and her belly is broader than it was with Joe at the same stage of pregnancy. When she thinks about the baby inside her, she pictures it as it was on the anomaly scan three weeks ago, a grainy, black-and-white creature moving in jerks and swivels as the sonographer clicked the mouse, stilling images, measuring, calculating, pointing out feet, hands, face. "You really don't want to know if it's a boy or a girl? You sure?"

After swapping between flats and heeled boots twice, she has gone with the boots, but now she wonders if this is the right thing to wear to a potluck party. Greg said, "Dress casually, but make an effort." She is not sure what this means here. She imagines stepping into a roomful of women in Nikes and T-shirts. Or, worse, cocktail dresses.

The trees above the Schechters' house look scratchy and thin against the glowering sky. She puts an arm around Joe as they step from the shelter of the porch, but he shakes her off. Farther down the road in the half-light she sees someone standing on the sidewalk, close to the shrubs. She squints.

"I don't want to go," Joe whines.

"Come on." She glances down at his grouchy face. "It's going to be fun." When she looks up again, the figure has gone.

Joe hauls himself along behind her like a little old man. She probably should have cleaned him up. His hair is all over the place, he has a rip in his sweatshirt, and she knows that in the light his cuffs will be filthy. There are holes in the knees of his jeans, which are only about two weeks old. But if she'd tried to make him change, he'd have lost it, so he will just have to be scruffy.

"We don't even *know* them," he says.

"We're getting to know them. This is what you do—this is how you get to know people. Anyway, you already know Kevin a bit, don't you?"

"I can't stand Kevin Schechter." He says it way too loudly.

"He's in third grade, isn't he? Bit younger than you?"

"He's weird. He only eats white food."

"What do you mean?" They start to climb the steep stairs to the Schechters' front door.

"Macaroni, vanilla ice cream, milk, white bread—only white things. His lunch is completely white every day."

She manages not to laugh.

"Plus, he's really mean. He calls me 'the British kid,' too."

"But isn't it quite cool to be British?"

"No! It's not cool! It's not cool at all! It's awful. They're laughing at me when they say it. I hate Kevin—I hate them all."

She can feel this escalating. "Listen, love," she says in a firm but soothing voice, "it's fine if you aren't keen on Kevin, but just pretend that you like him for tonight, OK? That's what I do. I pretend that I'm not shy and that I like everyone, and then it's over, and I can go home again."

They are at the top of the steps, and Sandra has thrown open the door already. Her smile seems fixed. She has no doubt heard their whole conversation. Then Tess realizes that she is empty-handed. "Oh, no—I forgot to bring the lasagna."

"That's OK." Sandra looks at Joe. There is a slight edge to her voice. "Kevin and the other kids are in the basement, Joe. Why don't you go join them while your mom runs back across the street?"

Joe glues himself to Tess's thigh. "Go on, love." She presses him between his shoulder blades.

Mike is advancing across the open-plan kitchen with a wine bottle. She has only ever seen him in his car, and in the flesh he is enormous. He looks as if he is wearing one of those shoulder-padded football jerseys, but it is just a simple navy sweater. He gives a wave and continues through to the living room. Sandra is in full makeup, a wrap dress, and heels. Despite the chilly evening, her legs are bare and tanned.

As she shoos Joe inside, he gives her a look that she hopes Sandra misses. She jumps back down the steps two at a time, hanging on to the banister, and runs across the road, into the house. It is only as she is kneeling at the sink cupboard, looking for a roll of tin foil, that she realizes that her front door was ajar. She must have failed to close it behind her when she was ushering Joe out. Somewhere in the back of her mind she registers an unfamiliar, slightly cloying smell. She glances over her shoulder. She cannot see into the hall or the darkened dining room from here, but she has the definite feeling that someone has just left the room.

"Greg?" she calls.

A gust of wind comes through the open front door, blowing leaves down the hall. She finds the foil and stands up.

There is nobody in the house—of course, there isn't. She pushes the feeling aside and covers the lasagna in foil, then hurries back out, pulling the door shut behind her, hearing the lock click.

As she is walking up the steps to the Schechters' again, she hears a high-pitched laugh from the front room, and a woman's nasal voice saying, "She did *not*. Seriously?"

"No sign of Greg yet?" Sandra takes the lasagna.

"No. I'm so sorry. I think he must have got stuck at the hospital."

"Don't worry—oh, your coat; just put it there, that's right—come on in, and let me introduce you to some people."

The room has tall, dark windows and a brass fireplace over which hangs a poster-size photograph of the Schechter family in a vibrant autumnal setting. Several people lounge on the chairs and sofas, and all of them are looking at her.

"So, Tess." Sandra touches her elbow. "Have you met the Bennetts from number forty-five?"

She recognizes the red-haired couple from the corner house across the road, though she has never seen them up close. The woman introduces herself as Muriel. She is wearing a powder-blue cable-knit sweater and a string of pearls.

"And this is my husband, Gordon," she says with a lisp.

The tall, thin man steps forward, holding out a hand. "You're going to make a joke about my name."

"Am I? Why?"

He shrugs. "It's some kind of curse in Britain, I guess."

"Gordon Bennett?" Muriel barks.

Tess can't help smiling. She covers her mouth.

Gordon nods. "Every time."

"No, it's just—I think it's Cockney rhyming slang or something." She tries to sound studious. "I can't remember what for."

"It's a minced oath," says Gordon. "A euphemism for an actual curse word," he elaborates.

She decides not to pursue this.

"So. Great!" Sandra says, as if something important has been resolved.

Tess notices Helena Vaux-Feldman in an armchair to one side, and two people she has not met before, looking at her keenly from the other sofa.

"This is Miriam and Bob MacAlpine, from number sixteen." Sandra gestures to the couple on the sofa. They get up. They are both short, with firm, sweaty handshakes. "Miriam and Bob have Deanna and Owen. Owen's Joe's age," Sandra says. "Fourth grade, right?"

"Oh, sure," says Miriam. "He's talked about Joe a lot."

"And, of course," Sandra turns Tess around, "you already know Josh and Helena."

Josh is standing by the fireplace next to Mike and an older man she doesn't recognize. He raises his beer and grins. Helena smiles lazily. She is wearing a draped cashmere sweater and long, ethnic earrings. Tess instantly feels wrong in her straining gray top.

But Sandra is turning her around again, introducing her to a white-haired woman whom Tess has seen walking a terrier. She realizes too late that she hasn't caught the woman's name.

"So, how are you liking American life, Tess?" Miriam has a strong Bostonian accent. "You settling in here OK?"

"Well, it's quite different, but . . ." She takes a glass of fizzy water that Mike is offering, and then Sandra appears with a platter of radishes carved into rose shapes. The conversations start back up. She glances at the carriage clock on the mantel. Greg is one hour and twenty minutes late.

"So, Sandy, I took your advice and signed Owen up for Russian Math." Miriam grabs a radish. "He hates it, but I told him he has to do it if he wants to study at Harvard like his dad."

"Yes, it's kind of brutal," Sandra says, nodding. "But effective."

They all hear a thundering sound, and children burst into the kitchen as if they've been summoned, which, as far as Tess can tell, they haven't. Their hands sweep over the table, piling their plates with potato chips, spilling Coke, elbowing one another. The group boasts several boys but only three girls, one with red hair and the other two she recognizes as Josh and Helena's daughters, both very pretty.

Joe hangs back from the group. His mouth is tight, his shoulders hunched to his ears. He radiates misery, and she wants to sweep him up and take him home, but then the children are gone again, back down to the basement. Joe brings up the rear, carefully balancing his Coke and a plate that holds only chips and pizza.

"I guess we should wait for Tess's husband to come before we eat," Sandra says.

"Oh, no—don't, please. He could be ages."

"Oh, don't worry." Sandra rests a hand briefly on her arm. Her voice is kind. "It's no problem to wait."

Her head throbs, and inside her the baby is restless, kicking, poking, turning. The adults walk back to the living room, and she hears the men talking about the Red Sox, while Muriel and Miriam begin to dissect members of the Parent-Teacher Association, and Sandra says something about Thanksgiving to the woman with white hair.

Tess excuses herself and goes to find the bathroom. She locks the door and leans both hands against its wood panels, closing her eyes, breathing out. A teenage boy's laugh filters down from the room above, and she catches a faint whiff of marijuana.

Greg is just arriving as she emerges from the bathroom. He is wearing his most urbane expression, holding a bottle of prosecco, and she hears him say to Sandra, "It was kind of a complex case."

"Oh, please! Don't give it another thought." Sandra laughs. "We're just glad you could make it. It's great to finally meet you properly."

"Here, let me take that." Mike swoops in and grabs the wine and Greg's coat, pumping Greg's hand.

Greg turns then and sees her—he kisses her cheek, giving her the briefest wink. He is immaculate in a blue-and-white striped shirt and dark pants.

"So, Greg—you know Gordon Bennett?" Sandra holds out an arm. Greg doesn't even flinch; he shakes Gordon's hand, saying, "Gordon, how are you?"

"And Muriel?"

"Gordon's in the medical world, too," says Muriel. "Though not humans."

"I'm a veterinarian." Gordon studies the ceiling.

"Oh?"

"Cats." He clears his throat. "I'm a feline vet."

"He chose cats," Muriel says, "because they're so self-contained, but it turns out, their owners really aren't."

Gordon nods morosely.

"And this is Bob and Miriam MacAlpine." Sandra touches Greg's forearm. He shakes hands with the short couple, using both their names.

"And then, of course, your own next-door neighbors, Josh and Helena Feldman."

Greg raises a hand to Josh, and then he turns to Helena. She gives him a slow smile.

"Sure, we all know each other," Greg says evenly. He turns to Sandra again. Helena recrosses her legs. The soles of her high black shoes are scarlet. Her eyes are fixed, hungrily, on Greg.

"Shall we eat?" Sandra says.

They all help themselves to plates of macaroni and pasta salad, garlic bread, limp salads. Tess takes a plate to the living room and hovers. Greg is deep in conversation with Mike now.

"So, Tess, I hear you're a photographer." Josh appears by her side. "What kind of pictures do you take?"

"Oh, portraits, mainly. I usually do editorial photography for newspapers and magazines. What about you? Are you a doctor, too?"

"I'm a professor at BU, but I'm interested in you right now, Tess. Who do you take pictures of?"

"Well, different people."

"Give me an example."

"It depends on who's commissioning me. For media work, it's whoever is being written about that day." She tries to spear a pasta shell, but it flies off the plate. They both ignore it.

"I had my photo taken for a book jacket recently, and I've got to tell you, Tess, it was painful. I bet that's the hardest part of your job—putting people at ease."

"In a way." She glances at Greg. He is going back to the table, and as he passes Helena, she reaches out and brushes her fingertips against his thigh. He stops and looks down, and she says something. He gives a curt nod.

"Wasn't it Sontag who said using a camera is an aggressive act?" Josh asks.

Whenever she talks to an academic about her work, it's never long before Susan Sontag surfaces. "'To photograph is to appropriate the thing photographed,'" she quotes, then nods and looks for Greg again. Helena is still talking to him, looking up and brushing her thick hair back. Greg glances at her exposed throat.

She certainly did not appropriate Greg when she took his picture the very first time, though he asked her to have a drink with him when she'd finished. They got a cab to a Pimlico pub, and then later, a little drunk, he walked her through Victoria station. As they crossed the concourse, she felt urgent messages buzzing between them, but she told herself that he must be married, even though he didn't wear a ring.

They said good-bye at the platform, a kiss on the cheek, both of them stepping back and laughing at the touch. Then the next day someone opened the main door below her studio and shouted up the stairs that she had a visitor. She came out, rubbing her hands down her jeans, shoving her hair back. Greg Gallo had driven down from

London. "I thought I'd take a look at those photos." He'd grinned, his shoulders filling the doorframe, blocking out the light.

Afterward, as she watched his car pull away, she felt as if a grenade had crashed into her studio, blowing out the walls, leaving the infrastructure exposed. It was just sex, she told herself—incredible sex, admittedly, but he really was not her type: too sure of himself, too inaccessible, and—surely—married.

But, of course, he wasn't. He came for her that day because he wanted her. And what Greg wanted, he got.

"I guess they have a lot to talk about, huh?" Josh is also looking at Greg and Helena. "He's a doctor, I hear?"

"Yes, he's a cardiac surgeon. Pediatrics."

"Long hours? Travels all the time?"

"Yes, actually, he travels a lot." But she doesn't want to talk about Greg's absences or his amazing career, and she certainly doesn't want to talk about herself anymore. "So, what is *your* subject?" she says. "What are you a professor of?"

"I'm a medical historian—I'm interested in eugenics."

"As in Nazi Germany?" From somewhere behind her she hears a low, throaty laugh. She decides not to look.

"Actually, I'm most interested in the origins of eugenics. I just wrote a book about Sir Francis Galton, the Victorian who coined the word. Have you heard of him?"

"I haven't—sorry. I'm very ignorant."

"He was Charles Darwin's cousin, heavily influenced by Darwin's work. He was a troubled genius himself. He once wrote that geniuses are 'within a measurable distance of insanity.' He proposed that successful, beautiful people should be made to breed."

Josh takes a sip of his beer, and they both glance at Helena and Greg, who are still deep in conversation. "He'd have put those two together, that's for sure."

She tries to laugh.

"Galton was a polymath. Among other things, he was the first person to devise a system for classifying fingerprints." Josh takes her hand suddenly and pulls it up to chest level, arranging it into a star shape.

His fingers feel warm and soft. She feels her face heat up. "He identified eight fingerprint types that are still used today—let's see if I can remember them. There's the plain arch"—he touches the tip of her index finger—"tented arch, simple loop, central pocket loop, double loop . . . um . . . lateral pocket loop, plain whorl, and . . ." He touches her thumb, adding, "Accidental."

She pulls her hand away—presumably this is Josh's way of getting to his wife. Before she can say anything, a terrifying wail rises up the basement stairs, and Joe bursts through the doorway, into the living room.

He stands still for a moment, swaying, scarlet-faced, his mouth a rictus of agony, looking for her. He spots her.

"That boy," he shouts, "can just FUCK OFF!"

The adults give a collective gasp.

CHAPTER NINE

She runs across the room to Joe. There is genuine panic in his eyes. He has never said "fuck" before—at least never in her hearing. "What happened?" She bends and takes him by the arms, and he tries to suck in a breath, but before he can speak, the other children burst into the room, all yelling at once, and for a moment there is mayhem. She hears the word "strangle" and sees Miriam rush to Owen, her breasts and belly jiggling.

Joe is sobbing and clinging to Tess as if he was a toddler. His whole body quakes. She kneels down so that she is at his level. "It's OK, love, it's all right. Are you hurt?"

Somewhere, a child says, "The British kid strangled Owen."

"He . . ." Joe is struggling to speak, his face purple. "He . . . hit . . . me . . . I . . ."

"Don't swear again," she says quickly. "Don't swear. Just talk, OK? Just talk."

Then Greg is at her shoulder, leaning over, his voice low and hard. "What you just said was not acceptable, Joe, not acceptable at all." This makes Joe sob even louder. Strings of saliva stretch between his jaw.

"Not now, Greg." She holds on to Joe as his enormous, loud, very un-cute sounds expand to fill the room. The other children are silent now, chastened by a shared understanding that Joe is out of control.

Greg reaches past her and takes Joe by both arms. "You need to stop this noise right now. You need to calm down." She sees Greg's fingers digging into Joe's arms and reaches out her hand, but Joe twists out of Greg's grasp.

"Get off me!" he howls. "Don't touch me! You are not my dad!"

He hurtles across the room, wrenches open the front door, and thuds away down the steps.

She glances at Greg. His face is a solid mask. She turns and runs out of the front door after Joe, but Greg is behind her; he pushes past her on the steps, forcing her to grab hold of the banister. It is raining properly now, thin, sharp, diligent rain. She peers over the railing and sees Greg reach the bottom in one leap and catch up with Joe in just two strides. He seizes him, whipping him around. Joe cowers, and in the dim streetlight she sees fear flash across his face. She hurtles down the stairs after them, shouting, "Stop it! Stop!"

Joe's upper body flips backward and forward in Greg's hands. She throws herself at them, yanking at Greg's arm, trying to force herself between him and Joe, but Greg is immovable, vast, bellowing into Joe's face: "How dare you use that word? How *dare* you? You get back up there right now. You get back up there, and you apologize to those people!" He begins to drag Joe toward the steps, one hand clamped around his upper arm.

She hits Greg's wrist. "Let go of him!" She tries to open his hand, but his fingers are too strong. "Greg, stop! You're hurting him! Stop this!" But he doesn't seem to hear—he doesn't seem to register her at all.

"Mum!" Joe's voice is high and terrified, his eyes enormous. "Mum!" The sound of his fear jolts electricity through her nerve endings, and she seizes Greg's thumb, jerking it back and twisting it hard before letting go.

Greg drops Joe's arm and holds his thumb, his jaw ajar, eyes startled. She grabs Joe and tucks him close against her side, sheltering him from Greg with both arms, one hand over his head. And then for a moment everything stops except the rain, which needles into her scalp. She hears Greg's harsh breaths and her own pulse, thudding somewhere at the base of her skull. Joe lets out a frightened whimper.

A vein in Greg's neck throbs, but he does not move or speak. He just stands rigid, as if he has been jerked back into the present and does not quite know how he came to be here—as if his mind is racing to work out what he has just done.

She lifts her chin. "Go away." Her voice is clear and sharp. "Go away and calm down." She takes a step back, keeping Joe wedged against her, as if they are one body. She takes another step back. "I am going to take Joe home now, and you are going to go somewhere else. You are going to go and calm down."

He nods once. She turns and steers Joe across the street toward the mock Tudor house. She doesn't look back to see what Greg does or where he goes, but she can feel him watching them as they go up the path toward the porch.

It takes her a long time to calm Joe down, lying next to him on his Arsenal Football Club duvet while he cries with his face buried in her chest. The image of Greg's face—his mask of fury and then, when she twisted his thumb, the shock as pain snapped him back into an awareness of himself, of her, of Joe—is lodged in her mind. She wonders if she could have dislocated his thumb. That would be a disaster for any surgeon.

When Joe can speak again, all he will say is that there was a struggle over an Xbox controller, everyone was teasing him, Owen punched him hard in the stomach, and he lost his temper and grabbed Owen around the neck.

"But I let go," he says. "I let go fast. I want to go home," he sobs. "Take me home. I want to go home."

"I know." She strokes his hand. "I know you do, love." It is all she can do not to say, "Me, too."

"Take me home." He looks up at her, and the combination of the desperate expression on his face and the words reminds her of her mother, who would pace the house saying those words over and over, bewildered, afraid, besieged by longing for a safety and stability that only ever existed in her imagination.

She strokes his hair. "This is our home right now, OK, Joey? Home is where people who love you are—and I love you. I love you so much. And Greg loves you, too, even though he got angry tonight and he scared you. Things won't always be this hard, love. It's not easy to settle into a new place, but it will get better. We'll make sure of that."

"It won't get better." He turns away, hunching under his duvet, a small creature in its burrow. "And I hate Greg. He scares me."

"I know you feel that way right now. He lost his temper, and it was very wrong of him to grab you like that. He was angry and upset because you said the *F*-word—that was pretty bad, you know; I was shocked, too, when I heard you say it. You mustn't swear like that ever again, OK? But even so, Greg shouldn't have done that, and I know he feels really bad about it now."

Joe lies very still. She doesn't have the heart to chastise him for swearing anymore. Greg's behavior was far worse than anything Joe did, and they both know it.

She is almost asleep herself, lying next to Joe with the baby dancing and twirling inside her, when she hears the key in the front door and the creak of its big metal hinges. She glances at her watch. It has been almost two hours since she left Greg in the street. She slides off the bed without waking Joe and goes to the top of the stairs.

He is taking off his coat in the hall. He looks up at her. His eyes have dark circles beneath them, but he does not look deranged anymore; he just looks tired.

She comes downstairs, folding her cardigan around her body. "Where have you been?"

"At the Schechters'." He frowns. "Where else would I be?"

"You went straight back there?" She imagines him taking his anger back up the stairs and into that front room. But of course he would never expose himself that way. He would have hauled everything back inside himself, and by the time he got to Sandra's front door, he would have appeared perfectly calm. He has probably spent the last two hours smoothing everything over, explaining that Joe has been unhappy, is having trouble adjusting. None of the neighbors will have any idea what happened in the street. None of them will have seen what she and Joe saw in his eyes.

She reaches the bottom of the stairs. "You hurt him—you terrified him. Don't ever do that again."

"I lost it. I'm sorry. He crossed the line, and I wanted to show him that it wasn't OK—but then I guess I crossed the line, too."

"You really did." She nods.

"I messed up, and I'm sorry." He looks up at her, but his face isn't soft or apologetic. He tilts his head. "But the thing is that these are nice, kind, and reasonable people, Tess. They were appalled: nine-year-old kids around here don't say *fuck,* and they don't wrap their hands around other kids' necks. Owen's mother is particularly outraged."

"Is Owen OK?"

"He has localized bruising around the windpipe and some superficial abrasions." He turns away and hangs his coat in the hall closet.

"*Superficial abrasions*? Why are you talking in medical jargon?"

"Joe's fingernails almost broke the skin on Owen's neck."

"OK, well, that's awful, but think about what it would take to make Joe do something like that. Owen punched him in the stomach, and before that they were all teasing him. Joe's not a violent boy—you know that. He's not aggressive, and he's never done anything remotely like this before. He's had months of teasing at school. He just lost it." The irony of defending Joe while attacking Greg for exactly the same thing does not escape her. But Greg is an adult, and Joe is nine years old. "He's never been in a fight in his life," she says.

"Well"—Greg shrugs—"he has now."

He turns away and double-locks the front door, putting the keys on the shelf above the radiator. Then he walks off down the hall into the kitchen. She pushes her hair back. A headache glimmers between her eyes. It is cold in the hall—there is a draft coming under the door, and she can hear the wind gusting down the chimney in the front room.

She hugs herself, feeling the baby flip and kick deep in her belly. A gust of rain hits the porch. She hears Greg in the kitchen, filling the kettle, putting it on the burner, the gush of the gas, the click and tiny roar as it ignites. She feels a sudden, irrational longing for a simple, efficient, electric kettle.

She does not want to follow Greg into the kitchen. She could just go up to bed. She is weary and chilly. But she knows she should not leave things the way they are. She walks down the hall and into the kitchen.

The lights bounce off the appliances. He has his back to her, and his hair glistens from the rain.

"Let's just hope the MacAlpines don't take it any further," he says without turning. It takes her a moment to realize that he is looking at her reflection in the kitchen window.

"What do you mean?"

"Well, when a child gets strangled here, the parents don't always sit around playing nice." He tosses a chamomile tea bag into a mug and slams the cupboard shut.

"What are you saying?"

"I've known people to litigate for less."

"OK, you have to be kidding me. That's bloody ridiculous."

He shrugs. "It is, but it happens."

"Joe was punched!"

"Owen's the one with the damaged neck," he says, "not Joe." He turns around, leaning on the counter. The kettle on the burner begins to rattle.

"This is nonsensical. They're in fourth grade."

"I'm not saying anyone's suing anyone. I'm just saying that there are some fairly major cultural differences going on here, and you don't seem aware of them. You need to go down the street tomorrow morning *with* Joe and smooth things over with Miriam. I spent a lot of time trying to appease her this evening, but she is clearly not the forgiving type."

The kettle is whining now. Greg snaps the gas off and pours steaming water over the chamomile tea bag. Then he turns and scoops coffee into the espresso machine, twisting the handle with a jerk of his elbow.

"You're making coffee? Now?"

"I have work to do tonight. The chamomile tea's for you."

The coffee machine shudders and growls. They both watch the thick brown liquid stream into the cup. He snaps the Off button, then walks across the kitchen, pausing as he reaches her, waiting for her to step out of his way.

She moves aside and hears him get out his laptop from the bag that's on the dining room table and the metallic ping as it switches on. Her lower back aches, and she feels faintly sick. He has left her chamomile tea on the counter, but she doesn't want it. She doesn't want anything Greg might give her right now.

No way is she going to drag Joe down the street tomorrow to apologize to that woman. If it ever came to anything as ludicrous as police involvement, then Greg—the pediatric doctor who witnessed this—would defend Joe. He is saying this because he wants to punish her. She has demonstrated to all the neighbors that she is not the beautiful English wife with the perfect little boy. Their family is messy, unpredictable, and slightly out of control.

She thinks about the shock on their faces when Joe shouted "fuck." In England someone would have made a joke or called out "steady on" or laughed or said something, anything, to defuse the moment, but the neighbors tonight had all been genuinely—understandably— aghast. They probably now think that she is the sort of mother who teaches her child to say *fuck* when he's annoyed. It would be funny if it weren't so awful. She rests a hand on the countertop, feeling the cold, smooth marble beneath her fingers. She has never felt as culturally adrift as she does right now.

Greg has sealed his rage back up, but in doing so he has shut her out. She hears him clear his throat as his fingers clatter lightly on the keyboard. She looks at him through the archway. The light of the screen illuminates his strong features. He works like a predator, his body terribly still, his brain arrowed in on the task. He will keep this up for hours now.

She remembers how he once described the intensity of emergency surgery: "It's not just my emotions that shut down," he explained. "Everything does—even basic needs like hunger, thirst, and tiredness. I don't need anything at all, no food, no bathroom breaks, nothing. It's like I only exist for one purpose: to get the job done."

It is clear that they won't resolve anything tonight. She couldn't get through to him now even if she had the energy to try. But whatever is buried inside him—the grief, loss, anger, self-blame, and terror—pushed its way to the surface tonight, and for those few moments out there in the rain she'd seen the part of him that she had, until now, only sensed intuitively.

She switches off the kitchen lights and turns away. Of all the people she has dealt with this evening, it is Greg who feels the most like a stranger.

CHAPTER TEN

The problem with a laundry chute is that you throw clothes down and then forget about them. She hasn't tackled the washing since before the potluck, ten days ago now. She gathers armfuls of dirty clothing from the concrete floor. It is just past eight, but Joe is tucked up in bed already, exhausted from whatever nameless tension he has experienced all day at school. Greg is still not back. She will put this load in, make a cup of tea, and go to bed with a book.

Since the potluck dinner she has felt listless and drained. She has struggled to get Joe off to school, and a couple of times after he has gone she has crawled back into bed and slept, dreamlessly, for another three or four hours. When she was six months pregnant with Joe, she felt alive, fecund, and energetic, but this is entirely different. Perhaps it is the contrast between a first pregnancy at age thirty and a second at thirty-nine. But she can't help suspecting that this perpetual weariness is some kind of fallout from the scene in the street.

They did talk, the day after it happened. Greg was apologetic; he took her hands and admitted that the pressure had built up, that he had snapped. He has been tender with Joe ever since, gently trying to rebuild trust, but the tension in the house now will not shift, no matter how nice they are to each other, how accommodating, how understanding—and now when Joe looks at Greg, he does so sideways, as if he can't turn his face full on to him.

She shoves stale clothing into the drum of the washing machine. It is top-loading, big enough that she could almost climb in herself. She straightens, rubbing the ache in her lower back and turning away, stretching, trying to shift the baby from its odd, uncomfortable position against her spine.

Greg's boxes are on the shelves, just above eye level. They will get damp down here with the moisture from the washing machine pumping out into the already clammy air of the tiny laundry room. She should move them, or at least transfer the contents into plastic crates. He has never specifically asked her not to open his boxes, but the masking tape is wound around each one several times. She would have to tear it off the soft cardboard to get inside, and the whole thing might disintegrate. Perhaps he has photographs of his childhood tucked away in there—memories that he cannot bear to revisit, even for her. He might not mind her looking, but, of course, she should ask him first.

Everybody carries grief differently, and it is not for her to dictate how Greg should cope with his, but she had hoped that being back in the States would allow him to talk about his childhood more, perhaps fill in some of the blanks. If anything, however, his past feels even more out of bounds here than it did before.

She turns back to the machine and shoves the last few things into it. As she is tipping laundry powder into the drum, a flash of scarlet catches her eye. It is sticking out of the pocket of Greg's pants. She digs down for it, thinking it must be a toy from the infants' ward at the hospital, and pulls it out. It takes her brain a moment to compute what she is holding between her thumb and forefinger. It is a woman's plastic hair clasp.

She drops it as if it is soaked in acid. And then everything crashes in: Greg's absences, his delays, his tension—the growing feeling she has that he is concealing something, never telling the whole truth. She remembers Helena's fingers brushing his thigh at the potluck dinner.

A coldness spreads through her torso, as if her ribs have cracked open to expose her heart and lungs. She slides to the floor, head in hands, knees splayed to make room for her belly. She remembers that he said Helena had been helpful when he was over here alone, letting the cable guy in, dealing with the mail. It is possible that he gave Helena a key to this house.

She thinks about the earrings, the moved stack of mail—and the feeling, when she rushed back from the Schechters', that someone had just left the room. Then she remembers the long strand of hair that she found on the sink on her first night in the house, coppery, dark. She imagines Greg pressing Helena up against the sink, running his hands up her firm thighs, his mouth on hers, her head thrown back, and that long hair falling like a waterfall onto the white ceramic.

And yet, though vivid, this image doesn't quite feel plausible. It feels more like a staged photograph than a reality. But what else would he be doing with a woman's hair clip in his pocket? No—he would not do this to her. Greg is not that kind of man.

But isn't that what all betrayed women tell themselves? They say that they always sensed something was wrong but refused to believe it, that they ignored evidence even when it was staring them in the face. Something is definitely not right with Greg—she is sure of it. So perhaps this is it.

She lifts her head, pushing back her sticky hair. She has to call him. She swallows against a rising nausea. The baby thuds inside her belly, booting with both tiny feet at once. Upstairs, the phone begins to ring. She presses her fingers into her eyeballs, then gets up, lurches up the stairs, into the kitchen, and picks it up.

"Hello?"

The line crackles. The kitchen lights buzz and whine overhead. Suddenly she feels sure that it is Helena on the other end. She could have gotten the number when she let the phone company in.

"SAY SOMETHING!" she shouts into the receiver. "WHAT DO YOU WANT? Stop calling! Stop this!"

The line, as always, goes dead.

She slams the receiver down, then picks it up again and dials Greg's number. It goes to voice mail. Her voice shakes. "I just found something in your pocket, and I have to talk to you, right now. I don't care what you're doing. Just call me."

She is very cold—her whole body is shivering. She walks slowly upstairs to the bedroom and moves from window to window, closing the blinds. She turns on the shower, stripping quickly and stepping under the scalding water, scrubbing shower gel over her skin, across the pallid mound of her belly and her tight, blue-veined breasts, between her legs.

As she steps out of the bathroom, wrapped in a towel, she hears voices and sudden, high laughter coming from outside. She goes over to the side window and peers under the blind. Helena's kitchen is lit up. There are lights in the backyard too—fairy lights strung on the half-starved limbs of the trees. She moves to the front window. Cars are parked in the street, and a couple is getting out of a black Mercedes SUV, a woman in silvery heels, a man in a dark jacket.

Back at the side window again, she stares down through the branches. She can see into Helena and Josh's kitchen—and suddenly there is Helena. She is wearing an aquamarine silk top with flowing sleeves, her hair in loose waves over her shoulders, her mouth set as she takes two bottles from an ice bucket on the kitchen island, and then Josh comes into the kitchen, too. He is wearing a light blue shirt; he says something, and she turns, and for a moment the two of them stand face-to-face, bathed in warm light from above. In their coordinating outfits they look like the most beautiful, perfect couple.

A sudden memory surfaces of Nell saying the same words to her when she told her Greg had proposed. "Oh, my God!" Nell's smile had been a little too wide, too fixed. "Wow! Wow, Tess! That's fast. But no—that's amazing news—really." She held out her arms. "You'll make the most beautiful, perfect couple."

She watches Josh and Helena exchange a few words in their kitchen, and then Helena shoves past him. He steps back, pauses, then follows her into their party, his shoulders bowed.

The night presses around the house. She can hear the distant music, the babble of voices next door as she struggles into pajamas, a sweater, woolen socks. Despite the hot shower she is still shivering; the house is so drafty, so chill.

Then she hears something, a rustling noise down in the hall—not claws, something papery, at the front door.

She knows, immediately, what it is.

She goes out to the upstairs landing and sees an envelope lying on the doormat, crumpled from being shoved beneath the door. She goes down the staircase toward it, hesitates, then throws open the door. A thin, shadowy figure is hurrying through the gate—she glimpses a long, dark overcoat, straggling hair flapping against the shoulders.

"Hey!" she shouts, stepping into the porch. "Stop! Hey!" Her voice echoes back at her, but the figure doesn't slow or turn; it runs, faster, down the street, around the corner, swallowed up by the hungry night.

Breathing hard, she looks at the silhouetted trees behind the Schechters' house, and then she goes back inside. She picks up the envelope, shuts the front door, double-locks it, then rips the envelope open.

I have not forgotten her. I will never forget. I am WATCHING YOU.

She checks the front door again, then moves around the house, checking the doors to the deck, to the basement. Then she goes back upstairs and gets into bed. She is sure, now, that the note-sender is female.

I am watching you.

But the way she fled, she seemed more panicked than menacing.

Minutes, then hours, pass, and still Greg does not call. He cannot, at least, be with Helena—she can still hear the party next door. Perhaps it is not Helena's hair clip in his pocket—it could belong to anyone. It must be so easy for Greg to meet women, with all the traveling, the early mornings, the late nights. Or it could be nothing. He might have found the clasp on the floor in the hospital and absentmindedly picked it up.

Her thoughts feel fantastical: simultaneously real and feverish, like a bad dream from which she is struggling to wake.

The balance between them has definitely shifted since they got here. She has not felt this exposed since childhood. She feels as if she has dropped her beating heart into Greg's hands and is watching to see what he will do with it next. But whatever is going on here, she will not lose her dignity, and she will not become weak and afraid—she will not let this situation undo her, whatever it is.

The baby shifts and then gives her diaphragm a sharp kick. She rubs the nub of a knee or the heel of a miniature foot. A gust of wind whooshes between the houses, making the bedroom windowpanes rattle. The words from the note run through her head. *I have not forgotten her.*

He must know who is sending these notes—who is not forgotten. If this woman is so desperate that she is watching the house, writing these things to him, never forgetting, then he must know exactly who she is and why she is doing this.

She is dozing when she hears the creak of the front door, but she sits up, instantly alert. She hears him moving around downstairs, opening and closing the hall closet, putting his bag on the dining room table. He must have had to walk up and around to the front of the house to let himself in because she bolted the door to the basement.

She gets out of bed and shrugs on the gray cashmere dressing gown he gave her last Christmas, folding it around her belly. She goes to the bedroom door. He is coming up the stairs. He has not switched on the light, and for a second they stare at each other in the gloom. His eyes are wide and startled. He reaches out a hand. "Tess? Honey? Why aren't you sleeping?"

"What time is it?"

"Past one."

She doesn't move. "What have you been doing?"

"There was an emergency." He steps toward her. She moves backward, into the room. "I was in the OR tonight."

"Didn't you get my voice mail?"

"I did." He stops, resting a hand on the doorframe. "But far too late—by the time I got out, I assumed you'd be fast asleep. What's the matter? You sounded upset—are you OK? What's happened? You said you found something?"

She turns and goes back into the moonlit bedroom. She does not want to switch on the light because she does not want to see whatever is in his eyes. He doesn't switch the light on either.

"What is it?" He steps closer. "Tess, honey, what's wrong?"

She gets the note from the bedside table and hands it to him. He squints at it, then turns it over.

"Either you tell me who wrote this, or I'm going to take it to the police tomorrow," she says.

"OK." He sits down, heavily, on the bed. "I wasn't going to say anything, because I thought it had stopped, but, yes, I'm pretty sure I know who it is."

She grits her teeth. "Who?"

"It's something that happened years and years ago. She was very young, kind of a mess—drugs, alcohol. Her baby died at birth. She caused some trouble at the time. I think she went to prison a couple of years later, maybe for a drug offense. She's an unwell person, Tess, but she's only a danger to herself."

"How can you know that?"

"I've asked around—I spoke to a psychiatrist friend about her, someone who treated her out of state. She couldn't give me any specifics, of course, but she did reassure me that the woman's only a danger to herself. Honestly, Tess, if there was any risk to you or Joe, I'd have told you all this, but there isn't. The best way to handle this situation is to ignore it—and it will stop." He steps toward her, holding out his arms. She moves back, out of reach.

"My God. When were you planning to tell me all this?"

"I know," he says, "that you must have been frightened tonight. But I honestly thought it had stopped. I didn't want you worrying about her."

"I'm not a child. I don't need protecting."

"No, of course you aren't, and I know you don't. Of course I know that. But you've had a lot to deal with lately, that's all. I was wrong not to mention it."

"I also found a hair clasp, in your pocket. Not mine. Do you think you might tell me why it's there? Or are you trying to protect me from that, too?"

"You what?" He looks baffled.

"A woman's hair clip. In your pocket."

He shakes his head. "I really don't . . ."

"Greg." She wraps the soft gown more tightly around her body. "Are you having an affair?"

He looks at her. And then he laughs. It is a genuine sound, not even nervous. "What are you *talking* about?"

"God! I feel like I'm going mad. I feel sick, Greg. I actually feel sick." She presses her palm against her forehead. He moves toward her again, touching her arm, but she jerks it away. "Don't."

"OK, OK. I have no idea what some woman's hair thing is doing in my pants, but I can't believe you'd think I was . . . Tess. You are the love of my life. I only just found you—why in God's name would I want to have an affair?"

She feels the blood beat against her temples. The thing is, she believes him. But this is what happens—this is what betrayed people feel. It is possible that she has married a spectacularly good liar.

"This is craziness, honey. You're upset about the note. I know I was wrong not to talk to you about it—stupid, really—but I honestly have no idea why there's a hair clip in my pants." The word—*pants*—sounds slightly comical, and for a moment she almost wants to laugh. She sits on the bed next to him.

The branches outside shudder behind the blinds, making shadows like long, bony hands signaling for help. Greg reaches for her.

"What's happening to us?" she whispers.

He tucks a strand of hair behind her ear. "I haven't been here for you, that's what's happening. These last couple of months must have been really hard on you, and even before that, when I was coming and going and you had to do all the moving, basically on your own, then deal with Joe and all the hassles of settling him in here—and then getting these notes. You've been amazing, Tess. You're the strongest, smartest woman I know. You're the only woman I want—I would do anything other than hurt you. I have no fucking idea how a hair clip made its into my pocket, but—look at me—it's me. You know me. That's not who I am."

She looks into his eyes, and something inside her crumbles, because he is right: she does know him. He is not having an affair.

"Could it be Helena?" she asks. "I've seen the way she behaves around you. And didn't you say she helped you when you were here by yourself? Did you actually give her a key to this house? Could she have been in here?"

He frowns. "I did give her a key one day—she offered to let the phone-company guy in for me, but I got it back the same night."

"She could have gotten a new one cut."

"Oh, come on, why would she do that?"

"I don't know. I have no idea. She's obsessed with you? I don't know."

"OK. She's flirtatious, she makes me uncomfortable, and I've tried not to encourage her. I refused to go running with her for a start, and I haven't really talked to her all that much. I really don't think it's likely that she'd come in and plant a hair clip, of all things. There could be any other explanation for that. The laundry chute—what about that? It could belong to a previous tenant. Maybe it was stuck in the chute and then dislodged by our clothes? I don't know." He puts his head in his hands. "This is all slightly insane, but the bottom line is that Helena—whatever she wants—is irrelevant."

For a while they sit in silence.

"I really don't like what's happening to us here," she says.

"Nor do I. But it will get easier, I promise. This is a huge adjustment, for all of us."

"You feel so far away all the time—I constantly feel like there's all this stuff you aren't telling me."

"I know." They sit in silence again. "I was wrong not to tell you about the woman. I should have told you. It was stupid to think I could protect you from worrying." He rubs his hand across his face, dragging the skin downward like melting wax. "The truth is, you're right: being here has brought some things up for me, things from the past, memories. I've been trying to shut it all down and not really succeeding very well. Maybe that's what you're picking up on."

"You mean memories of your parents? Of the fire?"

He nods. "That. Lots of things."

"Then maybe this is good, Greg. Maybe ultimately this needs to happen—you need to remember these things."

"The thing is, remembering is never helpful for me. It's just not how I work. It never will be."

"Fine, but you still have to talk to me. If all this is going on inside you, if you're struggling with memories, then you have to tell me, even if you don't want to talk about the actual memories themselves. I mean, how can we possibly feel close if you don't let me know what's going on inside your head?"

He nods. "I know you want me to open up and talk and talk and relive my past—I know doing all that helped you deal with your own childhood. I know it helped you come to terms with having an ill mother, and the terrible way she died, and all your own issues. But you have to believe me: it just doesn't work that way with me. I wish it did. But I don't want you to feel shut out. I love you so much."

She rests her head on his shoulder. "I know. I love you, too," she says. "But you have to let me in."

"I want to, Tess—you have no idea."

"Then *do*."

She allows her head to rest where it is. Perhaps this was always going to happen. They are not only adapting to this new country, they are adapting to each other, wrestling with each other's pasts and hang-ups and long-held habits. It is a normal process in any marriage, but circumstances have heightened everything. Loading an unplanned pregnancy, a stressful new job, and a relocation onto such a new relationship was always going to be fraught, no matter how much love there was, how much gut-level certainty.

She has always known that he was carrying something painful around inside him. She saw it the first time they met. The brief from the Sunday supplement was "Life Savers." The features editor had lined up five remarkable people for her to photograph, including Greg Gallo, and he wanted modern-day heroes—living gods. This meant power poses, noble gazes, subjects portrayed as untouchable, compassionate, and slightly battle-scarred. But what she saw in Greg's eyes when she raised the camera and looked at him through the lens for the first time was more than just the discomfort of being photographed. It was something far more complicated: something injured and raw. She'd started shooting right away without putting him at his ease or adjusting the lighting, focusing on his eyes, trying to capture the expression before he could paper it over.

After these initial shots, she had moved him around, helped him relax, adjusting the lighting to make him look regal and intense, focusing on his face with the background in darkness, shooting him slightly from the side and below to showcase the decisive shelf of his jaw, the lines of determination along his brow and cheekbones. She knew that he would be flattered by these handsome head shots and that the editor would love them, but she kept those first few face-on images for herself.

She only showed them to him when they had been together for a few months. And he was horrified. "Christ, Tess, I look almost frightened. Why have I got that look on my face when all I was thinking was 'this silent blond photographer in the scruffy jeans and boots with no makeup and those extraordinary blue-gray eyes is the most beautiful woman I have ever seen'?" He had tried to persuade her to throw the photos away, but she put them in her files, and they are still there, in the attic back home, in England.

Inside her, their baby rolls and shifts in a troubled nighttime dance, beating out its rhythms tirelessly. Greg pulls her closer. The damaged part of her recognized the damaged part of him the moment they met, and it shouldn't be a surprise, now, to encounter it again. He kisses her, softly, on the face, then on the neck, and eases her back onto the bed. She feels her body hum at his touch. His lips press against her throat, but as she closes her eyes, all she sees is a wall of fire and a panicking sixteen-year-old boy held back by the neighbors, unable to save the people he loves most in the world.

CHAPTER ELEVEN

The temperature is fierce, claustrophobic—it reminds her of the summer, when she arrived in Massachusetts and could barely breathe. This is not the sort of yoga she has done before. The teacher, a wiry Australian in a billowing shirt, does not demonstrate any of the postures but paces the studio, her straight black hair swinging, calling out instructions, often using Sanskrit names without explaining them.

The mats are only inches from one another, and she can hear exhalations, grunts, the squeak of feet on damp mats. The floor smells of sweat and tea-tree oil. "Inhale, forward fold, exhale, Chaturanga . . . Adho Mukha Svanasana, inhale, exhale, Urdhva Mukha Svanasana." She is sweating so much that her hands slip. The baby feels uncomfortable and heavy, like a dumbbell lodged inside her pelvis. A yoga class was Nell's idea, but it cannot be a good one. She gives up and folds herself into Child's Pose, resting her damp forehead on the mat, closing her eyes, breathing hard, waiting for it to be over.

She thinks of the yoga class she went to for a while in the drafty church hall at home, traffic rushing by outside. Sometimes it was so chilly that her feet would cramp up. She imagines getting up and rushing to the window, wrenching it open, and taking a breath of sharp, gray, Halloween air. She turns her head and opens one eye. Across the room she sees a strong body in a back bend, the crisscrossed straps of a purple yoga top revealing a network of muscles. The hair is rich brown with light caramel streaks. She cannot see the woman's face, but something about the hair makes her think that it is Helena.

At the end comes chanting, and then people roll up their mats in silence and walk, trancelike, from the studio. She tries to identify Helena in the crowd of bodies stashing mats and blocks, but there are too many purple yoga tops. She and Greg threw away the hair clip that morning, but she called Nell as soon as he'd gone to tell her what had happened.

Nell agreed with Greg that the barrette probably belonged to a previous tenant. But she also suggested that Tess confront Helena about the key, because there was a remote possibility that Helena did copy it and had been letting herself into the house. If she had done this, then something very unsettling indeed was going on, and it needed to be stopped.

"Go to that yoga class you talked about," Nell said. "Go—give it a try. Yoga will calm you down, and that'll be good for the baby. Then afterward, just go and knock on her door and ask her. You'll know if she's lying. Then you can change the locks."

She wraps her thick scarf around her neck and walks across the road to the bakery. Pumpkins squat outside the shop fronts, and store windows are decked out in black and orange with floating spiderwebs tangled on the signage. There are tombstones outside the bank, stretchy nylon webs across doorframes, and a life-size zombie looming from the hairdresser's window. She pushes through the bakery door, which is draped in black fabric with a witch's face peering out. She inhales the familiar smell of cinnamon and coffee, but the display cases are all Halloween-themed: orange-iced cupcakes decorated with black spiders and white skulls, cakes in the shape of black cats and witches' hats, muffins with veiny "eyeballs" on top. A massive cake on a stand perches by the tip jar, white-iced with dark-red spatters and a shard of bloodied "glass" gouged into the top. She must bring Joe here.

She is crossing the road with a decaf coffee and an undecorated fig scone, wishing that she had a warmer coat, when she hears someone calling her name.

"Hey, Tess! Tess? Over here!"

It is Helena, leaning on her Prius on the other side of the road, wearing a sporty fleece and a beanie. Tess's heart sinks, but she goes over to the car.

"What did you think of the yoga class?" Helena sounds bright and friendly.

"Oh, right; I thought I saw you in there."

"You walking home?" Helena smiles. "I can give you a ride if you like." Without makeup her eyes look smaller, puffier. Her face is glowing, but she has broken veins in her cheeks, and she looks almost gaunt and pale. Tess doesn't want to get into the Prius with Helena, but she can practically hear Nell telling her that she must. This is her chance to ask about the keys, to look Helena in the eye and work out what this woman is up to.

Two books lie on the passenger seat: *The Blood Sugar Solution* and *Madly in Love with Me*.

"Just toss everything in the back." Helena pulls off her hat and shakes out her thick hair.

Tess puts her things next to a large cream-leather carryall. The car smells faintly of coffee and of essential oils. She breathes in, trying to remember if this is the sweetish smell she noticed when she ran home from the potluck. She thinks it isn't, but it is hard to remember a smell, especially one only half-noticed at the time. The car is immaculate, and she thinks about the Volvo, littered with potato chip bags and moldering bits of sandwich, Joe's gym socks, footballs, crescents of dried mud. She must never allow Helena inside the Volvo.

"You seemed a little overwhelmed in there."

"In yoga?" She wonders if Helena was watching her. "It was so hot—is it always that hot? I wasn't sure if it was a good idea, being pregnant."

"It's 'heated flow,' but it won't hurt your baby. It's not Bikram. The heat opens the ligaments and protects the joints; it's very cleansing.

You sweat out the toxins—that's the theory—though from a physiological point of view, your kidneys mostly do that. But still, heat offers an emotional release, don't you think? I always feel like a different person after yoga. You really should drink water, though; you don't want to get dehydrated." She signals and pulls into the main street. "Oh, you know what, Tess? I just remembered, I have to pick up some dry-cleaning. I'm in Florida later this week, giving the keynote at a perimenopause conference, and I'll need my linen jacket. Would you mind if I took a short detour? Ten minutes, tops."

Tess feels a creeping sense of discomfort as Helena accelerates up the hill and the familiar street falls away. She does not want to be trapped in a car with this woman for any longer than is absolutely necessary.

"You OK with that?" Helena glances at her.

"No, sure, of course, that's fine."

In profile, Helena's nose is slightly plump and upturned, a little ungainly. In her publicity shots she always poses face-on to the camera: this is why. She knows her angles. People like Helena always do. She wishes she was looking at Helena through a viewfinder right now, with the bare trees flashing behind this unguarded profile.

She looks away, out the passenger window at the pumpkin-adorned porches. She has hardly taken a picture in weeks. The urge to get out her camera has faded here, for the first time in decades. In fact, it is when she sees Helena that she most wants to be looking through her camera—a protective mechanism, perhaps, a way of seeing without being seen. This is probably why she became a photographer in the first place: the world feels more manageable and controllable through a viewfinder. When she is taking pictures, she is invisible.

The street is lined with maples and oaks, which in summertime formed a bright green canopy and then, as autumn arrived, burst into gold and red flames. Now the branches look spiky, with clumps of rusted leaves clinging to them, as if afraid to fall. The silence in the car is becoming uncomfortable.

"It's cold now, isn't it?" she says.

"You think so?" Helena gives a low laugh. "Just you wait."

They pass the turn-off to the elementary school and continue up the hill. She has taken Joe to Boston Common and the Science Museum and dragged him, complaining, along the Freedom Trail. They've been to a shopping mall and a big downtown movie theater and eaten dumplings in Chinatown, but they have not really explored the suburban wilderness that surrounds their own home. The houses are all large, detached, well kept. They pass a house with a life-size Halloween galleon sinking into its front yard. Its ragged sails flap, and a skeleton pirate is standing at its tilted helm.

"So, Tess, you were having kind of a hard time last time I saw you—at the Schechters'. How's Joe been, the last couple of weeks?"

"Oh, he's OK now, thanks."

"He seemed pretty upset, huh? Greg says he's having trouble adjusting."

She opens her mouth, then shuts it. She will not ask Helena when, exactly, she and Greg were discussing her son. She has the feeling that this is just what Helena wants. "I think the . . . boys . . . whatever happened downstairs . . . must have pushed him over the edge." She is not sure why she is trying to justify Joe's behavior. She stops.

"Oh, hey, don't worry about it. Owen's a piece of work. You know he's a year older than Joe, right? He isn't really in fourth grade at all—he's just not very big for his age. Miriam and Bob held him back a year."

"Because of his height?"

"Oh, no, no, so he'd get better grades and excel at sports. If you're a year older than the other kids, you're going to be stronger and smarter, and, ultimately, you'll be offered more college scholarships."

"People hold their kids back a year in elementary school because of college scholarships?"

"Sure, they do. It's called 'redshirting'—it's a sports term."

They drive past a few more houses in silence.

"I'm sure Sandy was totally sweet about it," Helena says. "Right?"

Sandra had, in fact, had been gracious and kind, waving away Tess's apologies when she went over the next day. "Oh, hey. Really. Please. Don't give it a thought! I have two teenage boys, remember?"

Greg had clearly done a good job of smoothing things over. But no way was she going to go and apologize to Miriam MacAlpine; that was a step too far.

"Miriam can be a tough cookie," Helena says, as if reading her mind.

"That's what Greg said."

"He did?" Helena looks sharply in her rearview mirror, as if someone might be following them. "It must be hard for you, having to get your head around a whole new social system, new codes of conduct, new rules. I'm sure Greg is supportive, though, right? I'm sure he's really there for you."

"Yes, he is."

They have turned off into an unfamiliar neighborhood and are driving down a street with wide pavements and benches. The business establishments here are also decorated, with black-and-orange bunting and spiders and ghouls leering through windows. They pass a couple of clothes shops, a café, a Thai restaurant, and a bakery. Helena pulls up outside Green Clean Organic Dry Cleaners. The pumpkins on its steps have been carved into sinister grimaces with slanted eyes and pointy teeth. A sickly witch's face stares out through the glass door. Helena turns off the engine.

Tess braces herself and turns to look at Helena. "Listen, I was just wondering—do you still have a key to our house, by any chance? Greg says you let the cable guy in for him, before Joe and I got here. I just wondered if you still had one."

Helena gives a slow smile. "I don't have your key, Tess. I gave it back to Greg." She picks up her own bunch of keys. "Didn't he tell you?"

"He wasn't sure . . ."

"Poor guy." Helena gives an almost fond sigh. "He did seem a little stressed out on those visits without you. It was the least I could do, you know, letting the cable guy in and the cleaners, putting the mail inside for him, you know. Just being a good neighbor."

Tess feels her jaw tighten.

"Oh? Greg didn't mention I'd done all that?"

"No, he did . . ."

A faint smile lingers on Helena's lips. "You know what?" She leans in. "Greg said something to me at the potluck after you'd gone, and I just haven't been able to get it out of my mind."

"Oh, really? What?"

"Well, we talked, you know." Helena unbuckles her seat belt and turns the top half of her body so that she is facing Tess. "For quite a while, actually."

The image of Helena and Greg with their beautiful heads bent together rises in her mind; she stuffs it back down.

"He confided that you're struggling a little, too—not just Joe." Helena's opaque green eyes are watching her closely. "He's actually kind of worried about you, Tess. He thinks you're lonely."

"Greg said that to you?"

"He thinks you could do with a friend."

"He actually said that?"

Helena shrugs. "Sure."

"Well," she says, "I don't need anyone to find me friends." She imagines getting out of the car and walking away from Helena. It wouldn't take that long to get home on foot.

"Oh, don't be mad. He's just being kind. He always was the kindest person. Even when he was young and stressed out, he always had a kind word."

"Sorry, what are you talking about?"

"Oh." Helena looks at her with big eyes. "Didn't he mention that either? We were at medical school together, you know."

The car suddenly feels airless.

"He was a little older, of course, and kind of a legend—did you know he got a perfect score on the MCAT?"

She swallows. She isn't going to ask what an MCAT is.

"The standardized tests," Helena says. "Everyone who applies to medical school here in the States has to take them. Almost no one gets a perfect MCAT score. But you know that, I'm sure. Anyway, listen, Tess, I have a question for you." She jangles her keys against her palm. "You don't have to give me an answer, but I'd like to ask it. Is that OK?"

She wants to get out of the car. She cannot bear to be in a small space with this woman for a moment longer.

"May I?"

"What?" Tess snaps.

"OK. Do you trust Greg, Tess?"

"What?"

"No." Helena holds up an index finger. "Like I said, I don't need an answer." And with that, she swings her legs around and gets out of the Prius. Her hair ripples like the mane of a Thoroughbred as she hops over a snaggletoothed pumpkin and shoves at the witch's mouth.

Tess sits very still. Then she grabs her bag. She gets out of the Prius and starts to walk, fast, down the street, not knowing where she is going, only knowing that she has to get away from Helena. She ducks down a side road into a residential street and pulls out her phone. For once, Greg answers.

"You and Helena knew each other at college?" she shouts. A man passing with a black dog turns his head sharply. "How could you not tell me this? What the hell is going on here? How could you lie to me like this?"

"What?" He is walking, too. She can hear his feet echoing down a corridor. "I have no idea what you're talking about. Slow down."

"Helena! I'm talking about bloody Helena! She just told me you knew each other at medical school."

"OK, that's nonsense—she's mistaken."

"What's that supposed to mean?" She stops on the edge of the pavement, her heart thumping in her throat. The urge to scream is almost overwhelming. A six-foot ghost flaps on a porch next to her, its eyes and mouth big black holes.

"Tess—honey—seriously, it means exactly that. I did not know that woman at medical school. What the fuck has she said to you now?"

"She said you were at medical school together."

"OK, fine, maybe we were; it's a big school—and isn't she younger than me?"

"She said she was, but . . . ?"

"Well, maybe she knew me, but I did not know her."

"Then why—"

"Listen," he says, "if we'd known each other and I've somehow forgotten, then surely she'd have pointed it out, and she hasn't said a word to me. She's talking crap, OK? I have a meeting, and I'm there now. I'm outside the door, and I'm late—I've got to go in. Just ignore her, Tess. I have no idea why she's messing with your head, but she is."

She hangs up and walks on through the alien streets, past gardeners with leaf-blowers and past flapping Halloween shapes. She does not know what is going on, but she does know one thing: she needs to call a locksmith.

CHAPTER TWELVE

It was Amaal's job to transport the organ from donor to recipient. She had followed him in the brisk walk from the operating theater, through the hospital corridors, and out to the wet parking bay where the ambulance was waiting. The iced, preserved heart, which had until now pumped blood throughout the body of a fifty-nine-year-old mother of four, was to be driven at high speed across London and meticulously sewn into the chest of a twenty-year-old man who would die without it.

She is trying to organize the pictures she took of that portion of the heart's journey. With the other subjects she had systematically narrowed the choice of images until she knew, instinctively, that she had the right one, but with this final shot she can't make up her mind. She has printed out about twenty images now, and they are spread on the kitchen table. She lifts up one of Amaal's hand pushing the white box into the back of the ambulance. It's good, but it doesn't quite say enough. She slides the other photographs this way and that, holding them up one by one, tossing them aside.

Her lower back is sore, and she can feel a headache pressing behind her eyes. But she only has today and tomorrow to get this finalized.

Joe is watching movies in the front room, delighted to have two days off school for the Thanksgiving holiday. David is coming to get him first thing in the morning, and Greg has booked her and him a hotel in a fishing town an hour or so up the Massachusetts coast for the rest of the Thanksgiving weekend. It will be their first time away together in six months, and she has promised the editor that she will get this stage of the book finished—text and all—by tomorrow.

The sun is shining on the lawn, making the scattered leaves glow, deep reds and oranges. Cars are parked along the street: family gatherings, visitors, friends. Greg is at work; being married to a British woman has its advantages—he can then have Christmas off without a scruple.

She grabs her cardigan and goes outside, turning her face to the sky, blinking at the watery sun, looking up at the bare November branches. She can see her own breath. She closes her eyes. When she opens them, she sees a flicker of red across the road, behind the cars that are lined up outside the Schechters' house. She focuses on the shadows and feels a jolt of adrenaline: she knows the figure now, almost instinctively, but this is the first time she has seen her face. The woman is motionless, like a wild animal poised in the dimness. Dark-red hair straggles over her shoulders, half covering a skull-like face; she is scrawny, in a man's overcoat that trails almost to the ground. She does not move. She just stares.

Tess feels her skin prickle, and for a second they stand, eyes locked across the street. From inside one of the houses she hears the muffled roar of laughter. Somewhere farther down the street a car door slams and people call out greetings.

She takes a slow step toward the fence and holds on to it. "Who are you?" she calls. "What do you want?" The woman looks desperate, frozen, too, as if she has been waiting here for a long time, as if she has nowhere else to go. "Can I help?" Tess calls. "Do you need something?"

She turns to move toward the gate, but before she gets to it, the woman gathers her coat around her body, opens her mouth, and, like a threatened cat, lets out a guttural hiss. Tess stops, her heart thudding. Then the woman launches herself off, accelerating surprisingly fast, heavy black boots thumping on the pavement. She reaches the end of the street and flies around the corner without looking back.

As she is walking back toward the house, her legs trembling slightly, Tess hears Helena and Josh's garage door buzz. Her first instinct is to duck inside the porch—she can't face the neighbors now—but before she can get there, Josh's head appears over the bushes.

"Hey!" he says. "Happy Thanksgiving, Tess! How are you?"

"Did you see her?" She goes toward him. "Did you see that woman standing over there?" She points at the spot by the cars. "Red hair, in an overcoat?"

Josh glances in the direction of the Schechters' house. "Sorry— who? Where?"

"There was a woman—she was standing over there watching my house. Did you see her just now? Did you just get back? You must have driven right past her."

"Red hair? You mean Muriel?"

"No, no, not Muriel, definitely not Muriel—she was older, thinner, and kind of shabby, distraught-looking. She just ran away—literally just now, she ran off down there when I tried to talk to her."

"Sorry." He shakes his head. "I didn't see her."

"Oh. OK. Don't worry." She smooths her hair back, aware that she must look disheveled and slightly mad herself.

"Are you OK?" he asks. "Did she say something to upset you?"

"No, no, she didn't say anything. Honestly, I'm fine. Really."

"You look a little rattled."

"No, no, actually, I feel almost better for having seen her. I just came outside for some fresh air—I was working, and I've kind of hit a wall—and there she was, just watching my house." She realizes then that she does not want to talk to Josh about this. "Look, it's nothing, really. What are you doing here? Shouldn't you be eating turkey somewhere?"

"Actually," Josh says, "Helena took the girls to her mother's in Colorado, and I decided to stay here. I have a lot of . . ." His voice trails off, and he shrugs. "You know."

"Oh," she says.

"What about you? No Greg?"

"He's working. We both are."

"Is it your book you've stalled on?"

She nods. "I'm just trying to select the final pictures, but I can't seem to see anything very clearly anymore."

"What, exactly, are you stuck on?"

She tries to focus on Josh's face. "I have to decide on a picture to illustrate a particular phase of the donor heart's journey."

Josh shrugs again. "I could give you a second opinion, if that'd help."

She realizes that perhaps Josh wants company—and it might be good to have a fresh pair of eyes. "Actually, that might be really useful—if you have time."

As they pass through the hall, she is aware of Joe's shoes and a discarded hoodie that has fallen off the banister, her own boots, piles of books, a half-packed weekend bag. She picks up the sweatshirt and kicks the shoes aside. "Sorry it's such a mess. We're going up the coast tomorrow, and I'm trying to get organized."

Josh peers into the living room. "Hey, Joe."

Joe looks up and mutters hi but doesn't move.

"Wow." Josh gazes at the photographs spread across the table. "That's a whole lot of hands."

"I have hundreds more. This is it narrowed down. I'm trying to select one image for the transportation from the hospital where the donor was to the hospital where the recipient was waiting."

"I can see the problem."

"Yes, well, I need something that suggests urgency, motion, how extraordinary it is that this organ is outside the body, and how precious it is—and also, you know, the idea of a safe pair of hands. I have to find the one image to convey all that."

She picks up the couple of shots she is leaning toward: one of Amaal's hands pushing the cold-storage box into the ambulance, with the red letters HUMAN ORGAN FOR TRANSPLANT blurred but legible on the box, and one of his knuckles in close-up, folded around the handle, revealing the coarse hairs on the base of his fingers, his dull gold wedding band, the blur of a moving background.

Josh reaches for the two pictures. He looks at them, narrowing his eyes. He is clean-shaven, even-featured, with a fine, straight nose, hair cropped around neat ears. He is good-looking but somehow too ordinary for a woman like Helena. Perhaps that is the point: women like Helena might be drawn to powerful men like Greg, but what they want, at home, is someone safer—less challenging, more devoted.

But why would Josh put up with Helena? Her looks, status, and success cannot, surely, sustain a marriage. He must love her for deeper, less fathomable reasons. Then again, things between them must be bad if she has left him alone on Thanksgiving.

"This one." He raises the one with the visible lettering. "Though I don't know why."

She leans over and takes it from him. "Not the close-up of his hand?"

Josh looks at the other picture. "Hmm." He shrugs. "You know?"

"Thanks." She glances over his shoulder through the crisscrossed window. The street is empty.

"I'm no artist, though, so don't let my opinion sway you."

"No, that's OK, thanks—it's just useful seeing your reactions. It's helpful."

"These are all terrific pictures." His eyes flicker over the images on the table. "It's a cool idea for a book—the heart's journey."

"Well, it's about organ donation in general, not just hearts."

"Oh, sure, total body recycling . . ."

She laughs. "I haven't heard it called that before."

He smiles back and jangles his keys in his pocket, looking around. "It's kind of nice in here, lighter than it looks from the outside. We've lived on this street three years now, and I've never set foot inside this house before."

"I thought you'd been here for longer than that."

"Oh, no," he says. "We were in Scituate before this. My wife likes to uproot us every few years. She gets bored."

Tess looks down at the images on the table, all the hands—open, closed, grasping, letting go.

"She says she knew Greg at Harvard." She tries to keep her voice light and casual. "Isn't that funny?"

"At Harvard?" He frowns. "I don't think so."

"Oh?" She begins to gather the images up one by one.

He shakes his head. "No." Blotches of red have spread across his cheeks. "She didn't know him then."

"Yes, well, Greg doesn't remember her, so maybe she made a mistake."

"Listen, Tess . . ." He shifts and looks out of the window. "You should probably know that my wife is . . . she's, well, she has . . ."

"What?"

"She gets obsessions."

"She does?"

"And right now, well, she has kind of a thing for your husband."

"A *thing*?" The word seems so juvenile, so high-schoolish, that for a moment she wants to laugh. But this is clearly anything but trivial to Josh, who is rigid, his cheeks blazing, his shoulders high.

"This isn't the first time."

"The first time what?"

"Never mind." He sounds suddenly formal. "I shouldn't have said anything. I just didn't want you to, you know, you and Greg seem happy and . . . well, you know . . ."

"Wait, no—I don't think I quite understand what you're saying."

"Listen." He pushes his shoulders back. "Please—it's really not a problem for you guys." He lays a hand, flat, on the table. "It's an issue for me and my wife. And now I should probably get home. I have a stack of papers to grade, and this is my chance for some uninterrupted time."

"But—"

"Look." He attempts to smile, but his mouth is too stiff. He begins to walk around the table toward the hall. "Helena and I are having some marital issues right now, but we're working it out. Don't give this another thought, OK? I shouldn't have said anything, I don't know why I did."

"Wait." She skips around to stand between him and the door. "Please. I just want to be clear: Greg and Helena don't have any history, do they?"

He sidesteps her and reaches for the door handle. "No."

"Are you sure?"

He blinks at her. "Aren't you?"

She steps back to let him out, and as she shuts the door, she catches the image of her own face, miniature, warped, and huge-eyed, in the shining new lock.

She stands in the hall for a moment, listening to the chirp of cartoon characters on Joe's TV. Then she knows what to do.

The basement air is freezing, and she is shivering when she gets down to the laundry room. She stands with her back to the machine, hugging her arms tightly around her body. Inside her, the baby is kicking so hard that she can feel tiny thuds at the base of her neck. Greg's boxes are lined up just above eye level.

She has to stand on tiptoe to ease the first one off the shelf, but it is not too heavy. She kicks laundry out of the way and puts the box on the floor. She hesitates, then squats, making room for her belly, and rips off the masking tape. The cardboard is soggy. She'll tell Greg that she decided to repack his things into waterproof plastic crates. She will go and buy some of those before he gets home.

The box contains multiple black ring binders. She pulls one out. On the cover is a logo—a crimson shield with three books on it and *Veritas* inked across them, with *Harvard* underneath. She pulls out a few other files. All have the same Harvard University logo. She opens one and finds notes in Greg's measured handwriting: *The Trigeminal Nerve.* She turns a few pages: *Difference between Gram-negative and Gram-positive bacteria.* The pages are dense with complicated terminology, diagrams, and mnemonics. She puts the files back, shuts the box, and pushes it aside.

The next one contains more Harvard Medical School ring binders, as well as two box files with GMC written on them in marker pen—presumably Greg's UK certification paperwork. There are photocopies of documents: Greg's social security card, his birth certificate, his undergraduate degree certificate from the University of Pittsburgh, his Harvard medical degree certificate, visa forms in small type with UK government logos on them, grainy passport photos in which he looks thinner-faced with cropped hair but otherwise little altered.

She wonders what they would have made of each other back then. He was a ruthlessly ambitious resident working hundred-hour weeks, and she was a photographer, working in an independent bookshop, shaken and hollow after her father's death. They would have been completely incompatible, and yet, perhaps, even then, a mechanism deep inside them would have slotted together. She shoves the files back and stands up, reaching on tiptoe for the third box.

It contains more medical-student notes in Greg's handwriting. She sits back on her heels. A sheet of paper has fallen out, and she picks it off the floor. It is a typed poem, "Fair Harvard." She skims through its pompous stanzas:

. . . from the age that is past,
To the age that is waiting . . .
. . .

For the good and the great, in their beautiful prime . . .

She folds it and tucks it back into the file.

She sits for a moment longer on the cold, concrete floor. She doesn't really want to think too much about Helena and Greg in their beautiful prime. She is not sure what she thought she'd find in these boxes—evidence? Pictures of Helena? Love letters? Something to demonstrate that Greg has lied about knowing her? She tucks the files back in their box. She has no idea why her instinct is to doubt him, when it is clearly Helena who is making things up.

But now that she has started, she might as well see what's in the last box. It is light, as if it contains nothing but air. She rips through the seals and finds a child-size baseball glove inside. She lifts it out, feeling the cracked, stiff leather, turning it over: a little relic of his small-town Pennsylvania childhood.

She cradles it gently, and a heavy sadness folds itself around her. She has no right to be in this painful place, sifting through memories that her husband can only handle by containment. He has never invited her to witness this.

As she goes to put the glove back in the box, she sees something pale and cottony folded up on the bottom. She shakes it out. It is a pair of baseball pantaloons, about Joe's size, and below these a blue-and-white nylon baseball shirt with ROBESVILLE SLUGGERS and the number 16 on the back.

She tries to picture a ten-year-old Greg playing Little League like the boys she has seen in the local park. There are no photos of him as a child, because everything was destroyed in the fire. It is a miracle that these few objects survived. She lifts them up to her face. They smell of musty corners, tree bark, mouse pelt—but not smoke or ash. She feels shabby: she really should not be pawing through these things, uninvited.

But no wonder he has carried this box of memories all the way across the Atlantic and back. These things are precious. They shouldn't be left down here in the damp. That, at least, can be a justification for what she has done. She folds the baseball pants and shirt back up, and as she is laying them back in the box, she notices something shiny in one corner. She picks it out. It is a medal, on a striped ribbon, lightweight and tinny, with ROBESVILLE SLUGGERS, JUNIOR LEAGUE CHAMPIONS engraved on it. Again, she wonders how it survived the fire.

They had only known each other a month or two when he told her what had happened to his parents. His voice was controlled, but afterward he went out and ran for more than an hour. When he came back, sweating and loose-limbed, he stood in the kitchen with a glass of water and said, "I told you because you need to know, but I don't want to talk about it again. I am a different person now. It doesn't help me to remember; it never does." He tipped back his head and gulped the water without stopping to breathe, his eyes fixed on the ceiling.

Sixteen is a terrible age to lose both parents. She was sixteen when her mother died, but at least she still had her father, and he had always been the one who cared for her, so, in a sense, when her mother died, very little changed. She even experienced—something it took her many years to admit—a faint sense of relief, because life became infinitely simpler. Her father had continued to be her rock until his death nine years later. So, really, she can't compare her loss at sixteen to what Greg went through.

Shutting off his emotions has worked for him—it allowed him to get his undergraduate degree, his Harvard scholarship, then a medical degree. He has made a phenomenal success of his life, when it could so easily have gone the other way. No, it is not up to her to tell Greg how to handle his past.

She wonders what his parents would think if they could see him now. They were obviously good, loving, hardworking people, and they would surely have been so proud. The odd thing is that he can't even bear to remember the good things—the happiness and security of the first sixteen years of his life. He has shut all that down, along with the tragedy, as if the loss erased everything that went before.

As she puts the medal back on top of the pantaloons, she is overcome, again, by the enormity of what Greg must have gone through. He watched the flames consume his home, knowing that his parents were inside and he was powerless to save them. It's obvious, really, why he chose a career that is devoted to saving lives. In some way, every time he opens up a child's chest—every time he goes inside—he is rescuing them, mending the past.

She is about to close the box when she notices a plastic rectangle, about the size of a credit card, lodged down one side. She levers it out. It is a library card with a University of Pennsylvania logo. She turns it over:

University of Pennsylvania Central Library
Carlo Novak

She looks at it for a moment longer, then lays it back in the box with the other things. Carlo Novak must be a long-ago relative or a

friend, and, like everything else in these boxes, he is none of her business. She should not be squatting on the floor, going through Greg's
private belongings. This is all wrong.

She tries to stick the masking tape back down, but it shrivels away
from the cardboard. She puts the ruined boxes back on the shelves,
one by one, and then washes her hands with scalding water and soap.
She will have to go and buy plastic storage boxes, repack them, make
amends.

CHAPTER THIRTEEN

She is propped up by feather cushions in the middle of the king-size hotel bed, reading emails with the iPad on her knees. Greg is hunched over his laptop at the tiny desk, with his back to her. He is doing something vital to do with research funding that just came in and cannot possibly wait until Monday.

Nell has been googling again. Harvard Medical School, she says, had over seven hundred students at the time Greg studied there, and Helena—she found an online reference to a birth date—is three years younger than Greg.

> I'm sure he isn't lying when he says he didn't know her at Harvard—she might have heard of him because he was such a superstar, but there's no reason he'd have known her. You did the right thing to change the locks: the woman is a manipulator, best ignored.

Tess types a brief reply and looks up at Greg again. She hasn't yet told him that she repacked his boxes. It was impossible to talk to him about anything last night.

★ ★ ★

When he got back from the hospital, they had loaded the bags straight into his car.

"I'll drive," she said. "You look tired."

For once, he nodded and got into the passenger seat. But things began to go wrong almost as soon as they pulled onto the freeway. She had already told him over the phone about the woman with red hair, and he had persuaded her, once again, that this person was not a threat, just troubled. But in the car he seemed less patient, edgier, even less willing to admit that a stranger watching the house could be problematic.

"She looked ill," she said. "She's so thin and sickly. She shouldn't be on her own on Thanksgiving that way—she obviously needs help."

"I wish you hadn't tried to speak to her."

"Why not? You said she wasn't dangerous."

"She isn't, but talking to her is going to achieve nothing."

"How do you know? I mean, do you even understand why is she doing this? What does she actually want to achieve?"

"I'm sure even she doesn't know the answer to that."

"Then she needs help. We can't just pretend she isn't there."

"You can't help her, nor can I. Only a psychiatrist can do that."

"Then shouldn't we find out who her psychiatrist is?"

"I told you, I already did—I made some calls. Her doctors know what's happening."

"So we just turn a blind eye? It seems wrong. She looks ragged. Is she living in Boston? Is someone looking after her?"

"I don't know—I don't want to know. If we engage, it will only make things worse."

"That's all very well for you to say—you're hardly ever home. But I'm walking into the garden and seeing her standing there, watching me. It doesn't feel right to just pretend nothing's happening."

"You have to."

"Then you have to tell me about her. What does she think you did to her baby?"

"Nothing. My God, Tess, it was decades ago," he snapped. "She's just unwell, but she will eventually stop this if she gets no response."

She gripped the wheel and turned on the windshield wipers. "Well, I think she needs help."

"Maybe. But not from you." He closed his eyes and spent the next hour like that, with his head back. She couldn't tell whether he was asleep or simply intent on not talking.

When they arrived in Marblehead, it was past nine o'clock, and they were both hungry and irritable. The sea wind roared over the rooftops, and as Greg led her down a salty alleyway in the darkness, she wondered why he had brought her to such a brutally cold outpost.

They ate lobster rolls in a seafood bar, and Greg's mood disintegrated further. He glowered at the waiters, drank three large glasses of wine too fast—she had never seen him this tense. He seemed almost at a breaking point. And then, in the wide hotel bed, he switched off the light and kissed her hard, his mouth bitter with alcohol, and when her body responded, despite everything, he moved her beneath him, pinned her wrists above her head, pulled her underwear aside, and thrust himself inside her. Afterward he kissed her hair, muttered that he loved her, and fell instantly asleep.

She lay for what felt like hours—she had no clock—softly leaking his fluids onto the three-hundred-thread-count sheets. Inside her, the baby had retreated into a shocked stillness. She could have told him to stop, but she didn't. She gave herself over to the mixture of pleasure and pain, but buried beneath this surrender had been the tiniest seed of doubt: if she had tried to pull her hands out of his grip and roll away, would he have stopped?

He slept on like a dead man. She couldn't even hear him breathing. And when she finally slept, she dreamed there was an opossum curled on its side in a corner of the hotel room, baring fungal teeth in a masquerade of death, and when she bent to it, it rose, opened its mouth, and hissed. She woke in the blacked-out room with the words "playing possum" rolling around in her head.

Greg turned over and held her face in his hands. "Hello. I love you," he murmured. "I'm glad we came away. I'm so sorry about the crappy sex and my horrible mood last night. I'm so sorry. I love you so much. God, I need to spend time with you."

She felt the baby flex and tread down on her bladder. "I have to pee." She peeled his hands off her face and got out of bed. Under the unforgiving bathroom lights she rested her fists on the sink. Then she noticed a faint, violet thumbprint on the inside of her wrist. She remembered the mark she had found on Joe's upper arm, a stain on his babyish flesh, the day after the potluck supper. Then she remembered the terror on his face as he cried out for her, and the rage in Greg's eyes, the need to control, to dominate, to crush.

The memory of the night Greg proposed marriage suddenly surfaces now, out of nowhere. It was more of a statement than a question: "I want to take this job," he said. "But I can't go without you. I want you and Joe to come with me. I want to marry you."

Her head had felt unsteady when he said it, as if she was running too fast around a corner. He'd put down his pint of Guinness and covered her hands with his, pressing her fingers onto the sticky pub table.

"I always thought people who claimed to fall in love this fast were inadequate and deluded, but when you appeared in my office with your camera, I just felt as if I recognized you. It really was instant— almost before you'd even opened your mouth. I felt like my heart swelled up and burst open, and you were already there, inside it— waiting for me."

She had laughed, then, because that was how she had felt, almost exactly. She belonged with him.

And so, in such a short space of time, they were at the town hall, stepping out under a glowering sky with the first drops of rain making little stains on the pavement at their feet; Joe, a little dazed, next to Nell's boys, Ken smiling benignly, Nell with a box of confetti and her hair pinned up; the feel of her dress, slightly too snug around her middle already, and the knowledge of this baby—the other child— floating in the center of everything, a tiny magic bean: their future.

She is not sure how it has all become so complicated. Perhaps what they need, above all, is simply to spend time together. Before the job offer and the move, they used to go away for weekends when David had Joe. But with the pregnancy and the job offer and the move, their

time together, just the two of them, has been reduced to almost nothing. No wonder Greg feels so out of reach.

He is still hunched over his laptop, typing furiously. Today she
will tell him that she went through his boxes. She is not sure how
he will react to that, but she'll tell him anyway.

Suddenly, she remembers the Pennsylvania library card. It was an
odd, out-of-place thing to find among his surviving childhood treasures. She is sure that she has never heard him mention a Carlo Novak.
She looks at the iPad again.

A Google search brings up reports of tennis matches in Monte
Carlo. She adds "Pennsylvania" to the search and gets a funeral direc-
tor and a few more tennis reports. She adds "University of Pennsylvania" and gets an administrator called Carole Anne Novak. The
University of Pennsylvania, it seems, is in Philadelphia. There is no
mention of a Carlo Novak. She tries to think how people searched
before the Internet. Local papers, probably. Microfiches in libraries?

Perhaps he will be mentioned somewhere in a local paper—an academic award, a marriage, a community project. She finds a website
that gives access to local newspaper archives and finds the *Philadelphia
Inquirer* database. She glances up at Greg again—still hunched, intent
on his screen—and then she types "Carlo Novak" into the search box.
She starts fifteen years ago. *No results match your search criteria.* She
goes back one more year, then two.

Greg clears his throat. She stops, her hand poised, ready to shut the
iPad down. She could not explain to Greg what she is doing—she isn't
even sure herself. He shifts and begins to type again.

She starts twenty-five years ago, then goes back year by year to
twenty-seven years ago. And there it is: *Your search has 1 result.*

The website will only allow her to read the first paragraph of any
archived article without handing over a credit card.

Jurors in the "dead baby" trial of Philadelphia medical student Carlo
Novak were sent home today after the judge said a faulty air-conditioning
system was making the stress "intolerable." Novak, 23, a first-year medical student at the University of Pennsylvania Medical School, is accused

of murder, illegal abortion, and the unauthorized practice of medicine. Prosecutors allege that Novak is responsible for the death of a baby girl, born alive but six weeks premature to Sarah Banister, 21, at Novak's West Philadelphia apartment.

"Honey?"

She jumps. Greg is standing above her, stretching his arms up, his torso spread as wide as a flag. She switches off the iPad and throws it onto the pillow. For a tall and muscular man he moves so lightly on his feet. She tries to smile, but she feels as if a moth is trapped in her chest, brown and fat and frantic.

"You OK? You look a little pale. I'm so sorry, that took me forever—I had to respond to their query, or we could lose thousands of dollars of funding literally overnight." He looks down at the iPad. "What were you so engrossed in there?"

"Just emails." She slides off the bed and reaches for her coat, turning her back on him. "I was replying to Nell."

"You two should Skype."

"We do sometimes."

"She could come over and visit."

"She's going to, after the baby's born."

She tries to do up the coat, but it won't stretch over her belly. The baby Carlo Novak was accused of killing was the same age as the one inside her. She feels gargantuan as she tugs her boots on. She glances back at Greg. He looks handsome in his gray cashmere sweater, winding a scarf around his neck. Novak is a Polish name. Perhaps Greg has a relative with a disturbing past. She feels the baby change position.

She should ask him, but first she has to tell him that she's looked in his boxes. Suddenly she badly needs to get outside—to breathe sea air and sweep this mess from her head.

They step into a street lined with painted clapboard cottages, some in cheerful pinks or yellows. He puts an arm around her and pulls her close to him. She realizes that she is hungry. She couldn't stomach the hotel breakfast, with fat slices of coffee cake, muffins, bagels, silver trays with glistening scrambled eggs and strips of fatty bacon, but now her stomach feels empty, her legs unstable. The air is bitter; their breath makes plumes above them. Greg, zipped into his black puffy jacket, is talking about the first British settlers coming up the coast to escape the Salem Puritans.

"This area was ruled by the Naumkeag tribe. You'll like this: they had a squaw chief . . ." He squeezes her hand, crushing it, as if forcing her to pay attention to him instead of to the questions roiling in the back of her mind. Gulls the size of small dogs swoop across the rooftops. He is talking about smallpox now, an epidemic brought by the Pilgrims that wiped out the native population. He sounds as if he has recalled, almost word for word, a guide to Marblehead. His memory seems all-encompassing, almost photographic.

"This place has had a lot of names," he is saying now. "It was Massebequash first, then Foy, then Marble Harbor, then Marvill Head . . ."

Her breathing echoes inside her skull. She needs to tell him she has been through his boxes, but she can't bring herself to, not yet, not without understanding what she has just stumbled across. She could type in her credit card, later, and read the rest of the *Philadelphia Inquirer* article.

"You OK, Tess?"

She can't meet his eye. It might not even be Greg's Carlo Novak in the report. It might be someone with the same name, completely unconnected to Greg.

He slows down. "Listen, give me a break, OK? I'm trying here. I'm sorry I had to respond to that email this morning; I'm sorry I was in such a horrible mood yesterday; I'm sorry I've been so preoccupied. There's a lot going on right now. I don't need to talk to you about it, but—"

"Why not?" She stops. "Why don't you need to talk to me, if something is going on with you? Why? Why can't you talk to me?"

"OK," he says, slowly. "You're right. No, you're right." He takes a deep breath. "There's a lot going on because the parents of that four-year-old who died have filed a lawsuit."

She squints up at him. "They're suing the hospital?"

"Not the hospital, me. We're in negotiations with the family's lawyers. It's going to drag on forever, and it's a pain in the ass."

"Oh, shit, Greg, that's awful. Why? I mean—what are they saying you did wrong?"

He starts walking again; she follows.

"I didn't do anything wrong," he says. "Being sued is a hazard for any surgeon, particularly in pediatrics. Virtually every pediatric surgeon gets embroiled in a lawsuit at some point, many more than once. But it's a monumental hassle right now, that's all. It's not what I need when I just got here. I'm going to have to waste time on it, and time is the last thing I have."

"Wait . . . you weren't even going to tell me about this?"

"It's not that huge a deal."

"But what, exactly, are they threatening to sue you for? What are they saying you did wrong?"

"It's supremely technical."

She grits her teeth. "Then dumb it down for me."

"OK—sorry—I don't mean it like that. The summary is that I knew the child was going to die, and I tried a controversial and fairly experimental technique that has a high chance of failure. And it failed. If I hadn't tried, he'd have died anyway, but the parents want someone to blame, so they're blaming me. They're questioning that decision."

"But you did nothing wrong."

"Yes, I know that. In fact, the irony of all this is that I was their one, very remote hope. If the procedure had worked, I'd be a deity in their eyes right now. But instead I'm a demon. They can't see that the failed procedure isn't really the point."

"Well, for them it's the point. They've lost their little boy."

"You know I don't mean that."

She sees how fierce he must be at work, how untouchable.

She remembers reading an article once about the top ten psychopathic professions. Surgeons were high on the list. Greg had laughed as she read it out to him on the sofa in England, her feet resting in his lap.

"'Surgeons and psychopaths share several key qualities: they are decisive under pressure, ruthless, fearless, and entirely lacking in self-doubt. When surveyed, ninety-eight percent of surgeons considered themselves to be at the top of their field . . .'"

"Of course we do." Greg had looked at her over the rim of his glasses. "We have to, or we couldn't do the job."

"Isn't that just a tiny bit delusional and potentially dangerous?"

"No, it's really not. It's actually the opposite. In the OR, the moment I make an incision, I'm completely alone—even if there are twenty people in the room, the moment my knife goes through skin, it's just me and the patient. I have to be the best surgeon in the world for that child, every single time. It's not like most jobs. I mean, if you take some crappy photos, you might not get hired next time, or you might even piss off an editor. But if I lose confidence in myself, if I mess up, a child might die."

She looks up at him now, his dark hair framed by a pewter sky. He is waiting for her to agree with him that the death of this child is not the point.

"I'm sorry," she says. "For them and for you."

He looks away. "I sound like a monster, but I'm not. I know they're in agony, and they need to be angry with someone, and that someone has to be me." His voice is strained, and she realizes that, of course, he is nowhere near as cut off from this as he wants to appear.

She reaches for his hand. "This must be horrible for you. No wonder you're upset and distracted."

"I'm upset about losing the boy, not about their reaction. I'm a little annoyed, that's all, to be part of a system where people can sue me for making a perfectly legitimate surgical decision."

"But I don't really understand how they can they sue you."

"Well, surgically, it's kind of a gray area."

"A gray area? What do your colleagues say? Are they supporting you?" This must, she realizes, represent a massive loss of face so early in his new job.

"I sent an email out to the whole department yesterday, laying it all out. I told them this litigation threat is nonsense and there was no error whatsoever on my part, and I pointed out that I'm the best there is—nobody else would have had the skill to do what I did. I hope that's the end of it, as far as they're all concerned."

"You actually emailed *that* out to your colleagues?"

"Listen." His voice softens a little. "I know it sounds arrogant, but it's necessary in this context. If I shrank away, I'd look weak—I'd look guilty, to be honest. It's much better to come out with your head up. They all get that. And they'll all know that most top surgeons in my position would have tried the procedure, too."

"But they could turn against you?"

"OK, Tess, see? This is exactly why I didn't tell you—I didn't want to ruin our weekend. You aren't a surgeon, you aren't in the medical world—you need to trust me when I tell you that it'll be fine. I'm not worried. I'm just unhappy at the amount of time this is going to suck up. I really don't need to talk about this—not for myself. In fact, right now I'd kind of like to *not* talk about it—I'd kind of like to get away from this and forget about it for the next twenty-four hours, if that's OK by you. I just need a break, honey. It's not a big deal; it's just an administrative pain in the ass, and it's going to go on for months, if not years."

A dead child is surely the biggest deal of all, but she does not say so. A gust of wind pushes between them, and his hand tightens around hers; it feels like a restraint. He can rationalize all he likes, but deep down he must feel responsible for the death of this little boy. She cannot imagine what it must be like to carry that around inside you every day.

They walk up the main street toward a lemon-yellow town hall, built on a triangle where two roads converge. It has stairs leading up to a double door that is decorated with lavish Thanksgiving wreaths. This is one of the most historic towns in Massachusetts, but she feels as if she has stumbled onto the set of a Hollywood romantic comedy. They pass shop windows displaying storm lanterns and cashmere throws, dog collars decorated with stars and stripes, Adirondack chairs and sea-glass earrings. She thinks about the poor parents of the dead boy. She would be the same if it happened to Joe: she would need someone to demonize. She looks up at Greg again. His chin is lifted, his shoulders thrown back, his dark hair swept off his strong brow. His lack of self-doubt really can be breathtaking.

They pass other weekenders—smart Bostonians holding takeout coffee cups, with copies of the *New York Times* tucked under their arms. He can't really be this sure of himself. He must be questioning every moment of that operation. That might, at least, explain his recent behavior: his outburst with Joe, his remoteness, his inability to talk to her, and, of course, last night's horrible mood. He must be under phenomenal pressure.

Pebble-colored clouds skate overhead, and gulls cry, a lonely, heart-hollow sound. It is bitterly cold, and her hands, without gloves, feel stiff and sore. The seasons are so much more brutal here, more definite and delineated: summer was sweltering, broken by the occasional wild storm, and then autumn kicked in, and everything exploded into hysterical colors, and now winter is closing in, sweeping punishing winds across everything, and—Greg says—soon there will be snow, blankets of it: whiteouts, snow days, blizzards. This assertive, cyclical progression ought to feel reassuring in some way, but it does not. These stamping, huge East Coast seasons only make her feel small, exposed, far from home. She never thought she'd miss the dithering English wetness, but she does, on an almost cellular level.

Greg guides her down an alley that smells of dog pee. He has never been to Marblehead before, but he seems to know exactly where he is going. He always knows where he is going. His chin, unshaven, square, juts out, the tip of his nose is red, and his breath rises, dragon-like, from his carved nostrils. His eyes are fixed straight ahead. Greg would never allow himself to look lost.

It is almost impossible to imagine him making a clinical mistake. He may make lightning-fast decisions, but they will be based on a watertight series of judgments and microanalyses. His decision to try that particular technique on that little boy at that moment will have been perfectly calibrated. The chances of anyone successfully suing Greg must be extremely small.

What she can't understand is why he couldn't talk to her about this. Why keep it all to himself? They emerge onto a grassy, windblown slope, and he puts his arm around her. She inhales sharply, and the freezing air stings her lungs. It is almost a hostile act, to have kept this litigation threat to himself. The Atlantic wind bowls in at them, shoving at her face and body, biting through the thin wool of her coat. Ahead of them, the gunmetal sea flexes toward the horizon. Despite the cold it is a relief to be looking out at something bigger and louder than the thoughts inside her head.

She tugs her hat down and shakes herself free of Greg's arm. But he takes her hand again. They walk up the grass and stand above the ocean. There is a lighthouse on a promontory far over to the right. The sun appears from behind a cloud, and the sea glitters as if there is a spark on the tip of each wave.

She watches a boat grow smaller and smaller until it is swallowed up by the horizon. She thinks about England, across these miles and miles of ocean, and she feels a pull deep down, as if an invisible umbilical cord, stretched whisper-thin, attaches her to home. Inside her, the baby somersaults. She feels light-headed, hungry, empty. Greg's hand, gripping hers, is as hard and cold as granite. He starts walking again. He is half a step ahead of her, but the space between them feels vast. She remembers him telling her once that the human heart is the size of a fist, and hers feels like that now, a fist thumping against her ribs, angry and trapped.

He drops her hand and climbs up onto a big flat rock, then turns and holds out his hand for hers again. She looks up at his face, all planes and angles, paved with stubble, his cheekbones picked out by the light. He is so certain that she will follow, take his hand, scramble up there after him—he looks at her expectantly, and suddenly she feels as if she doesn't know him; he is a stranger, expecting her to follow him onto the slippery rock, without question.

She turns and walks away, leaving him there. She needs to get away. She needs to be alone, to think. She supports her belly with both hands and walks very fast, head down. She hears him calling her, his voice booming across the grass.

The wind thumps her eardrums. She stumbles over a hillock and reaches the edge, teetering for a moment above a magnificent, glittering sea, the sky streaked with white clouds, sweeping out to the horizon. To her right is a path through some scrubby trees. She hesitates, then heads toward it, pushing through scraggly branches, leaning backward to stop herself from toppling over rocks. Her ankles wobble as the path plunges toward a beach, which is no more than twenty yards of dark sand littered with gray stones. She reaches the bottom and jumps down onto it, feeling the jolt of the baby against her spine. Waves crash and flatten, hissing toward her, and she hears Greg's feet following her.

The wind shoves at her face; she turns. His eyes are anxious but dark, too, angry, demanding. "What's gotten into you? Why did you run off like that?" Her belly feels taut, her limbs shaky, and suddenly she can't get enough air in; it feels like drowning. His hands grasp her upper arms, but a mist is oozing around her eyeballs—the sea, his blackened eyes, the stones, the sky are saturated in gray mist, and she is alone in space, her heart softening, beating more slowly, its chambers unfolding like wings.

CHAPTER FOURTEEN

The first thing she sees is a single white cloud, rushing overhead. She smells seaweed. The light is white, and it cramps her eyes. Waves hush and suck nearby, and a fat gull glides overhead, peering down at her with a pebble eye. Stones press against her spine, but she feels rested and warm, as if she has slept like this, undisturbed, for hours and hours. Only her fingers are cold, spread on sand, and her, toes too— she cannot feel her toes. Greg's face appears, blocking out the light.

"It's OK," he soothes her. "You're OK. You passed out. You're fine. Just lie still for a moment, come around slowly, and then we'll get you somewhere warmer." She lifts her head. His jacket is spread over her, protecting her body from the wind. He is kneeling by her thighs with her legs raised on his lap. She tries to sit up, but he eases her shoulders back down.

"Don't try to get up just yet, Give yourself a moment, OK?"

Her right hipbone aches, and her leg feels itchy. She touches her belly, beneath his jacket, with both hands. The baby is very still.

"You'll be fine." He presses her shoulder gently. "Just take a moment."

She thinks of her body thudding onto the beach.

"I want to sit up."

"OK, but take it slow . . . take it easy . . . easy . . ."

The sun comes out from behind another cloud, much too bright. She blinks, and then out of the corner of her eye she sees a movement on the cliff path, behind Greg. She cranes her neck. A man with a black dog jumps onto the beach and crunches across to them, moving purposefully, hands in the pockets of his dark pea coat. The dog gallops off toward the sea. The man has a bushy beard and cropped hair. He stops above her.

"I saw you go down," he says. "Are you OK?" He looks right at her as if Greg isn't there.

Greg's face adopts an urbane smile. He eases her legs off his lap and stands up, facing the man. He is an inch or two taller.

"She's fine, thanks. My wife's pregnant. She felt a little faint for a moment, but she's going to be just fine."

The man steps closer to her. He is about the same age as Greg, with wind-stung cheeks and eyes as gray as the rocks behind him.

"You really OK?"

"I'm a doctor." Greg's voice is brittle. "And I'm telling you, she's fine." But the man still does not look at Greg; he is waiting for her answer.

"Yes, honestly, I'm completely fine." She tries to sound normal. "Thanks."

The black Labrador bounds up the beach and stuffs its nose into her face; she smells salt water on its wet fur, fishy dog breath. "Off." The man grabs his dog's collar. "Sorry. Go on, go!" He sends the dog away. Only then does he look at Greg. His eyes are hard and, she realizes, hostile. She wonders if she should reassure him that Greg has done her no harm, that nothing threatening is happening here.

"She's just resting for a moment." Greg's voice is suddenly tense. The man's eyes are still fixed on Greg's face.

"I know you . . ." he says. "You're—"

"You know what?" Greg cuts him off. "Maybe you could take her other arm, because I need to get her somewhere warmer—can you stand up now, honey? Come on, let's go."

He takes one of Tess's arms and tugs as if she is a stubborn donkey. The ground slides away, but she feels the stranger's hand around her other elbow and forces herself to stand up. Then she twists herself out of the men's hands and looks from one to the other. Greg's jacket has fallen onto the stones at her feet. He bends, slowly, to pick it up, taking slightly too long.

The dog is back in the water behind them—foam splashes around it in great, hilarious arcs. Greg straightens. The two men are looking at each other again, over her head. Greg slides one arm into his jacket. This is not about her anymore; this is something else.

The man opens his mouth, but Greg speaks over him. "So, we're good to go. Thanks for stopping. Bye." He turns, taking her arm, pulling her away.

"No. Wait!" the man shouts after them, suddenly furious. "What the hell are you doing here? What are you doing here? Don't you walk away from me! I know who you are! I know you!"

Greg pulls her arm; she stumbles on the stones.

"You know me, too, don't you?" He is following them, a few paces behind. "I'm Alex Kingman. I know you recognize me."

"Sorry." Greg stops and turns, abruptly, "I don't know you. You have the wrong man."

"No, I don't."

"Listen, buddy." Greg's voice booms, making her jump. "You're making a mistake here. We've never met, and I need to get my wife inside now, so thanks for stopping, but we have to go. Good-bye."

She has never heard Greg call an adult "buddy" before. He puts his arm around her, steering her toward the path.

The stranger says nothing more, but as they head up the cliff path, she can feel his fury unfurling behind them like a lurid banner.

She looks up at Greg. He is staring straight ahead, his chin jutting.

"What on earth was that about?" she says. "Who was that man?"

"I have no idea. Come on, let's get you out of here."

Her shoulder hurts where Greg is gripping it. She shakes him off. She must have bruised herself when she fell, because her hipbone feels sore. "Did I hit the beach very hard?"

"No," Greg growls. "I caught you."

They walk through the back alleys and emerge again on the main street. She is shivering. It is the sort of cold that burrows deep inside the bone marrow. She remembers Helena saying, "You'll be freezing your ass off before you know it," and all at once she realizes that Helena is irrelevant. She is not a threat; she is just a distraction, a stone skimming the surface, catching their attention, then bouncing onward. Something else is going on here—something that has nothing to do with infidelity, something much less obvious than that. Helena is not the point.

"You're shivering," he says. "Come on, let's go in here and get you a hot chocolate. We need to get your blood sugar and body temp up. Doctor's orders." His voice is falsely cheerful, as if they've enjoyed a lovely stroll together along the coastal path. He steers her into a café, to a scuffed leather armchair, then goes off to the counter for drinks.

It is the sort of café that Americans do so well, with sofas and bright paintings, an old piano, big jars jammed with cookies, different types of tea. The air is a mess of steam, cinnamon, sugar, and discordant sounds—a folksy soundtrack, the squeak and hiss of a coffee machine, chatter, a feral laugh, the squeal of a chair leg on the wooden floor.

She struggles out of her coat and unwraps her scarf, suddenly sweating. She tries to push her hair back into its ponytail, but it feels static and wild. She puts her hands on her belly. There it is: a little shift, and there—again—the poke of a knee, an elbow, a foot. Relief shimmers through her. The baby is fine. Nothing is wrong with the baby.

She thinks suddenly about the report from the *Philadelphia Inquirer*—the baby girl, born alive at thirty-two weeks, possibly killed by this man, this Carlo Novak. It didn't say how. She touches her belly. An elegant woman at the next table catches her eye and gives a fond smile. The smell of the woman's latte wafts over, and a wave of nausea rises in her throat. She pushes her hair off her forehead, taking slow breaths until the clammy feeling passes. There is a dull, tight ache in her stomach. Lack of food. She must eat. All she has had today is the tea Greg made her in bed that morning and a thin slice of toast in the breakfast room.

She has only ever passed out twice before—once at age twelve at a German gas station, when her mother took her out of school and drove her to Newhaven, crossing the Channel at night in a storm, and then driving on, taking an inexplicable road trip to Nuremberg. They forgot to eat for two days. She passed out, and when she came to, her mother was holding her, weeping, saying, "Sorry, sorry, sorry," and they called her father. He was distraught, not knowing where they'd gone, whether they were even alive. The second time was more mundane, at the GP's office when she was pregnant with Joe and having a blood test. Both times the predominant emotion had been embarrassment. But this time all she can think about is how exposed she must have been on the beach. She imagines Greg laying her out, arranging her limbs, tilting her chin, lifting her knees, one by one.

He comes back to the table. "I got you hot chocolate and a scone." He places the offering in front of her. "Fig and orange—your favorite, right?"

She tries to smile.

"This hasn't been the best start, has it?" He unwinds his scarf. "I was a complete pig last night, and now you're freaking out on the beach. Shall we just stay in bed for the rest of the weekend? It might be a lot more fun."

"Are you sure you didn't know that man?"

The smile freezes on Greg's face.

"He said his name, didn't he? Alex something. Kingston? Kingman? Alex Kingman."

Greg picks up his espresso cup and takes a sip. "I just wanted you off that beach."

The painful knot in her stomach tightens. "But he seemed completely certain that he knew you."

He looks away. "Well, he doesn't."

It is a lie. She can hear the tension in his voice; she feels it radiating from him. And he knows that she knows it—he can't look at her; he looks just past her. A sharp disk of panic begins to spin in her chest. He is still trying to smile, but his eyes are too tight in his head, his jaw too tense. Her stomach cramps, and then saliva gushes into her mouth: she is going to be sick. She leaps out of the chair, pushes past Greg, and looks for the bathrooms, covering her mouth with both hands, feeling everybody's eyes on her, all the concerned strangers, as she hurtles across the crowded room.

CHAPTER FIFTEEN

Joe is on tiptoe, bouncing, eyes shining, as the three of them stand in the hall.

"We went to the Museum of Science and saw an IMAX movie about tornados," he says. "It was awesome." He sounds quite American. She smiles and hugs him tighter.

"Then what did we do?" David puts a hand on Joe's head.

"We had a foot-long hot dog on the beach!"

"You didn't!" Tess feels the relief of Joe's arms stretching to reach around her belly, his face against her side.

"I ate the whole thing."

"You went to the beach? In November?"

"And we had ice cream from this shop with a huge dancing cow."

"Lizzie's, in Cambridge," David says. "Not a real cow. Best ice cream in Boston."

"Then we had room service in the hotel and watched a war movie called *Saving* . . . something . . . what was it, Dad?"

"*Saving Private Ryan.*"

Tess is sure that *Saving Private Ryan* is completely unsuitable for a nine-year-old, but Joe is looking at David as if he is a god. She wishes she could protect him from the inevitable wrench of their separation. It is best not to think about that, or about the conflict zones David goes into and out of all the time. Today Joe's eyes are bright, his cheeks pink. He looks better than he has in weeks—he looks like a normal, happy child as he unpeels himself from her, wanders into the living room, flops onto the sofa, and turns on the Disney Channel.

The energy in the hall changes—she and David are now standing too close. She steps back.

"Well, he was great." David hands over Joe's backpack. "Though he's bankrupted me." There is an awkward pause. "Actually, I meant to ask: do you need me to put some money into an American account? I know it's been a while."

"No," she says. "If you're going to contribute, just put it into my British account."

"OK, right, will do, as soon as I get back. Sorry, you know what it's like, setting up American bank accounts and all that crap . . ." His eyes crease at the edges. She loved him once, in a calm and friendly fashion, but, looking back, she can see that they were never really going to make it. She never felt anything like the passion for David that she does for Greg, or the deep-seated pull, the need, the sense of belonging. But equally, she never felt this unsettled with David. She never wondered what he was hiding, and, even though he lied to her toward the end, they felt like lies of kindness rather than deceit. They both knew it was over by that time, and they both wanted to minimize the hurt. She never felt afraid of David, even for a second.

"So, I should get going."

"Yes, sorry. We'll see you in—what—two weeks?" She goes to open the front door for him.

"Ah, yeah, I have to check that, actually. I may have to go away. I'm not sure yet, but I'll look into it, and we'll work something out."

"OK, but what have you told Joe?"

"I said I'd see him soon."

"I think he needs specifics, David. Right now, he really needs to know what's happening." She grips the doorframe.

"Yes, yes, OK. Don't worry. I'll email you the moment I'm sorted." He doesn't go. "Are you OK, Tess?"

She lets go of the doorframe and folds her arms around her belly, tugging her cardigan closed, pushing back her hair. "What? I'm fine."

"You just seem a bit—I don't know—edgy? And you still don't look very well. Is Greg here?"

"He had to go into the hospital for a bit."

"On a Sunday afternoon? Is everything OK with you guys?"

"Everything's great, David."

He holds up his hands. "OK. Sorry. None of my business. I get it."

"Look, really, it's all fine. Greg and I had a lovely time in Marblehead. There's nothing wrong. I'm just tired, that's all; we only just got back ourselves. And I'm seven months pregnant. I'm allowed to be tired and grumpy."

"Fair enough." He steps out onto the porch, then stops, turns, and looks back at her. "But take care of yourself, Tess, OK? If you need anything, anything at all, you can always call me. You know that, right?"

"In Bahrain?"

He laughs. "Definitely not. I'm currently banned from Bahrain."

When David has gone, she heads upstairs to the bedroom and opens their bags to sort the laundry. It is irritating that he picked up on her unease, and that instinct led him straight to the trouble spot. He knows her too well. She thinks about Greg's lie in the café. She did not imagine it. He recognized Alex Kingman; she is certain of that.

After she threw up, they went back to the hotel, and a profound tiredness hit her—she slept for several hours. At one point she surfaced, sweaty, thirsty, with a numb arm. It was getting dark already, and as her eyes adjusted to the grayness, she saw Greg in the chair by the desk. He wasn't working. He was sitting very still, watching her. In the gloom his face was completely blank. She murmured hello, tried to sit up, rubbing her arm, but the pull of sleep was too powerful, and she lay back down, feeling the darkness fold back over her.

When she woke, it was early evening, and Greg was gone. She found a note on the bedside table. *Gone for a run. Back in 30 mins.* He had not put the time on it, so she couldn't tell when he'd left. She got up, went to the bathroom, washed, checked her phone, then sat on the bed and switched on the iPad. She was about to type "Alex Kingman" into Google, when the door burst open, and Greg came in, pumped up and flushed from running.

"Hey!" he said. "You're awake!" His eyes were bright, his face taut, his movements jerky. He went straight to the bathroom. She shut down the iPad.

That evening, ravenous, they ate at a different restaurant, a place with linen napkins and charming, college-student waiters. Greg behaved as if there had been no fainting, no lies, no strangers on the beach. He talked almost nonstop, telling her how he used to drive up to Maine when he was a medical student, how next summer he would like to take her and Joe cycling in Acadia National Park. He talked and talked, describing the park and its history: how, in the early 1900s, Rockefeller cut fifty miles of carriage trails into its wilderness. Joe, he said, would love it up there. After a while she put her hand on his and said, as calmly as she could, that they would have a six-month-old baby next summer. A cycling vacation might not be the best option.

But he started talking about skiing then: how New Hampshire was on the doorstep, he could take Joe up there one weekend, Joe should learn to ski—and she did not stop him, because she knew that if he stopped talking, then she would have to ask him about the man on the beach, or about Carlo Novak, and she did not want to, not yet. She did not want to tell him that she had opened his boxes. It seemed too unsafe to confess to this, when everything between them felt so off-kilter. And so they sat eating, and Greg talked, and the sea wind raged outside, muffled by the thick restaurant glass.

"Honey?" She jumps at the sound of his voice now, booming from the bottom of the stairs.

"I thought you'd gone!" He must have been hiding in the kitchen all that time, avoiding David.

"No, no, I got waylaid by emails, but I'm heading in now for a couple of hours. That OK?"

She comes to the top of the stairs. He is putting on his coat, smiling up at her.

"Don't be too long."

"I won't. I just have a couple of patients to check on, and then we can have dinner, all three of us. Shall I pick up takeout on the way home? Thai? Vietnamese? Sushi? Pizza?"

"Pizza!" Joe calls from the sofa.

"Pizza, it is. Sloppy Giuseppe?"

She goes back into the bedroom and throws an armful of clothes down the laundry chute, then peels off her jeans and T-shirt. Her skin is creamy, but the livid stretch marks have crawled farther up the tight mound, and her belly button is knuckling out now, like a minuscule fist. She can hear Joe's voice through the floorboards, saying something to Greg.

She hears footsteps and the door closing, as Greg goes down to the garage. She goes through to Joe's room and empties his backpack onto his bed, pulling out the dirty clothes. Through the window, she sees Greg's car pull out of the drive, then slow. Helena is approaching the driver's window, in running gear; she bends, waves, but Greg doesn't stop. Helena watches his car disappear down toward the bigger road; then she turns and begins to run again.

She feels almost sad, suddenly, for Helena. The woman is clearly unhappy with her marriage, and, despite her successes—the Harvard Medical School degree, two businesses, her health-guru status—she is still grasping for something, someone, that can make her feel that she has really made it. It is no way to live.

She picks up her laptop from the bed and switches it on, but then she hears Joe calling, "Mum? Mum? May I have a cookie?" She puts away the laptop. She should not be up here with her computer; she needs to be with her son.

An hour later, Greg texts to say that he is caught up in something at the hospital; he will be more than an hour. So they order pizza themselves and curl up with a blanket over them. They watch *Toy Story 3*, then a couple of episodes of the Disney Channel shows Joe is addicted to—peopled entirely by cloned pseudo-adults—and then she runs him a bath. He is getting self-conscious now and will not let her be in the bathroom as he undresses, so she has to hand him his pajamas around the door. She looks at his stocky legs as he pulls them on, and she sees a bruise near his hip. It is dark blue, with purplish edges, and it is big, the shape of a heel—or a fist.

She says nothing, just waits for him to clean his teeth, and then asks if he would like a story.

Joe still sleeps with the teddy bear David gave him when he was born. It is matted and grubby, never washed, and he uses it as a pillow. She sits on the edge of the mattress and lays a hand on his leg. He flinches.

"Is your leg sore?" she asks.

"No."

"I saw you have a really big bruise. Did something happen when you were with Dad?"

He widens his eyes, baffled. "No!" Then he frowns. "Don't watch me when I'm getting dressed."

"I wasn't watching. I just glimpsed it—that's all. How did you get it? Was it at school?"

He folds both arms over his eyes.

"Did someone hurt you, Joey, on the leg?"

"No."

"It's a really big bruise."

"I banged my leg in PE."

"Love, if any kid is hurting you at school, you have to tell me, because I can make it stop. I can talk to the teachers without involving you at all."

"Nobody hurt me at school!" His voice is high, trapped behind his arms.

She strokes his hair. "It's OK," she whispers. "It's OK."

She will go and talk to the PE teacher first thing tomorrow. She kisses him on the forehead. But there is another thought hunched at the back of her mind, and she has to make herself examine it, even though it feels wrong to do so. Greg would never hurt Joe.

But he did hurt Joe. She remembers the bruises on Joe's upper arm, Greg's fingermarks in his soft flesh. He grabbed Joe and shook him; he terrified him. It is a sickening thought, but she knows that she has to keep steady and think it through. She cannot ignore it just because the answer is potentially monstrous.

So she forces herself to go through the process: the bruise on Joe's leg is four or five days old, and Greg has not been alone in the house with Joe for a week at least, maybe more. Greg could not have hurt him. She rests her hand on Joe's head, feeling sullied by her own treacherous mind.

"When's Greg coming home?" Joe mumbles, as if he has listened to her thoughts.

"Really soon," she says. "Joey . . . if someone ever hurts you, whoever it is—at school, or even . . . or even at home—you must promise to tell me, OK? I am always on your side, always, always."

"When am I seeing Dad again?"

"Two weeks' time, I think. He's going to call when he knows about his next trip."

"I want Dad." He turns over so his back is to her.

She strokes his shoulders in circles. "I know you do. You can call him tomorrow, when you get up. I know he misses you so much. But what I just said—about anyone ever hurting you. It's my job to protect you."

"I want to see Dad right now."

"I know you do," she murmurs. "I know you miss him a lot, don't you, and you had fun together this weekend. Sometimes the more you see someone, the more you miss them when they aren't around."

Joe does not move.

"Joey," she says, "who gave you that big bruise?"

"I already told you." His voice is muffled by his pillow. "PE."

She picks up *Treasure Island*. "OK," she says, "let's have that story now, shall we? They're about to be ambushed by Silver and the pirates, remember? They're outnumbered, they've made a barricade, and they're under attack."

When Joe is still, his breathing heavy, she switches off his bedside lamp and goes to her room. She gets her laptop and sits on the bed, wrapped in a blanket. She types "Alex Kingman, Marblehead" into Google.

"I can't sleep."

She looks up, startled. She didn't hear Joe cross the landing. He looks very pale and small in his Arsenal pajamas. She was sure he was sleeping when she crept out, but he must have been faking. His eyes have big dark circles under them, and he looks cold.

"Come on, come into the bed with me." She pushes aside the laptop and makes room for him. They both get under the duvet. She puts an arm around him.

"I don't want to go to school." His voice is small.

"I know." She pulls him closer.

"They all laughed at me on Wednesday when I cried."

"Oh, love. You cried? What happened?"

"I didn't want to cry, but the tears just came out of my eyes, and I couldn't stop." He touches his eyes as if checking that they were not about to do it again.

"What made you cry?"

"They said I was dumb because I didn't know the rules of this game they were playing. They all laughed at me, and then I cried, and they called me a baby."

She strokes his hair off his face. "Did someone kick you?"

Joe says nothing.

"Love, if you tell me what happened, then I can help to sort this out. It doesn't have to be like this, Joey. It's not fair to you. Your teacher can sort this out easily."

"No!" He struggles away from her hand, panicked. "Don't, don't— don't tell him. Please—please. You'll only make it worse!"

"OK. It's OK. But the school can stop these kids without involving you, you know. They're really good at that." She wonders if they actually are good at that, here. She actually has no idea how the elementary school would handle bullying.

"I wish I'd never told you now."

She folds her arms around him. "You can always tell me. I won't talk to the teacher if you don't want me to." As she says it, she knows that it is a lie. If she tells him that she is going to see his teacher, he will only be more stressed. But she can't not go and talk to the school now. He buries his face against her, and she holds him tightly. Sometimes loving someone and lying to them are not as contradictory as they ought to be.

The baby gives a massive, powerful kick.

"What was that?" Joe looks up with huge eyes.

"It's the baby kicking. Really hard. Here . . ." She guides his hand onto her belly. The baby kicks again. He laughs. It kicks again. "I think we have a footballer in there," she says. "Don't you? Are you excited? It's not that long now till January."

"It's *ages*. That's even after Christmas."

"It's not that long, really. We'll be putting up Christmas decorations before you know it."

"It's *ages* away."

"It's only a month. You need to write a list. Tell me what you want for Christmas."

He begins to list things: LEGOs, Nerf guns, magic tricks . . .

She could start Christmas shopping this week. She needs to be organized. She'll have to post things for Nell and the boys in advance and write out cards for friends in England. And they have not yet bought any baby gear: they'll need a Moses basket, a cot—crib, stroller, diapers, onesies, a sling, a car seat. Earlier, it had seemed like tempting fate to buy things for the baby, but now it is definitely time.

"How about next weekend we all go shopping? We can get some Christmas presents, and we also need to buy some things for the baby. Would you like to do that? You can help me pick some stuff out for the baby's room, and we can get some things for your room, too. You wanted a football beanbag, didn't you? And you know what? We need to think of names, too, for the baby. What shall we call it, if it's a boy?"

He thinks for a moment. "Ronaldo."

"And if it's a girl?"

He frowns. "I don't like any girls' names."

"It might be a girl, you know. It might be a sister in here."

"I don't mind if it's a sister. I just don't like girls' names."

"OK, fair enough," She kisses his head. "You know I'll love you just the same, don't you, when our baby's born? It will change things, but it will never change the way I feel about you. You'll always be my first boy, my special one."

He doesn't answer.

"I was thinking if it's a girl, we could call her Lily. That was your granny's name, my mum, who you never met."

"Was she nice?" He has asked this before, and she gives the same answer.

"She was lovely. She was ill for a long time, but before she got ill, she was the loveliest mum you could hope for. She was kind and funny. And she would have loved you so much. She always said she wanted a little boy after me, but it never happened."

"How old were you when your mum died?"

"I was sixteen."

"How did she die?"

He has never asked this before. But she has always known he would.

"She fell under a train, Joey."

He lifts his head, alarmed. "I don't want you to fall under a train!"

"I'm not going to do that." She kisses his head. "I promise. I am very careful. So, what do we think of the name Lily?"

He rests his head back on her. "It's OK, probably."

There is a rattling downstairs. They both jump. The door to the basement slams.

"It's just Greg!" She laughs, pressing her hand to her heart. "It's OK. It's only Greg."

But Joe's face shows only alarm.

It has been snowing all night, but it is easing off now, the flakes turning from heavy clumps to intermittent, weak structures that float to earth one by one, like ghostly parachutes. When she walked Joe to school, in his new snow boots, he was swept away by the excitement—chucking snowballs with other kids, skidding down the road, the anxiety of the night before erased by the unexpected magic of the weather.

While he is playing in the snow, she slips into the school's reception area and makes an appointment to see his PE teacher.

Back at home, she makes a cup of tea and takes it to the sofa. Folding her legs under herself and shifting until she finds a spot that works for both the laptop and her belly, she opens up Google and types in "Alex Kingman, Marblehead."

The first link is to an article from a Marblehead newspaper about a planning application protest, led by "landscape architect Alex Kingman." She peers at the grainy picture: beard, pea coat, woolen hat. It could be him. It's a bit blurred.

She tries "Alex Kingman, Landscape Architect," and the website of a Boston-based landscape-architecture firm appears. She clicks through descriptions of impressive projects: a university campus, a downtown park, an arboretum. Then she finds a button for "Team Members." And there he is. She recognizes the beard and the steady eyes. In the photo he is wearing a white shirt and linen jacket and sitting at a desk above spread-out plans that show lots of greenery and trees. There is no text to go with the picture. She clicks around, but the website is so trendy that she can't find a button giving actual written information about staff members. There is a "Talks and Lectures" link—she clicks that and reads down a list of forthcoming events.

He is to give a guest "Landscape Lecture" in mid-December, a few weeks away, at the Isabella Stewart Gardner Museum in downtown Boston. It is a place she has wanted to visit; she has read about it—a house of treasures collected over a lifetime by a wealthy nineteenth-century art-lover. She clicks into her calendar. Greg is on call that night. She could ask Sandra's nanny, Delia, to babysit for Joe. She could go and visit the museum, listen to Alex's talk, maybe catch him afterward and ask why he is so sure that he knows Greg.

She jots down the time of the talk; then she goes back to the *Philadelphia Inquirer* archives—the ones she visited briefly when she was in the hotel room. She types in the name Carlo Novak and the dates, as she did before. There are three news items. She reaches into her bag for her wallet and enters her credit card details to get access to the full reports.

They are all disappointingly brief. She rereads the first one, which has no further paragraphs. The details feel more stark in the daylight: a young man accused of a macabre crime, the judge's decision to adjourn because of the intolerable stress of an overheated courtroom.

She clicks back to the search. The next article was written a few months beforehand.

University of Pennsylvania medical student Carlo Novak was charged yesterday with murder, illegal abortion, and the unauthorized practice of medicine in a case centering on an alleged abortion performed on Sarah Banister, 21, at Novak's West Philadelphia apartment. Prosecutors allege that, after inducing the abortion, Novak, 23, allowed Banister's baby girl to die shortly after birth. The alleged termination was carried out thirty-two weeks into the pregnancy.

Said Philadelphia District Attorney Geoffrey K. Arnold, announcing the charges at a news conference yesterday: "This young man coldly decided fatherhood was inconvenient to him. He took the law into his own hands, coercing Ms. Banister to abort. It is the Commonwealth's case that when the child was unexpectedly born alive, Novak failed to adequately care for her. Despite Ms. Banister's desperate pleas, Mr. Novak watched his own daughter die. He sought to play God."

The third article is dated just a week after the one about the jurors being sent home.

The case of University of Pennsylvania medical student Carlo Novak was dropped yesterday. Novak had been charged with murder, illegal abortion, and the unauthorized practice of medicine, but the retraction of a key witness statement led prosecutors to withdraw the charges. Novak was accused of performing an illegal abortion on his sometime girlfriend Sarah Jane Banister, 21, of West Philadelphia, who was thirty-two weeks pregnant, and unlawful killing through failure to adequately care for the child, born alive but who died approximately three minutes after birth.

Banister this week retracted her statement, however, attributing it to stress and depression.

Banister, originally from Scranton, NJ, told the court that she had falsely accused Novak due to mental instability following the premature birth and subsequent death of their daughter, saying she had been distraught when, shortly after the infant's death, Novak terminated their relationship. Jurors heard that Banister had a history of drug use and psychiatric problems. Without Banister's testimony, and without conclusive medical evidence to support the charge of illegal abortion, the Commonwealth withdrew the charges against Novak. "You are free to leave," the Honorable Anna Coulson told Novak at the conclusion of yesterday's hearing at the Philadelphia Court of Common Pleas.

She stares, for a minute or two, at the screen. This could be nothing—just a coincidence, just a name hooked from the past, a random event in someone else's grim life. But of course it can't be: the library card in Greg's box was from the University of Pennsylvania. She looks again at the dates and makes some quick calculations. Carlo Novak would have started medical school two years before Greg. Greg was accelerated through his Pittsburgh undergraduate degree, so he would have been three years younger than Novak. It is not clear how their paths would ever have crossed. The two men were at separate universities, in different cities, academically two years apart.

She shuts down the computer. There is, of course, another possibility: Novak is a Polish name, and Greg's mother was Polish, so Carlo could be a relative. If this is the case, and it seems the most likely connection, then Greg's failure to mention him has to be more than forgetful—it feels slippery, almost deceitful, not to have said anything. It is like looking over your shoulder to see a shape rising out of the fog but not knowing what it is or how menacing it might prove.

That night, when she comes downstairs after putting Joe to bed, Greg is at the dining room table with his papers spread out around him. She brings him a cup of tea, and he looks up, smiles, and murmurs, "Oh, thanks, hon."

"I saw Joe's PE teacher today," she says.

"You did?"

"She says she's noticed some of the other kids are ganging up on him—well, her words were 'being a little hostile at times.' She hasn't noticed any physical violence, but she's going to talk to his class teacher about it and bring it to the staff meeting, and they're all going to keep a close eye on things."

"That's great. They're good at this stuff. Don't worry: if something's going on, they'll be on it now."

"I can't bear it that it's been going on all this time and I haven't protected him from it."

"It's only been a few months."

"A few months is an eternity for a nine-year-old."

He reaches for her hand. "I know it is. But you've done everything you can—you've been to see them several times, haven't you? And it's notoriously hard to pin this stuff down—kids can be sly. But if something is going on, then they won't tolerate it."

"Something is *definitely* going on."

"You want me to come with you, to see the school?"

"No, I've got it. I'm going to go visit his class teacher tomorrow, just to make sure."

"You want me to talk to Joe?"

"No, God, no. Don't say anything. I don't even want him to know I've spoken to them. He'll only worry more if he knows."

He lets go of her hand and sips the tea. "Wouldn't it be better to be honest?"

"Not about this, no. Not yet."

He shrugs and nods, putting down his tea.

"Greg." She stands by his shoulder. "Talking of truth telling—I keep thinking about the man on the beach in Marblehead."

He flicks through some papers. "Uh-huh."

"I got the feeling you recognized him."

He glances up at her, over the top of his reading glasses. "Tess." His voice is heavy with exaggerated tolerance. "Why are you obsessing over this?"

"I'm not obsessing . . . I just had the feeling, when I asked you, when we were in that café, that you weren't quite telling me everything."

"OK, you'd just passed out, you were freezing cold, your BP had crashed, your blood sugar was low, and you were about to throw up: I'm not sure you were at your most clearheaded."

"So you didn't know him, then?"

He flicks through his papers again, plainly irritated. "Listen," he says, "I've got to go through a deposition tomorrow at seven a.m. with the legal team—do you think we could do this another time?"

She stiffens. "Fine. But, also, I wanted to let you know that I put your stuff—you know, from your boxes? I transferred it all to some waterproof containers. It was getting really soggy down there, and—"

"You did what?" He looks up, sharp-eyed.

"Your boxes in the basement. I bought some watertight containers."

His jaw is tight, his face suddenly thunderous. "Those are my personal files, Tess, all my vital documents and certificates, my . . . just about everything's in there."

"I know that. And they were getting damp. Have you been down there lately? The walls are almost wet."

He slams his hand, flat, on the table. "What the hell, Tess?"

She jumps. Then she squares her shoulders. "Don't shout at me."

His nostrils flare, and he looks at her for a moment longer; then he turns his head away and swallows hard. "OK. I'm sorry." His voice is controlled again. "I'm not . . . I can't . . ."

"What can't you?"

"I can't do this right now. I have to think about this deposition . . . Could I please"—he takes a long, slow breath—"get on with this now?"

There is no point in asking him about Carlo Novak's library card now. He will only be hostile. He will never open up in this state. She turns and walks back into the kitchen, picking up her mug of tea. It spills on the countertop. She realizes that her hand is shaking.

This is very wrong. She feels as if she keeps discovering doors and pushing at them, only to find that he has gotten there first and turned the key. She makes up her mind, then, to go and meet Alex Kingman. She will ask him how he thinks he is connected to Greg, and then she will know for sure whether Greg lied to her in Marblehead. Once she has established that, she will be able to confront him about it, and about Carlo Novak, too—get to the bottom of this, whatever it is. She switches off the kitchen lights and goes upstairs, leaving him at the dining room table with his laptop and his papers, preparing his defense.

CHAPTER SIXTEEN

The Back Bay Fens is a part of the city she has not yet visited. She steps out of the T into sleet and peers at Google Maps on her phone, trying to make sense of the tangle of streets as she dodges the cars and buses that carve up slush, their yellowed eyes looming at her out of the gloom, tires hissing on the pavement. The museum is uncomfortably close to Children's Hospital, just a few blocks away. She wonders how she would explain what she is doing if she bumped into Greg. She has told him she is going to the Museum of Fine Arts to hear a talk about the Alfred Stieglitz photographs tonight. She told Delia, the nanny, that she'd be home by ten, so if there is time, she will go across to the MFA, and then it will not be a lie. But of course she isn't going to bump into Greg here in the street, because he will be inside the hospital complex, in a surgical mask and scrubs, moving meticulously through his other, unimaginable world.

After the suburbs, the city feels colossal and booming; it towers and teeters and roars. Someone bumps against her shoulder—she is blocking the pavement, peering at her phone—so she keeps moving, squinting through the sleet at the brick buildings. None looks like a Venetian-style palace. She calls out to a passing woman walking confidently in heels over the icy pavement, "Excuse me? The Isabella Stewart . . . ?" The woman points upward but doesn't stop. On the brickwork above her head foot-high letters spell out ISABELLA STEWART GARDNER MUSEUM.

The lecture is in the museum's concert hall, a tall, cubelike structure with red velvet seats going up in layers of balconies. She spots an empty seat on the same level as the stage, third row back, and squeezes her belly past women with expensive hair, men in jackets, students with slashed red mouths, heavy fringes. Everyone seems to be wearing interesting glasses.

The room hushes as Alex Kingman walks onto the stage with a handsome woman in a pantsuit. His hair is more gray than she remembered, his beard bushier. He is wearing a navy shirt, a tweed jacket, and square black specs. She watches him as the woman gives her introduction, listing his achievements, including a design award and a visiting professorship at Harvard. His gaze travels from face to face as she talks—and then he gets to her. Their eyes lock; he looks briefly startled, but people are clapping now, and the chairwoman is holding out an arm to welcome him to the microphone.

She half expects him to take the stand and address her directly, demand to know what she is doing here, why she has come. The room suddenly feels extremely hot. He clears his throat.

"Van Valkenburgh has called this garden 'a place to get lost,' a place for thoughts—as well as feet—to meander through associations, memories . . ."

Inside her, the baby's feet dig into the cushion of her gut, and she moves her hips so that she is perched on one buttock, trying to rock it off this axis. It gives another jab, then settles on her bladder. She tries to refocus on the stage.

". . . Instead of being a means to get from point A to point B, the path curls back on itself, crossing and recrossing. It is designed for play, because Isabella Stewart Gardner herself was famous for her sense of humor, her adventurous spirit, her defiance of stuffy Victorian conventions. She walked through Back Bay with a tiger on a lead, she loved the Red Sox, she was scandalous and outspoken and famously said, 'Don't spoil a good story by telling the truth.' It is this spirit of irreverence and play that the garden captures so perfectly . . ."

His face is animated, his head held high. He has a strong nose and intelligent, deep-set eyes, but his small mouth is lost in his beard. She realizes that it was slightly crazy to come confront Alex Kingman this way. She should have emailed him. This feels far too public.

"Gardner built this place from nothing. She called it her 'memory palace.' But memory is never linear," he is saying. "Our memories fold back on themselves, they recur and repeat, there are variations and overlappings, and that is, I believe, what Van Valkenburgh set out to achieve here, a small space that would honor the memory palace. Like memory, the Monk's Garden is confounding, impractical . . ."

When the talk is over, Tess urgently needs to go to the bathroom, and when she gets back to the lecture hall, most people have gone already. There are small groups chatting here and there as they gather belongings, but the stage is empty. She feels a wave of relief that Kingman has gone. She will email him—that will be much easier than a face-to-face conversation.

She glances at her watch. Joe will be asleep; there is no need to hurry home. She doesn't have the energy to walk to the MFA—she'll see the Stieglitz photographs another time—but she might as well take advantage of the ticket and have a look around this museum, which has been kept open specially for half an hour after the talk.

She passes along a glass corridor from the modern extension to the original building and finds herself in a cloister that looks out onto a palatial, glass-roofed, indoor courtyard. She stops and gazes at the unexpected greenery. The courtyard is dotted with Roman statues and plinths, tall ferns, a mosaic with Medusa's head at its center. At one end, two fish spout water from an ivy-covered wall. Looking up, she sees tall arched balconies leading from rooms that are packed with the art and artifacts collected over a lifetime of travel. A few people are wandering through the cloisters on the other side, but the place is hushed, churchlike, and very chilly.

She perches on a low wall next to a Roman tomb featuring carved figures gathering grapes. Perhaps, between restless bouts of travel, society dinners, trips to the opera, the symphony, Fenway Park, Isabella herself sat in this spot to remember the husband she lost, or the little boy, her only son, who died when he was not even two years old. The courtyard has the hallmarks of a sanctuary, but there is something lonely about these echo-y shadows. It must have felt desolate when all the guests had gone.

She hears footsteps behind her and starts as a man clears his throat. "Magical, isn't it?"

She turns. His shoes click on the stone floor as he comes to a halt in front of her and the light falls on his face.

"I'm glad I found you—I thought maybe you'd left," he says. "I saw you at my talk. We've met before, haven't we, in Marblehead? Alex," he says, introducing himself.

"Yes, yes, we have." She stands up and holds out her hand. "I'm Tess." His hand is smaller than she'd expected, soft-skinned. Up close his face looks weary and his beard coarse, as if it's sprinkled with iron filings. The urge to photograph him, exactly like this, close-up, with the shadows of the cloister etching the lines around his eyes behind the thick-framed glasses, is briefly overwhelming.

"So, is this just a coincidence?" he asks.

"No, not really. I saw you were speaking, so I came."

"And did you enjoy hearing about the Monk's Garden?"

"Yes. I've never been to the museum before." She looks around at the courtyard. "It's quite a place."

"She certainly left her mark." He looks around and puts his hands in his pockets. "I sometimes feel that this place is more about loss than memories, you know? She's built it and filled it with timeless objects, but there's still this sadness at its heart." He straightens and looks at her. "But listen . . . Tess, did you want to talk to me about something?"

"Well, sort of. I just . . . I kept thinking about bumping into you on the beach. You were so convinced that you knew my husband, and . . . I don't know . . . I suppose I just wanted to know why."

"Because I do know him." He maintains steady eye contact.

"He says you mistook him for someone else."

"And you don't believe him."

"Oh, no—yes, I do, of course I do."

"Then why are you here?"

She looks across to the other side of courtyard. A man is photographing a woman leaning against a pillar. The camera flashes, illuminating the cloister and the shadowy stone figures behind them.

"You want to know how I know your husband?"

"Well, yes, I want to know how you *think* you do."

"Did you see the Monk's Garden yet? It's cold out there, but you have a coat, and you really can't come here without seeing it."

He guides her through the cloisters, then through a door into a garden. A gray brick path winds away through spindly trees. In the distance traffic hums and roars, but the sounds are muffled by high walls. The sleet has stopped, but it is bitterly cold. She struggles into her coat, and they begin to walk, their feet crunching on sprinkled salt and grit.

"OK, so," he says, "years ago, when your husband was a student at the University of Pittsburgh, he was in the same class as my brother."

She feels the chill spread through her chest.

"So?" Alex slows down. "Do you believe me now? They were classmates for a while, until your husband transferred to another school."

"No—wait—there you go. He didn't transfer to any other college. He did his undergraduate degree at the University of Pittsburgh; it was accelerated. He was there three years, not four, and then he went to Harvard Medical School."

Alex shakes his head. "He did a semester and a half at Pitts, and then he left."

She feels her shoulders relax. "It's the wrong person, Alex, see? You've mixed him up with someone else."

"I really haven't." Alex shrugs. They both wait, almost patiently, at this impasse. The trees are like tall, silent waiters, balancing frost on their thin, outstretched arms.

"I think this is what I'm most curious about," she says, eventually. "Why you're so sure you haven't mixed him up, when you so obviously have."

"I recognized him the moment I saw him. He hasn't changed that much. He's aged, of course; his hair is receding a little." Alex's hand flutters toward his head. "But he still looks pretty much the same as when my brother brought him to Florida, when I was twenty years old."

"Honestly"—she can't keep the exasperation out of her voice—"you're thinking of someone different."

He slows again and looks at her. "I promise you, Tess, I'm not."

She walks on, stepping ahead of him.

"This is really silly."

"I'm telling you, he was only an undergraduate at Pitts for one term."

Alex doesn't have a coat. He must be freezing in his tweed jacket, but he doesn't seem bothered by the temperature. She clutches her coat around her belly. "Why on earth would you keep saying this, Alex?"

"Because I could never, ever forget his face."

"Why not? Why couldn't you mix his face up with someone else's? Why couldn't you have forgotten someone's face?"

"I could never forget his face, Tess, because he almost killed me."

She stops.

"You want the whole story now?" Alex shoves his hands into his pockets, his eyes fixed on her face. She nods.

"OK," he says. "I was on spring break with my girlfriend, Patti, my brother, and a couple of my brother's friends, including Chuck."

"Chuck? My husband's name is Greg."

"Well, in those days he was called Chuck, and he'd zeroed in on Patti; he was constantly by her side, making her laugh, bringing her cocktails, rolling her joints. I could tell she was attracted to him—why wouldn't she be? He had supreme self-confidence, he was very good-looking, athletic, charismatic, slightly wild, and very, very smart. He seemed to know something about everything, like he had a photographic memory or something. Anyway, I pretended not to take him seriously, but there was a lot of tension between us, for obvious reasons."

The path twists back on itself, and she realizes that they are crossing a spot where they'd walked just a few minutes before. The garden is tiny. She hugs her coat tighter, burying her chin in her scarf.

"So, one day," Alex continues, "he offered to take me cave diving—he said he had a license. I knew he probably didn't, but I didn't want to lose face in front of Patti, so I went. We hired the gear and drove down the coast. Chuck went in first, and I followed, but I had a bad feeling; I knew how stupid it was. There was an underwater sign saying, 'Go no further. There is nothing in this cave worth dying for.' We went past it, into a tunnel. Chuck went first, and I followed. It was only just wider than my body with the air tank, and there wasn't even enough room to bend my knees, so I just focused on the inch of rock ahead of me. And then I got wedged. I couldn't turn around, I couldn't move, and I felt the beginning of panic—I don't know if you've ever felt real panic, Tess, but it's like this electric feeling in your spine, this icy blankness spreading through the back of your brain. I was trying to calm myself—I already knew that panic kills divers. I've read up about it since, and a lot of divers drown because they panic. Sometimes they remove their own air tank."

"They do that?"

"Nobody knows why—it's maybe the body's instinct to be free? I don't know. But anyway, I was tugging on the lead rope, and after a bit I saw Chuck's mask. He came up so his face was against mine. I remember there was this dead look in his eyes—no warmth, no reassurance, no emotion, nothing. He shoved a hand past my shoulder to my air tank. I guess he released it, because I could move again."

"So he saved you."

Alex ignores her. "We got through the tunnel and dropped into a cave, but there was a lot of silt. The water was thick with it; there was no visibility at all. I'd already decided to go back, but I was feeling really panicky, and I couldn't see Chuck. I somehow made it back through the tunnel, but then I couldn't move; I couldn't get up to the surface. The last thing I remember, I was standing in a beautiful garden, talking to my mom and telling her I loved her."

"You were drowning? How did you survive?"

"Pure luck that a couple of experienced divers found me and got me out. I was in bad shape; I had to be airlifted to a hospital."

She realizes she has been holding her breath.

"And what about Chuck?"

"I don't know."

"He must have come up after you."

"He did, but I never saw him again. People saw him, and he returned the rental car, but he didn't show up back at the condo, didn't collect his things, didn't come to the hospital, and after the break, he wasn't at Pitts anymore. Nobody knew where he'd gone."

"You never saw him again?"

"Not till two weeks ago on my local beach."

There is no point arguing with the man. He has clearly convinced himself that his nemesis had returned. She can see how a claustrophobic, near-death experience like his might leave emotional scars.

"It sounds terrifying," she says, "but you should know that Greg doesn't scuba dive. He really doesn't."

"Yeah?" Alex gives a hollow laugh. "Well, nor do I. Anymore."

She is beginning to shiver, and her feet are growing painfully numb.

"Alex, you really have got the wrong man. If it makes you feel better, I've seen all Greg's college paperwork, from Pittsburgh and Harvard. He is not a cave-diving lunatic; he's a pediatric cardiac surgeon."

"He is, huh? Well, I guess he did something good with his life after all." They are back where they started by the museum door. Alex stands in front of it, blocking her way.

"He isn't your man, Alex."

"Then why," Alex says, "did he threaten me?"

"Sorry?" She folds both arms around her belly and shakes her head. "What?"

"I followed the two of you back to your hotel after you left the café—I guess he didn't mention that either, huh?"

"What do you mean?"

"You looked kind of fragile. I just didn't have the heart to confront him again in front of you, so I waited in the hotel lobby. I was still there, an hour or so later, when he came out for a run—and that's when he threatened me."

She remembers sleeping that afternoon, the dull, dead sleep, and Greg coming back into the room, flushed with adrenaline.

"I confronted him—I was angry—and he forced me outside and around the corner, into the alley. That's when he put his hand around my throat and told me that if I didn't leave him alone, I'd regret it."

She can see the tension in Alex's face, a mixture of fear and outrage. He is not making this up.

"Listen, I don't make a habit of identifying Chuck on random beaches. This is the first time in thirty years that I've seen him, and I knew him right away."

"OK, I need to get going." She steps forward in the hope that he will let her through the door, but he doesn't move.

"What was he doing in Marblehead, Tess?" Alex narrows his eyes. "Was he looking for me?"

"No—what? No. Look, Alex, it's really cold, it's getting late, and I'm very tired. I have to get home to my son. The babysitter will be—"

"A son?" Alex frowns. "You have a son?"

"Yes, yes, I do, and I need to get back to him now." There is nobody else in the garden. Some of the lights in the museum have been switched off, and the two of them are standing in shadows.

Alex glances at her belly. "When's your baby due?"

"In five weeks." She lifts her chin and looks into his eyes. He blinks and looks away, perhaps suppressing whatever unpalatable thought has just crossed his mind. "I'm cold, Alex, I need to go."

There is a pause, and then he says, "Of course. I'm sorry." And he steps aside, holding the door open for her. She moves quickly through it and into the cloister, but he keeps up with her.

"Ever hear of Jacques Cousteau?"

"The deep-sea explorer?"

"Yes. And you know the closest he ever came to death?"

"No, no, I really don't." She wonders how stable Alex actually is.

"It was on a cave dive."

"Really?" She looks around for the exit, barely listening, just wanting to get away.

"There's this spring in the South of France." Alex walks next to her and keeps talking. "Every year, for just a few weeks in early springtime, it turns into a huge gushing fountain. For generations it baffled the village, and then in the nineteenth century an underwater explorer, Nello Ottonelli, built a little zinc boat and went down into it to solve the mystery. He died."

"Oh, dear." She decides it is best just to let the man talk. The rooms they are passing are dark, and the corridor feels longer than it did on the way in.

"Later on another diver, Signor Negri, decided to try. Negri didn't solve the mystery of the spring either, but he did make it back up and gave a detailed account of a network of underwater caves; he even described finding Ottonelli's zinc boat."

She spots the lobby and a security guard and feels herself relax. Alex is still talking.

"A few years on, Cousteau decided to try. He used Negri's detailed directions, but, fifty feet down and very confused, he realized he'd been duped. Negri's descriptions bore no relation to the topography— and there was no zinc boat. Without the right equipment, Cousteau was in big trouble. He wrote in his autobiography that it was by far the closest he ever came to death."

"I don't get why anybody would want to squeeze through underwater caves or tunnels to begin with."

Alex isn't listening.

"He worked out that Negri hadn't got any farther than a ledge fifteen feet down—he'd made everything else up."

She sees the cloakroom.

"Really? Well, I—"

"Tess." Alex stops and puts a hand on her arm, squeezing it, looking into her eyes now. "Negri drew a map of every tunnel, ledge, and turn. He gave measurements, precise depths, a poetic description of Ottonelli's zinc boat—it never occurred to Cousteau to question

Negri's story. If a story is outrageous enough, complete enough, we just assume it's true."

She realizes, then, what Alex is saying. "I know my husband," she says, "if that's what this is about."

"Do you? Well, I thought I knew my wife—my soon to be ex-wife—until I discovered that she'd been having an affair with my closest friend. For twelve years." He rubs a hand over his beard "Twelve years, Tess! We have three children—eleven-year-old twins, a fifteen-year-old daughter, a beautiful apartment in Back Bay, a weekend place in Marblehead, our careers are great, our kids go to great schools, we have a charmed life—and it's all an elaborate lie."

His skin has gone gray, his eyes sunken. She realizes then that this is not about Greg at all; it's about Alex's disintegrating life: the shock, pain, and grief of betrayal—the loss. She doesn't need to be afraid of Alex's memories—they are obviously warped by his current nightmare. Memories are always shaped by the present, and Alex's present is clearly a mess.

"I'm really sorry. It sounds incredibly painful."

"Yes, well, it is. I guess I knew deep down that things weren't perfect, but it never occurred to me that the two of them were capable of that level of deceit. My God . . ." He swallows, as if struggling to breathe. "The lies they told, Tess . . ."

Alex Kingman is, she realizes, effectively back in that underwater cave—trapped, abandoned, blinded, facing what feels like annihilation. She wants to comfort him, but there is nothing she can do or say that would make this any easier for him. They hover by the glass doors. The last visitors are pulling on hats and gloves, winding scarves around their necks, talking in low voices. Behind them, a guard says, "We're closing now, sir, ma'am."

Alex's eyes are bloodshot. "I'm sorry, Tess," he says. "I know I've talked a lot, but you seem like a nice person, a kind person, and you have your baby on the way—and a little boy, too. You need to know what kind of man you're married to. We should exchange numbers."

She finds herself agreeing, even though she has no desire to see Alex again. He puts his phone back into his pocket after they've swapped numbers, and he looks into her eyes. "You know, to see Chuck Novak again in my hometown, on the beach where I walk my dog, it was—"

She recoils. "What did you just say?"

"What?"

"Chuck Novak?"

"Yes—"

The glass walls seem to shift, closing in on her, and she turns, without saying good-bye, and steps through the doors, out into the freezing night. She walks as fast as she can, though her boots are slipping on the ice, and sleet needles her scalp. The city roars and belches all around, and as she gets to the corner, she stops, disoriented by the lights and the noise, the teetering buildings, the smoky sky. She has to get home—she has to get home to Joe—but she can't remember the way; all the roads look the same, and she has no idea which one to take.

CHAPTER SEVENTEEN

It takes a while, on the phone to Nell the next morning, to explain what happened with Alex Kingman.

"The main thing is, he called him Chuck Novak, Nell. Chuck—Charles, Carlo? This is feeling less and less like a coincidence." A pallid winter sun appears low in the sky, illuminating the cold steel of the kitchen.

"All right, OK, but this is so confusing." Nell takes a sip of something. Radio 4 is burbling in the background. Tess imagines Nell standing in her messy kitchen with a cake in the oven, the woodstove crackling. "Carlo Novak's library card was from the University of Pennsylvania, wasn't it? Is the University of Pennsylvania in Pittsburgh?"

"No, the University of Pennsylvania is in Philadelphia. I googled it on the way home last night."

"But Pittsburgh's in Pennsylvania, isn't it?"

"Yes, but Philadelphia is in Pennsylvania, too."

Nell laughs. "This is baffling."

"I know, but the geography doesn't matter. The point is, they're two different universities, in cities hundreds of miles apart. Greg was never at college in Philadelphia; he was an undergraduate in Pittsburgh, and then he went to Harvard Med School." She reaches up and tucks a loose strand of Christmas lights back over the window ledge.

There is a pause. "So Alex Kingman is wrong, obviously."

"Yes, of course, he is. But there's got to be some connection between Greg and Carlo Novak—given the library card, there has to be. So, what am I missing here?"

"What you're missing," Nell says firmly, "is Greg. You have to ask him—you have to tell him what Kingman said and talk to him about all this."

"I was going to last night. I was planning how to talk to him all the way home from the museum, but when I got in, he was still at the hospital. I made myself wait up for him, but the later it got, the more unhinged this whole thing felt, and eventually I fell asleep and didn't even hear him come in. Then this morning he was in a rush—he left at six-fifteen."

"OK, fine, but you have to ask him tonight. It's the only way you're going to clear this up."

"I know. I will."

"Listen," Nell says, "there are all sorts of reasonable explanations for this, I'm sure. All you've got is a library card and Alex Kingman, who is hardly reliable, since he's going through a massive midlife crisis. This Novak thing could still be a weird coincidence. I mean, *Novak* could be the Polish equivalent of *Smith* for all we know."

Tess feels the tension in her neck ease.

"Just ask him, for God's sake, because this is getting out of hand. You're starting to hide more from Greg than he is from you."

They change the subject then and talk about normal things: Christmas plans, the twins' squabbling, Joe's problems at school, Nell's frustrations with Ken, the urgent need to get a Christmas tree. It is almost like being home, sitting at Nell's kitchen table, with the boys at the Xbox in the front room, Nell's spaniel resting his nose on her feet, a pot of tea or a glass of wine and whatever cake she made that day in front of them. Missing Nell feels almost physical at times, an ache in the pit of her stomach, a longing not just for a person but for a place, a life that has suddenly slipped into the past.

"I wish we could go get our Christmas trees from the Scouts like we always do," Tess says. "I think that's why I haven't gotten one yet; it feels too sad without you and the boys. I've got almost all Joe's presents now, and we've put some lights up but no tree yet."

"I know. I'm sure that's why I haven't got ours yet either. It just isn't the same here without you."

When they hang up, Tess goes down to the basement to bring up the box of tree decorations. The plastic crates containing Greg's things are neatly lined up where she left them. She hesitates, then reaches up and pulls one down. She digs through it until she finds a file with *Harvard Scholarship* written on it in Greg's handwriting. She flicks through the paperwork.

All the dates stack up—of course they do. Greg finished high school at seventeen, went to the University of Pittsburgh for three years, then to Harvard Medical School. It is all here. As she repacks the file and clamps on its plastic lid, she realizes that something must be badly wrong in order for her to be crouching like this in their freezing basement, checking up on his dates.

This is definitely not how a healthy marriage should feel. She heaves the box back up onto the shelf. As she pulls down the cardboard box of Christmas decorations, she dislodges another of Greg's crates, knocking the lid loose. She pulls it down. It is the box with the baseball things. She can't stop herself. She reaches inside again, and her fingers touch the medallion. She pulls it out and holds it between her fingers: ROBESVILLE SLUGGERS, JUNIOR LEAGUE CHAMPIONS. Slowly, she turns it over: CARLO NOVAK.

It is as if she already knew that the name would be engraved there. It feels unsurprising, almost matter-of-fact to see it inscribed in the cheap metal. She slowly folds the ribbon around it and puts it back. Carlo Novak is a relative; he must be.

She feels a twinge down one side as she reaches the top of the basement steps. She should not be lifting boxes at this stage of pregnancy. The baby shifts. She puts the box of decorations down on the top step, rubbing her sides, waiting to get her breath back.

She tries to remember the things Greg has told her about his family. He told her that when he was a little boy, they would walk through the town every Christmas Eve and look at all the Nativity displays people had in their windows. But he never told her about Christmas Day itself. He didn't even tell her what they ate—though, when she thinks about it, many of his other childhood memories involve food. Food is presumably safer to remember than people.

He has mentioned the Gallo family meatballs, the bread dipped in "sauce" that they would eat on Sunday after Mass, the kitchen garden with rows of tomatoes to be picked and canned every year, the *paczki*—deep-fried, sugar-dusted Polish pastries that he would eat warm.

Other childhood memories are sparse. He has told her about the network of waterfalls where the kids would go on summer vacation, half an hour's hike out of town. They'd stay there, unsupervised, until sundown day after day. He has mentioned wildlife, too—wild turkeys and deer, black bears, bald eagles. He told her, once, about a bald-eagle statue on the high school playing field. But that was about it.

And when it comes to his undergraduate days in Pittsburgh or his Harvard degree, she knows next to nothing. He took more courses than other people as an undergraduate, because academic study was the only thing that seemed to help. But he was too modest even to tell her about his perfect MCAT score.

The only thing he has told her about in any detail is the fire. And he told her everything about that: how he was cycling home with his backpack on, his baseball cap pulled down against the evening sun, and how he smelled burning even before he saw the smoke billowing over the rooftops. How he turned the corner into his street and heard the wail of fire trucks, and people were running toward him, holding up their hands, shouting at him to stop. And he told her how he'd fought them to get to front door—and then a wall of heat hit him, and hands pulled him back, dragged him away, held him down.

Whatever else he is concealing about his past, this, at least, is complete and true. The memory was so real to him, even thirty years on, that the telling of it altered his face and body: his shoulders collapsed, the angles of his brow sharpened, and his eyes became hollow and haunted.

He was less willing to talk about the unspeakable year that followed the fire. It must have been unbearable, living in his alcoholic aunt's apartment while he finished his senior year of high school. He can't even say her name. The only thing that kept him alive that year, he said, was the prospect of college. He had been accelerated a year at high school, too, so when he left his aunt's apartment, he was only seventeen years old.

He will always be damaged by loss: no matter how many lives he saves, how many clinical breakthroughs he makes, how many prizes he wins, he is going to carry this traumatic memory around inside him until he dies. But Alex Kingman is wrong: there is no reason to doubt Greg's story, because she has seen it written on his face and body. In fact, she saw it in his face the first time she looked at him through the viewfinder of her camera.

Greg must have been an extraordinarily resilient teenager. He didn't let the loss destroy him. He turned the tragedy around and let it propel him to where he is now. It is an extraordinary achievement. She picks up the decorations box and steps back into the kitchen.

When Greg finally gets home, it is past midnight again. She has been dozing fitfully, determined to stay awake, listening for his key in the door between brief, rapid dreams of tunnels, high walls, and the smell of burning. She hears his feet treading lightly up the stairs. He goes into the main bathroom so that he won't wake her, and she hears him crank on the shower, water hissing through the pipes. After a while the smell of his shampoo floats through on the steam. She knows that she should get up, go to the bathroom, and demand to know who Carlo Novak is, why his library card and medal are downstairs in his box, and why Alex Kingman thinks they are the same man.

She has to do it. She waits for him to come into the bedroom. He is barefoot. She can smell his damp, clean skin. She forces herself to sit up.

"Greg," she says, "I've got to talk to you."

He stops in the middle of the room, a towel around his waist, broad chest bare, its dark hair massed in a crucifix over his heart.

"Shit, Tess! I thought you were sleeping."

"I was, sort of, but I need to ask you about something."

He does not move, and for a moment, for too long, he doesn't respond. She can almost hear his brain spinning.

"Greg, I—"

"It's late," he says in a low voice. "You really should be asleep."

"I know, but I have to talk to you."

"Honey, I have to sleep now. I can't even think straight, let alone talk—do you know what time it is? I have a full schedule tomorrow, and if I don't get some sleep now, I'm not going to be able to function properly. Maybe we could talk in morning, early, before I go? Could we do that? Or tomorrow evening?"

She can't see his eyes; it is too dark.

Her mouth suddenly feels dry and cracked. She knows he is avoiding her now. She knows he is hiding things. She turns to look for water on the bedside table, and he disappears into the walk-in closet. She shouldn't let him walk away like this; she should get up, turn the lights on, follow him in there, and demand answers, but it is the dead of night, they are both exhausted, and right now everything feels very breakable indeed.

This could wait another few hours. They will both be able to think more clearly in the morning.

She lies down and turns onto her side with her back to the walk-in closet. The baby swivels and stretches busily, pushing, elbowing, poking at her sides. She hears Greg come back into the bedroom. She wonders if he was stalling in there, folding clothes, hanging up ties, uniting stray socks, hoping she would be asleep when he came out.

He gets under the duvet, and the mattress tilts into his weight. He lies on his back, motionless. He does not try to touch her. Perhaps he thinks she is sleeping. It is as if they are suspended, side by side, in separate cocoons of tension.

But Greg can fall asleep in an instant, no matter what, with no twitching or sighs, no need for reading, release, or winding down. It is the result of years of medical training, of broken nights on cots in hospital break rooms during forty-hour shifts, alert, high-functioning, snatching sleep only to reboot. And yet right now his stillness feels watchful.

She keeps her breathing even. In the morning, in daylight, they will both be calmer and more rational.

After what feels like a long time, she hears his lengthened, whispery exhales. She waits for a few minutes more and then, gingerly, turns onto her back. The baby sinks heavily against her spine. She can see Greg's profile in the moonlight, the carved, almost noble features, his lips slightly parted. Perhaps she is looking at his father's Italian nose and square jawline, his mother's Slavic cheekbones. She wonders if their baby will inherit any of these features. Or maybe it will look like her side of the family, with the light blue eyes she inherited from her mother, the wavy blond hair from her father.

She closes her eyes, feels the walls of the house brace themselves against a gust of wind, and the questions rise up, like faces pressed against a window: Greg's parents emigrated—separately—from Italy and Poland for a better life, but how did they meet? How did they end up in that Pennsylvania town? Did they fall in love there? Or did they meet in a big city—New York, Philadelphia, Chicago? Were they happy? Did they love each other? And why—both Catholics—did they have only one child? And what about his aunt—why did she have no children of her own? The questions crowd her head, and then there is a cracking sound, and the skewed brickwork of the house begins, very slowly, to tilt, collapsing inward. The walls are toppling around her—the house is being sucked into the basement—she smells brick dust, and the floor beneath her drops. Her limbs jerk—her eyes flip open—she takes a sharp breath.

She thought she was awake, but she must have been sleeping. Her heart is thumping now, and she feels sick, trembly. She is wide awake. Greg grinds his teeth, just once: a sharp, gravelly shriek.

She slips out of bed and tiptoes shakily across the room, pushing through shadows to take her robe from the back of the bathroom door. She lifts her laptop from the chest of drawers and glances back at Greg. He does not move. As she closes the bedroom door behind her, it gives a little click.

The house is terribly cold. Down in the living room, frost patterns each diamond-shaped windowpane. She grabs a blanket from the arm of the leather chair and wraps herself in it, wiping condensation off the glass. She peers out. Snowflakes drift from a canopy of darkness, illuminated only by the funnel of light from the Schechters' porch lamp. Greg said that snow this early is rare—it is going to be a brutal winter.

Joe will be excited. The white stuff is already lying thick on the road and the front lawns, balancing on branches and fence posts. The plows will come soon, growling through the night like slow, determined beasts, scraping everything aside, staining everything they pass. She wipes her breath off the glass and peers across the road, half expecting to see a red-haired figure in the snow, staring back. But, of course, the street is empty.

She goes to the sofa and switches on her laptop. There is an email from Nell marked "URGENT—look at this." She sent it at what would have been about four o'clock in the morning, her time. Tess opens it.

> Insomnia strikes again, so I've done a bit of digging about this Carlo Novak thing tonight, and look what I found; it was on some Deep South, rabid, pro-life blog (scary). It's a newspaper picture from that Philadelphia baby trial. It's obviously very blurry and hard to see but—just have a look. Then call me. N x

She opens the link and scrolls through a virulent pro-life blog that has a post devoted to "men who got away with murder." In it is a blurred black-and-white image of a young man on the steps of a grand public building. He is looking over his shoulder at the camera, which is below him, as if somebody in the street has shouted out his name. His features are indistinct. She squints at the screen, trying to make sense of the pixels. Then she pulls her head back. Suddenly, the bone structure comes into focus.

For a moment the living room walls seem to bend outward, as if the air around her has expanded. She shoves the laptop aside, hauls herself onto her feet, and stands, pressing both hands against her head. Her belly clenches.

It cannot be. She is seeing things. The image is years old, blurry. It must be an odd photographic effect of angle and lighting. Her eyes must have picked up patterns they want to see—or don't want to see. She looks at her watch. It is past one in the morning. She tips everything out of her bag to find her phone, scattering wallet, keys, hairbrush, lip balm, pens, papers, and crumbs onto the parquet. She finds the phone and calls Nell.

"Did I wake you?" she whispers.

"What do you think?" Nell croaks. "It's six in the morning, and I was up till four."

"Sorry, sorry—but I had to speak to you, I just got the email. I just saw that picture."

She hears rustling over the phone.

"Wait—hang on . . ." Nell says.

She hears faint footsteps. She pictures Nell sliding out of bed, leaving Ken snoring, creeping down the creaking stairs, trying not to wake the boys or the dog.

"Right," Nell says, in a louder voice. "I'm in the kitchen now."

"How did you find this?"

"I wanted to see if there was anything online about Carlo Novak. I stumbled across it."

"It looks so much like him, Nell." She keeps her voice to a whisper. The last thing she wants right now is for Greg to wake up and come downstairs.

"I know," Nell says. "I mean, I wondered if it was just me. I almost didn't send it to you."

"No, it's not just you." She sits back in the sofa, wrapping the blanket around herself again. The baby lurches, changing position. "God, Nell. It's the bone structure, it's the cheekbones—they're so much like Greg, the likeness is freakish. I can't get my head around it." She is shivering now, properly, as if the temperature in the front room has plummeted.

"What did Greg say when you asked him about Carlo Novak? Did you tell him you met Alex Kingman? What did he say?"

"He only got in about forty-five minutes ago. I was half asleep—I tried to talk to him, but he said he was exhausted and we should talk in the morning. He's asleep now, but I couldn't, so that's why I'm down here, reading your emails."

"OK, well, you've got to talk to him now. This is bonkers."

She hears a rushing sound. Nell is filling the kettle.

"What the hell is happening here, Nell?"

"It has to be a relative. Wasn't Greg's mother Polish?"

"Yes, yes, she was, but he's an only child, and he's never mentioned any relatives."

"There are *always* relatives."

"There was an aunt," she hisses. "After his parents died, he had to live with her. It was awful; she was an alcoholic."

"What was her name?"

"Julianna . . . I don't think he's ever told me her last name. Clearly it was a hideous time for him—he just says it was appalling, and he'd rather not remember it."

"So, then, he could have cousins. This Julianna woman could have had kids."

"But he'd have told me that."

"What was his mother's maiden name?"

She tries to think, but no name surfaces. "Jesus, I don't know—I can't remember. I honestly don't know if he's ever said." She forces her voice back down to a whisper. "He just won't talk about his family—he always says it's not helpful, it upsets him to remember them, and he's coped all these years, really well, by shutting it all off and not looking back. It might not be fashionable, but it works for him."

"Well, he's got to talk to you now, hasn't he? If Carlo Novak is a close cousin, then the family resemblance makes sense, and the library card, the medal, Alex mistaking Greg for Carlo. Cousins can sometimes look really alike, can't they? If Carlo is Greg's cousin, then all this is explained, isn't it?"

Tess picks up the laptop and makes herself look at the picture again. The man on the courtroom steps is young and beautiful, though his expression is hunted. She feels a shiver pass through her and pushes the laptop away.

"It's just *so* much like him, Nell."

She hears the clanking sound of Nell's cutlery drawer: Nell is looking for a teaspoon. She will be in her checked pajamas, barefoot on the terra-cotta tiles with her dark, curly hair all over the place. The longing to be there, with Nell, is almost overpowering. She can feel herself holding out her hand for the mug of tea, warmth radiating from the woodstove, going over to the big table, pushing back the mess of Christmas cards, newspapers, school consent forms, exercise books, baking trays, dog leads, magazines, and rolls of Scotch tape, and sitting down. But Nell is three thousand miles away, in a different time zone, on a different land mass.

"Or a brother?" Nell says. "Could he have had a brother? A twin, even?"

"A brother wouldn't be a Novak; he'd be a Gallo. And anyway, for God's sake, Greg would have mentioned it if he had a twin, even one he was ashamed of."

"Would he?" Nell's voice is distant and troubled.

"Yes." She wraps the blanket tightly around her shoulders and shivers. "Of course, he would."

After they hang up, she climbs the stairs, but at the top of the landing she turns right, into Joe's room. He is hunched under the duvet, hair sprouting, snoring lightly. She sits on the edge of his bed, rubbing the sides of her belly, her hands pressing on what feels like a little heel. The branch of a tree casts a shadow through the window onto the floor. It moves across her toes like a black claw. The skin on her belly feels very tight, as if the baby is expanding too fast. She'll have another checkup in two days' time; there are weekly checkups with the ob/gyn now. Suddenly it feels urgent to sort this out. She has to know what she is dealing with before she brings their baby into this house.

The photograph makes no sense at all. Perhaps it is her mind connecting the dots, seeing facial patterns that don't exist. Cameras can alter reality; she knows this—she's done it herself many times. She has made plain people beautiful, old people younger. Certain shadows and lines of a face can be emphasized, features heightened or diminished by light, angle, focus, settings. She can make a camera lie anytime she wants it to. A photograph is no more reliable than a memory, really: both are stories told about the past, rooted in the moment, warped by the teller.

She tucks the duvet around Joe's shoulders, then gets up and crosses the landing to their bedroom door. Greg is lying as she left him, on his back. He reminds her of a statue of a medieval knight carved in marble on a tomb. In the morning she will tell him about meeting Alex Kingman. She will show him the photograph and ask him what it means. She will demand to know how he is connected to Carlo Novak. She glances at the luminous hands of the bedside clock. It is almost two now. The lack of sleep is not helping. She has to get some rest and face this—whatever it is—in the morning.

But she can't bring herself to go over and climb into bed next to him. She stands, shivering gently, and then goes back to Joe's room. She eases his little body over and tunnels into his warm spot. He wriggles, turns, and burrows against her belly, and she folds her arms around him, holding him tightly, waiting for sleep to come. Deep inside her, the baby struggles and kicks as if it is trapped and panicking—as if its oxygen is failing and it must find a way out.

CHAPTER EIGHTEEN

She must have slept, because light is flooding into the room, hurting her eyelids. She is stiff, and the Arsenal duvet is folded back, exposing her right side to the air. She remembers vivid dreams that the baby died—she can still feel the weight of it in her arms and see its waxy little face—and then she remembers the other thing that has been racing through her brain all night: the young man on the courtroom steps. She sits up.

She looks at the empty mattress next to her. Joe is not there. She gets out of the bed, unsteady. "Joe? Joey?"

Out on the landing she calls for him again.

"What?" His voice rises up from the kitchen, and she feels a wave of relief—she does not know why—and she hurries downstairs, the weight of the baby throwing her off-balance, forcing her to grip the banister to stop herself from falling forward, crashing down to the white tiles of the hall.

Joe is sitting at the kitchen counter with an empty plate next to him, reading *National Geographic Kids* magazine. His hair has been combed with a side parting, and he is in a blue checked shirt, a proper one with buttons, which she does not recognize. She looks at the stove clock. It is 7:55 a.m.

"Goodness, it's late." She tries to sound calmer than she feels. "Why didn't you wake me up?"

"Greg took me out in the snow!"

"He did?" She rubs her eyes.

"We made a snowman." He leaps up and drags her through to the dining room, pointing out the window. There is a fat snowman, with Greg's hat on it and her scarf. A carrot nose.

She laughs. "Wow!"

"Then he said I had to get ready for school."

"Why didn't you wake me up?"

"Greg said I had to let you sleep. Why were you in my bed?"

"I think I must have had a bad dream," she says. "Did you have breakfast already?"

"After we made the snowman, Greg made French toast with cinnamon and maple syrup."

"He did? Has he gone to the hospital now?"

"Yes." Joe gets up. "He said to tell you he loves you very much, but he had to be at the hospital, and he's going to call you later. I'm going to brush my teeth now."

"Good boy. Look at you—you look so smart today. What's this nice shirt? Where's it from?" She resists the urge to mess up his hair. It has been dampened before the combing.

"Greg gave it to me."

"He did? This morning?"

"Yes. He bought it for me—there are four more and a couple of T-shirts, too. He says they're what American boys wear."

"Is that right?"

He shrugs. "Some of them do."

She touches his neck and glances at the label—Gap Kids. She has no idea how on earth Greg found time to go to a Gap. She feels a prickle of unease—it feels slightly controlling for Greg to buy Joe clothes without saying anything to her. But she must not be so defensive. It was a touching thing to do; Greg is just trying to help Joe to blend in.

"Well, you look great," she says. "So handsome."

He groans, rolls his eyes, and goes upstairs. She puts his plate and cup in the dishwasher. Greg has washed the frying pan and left it on the draining board. He must have gone in later than usual if he was making a snowman and cooking French toast. Perhaps he was waiting for her to wake up so that they could talk but then decided that, on balance, it was more important for her to sleep.

She realizes then that she left her laptop on the sofa. She can't remember whether she shut it down before she went up to bed. If he has opened it, then he will know what she has seen. She catches sight of her reflection in the kitchen window. Her hair is tangled, her eyes hollow, her face as white as the T-shirt she is wearing.

She goes into the living room, passing Joe's snow boots and a puddle of melted ice. She hangs his coat, which is damp, on the newel post. She can hear him brushing his teeth. The laptop is where she left it on arm of the sofa. She remembers spilling the contents of her bag onto the floor, looking for her phone, but her bag is sitting by the sofa, and everything is back inside. She does not remember doing this, but perhaps she did.

The light of the computer winks up at her. She opens its lid and types in the password, which Greg knows. The page is still open on the blog, with the photo of the young man. She presses the Off button without looking at the image.

She remembers a BBC documentary she once watched about a middle-aged divorcée who had been taken in by a con man. The woman was intelligent, articulate, educated to master's-degree level, and had fallen in love with a man she met online. He seemed utterly plausible—even her mother loved him—and they became engaged. It turned out that he had five other fiancées. The women were all educated, attractive single mothers. They accepted his frequent absences because they believed that he was busy setting up an international recruitment business. They had each "lent" him thousands of pounds. Then he vanished.

After she has taken Joe to school, she leaves Greg a voice mail. "I need you to call me back," she says. "The minute you're done. I have got to talk to you. Even if it's just for five minutes before you go into your next thing. I need you to call me."

She eats an Oreo from the cookie jar. Then another. Her head feels murky, and the brightness of the snow outside hurts her eyes. She makes herself an espresso in Greg's machine and gulps it down, not caring about the caffeine. Soon she feels a rush of shaky energy—everything sharpens. She is so unused to caffeine, it feels as if she's taken a powerful drug. The baby buzzes inside her like a fat hornet.

She will get on with tasks around the house until he calls her back, and then she will just ask him, over the phone, who Carlo Novak is. The Volvo is booked for servicing at the local garage. She'll take it in, then walk back to the house to clean up; then, when she gets the car back, she'll drive over to Whole Foods and get a Christmas tree. She has left it far too late—Christmas is only five days away. Greg had a romantic idea that they'd drive out to a Christmas tree farm for one, but every time they've planned it, something has come up. She has never left it this late before. It is not fair to Joe. She'll surprise him. She goes back to the hall and shoves her feet into her boots, takes her coat, and wraps herself in a scarf.

The path has been shoveled clear of snow. Greg must have done it this morning. It is as if he is making an effort to do everything right— build a snowman with Joe, shovel the walk, buy clothes for Joe, make French toast, allow her to rest. The snowplows have been through the neighborhood overnight, and the roads are clear and sanded. Somehow the plow avoided hitting the Volvo, but it is wedged in now by a dirty snowbank, up over the wheels. She is sure it shouldn't have been on the street—no other cars are. From now on, she'll park it in the garage.

She goes back to the porch for the snow shovel and digs at the snow packed hard against the car. Her head is pounding, and her sides ache. She straightens, putting the heel of one hand to her forehead and pressing it hard.

After she has dug a channel for the tires, she gets into the car. She is sweating and breathing heavily. She puts the Volvo into Drive and edges forward, looking over her shoulder to check that nothing is coming, glad that Greg has put snow tires on it, feeling them grip and lift the heavy body of the car onto the road. As she turns to look forward again, a hooded figure is standing right there, in front of the car. She stabs the brake and wrenches the steering wheel—the tires shriek—and the figure, in a long black puffy coat, scrambles out of the way, up onto the snowbank. The Volvo stops.

She cranes her neck to look behind her, her arms shaking on the steering wheel. The person is getting back off the snowbank now, pulling the hood down to reveal a furious face: Helena.

Tess reaches for the button to buzz down the window but then stops. Helena is almost at the car, and she is obviously angry but unhurt. Tess shoves the Volvo into Drive again and moves away slowly, leaving Helena in the middle of the road in her long black coat, hands on hips, shouting something.

The walk home from the garage, across the snowy park, passes in a blur. A heavy, khaki-colored sky presses down, and there seems to be a pause to the air, a tension—more snow is on the way. Her boots crunch and squeak, and her belly feels hard and tight. The ache in the base of her spine and around her sides is more intense now, perhaps from shoveling out the Volvo. She checks her phone: no missed calls. She reaches their street—no sign of Helena or anyone else.

Back in the house she can't rest, even though she knows that she needs to. The urge to clean the house is overwhelming. She scrubs the kitchen, loads up the dishwasher, sweeps and mops the floors, and clears away stacks of papers and socks and shoes, coloring pens and school-books and Joe's crusted snow boots, which he should be wearing today but somehow is not. She mops the hall so that the white tiles gleam. She opens the front door and throws the dirty water out. It brands the snow in the shape of a small dark country.

She has to keep moving, despite the dragging around her sides and the burning in her lower back. She will do the laundry. It seems vital that the house should be organized, all domestic tasks completed.

The air temperature drops with every step into the basement, and she feels her belly clench, as if the baby has curled into a tight ball for warmth. As she opens the laundry-room door, she hears a thump, high above her in the house: the wind pushing the snowstorm closer.

The laundry room is pitch-dark. She feels for the switch, and in the instant before the lights flicker on, she is sure that someone will be there, standing in the tiny room, facing her.

But, of course, the room is empty. Just a heap of unwashed clothing spewing from the laundry chute, the smell of mildew and Tide and stale clothes. As she bends over to heave the dirty things off the floor, she hears it again—a thud upstairs. She stops. The sound was more localized than the wind. Something is moving across the floor above her: rapid footsteps.

Somebody is in the house.

It isn't Greg; she knows the sound of his feet, and, anyway, Greg would have called—he wouldn't just come home like this. She feels for her phone in her back pocket and then remembers that it is on the counter in the kitchen by the coffee machine. Did she close the front door after washing the floors? She isn't sure. She imagines Helena shoving her way in, pacing angrily through the rooms, looking for her. If it is Helena, she must go up there and face her. But what if it isn't Helena? It could be anyone.

She stands rigid, every hair on her body raised, listening. She hears feet, very clearly now, walking along the hall above her head, a flat-booted tapping sound, definitely not Greg's purposeful stride. If it was Helena, she would surely be calling out to Tess by now.

She can get out of the basement by going through the garage and onto the back driveway, but the electronic garage-door opener is in the car—and the car is at the mechanic's. She is not sure whether it is possible to open the garage from the inside without the electronic device.

Greg's crates are lined up front of her, neat, plastic squares. She listens, her head cocked. The house braces itself against another gust that shoves the bricks and boards so that they shift fractionally. She could go up and confront the intruder, order whoever it is out of her house. She suddenly pictures the thin, red-haired woman hissing at her in the street.

Then she hears her cell phone ringtone. It is loud, as if it is coming from behind her, as if it's in the laundry room—perhaps she did bring it down. She scrambles through the clothing looking for it, but it is not there. The sound cuts out. The laundry chute travels all the way through the house, like its spinal column, from top floor to basement. There is an opening in the hall by the kitchen and one on the upstairs landing. The sound must be traveling down the steel pipe.

She scrapes piles of clothing from mouth of the chute and bends her head to the metal, listening.

"Hey." The voice—a woman's—makes her jerk her ear away. "Where d'you go? I only want to speak to you. I just need to . . . just need to . . . you know . . . it's all I need . . . all I need is . . ." The voice, babbling, rapid, is warped by the chute. "Come on! Where are you? Where'd you go, lovely pregnant lady? Pregnant lady, where are you?"

It has to be her. She recognizes the instability in the voice; when her mother was bad off, her voice had this same feel, the same pitch and rapidity, the same syllabic tumble. The footsteps are moving again overhead, suddenly fast. She imagines the ravaged face, the dyed red hair, the overcoat, those black boots. It can only be her, and in a minute she is going to notice that the door to the basement is open, and she is going to come down. Tess lunges at the laundry-room door, grabs the key from the outside, shuts the door, and locks herself in.

She hears boots coming down the basement stairs and landing, heavy and flat, on the damp concrete floor. She wraps her arms around her belly. The baby gives a monumental kick with both feet. The boots are coming across the basement toward the door now. They stop. The two of them are separated only by a thin layer of plasterboard. There is a faint, cloying smell, somehow familiar. The wind hits the house again like a big flat hand.

Tess holds her breath. The doorknob turns. Her eyeballs strain in their sockets. The handle releases. Her head feels light. She looks around for anything to use if the woman breaks through the door, but there is nothing in here—absolutely nothing that she could use if she needed to defend herself.

There is a scratching sound. The woman is scratching at the wood, maybe with a fingernail—rapid little *scratch-scratch-scratch* sounds. She squeezes her eyes shut. And then the scratching stops. She hears the boots shuffle, a sigh, and then the woman moves off again. She crosses the basement floor, moving away, going back up the stairs.

Tess sucks in a breath, then sinks onto the bed of dirty clothes, her heart hurling itself around inside her chest. A few minutes later she hears the distant slam of the front door—the thud of mahogany, the rattle of the doorframe. The intruder has gone.

She clambers over the strewn laundry, unlocks the door, and goes across the basement and up the stairs. The door at the top is shut now. She tries the knob. Nothing happens. She shoves her shoulder against the wood, tugging the knob, then pushing as hard as she can, but it will not move. The woman has locked her in.

She can see back down the steps and into a portion of the empty basement but not around the corner. The baby somersaults, and a wave of giddiness hits her, as if she, too, is spinning in circles. She hurries back down the stairs.

The garage is dim and smells of oil and soil. She does not want to think what might be hiding in the dark corners. A draft rattles through the gaps around the door and licks at her ankles with an icy tongue. She looks for a light switch on the exposed brick, but there does not seem to be one. The door is framed by gray daylight, and she moves toward, it but there is no latch, just a handle. She tugs and tries to wrestle it upward, but the door will not budge. She smashes both fists against it, and it clangs stubbornly. She kneels down, snagging at the bottom edge with her fingers, trying to heave it up. She pulls again and again. The wind howls in the trees and whacks into the house. She crashes both hands against the door.

"Can anyone hear me?" she shouts. "I can't get out!" She hits the door again. She heaves at it from below. "I'm trapped! Hey? Help!" She rattles the door, her panic rising.

And then someone is tugging at it from the outside. She steps back, covering her mouth with both hands.

"Tess?" It is a man's voice—familiar—Josh? It is Josh! "Tess? Is that you?"

"Yes! It's me. Can you open the door? I'm stuck. I can't get out!"

"OK. Wait a moment." The door rattles, and then its hinges shriek, and a rectangle of gray light appears by her feet, grows taller—she sees Timberland boots, jeans, a puffy jacket, and finally Josh's concerned face.

"It's OK," he says. "You're out now."

"I couldn't open it; there's no handle on this side." She is breathless, shaky.

"There's usually a pull mechanism on the ceiling—over there, behind you, look."

"Someone was in my house."

"They were? When?"

"Just now—literally just now—but she's gone. I heard her leave. She locked me in the basement."

"She? Who's she?"

"I didn't see her, I just heard her voice, but I think I know who she is—did you see her? Coming out the front door?"

"I didn't see her coming out, but . . ."

"I'm sure it's the woman I saw before—remember? red hair?" She gestures as if she can somehow convey color with her hands. "Thin face, ragged-looking features?"

"OK, listen, Tess, let's get you inside and warm you up; you're shivering. Come with me; I just put coffee on. Come on."

He guides her across the icy ground and through the cypress branches, which poke at her face with spiny fingers, dropping clumps of snow into her hair, and into his backyard. A bird's feet have made sharp little rail-track prints across the snowy patio.

She stops. "Where's Helena?"

"She's at her clinic." He steers her to the French doors, peeling them open. "Come on, come on in."

The house smells of fresh coffee. The dining room is minimalist and tidy, with tasteful, red-and-white-themed Christmas decorations. A garland of fake fir graces the mantelpiece above the fireplace. She glimpses a front room through an archway, the edge of a cream sofa, a pinkish Turkish rug, a limb of a Christmas tree, white baubles.

"I heard you from my kitchen, and I couldn't think what it was at first," he says. "Here, sit." He pushes a stool toward her, goes to the coffee machine, and pours some into a Grand Canyon mug, putting it in her hands. She takes a sip—it is hot, powerful, and bitter. Josh and Helena's kitchen is familiar from her having peered into it so many times—she recognizes the green mosaic tiles, the shining blender. It is more spacious than it looked from across their yards. From where she is sitting now, she can see directly into their dining room. She knows that if she were to go to the window and peer up, she would be looking right into her own bedroom.

Josh says, "So you're sure that a *woman* was in your house?"

"Yes, I was in the basement, and I could hear her, going through the house, calling for me."

"So you know her?"

"Not really."

"You want me to go check in there for you?"

"No, it's OK. She's gone now. I heard her leave—the front door slammed."

"So she broke in, then? You want to call the police?"

"I don't know . . . maybe."

"Who is this woman, Tess?"

"It's complicated. We think she's someone whose child Greg treated years and years ago. I need to call Greg and tell him she was here."

"But wasn't he just here? That's what I was going to say." Josh wipes his hands on the tea towel. "His car was out front just a moment ago."

"What?"

"Just before I heard you in the garage, I saw it out there, but then, when I came out, it was gone."

"You can't have seen Greg's car." If Greg had been home, he would have heard her battering on the garage door—he would have let her out.

"Tess?" Josh folds the tea towel and puts it down, resting one hand on it. "Did something happen just now between you and Greg?"

"No, no, I haven't even seen him."

"You two didn't just have a fight?"

"No. Look, are you sure you just saw his car?"

"Pretty sure, yeah, out front, just before I heard you."

"OK, look, I have to go. Thanks for getting me out—and thanks for the coffee. I'm fine, honestly, but I have to go call Greg."

As he shows her out, and she thanks him, it occurs to her that she and Josh have something in common: neither of them trusts the person they love. But that is where the similarity ends, because Josh, at least, seems to understand Helena; he knows what's going on and is doing his best to fix it, whereas she has no idea what she is dealing with. She feels like Alex Kingman in the underwater cave, blinded by silt, feeling for the guide-rope, panic rising.

Somewhere, far off, she hears distant sirens. She needs to call the police, even though she is not sure what they can do other than tell her not to leave her front door open. But she'll report this anyway. Whatever Greg says, she is not going to ignore this anymore. The woman needs urgent psychiatric help.

Her belly feels like a huge tight fist, clenched in front of her as she walks out into the freezing air. She can feel Josh watching her from the porch as she crosses the icy lawn in her thick socks. He obviously doesn't believe that there was an intruder. He thinks it is Greg who is the threat. He will be wondering whether he should intervene. She crunches across the snow to the front porch and shakes her feet angrily, watching clods of dirty snow cling to the woolen soles.

She hasn't got keys, but the door pushes open. She must have left it on the latch when she was washing the floors earlier, which is how the woman got in.

She steps inside and looks around. The living and dining rooms are definitely empty. She heard the front door slam; the woman left. She could, of course, have come back. But the house feels empty. Everything in the hall seems intact. Her keys are in the blue ceramic bowl on the radiator cover. As she gazes at them, it occurs to her that it might not have been Helena who duplicated the key. The red-haired woman might have been coming in and out all this time, looking through mail, opening the jewelry box, putting hair clasps into Greg's pockets, or simply standing in the shadows, leaving that sickly, odd scent.

She feels a coldness spread up her spine and goes down the hall, forcing herself to look through the arch into the kitchen. The appliances shine back at her. She grabs her phone from the countertop and goes back down the corridor, listening at the bottom of the stairs.

She goes halfway up, then listens again. She can hear the wind thudding against the bricks, the creak of pipes, but nothing else. She forces herself to go all the way up to the landing, pushing the bathroom door open with a straight arm and peering around it. She goes and looks through Joe's door, then into the room that will be the baby's—empty—and then, finally, she goes into the master bedroom.

The bed is unmade; her T-shirt is on the floor where she left it that morning. She stands outside the bathroom and takes a breath. A dripping tap makes a slow *plink-plink* in the sink. She shoves the door open with one foot and jumps back. The tiny room is empty. She lets out the breath and moves away. Then she sees the walk-in closet. The door is only open a crack, and she usually leaves it wide open. Her heart pumps, and she stands very still. There is the faintest, sweet, off-smell. And then, all at once, she is sick of being afraid, sick of creeping around her own house. She lifts her foot and slams it into the door. It bounces back against the wall, revealing lines of shoes, Greg's hanging jackets, shelves with sweaters folded on them: nothing more. The closet is empty. There is nobody in the house.

The blanket on the end of the bed has slipped onto the floor. She picks it up with a shaking hand and puts it back on the rumpled duvet—and that's when she notices a small face on the pillow. It is staring up at her. She jumps backward and hears herself yelp.

It is not real, not a real baby—just a doll. She takes a step closer: a doll's head, a small china-faced doll's head. One broken eyelid droops, sickeningly, over a bright blue eye, and the other eye is open, fixed on her. The cheeks are stained lurid pink; there are chips and scratches in the painted skin. The head is not attached to a body.

She lifts her phone. There are four missed calls from Greg. She does not even listen to them—she calls his number.

He answers on the first ring. "Tess? Where are you?" He sounds breathless. "Are you all right?" There is fear in his voice—she has never heard Greg sound afraid before, and it shocks her.

"I'm at home; where are *you?*"

"I'm just around the corner, sweetheart; I'm on my way back to find you." He is on speakerphone in the car; his voice is echo-y and blurred.

"Were you here? Did you come home just now?"

"I'm on my way—where are you?"

"I'm in our bedroom. That woman was here!" Her voice rises. "She's been in the house. She's left this . . . this doll head in our bed. She locked me in the basement. I got stuck in the garage. For Christ's sake, Greg, I'm calling the police. This is too much. I'm reporting this."

"No!" he barks. "No, wait, Tess, don't, OK? Just don't. I'm almost there."

"She was here! In our bedroom! I'm looking at a doll's head on my pillow right now. This time I'm calling the police—"

"She won't come back, Tess. She just—something just happened, literally just now. Wait, OK? Wait there for me, and I'll explain in a minute—please—I'm almost there. You're totally safe—I promise."

"How can you *possibly* promise me that?" She looks at the head nestled on the big white pillow, the single blue eye staring up at her.

"Hang up now. Don't call the police—I'm almost there."

She hangs up. She can't bring herself to pick up the doll's head, so she leaves it where it is and goes back downstairs. She picks up the kettle and fills it with water—a reflex; she is trembling, from cold or anger or shock or perhaps all three. Then she hears Greg on the porch, his key in the door. She steps into the hallway.

He bursts in and sweeps down the corridor toward her, stretching out his arms for her. She lets him hold her for a moment, and he squeezes her so tightly that she feels the baby squashed against her spine. "OK," he says, as if talking to himself. "It's OK." He kisses the top of her head. She pulls away.

"What the hell's happening, Greg? Why are you even here? Why aren't you at the hospital?"

He guides her to the kitchen, to a stool.

"I got your voice mail, and you sounded . . . I know we said we'd talk today. I tried to call you back, but you weren't answering your phone, and I had an hour free, so I just came home." He pushes back his hair. His fingers, she notices, are trembling, too. "I saw her in the street."

"You saw her?"

"Just now, around the corner—she spotted me and took off, so I turned the car around and went after her. She crossed the road, and I had to wait, so she got ahead of me. Crossing Walnut, she was looking back at me—the poor guy couldn't have stopped in time. She just kept looking at me, then stepped out into the road, and he ran right into her. She's been taken to the hospital. I need to go find out what's happening, but I had to come and make sure you were OK first. Jesus, Tess." He leans his forehead against hers, and his gray scarf slithers to the floor. He does not pick it up.

She tries to absorb what he has just said. "A car hit her? Is she dead?"

"No, she was unconscious but alive. An ambulance was there in just a few minutes. She's pretty bashed up."

"How bashed up?" She remembers hearing sirens as she drank Josh's coffee. In the snow-refracted light from the kitchen windows Greg looks ghastly: unwell, shocked, his face ashen.

"I don't know. Fractured pelvis, I think, probably some other broken bones. I don't know, maybe worse. But she's in good hands, the best."

She shakes her head. "But she was just here . . ."

"She's not coming back," he says. "I promise."

"Jesus, this is horrible. This is terrible. Will she be OK?"

"I think so."

"She put a doll's head on our pillow! Go and look! My God, Greg, what if Joe had been here?"

"But he wasn't, OK? He wasn't." He tries to reach for her, but she pulls away. "I know we have to talk about this—"

"Too right we do." Carlo Novak had been, briefly, a long way off, like a one-time enemy, but now, suddenly, he is back, filling the space between them.

"I'm going to go look in our bedroom." He runs up the stairs and comes back a moment or two later with the doll's head in his hand.

"OK, listen." He sounds suddenly efficient. "I have patients to see this afternoon, and I need to go check what's happening to her in the ER first, but you're safe—that's the main thing. You're all right. She's going to be in the hospital for a long time, and she isn't going anywhere, I promise; she's no danger to you whatsoever." He drops the doll's head into the kitchen wastebasket. The lid clangs shut.

"I can't do this anymore." She shakes her head. "I just can't."

"Please—please, Tess. The last thing on earth that I want to do is leave you right now, but I have to go back, for my patients, their families—I have to take care of them, too. I need you to hang in there till this evening, and when I get home, we will talk . . . about all of this, OK? About everything."

"But—"

"Tess"—he presses her hand—"I know. We'll talk about everything tonight, I promise, *everything*. There are things I need to tell you, too. Can you rest for a bit now? Go lie down till you have to go get Joe, OK? You look pale; you've had a shock. You need something sweet—can you eat a cookie? Have some tea?" He takes her wrist, and she realizes, after a second, that he is checking her pulse. She rips her hand away.

"The moment you have finished—the very moment—you come back home. OK?"

"I will, I will. Eight at the very latest. But remember, the woman is in the hospital, she's in bad shape, and she's not a threat. Just hang on till I get home, OK? I'll call you or have someone call you the moment I can get an update on her condition; the second I know anything, you'll know, too." He bends to pick up his scarf, then kisses her.

"I don't even know her name."

"What?" He is making for the door.

She stands up, calling after him, "What's her name, Greg?"

"Does it matter?"

"Of course it matters!"

"Sarah," he calls over his shoulder. "Her name's Sarah." But before she can ask for a surname, he has gone.

CHAPTER NINETEEN

She waits for the sound of Greg's feet coming up the basement steps. It is 8:55 p.m., and he has texted her twice in the last half hour: he is on his way. It is probably a good thing that he is later than he said he would be, because Joe is, thankfully, asleep now—exhausted by whatever unspoken conflicts he has been through today.

The house is quiet. She has taken the bag containing the doll's head down to the outdoor trash can, but even now she can feel it down there, nestling in the darkness. The wind has dropped, and snow is no longer tumbling, but it feels as if a great thumb is pressing down on the suburb, keeping everything still.

There is a persistent, burning ache in her lower back. The baby's head rests heavily on her pelvis, and from time to time her abdomen tightens—a Braxton-Hicks contraction; she remembers these, but she also feels as if her body is bracing itself for Greg's homecoming.

After she made the call to the hospital, her first impulse had been to call Nell—she picked up her phone, but then she hung up before the call could be connected. The conversation with the ER receptionist had only confirmed what she already knew: Greg is tangled in lies. Nell can't help. The only person who can straighten this out is Greg.

She has had two updates from him on Sarah's condition: a broken pelvis, broken tibia, smashed knee, three fractured ribs, but no internal or serious head injuries. She was very agitated and is now under sedation. They have traced her out-of-state records, and the psychiatrist is with her. Greg was right, in other words: the poor woman is going nowhere. At least she is getting help.

Her phone vibrates on the marble countertop. She peers at the screen—not Greg this time but Alex Kingman. She waits for it to stop ringing. It shudders to signal that a voice mail has been left. She picks it up and deletes the message. She does not want to hear from Alex Kingman; she does not want to know what he has to say. He is the last person on earth whose voice she wants to listen to right now.

She hears the buzz of the garage door beneath the kitchen and, after a moment, Greg's footsteps coming up the stairs.

"Tess?" His voice at the basement door, his fingers tapping. "Honey? It's just me. Can you open the door?"

Her belly contracts again as she gets up and unbolts the door, letting him in. He looks uncertain, exhausted, and for a second everything falls away, and it is just Greg: she has the urge to sink into his arms, feel his chest against her cheek, breathe him in, let all of this melt away.

But she will not allow herself to do that. If she does, he will somehow persuade her that the call she made to the ER this afternoon was a misunderstanding, that the photos and reports she has seen online are errors and muddles, that Alex Kingman is deluded.

She has to get answers now, because whatever Greg is hiding, it cannot be worse than the fact of its concealment.

He steps toward her, frowning. "Are you OK?" He sounds nervous, and the faint nausea she has been feeling all evening moves closer to the surface. He pulls off his coat. He is wearing a black turtleneck sweater that she doesn't recognize. His body seems to expand to fill the space in front of her.

"I've been calling you," he says. "Didn't you hear your phone?"

"I was probably reading Joe a story." Her belly clenches again. She has ignored his calls all evening—put her phone on silent, watched it buzz and vibrate angrily across the countertop.

"Is he asleep now?" Greg goes to the counter and reaches for the wine bottle. He pulls a glass down and sloshes some into it. She watches him take a swig, with his back to her.

Then he lowers the glass and turns to face her. "I am so, so sorry about what happened to you today. I'm so sorry she came into our house. It must have been scary for you." He reaches out a hand, but she steps back. His fingers hover in the air, then drop to his side. "Do you know how she got in?"

"I left the door unlocked." She examines his face. Erase the lines, the shadows, the years, and the bone structure is right there. It isn't photographic trickery. She is looking at an older version of the face on the courtroom steps in Philadelphia: the medical student whose girlfriend accused him of killing their baby.

"You have every right to be upset with me—"

She grips the breakfast bar that separates them. "I know who she is, Greg."

The overhead lights form two tiny, glinting triangles in his dark eyes. "What do you mean?" He tips his head back and takes another gulp of wine. His face has reddened. The wine stains his lips.

The ache spreads through her belly.

"I know her name."

"What?"

"Her name is Sarah Banister."

"OK, listen. This sort of stress is really not good for you right now!" He says it abruptly, almost madly. "It really isn't good for the baby either." He puts down his wineglass. "I'm going to make you some hot chocolate. We both need to calm down. We have to sit down and talk about this. It's been a rough day. We both need to calm down, sit down, talk."

She grips the kitchen counter. He goes to the fridge, gets out the milk, a mug, a small pot. His movements are taut and sprung.

"I know who Sarah Banister is," she says.

He doesn't turn around. But his hands stop moving.

She tries to keep her voice low, because they mustn't wake Joe. Joe can't witness this—whatever this is. "Almost thirty years ago in Philadelphia, Sarah Banister accused a medical student called Carlo Novak of giving her drugs to abort their baby, then watching the baby die."

Greg turns his head, quite slowly. His face is a mask. His jaw is clenched, his eyes small and unblinking.

She lets go of the countertop, steps back.

He moves around the breakfast bar toward her, very fast.

"No!" She holds up both hands. "Don't—don't." Her spine is pressed against the kitchen cupboard. He stops just in front of her. "Carlo Novak's library card is in your box in the basement. And a medal with his name on it. Alex Kingman recognized your face—right away. He thinks you're Carlo. And I've seen an old picture taken outside the Philadelphia courtroom." She lifts her chin. "It's your face. It's your face in that photograph."

He towers over her. "This is not what you think. It really isn't."

"What? What do I think?" She slides along the cupboard away from him. "My God, I have no idea what I think except that you've been hiding things from me, and lying. I called the ER this afternoon. I told them my sister had been hit by a car on Walnut Street—I asked for her by name. I asked for Sarah Banister."

"They aren't allowed to give out that sort of information."

"He didn't; he said he couldn't tell me. But I suppose he felt sorry for me, because when I begged him for information about my sister, he said, 'I'd urge you to come down here right away.' And I said, 'Is that a yes? Does that mean you have Sarah Banister there?' and he said, 'Miss, you should come right now.' So, yes, Greg, yes, it's Sarah Banister who was hit by a car on Walnut Street—running away from you."

A part of her wants him to say no—to explain this away, to make it all vanish. But he doesn't. There is an awful silence.

"Who is Carlo Novak, Greg?"

His mouth gives a panicky spasm; his brows lower. He moves toward her, and all at once the fear that has been coiled in her belly all day explodes inside her. She ducks out of his way, her socks slipping on the tiles. He shoots out a hand, maybe to steady her or maybe to restrain her—she doesn't know. She feels his fingers clamp onto her wristbone, and she twists her arm out of his grasp. She darts through the archway into the hall. He is coming after her. If she goes upstairs, Joe will be brought into this, and she can't have that—she cannot have Joe wake up. She is at the front door, so she wrenches it open, steps onto the porch, and slams it behind her before he can follow her out. She feels it bounce off something—his fingers?—and hears his brief bellow of pain. Then she runs into the bitter night, supporting her belly with both arms.

CHAPTER TWENTY

The snow needles the soles of her feet as she goes around the side of the house. She does not know what she's doing. She can't think clearly anymore. She ducks into the bushes and feels a sliver of ice slide from a branch down the back of her neck.

She can't leave Joe—she has to go back in. The urge to run was instinctive, but she has to calm down. Go back. Face this. Face Greg. She sees his dark shape over by the porch.

"Tess?" he calls, but not too loudly. He wouldn't want to involve the neighbors.

She crouches between the houses, and her belly tightens. A persistent pain is spreading around her middle; she feels as if a huge hand is squeezing, tightening. She bends her head, tries to breathe, tries to think. The branches crowd closer. The fresh snow smells otherworldly beneath the earthy, darker smell of the frozen trees. The baby's head presses onto her pelvis like a big metal bullet.

"Tess?" He is coming around the side of the house now. He can't see her. "Tess, honey? Please, this is crazy—where are you?"

He is right. But she can't move; it is as if she has frozen solid, with only the pain alive, burning low in her back. She hears his feet moving past, crunching down the snow. His shadowy shape flickers through the branches. She has to get up. She takes a breath. She has to get out of the shrubs.

She tries to rise, but nausea surges through her, sticky and grim. Her belly tightens again.

And then she understands what is happening.

It has been going on for hours, if not all day—of course it has—but she has been so distracted that she has not allowed herself to tune in to it. The low pains, the backache, the tightenings, the nausea. But it is far too soon. This baby is not ready to be born—it still has almost five weeks to go. This cannot possibly happen now.

She hears his feet in the snow again. She tries to think. First she has to go and get someone to look after Joe, and then she has to get herself to the hospital. The pain builds, rakes through her, peaks to burning, and for a while she can't think anymore.

As the pain subsides, she becomes aware of the cold again, the frozen branches by her face, Greg's footsteps fading. She can't have him holding her hand as she gives birth, not tonight. Sandra will help. But she might not make it across the road to the Schechters' before another contraction comes, and Greg will see her if she tries to cross the road; he will catch her.

She can hear him calling her name in a quiet, low voice, but he is farther away now. Maybe he is going around the back of the house, under the deck and down to the garage. She crouches, clutching her sides, trying to breathe, waiting for the pain to ease off. This baby isn't ready to be born. Its lungs might not be fully developed. It will be far too small, too fragile; it will need medical help. Of course she must get up—she must get Greg. And then a terrible question rises in her mind: would he save this baby?

But of course he would. She is not thinking straight. She is confusing two men—Carlo Novak and Greg, her Greg, who would never harm their baby, no matter how complex his emotions toward it might be.

When the pain has gone, she slithers out, staggers to her feet, and calls for Greg, but before she can get to the front of the house, the

pressure begins to build again—already—to expand through her pelvis and intensify. The contraction is far too close to the last one—
almost on top of it. She knows what this means. She puts her head
down and moans, swaying, trying to breathe. This is very bad indeed.
She has to get to the hospital right now.

She manages to stand, and then there is a sensation of falling, and
warmth spreads down both thighs. Her waters soak the snow. Her
leggings are sodden, and the baby is screwing itself against her pelvis even harder, bone grinding against bone. She has to get Joe to
the Schechters' and herself to the hospital. These two tasks feel both
simple and overwhelming.

She shouts for Greg, as loudly as she can. She takes a step or two
forward and shouts again. She can hear her own breathing bouncing
off the snow. The weight in her pelvis is enormous now. She tries
to waddle, her legs slightly apart. A bright security lights flashes on,
and she is spotlit, bewildered. She realizes she is on Helena and Josh's
front lawn. She both longs for and dreads the sight of Greg pushing
through the bushes.

She drops to her hands and knees. She isn't cold anymore; she is
sweating. She needs Greg, because this baby is going to be born,
and it is going to be too small, and she doesn't even know if she
will make it to the hospital. She tries to call out again, but instead of
his name a long moan rises from her chest as the pain swells. Then,
somewhere far off, she hears a rhythmic sound.

At first she thinks it is her own heartbeat, and then she realizes it
is the crunch of feet on snow. She sways as the fog closes in and the
pain spreads, and she is dimly aware of hands closing on her shoulders.

"Tess? Tess? Honey?"

She peers up. Greg's face wavers into focus. She bends her head and
vomits over his shoes. "Call an ambulance," she spits. "Now."

CHAPTER TWENTY-ONE

Their baby is like an unexpected visitor, bringing sudden lightness and relief to a troubled house. They gaze at her through the glass sides of the incubator. She has a pointed chin and fingernails as delicate as petals; her movements are slow and otherworldly; penciled blue veins pulse beneath her skin; her eyelashes have not yet developed; there is an oxygen tube in her nose, sticky sensors on her chest and belly and foot, and she has to lie on a heated pad—but she is whole and miraculously healthy, all her organs function, she breathes on her own, and her plum-size heart keeps perfect time.

Tess feels as if her body has been flipped inside out and torn from front to back, but she is oddly calm. The light coming through the slatted blinds is crystalline, as if minute particles of frost are suspended inside it, sharpening all the edges and brightening the air.

"She's amazing." Greg sounds hoarse. "We're unbelievably lucky; just look at her. She's a great size, nice and pink, her lungs are in amazing shape, all her reflexes are good, the cord gases were all normal. My God, we're lucky, Tess; she's going to be OK. She really is." He sounds as if he is trying to reassure himself, to pin down this mind-blowing experience and talk his way onto safer, more medical ground. His hair is sticking up, and his face looks pale behind a dark wash of stubble. He is, she supposes, in some kind of shock.

Perhaps watching her in the rearview mirror as she gave birth five weeks early in the back of his speeding car was more disturbing than the actual delivery was for her. For her there was no time for fear, because the baby was coming, and the force of that was far bigger than anything her conscious mind could come up with. But Greg would have had all sorts of frightening medical scenarios running through his head as he sped through the snow.

The machines monitoring the baby's heartbeat and oxygen levels beep constantly. Greg is sitting on a high-backed chair with one leg crooked. Anyone glancing at them now would think that they were the perfect new family.

She needs Joe. Joe has to meet his sister, and she needs to hold on to him and reassure herself that he is OK. It must have been so frightening for him to be woken in the night by Josh, a virtual stranger, and taken across the road to the Schechters'. She had not prepared him for this—she'd assumed that there was still at least a month in which to have these practical conversations. Suddenly she remembers the panic she felt in the kitchen when Greg came at her. Birthing hormones must have skewed her mind, triggering the deep, primitive urge to flee.

She looks down at her baby again. The neonatologist, a woman with cropped hair and a strange, soft accent, has explained about oxygenation levels and blood sugar, about the possibility of unsteady breathing patterns, the risk of jaundice, the need to express milk until a stronger sucking reflex develops. She also explained that they would need to stay in Special Care until Christmas Eve, as it was against hospital policy to release a baby before a gestational age of thirty-six weeks. Greg says he will fix things so he can be at home before and after school with Joe. At least in Massachusetts the schools are open right up to Christmas Eve.

Nurses come and go, checking and rechecking vital signs—in both her and the baby. But she feels oddly well, perfectly alert.

"Can you go and get Joe when he wakes up?"

"Of course," Greg nods. "Absolutely." She has a feeling that he would do anything she asked of him right now—except, perhaps, tell her the truth.

"I don't want him going to school today."

"No, of course not. He should be here with us—I'll go get him." He glances at his watch. "It's almost six-thirty; you want me to call Sandra? I'm sure they'll be up by now."

"OK."

He reaches for her hand. "Tess"—his voice wavers—"you were incredible. You really were."

The birth is like the memory of a drunken night out—flashbulb scenes, extreme sensations, odd smells, interspersed with periods of blankness. She remembers Josh helping her up, after she was sick, then Greg saying something about "preterm" and "transition," and Josh, somewhere farther off, talking on the phone: "Her husband's bringing her in by car—they can be there in ten, twelve minutes."

She remembers the smell of the leather seats in Greg's car and shouting at him about Joe—and Greg saying Joe was with the Schechters, that he was fine, not to worry, he was safe. Then the hospital parking lot: on her hands and knees on the backseat, the urge to push overwhelming, feeling the baby's head between her legs—and paramedics everywhere, suddenly, bitter air sweeping into the car with all the doors flung open, and thinking Greg had gone and then realizing that the arms around her, holding her up, were his, that she was on her back now, with Greg supporting her torso.

She remembers looking up at his face and thinking that he did not look like someone who had witnessed childbirth countless times: he was barely holding it together. She wanted to reassure him that it was going to be fine, but then she had to push again, and the rest of the baby came out—she reached down to lift the tiny, limp body, and suddenly there were people everywhere in scrubs and someone said, "It's a girl!" and gloved hands whisked her baby out of her arms—strangers—and a man in a mask with an African accent of some kind was introducing himself as an ob/gyn, peering between her legs. Then hands lifted her onto a gurney, and there were bright lights flashing overhead, and Greg was gripping her hand, saying, "It's OK, she's going to be OK, they're just checking her over—she needs a little oxygen, everything's going to be OK"—and panic bloomed in her chest, because someone else had her baby: she couldn't see her baby among all these strangers in scrubs.

She feels her throat and chest tighten and looks down into the incubator. Thin wires snake from the swaddling. She will never let anyone take her baby from her again.

"I need to call Nell."

"Sure. You want to call her right now?"

"I'll call her when you go for Joe."

The rims of Greg's eyes are red. She looks down and realizes that she is wearing a gown with teddy bears on it. She has no idea where her clothes went. Her whole body throbs.

"My God, Tess," he says. "She's . . ." But he can't find the words. "We have a daughter."

They look at each other and start to laugh, and she realizes that in all these months she has never actually allowed herself to imagine this baby as either girl or boy. It has been a genderless, separate being. And now its position in the world is staked out. She is a she—daughter, sister.

"She has such dark hair," she says. "Joe only had a blond fuzz."

"That'll be the Italian genes."

For a moment all the unanswered questions close back in and swing between them. They stop laughing and stare at each other.

"We haven't even talked properly about names." Greg looks away first.

"We haven't talked about anything."

"I know. Do you want to? Do you want me to—"

"No, God, no—not now, but . . ."

"Later, then."

"Yes." She looks down at their baby again. "I'd like to call her Lily." The process of choosing a name must have been going on somewhere in her subconscious, because this feels like a solid and well-considered decision.

"Lillian? After your mother?"

"After my mother but not Lillian, just Lily."

"Lily—Lily—you mentioned that before. Actually, I love Lily. It's a beautiful name."

"Then she's Lily? Lily Harding Gallo?"

"She is." Greg looks slightly dazed, as if he cannot quite take in that she is real, his daughter—let alone that she has his name, Lily Gallo.

"Do you want your mother's name, too, though?" she asks. "Natalia's beautiful. It could be her middle name. Lily Natalia?"

He frowns. "No, no, I don't think so. No."

"Really?"

"Really—no." He looks away. "No."

"OK, then. Maybe Joe should be involved in choosing her middle name anyway."

"Good idea." He looks back at her and grins. "Lily Ronaldina. It has a certain . . ."

They both laugh again, and she feels a powerful ball of well-being dilate from her heart, push through her veins, filling her with strength. *Everything will be OK.* She looks down at Lily. *You are safe. I will keep you safe.*

The icy Charles River flashes past as they speed along Storrow Drive. It is Christmas Eve, and they have broken out of the cocoon of the Special Care Unit at last. For three days she has longed to get out—Christmas Day in the hospital would have been tough for Joe—but now the city feels vast and perilous, no place for a frail newborn.

She knows that they have to talk. A speeding car feels like the wrong place, but she can't bring Lily home without first understanding how Greg is connected to Sarah Banister, Carlo Novak, and Alex Kingman—and why he has tried to conceal it from her.

She looks over her shoulder. Lily is dwarfed by the car seat, chin to chest, a little pink gnome. She looks closely to check that Lily's chest is rising and falling evenly. The responsibility of bringing her home feels overwhelming, suddenly. In the context of the other Special Care babies, Lily seemed relatively big and healthy, but now, in the real world, she feels incredibly tiny and exposed.

In Special Care, she and Greg had made a list of all the things they needed for Lily, and then Greg and Joe went to the mall. They bought the car seat, a Moses basket, an electric breast pump, a white wooden crib, and a baby sleeping bag covered in stars, packs of cotton sheets and muslins, onesies and nappies—diapers—changing things.

"Everything," Greg said when they came back, "is at home and waiting for you."

Joe held up a monochrome mobile. "Right now she can only see black and white," he explained, looking serious. "Her brain needs to develop more before she can see colors."

She realized, then, that they didn't even have a Christmas tree. "We have to get one!" It suddenly seemed vital.

Joe opened his mouth, then looked up at Greg.

"A Christmas tree," Greg said, "is the last thing you should be worrying about."

Joe nodded, bravely.

She opened her mouth to argue, but then the nurse came over.

"Greg," she says now, "we've got to talk before we get home. I can't go home with it all hanging over us like this."

His elbows stiffen against the steering wheel. "OK . . ."

"So—I need to know who Carlo Novak is."

He signals and pulls into the fast lane. "My cousin."

"Your *cousin*? You had a cousin? Then Nell was right." Greg's chin jerks in, and she realizes that it has not occurred to him, until now, that she will have talked to Nell about any of this.

"How could you not tell me that you had a cousin?" She tries to straighten this fact in her mind. "There's a picture of him from the *Philadelphia Inquirer*, and it looked so much like you, I thought it *was* you."

He nods. "I know. Everyone used to say that."

"You couldn't look *that* similar."

"Well, we did. Our parents were siblings—all four of them: the Gallo brothers married the Novak sisters. Carlo and I shared all four grandparents, so we did look a lot alike, particularly in photos. Even our mothers would sometimes struggle to tell us apart in an old photo. But there was a three-year age gap, and we were slightly different builds, and there was a couple of inches height difference, not to mention some fairly major personality traits. But in a photo I guess none of that was obvious."

She thinks about the picture. It is true that the camera will love certain lines and angles of a face; it will bring out likenesses that are much less obvious in the flesh. If Greg and Carlo had matching bone structures, then they really could look almost identical in a photograph, or even perhaps in a thirty-year-old memory. She feels the tendons in her neck release slightly.

"That's why Alex Kingman mixed you up, then?"

He glances at her and looks back at the road. He is driving too fast.

"I went to see Alex," she says. "I found him online. He's convinced that you are Carlo Novak and that you almost killed him when you were students."

"You saw Alex Kingman?"

"He was giving a lecture at the Isabella Stewart Gardner Museum. I spoke to him afterward."

"Jesus, Tess." He looks genuinely rattled. "When did you do that?"

"The other night. I didn't go to see the photography exhibition. I went there instead."

"You lied to me?"

"I was going to tell you, only you got back so late that night, and then I tried to tell you again the next night, and you got back late again—remember? You wouldn't talk to me? You said you couldn't think straight."

He opens his mouth to argue but stops himself, perhaps realizing the irony of accusing her of evasion and lies.

"How on earth did you find Alex Kingman?"

"He's a partner in a Boston landscape-architecture firm; he was easy to find."

"But he could have been anyone, Tess. You know nothing about him. I wish you'd told me first."

"Really? Well, I wish you'd told me about your cousin. And I wish *you* hadn't lied about Alex. You went back out to find him while I was sleeping in the hotel room. He says you threatened him in an alley."

"Oh, come on! That's bullshit. He was waiting in the lobby when I went for my run. *He* accosted *me*. He was very aggressive. I just told him to leave us alone."

"So why didn't you tell me about it, then?"

"I didn't want to make things any more stressful—you'd had a bad enough day as it was, and I just wanted us to have a nice time together."

"He told me this long story about a cave dive, years and years ago in Florida. He said he could never forget your face because you tried to drown him—thinking you were your cousin, presumably."

Greg's jaw stiffens, and tiny beads of sweat glisten on his hairline. "Nobody tried to drown that man." He changes lanes again, cutting in front of someone, then accelerating up close to the bumper of a BMW.

"He said Carlo took him to an underwater cave and then vanished. He's only alive because two experienced divers found him and saved him."

Greg gives a snort. "He said that, did he? Well, I guess he's forgotten a few crucial details. One, Carlo was already getting him to the surface when the other two divers came down, and two, Carlo only took off after the air ambulance arrived. It was reckless and stupid to try cave diving, but he did not leave Alex to die. He got him out of the tunnel."

"Why did he disappear, then?"

"Because Alex Kingman was a rich kid, Tess, and it's generally a bad idea for a poor kid to endanger a rich kid's life."

She thinks about this for a moment. It is certainly possible that Alex's memory of that day might be selective.

"OK, fine, but whatever Alex does or doesn't remember about your cousin doesn't change the fact that you lied when I asked you about him. You've hidden Carlo from me. And you've also lied about Sarah Banister."

He shakes his head. "I didn't lie about Sarah. I told you I thought she was someone whose baby had died. I said I believed she had a grudge, and she was unstable. That's all true."

She opens her mouth to quibble about lies of omission but then stops. They are both guilty of this, to varying degrees. The more they talk, the more slippery everything feels. Greg is driving way too fast now, skimming past the other cars.

"Greg," she snaps, "you need to slow down." She thinks about Sarah Banister walking through their house, calling for her. "Is it possible," she says, "that she's been coming into our home for months? I know someone has; remember when I asked you about my earrings that were out? And the mail being moved in the kitchen. And the hair clasp—Helena would never wear anything cheap and plastic, would she? And before the potluck supper, I rushed back to grab something, and the front door was wide open, and I had this feeling someone was there, there was this smell . . . I think it was Sarah."

"Well, she might be able to pick a lock, but I don't know, Tess. What I do know is that she won't be coming near us anymore."

"We should have called the police the first time you got her note."

"Maybe." He nods, but she knows he doesn't mean it.

Her breasts are heavy and aching, and despite the extra-strength Tylenol it is painful to sit on the hard leather car seat. Greg drives right up to the bumper of an SUV and has to jab his foot on the brakes, making her jerk forward. She looks back at Lily, who is sleeping still.

"Greg, you have to slow down." She pushes her hair off her face. "You're being reckless."

"Sorry." He eases his foot off the accelerator.

"So Sarah thought you were Carlo, too."

He takes a deep breath. "Yes. My best guess is, Sarah saw the news about my appointment, and the prize, and it brought back the trauma of her baby's death. She confused our faces. I have no idea what she was hoping to achieve, but I suspect she didn't either. She's not a well person."

"She could have done anything to me—or, worse, to Joe. You left us wide open."

"I understand why you feel that, I really do, but I'd never do that. After that first note, I got in touch with an old friend in Philadelphia, a psychiatrist who works with Sarah's psychiatrist. There's patient confidentiality, obviously, but I was able to get emphatic assurance that Sarah is only a danger to herself."

"Emphatic assurance?"

"I was trying to find her, Tess. I just didn't want to involve you. You had enough on your plate."

"I'm not a bloody child!"

"I know. I'm sorry." He shakes his head. "You're absolutely right. I should have told you who Sarah was from the start, and about Carlo. I am so sorry. I was trying to protect you from unnecessary worry."

"I don't need protecting. And the unnecessary worry, here, is that you could hide this sort of thing from me."

"It was a huge mistake to think I could deal with her without involving you."

"I think you didn't tell me," she says, "because you didn't want me to know about your cousin."

He nods. "I know. You're right. I didn't want to think about him. I'd shut him away along with everything else, and I didn't want to open it all back up again."

"Did he kill his baby? Is that why you couldn't face telling me about him?"

"No, God—no, of course he didn't. He did nothing wrong, except get involved with a delusional drug addict in the first place."

"But it's just not normal to hide this sort of information, Greg. We're married. I need to know about your family, because, good or bad, they're part of you. I've told you about my mother, haven't I? I've told you everything."

"I know you have."

"Right, then, tell me about him—tell me about Carlo."

"What do you want to know?"

"Did you know each other growing up?"

"Yes." Greg nods. "We were close. His father died when he was just a little kid, and Julianna"—he swallows, as if the name might actually choke him—"slowly fell apart. So we were together a lot."

"Your parents took him in?"

"Well, not exactly, but they looked out for him and cared for him when she couldn't."

"Did all that damage him? If he was illegally cave diving, he must have been a bit unhinged already."

"You can't come out of a childhood like that unscathed. He definitely had a self-destructive streak."

"What does that mean?"

"I don't know, exactly. In high school he hung out with the wrong crowd, and he made some mistakes. But he made it to college; he got himself out of there."

She thinks of Alex Kingman's account. "Which college?"

"He started at the University of Pittsburgh, then transferred to UPenn in Philadelphia, after the Florida thing with Kingman."

It all slots together—Alex's story is at least rooted in truth.

"And he met Sarah Banister in Philadelphia?"

He nods. "You wouldn't think it from the way she looks now, but she was incredibly beautiful. She was also magnetic and charismatic, you know—the way very smart, unstable people often are. He was drawn to her for all sorts of unhealthy and probably Oedipal reasons. It was a huge mistake, obviously, but by the time he'd worked out the extent of her drug use, she was pregnant with his child."

She glances back at Lily, tucked into her blanket, her pink hat almost covering her eyes.

"How did that baby actually die?"

"Sarah went into premature labor, probably as a result of substance abuse during pregnancy." His jaw is tense, his hands clenched on the wheel. "She'd been trying to come off opiates, and she called him saying she didn't feel well, that she had stomach pains. Stomach pains are common in opiate withdrawal, but he told her he'd meet her at the hospital just to be sure. She refused to go, so he went straight home. He realized she was in premature labor, called an ambulance, but"—he swallows—"the baby died in his arms before the paramedics got there."

His eyes are fixed on the road, but she feels as if he is no longer seeing it. Trees and buildings are flashing past.

"Can you slow down, Greg? You're driving way too fast."

But it is as if something has been unleashed, and he can't stop, can't even hear her—he is shaking his head.

"He was innocent, but it was impossible for him to carry on at med school after that—who wants to be treated by a trainee doctor they recognize from an infanticide trial?"

"So he dropped out?"

Greg's skin has turned a disturbing shade of gray. "He felt as if his life was over."

He jerks the wheel just in time to miss the bumper of a silver car—a horn blares.

"Greg, please, please—we have Lily in the car. Just pull over; we shouldn't talk about this while you're driving."

"No, no. You're right. It's OK," He eases his foot off the accelerator. "Sorry." He takes a big breath, signals, and pulls into the slower lane. "It's OK. I'm OK."

She looks around at Lily again. She is still sleeping peacefully, unaware of the fast-moving vehicles and the icy road or her father's agitation, his profound distress. Tess presses her fingertips against her forehead.

"What I just don't get is why you couldn't tell me any of this. Why would you possibly hide this from me? Did you think I'd judge you for Carlo's behavior? I mean—my God, Greg—me, of all people? I grew up with a mentally ill mother—she killed herself. I'm hardly going to judge you for your own messed-up family members."

"No, it wasn't that." Greg shakes his head. "Of course it wasn't. I just made the decision long ago that I needed to put it behind me. It's what I had to do."

She realizes that all this time they have been talking about Greg's cousin in the past tense. "Did Carlo die?"

Greg nods.

"How?"

He glances at her. "I don't know."

"What do you mean, you don't know?"

"He vanished soon after the trial proceedings."

Red blotches have appeared on Greg's neck, but she is not going to stop. "I know this is horrible for you, but you can see why we have to talk about this, can't you?"

"Yes."

"OK, so he disappeared?"

Greg nods.

"In theory, he could still be alive, then."

"No, he isn't alive, Tess. I'm absolutely sure of that."

"How can you be sure?"

"If he was alive, he'd have contacted me."

"Where were you when all this was happening?"

"It was the summer before I started Harvard."

She tries to line up what she knows. There is Greg, orphaned, staggering through an undergraduate degree in Pittsburgh before making it to Harvard just as Carlo's Philadelphia medical-school career implodes.

She tries to think of a gentle way to say what she's thinking, but there isn't one. "Is it possible that he vanished because he couldn't face you? I mean, you still had a brilliant future at Harvard, and his career was over before it had started."

Greg's jaw tightens. "It's not like that. It was never like that. He loved me—and there's no way, believe me, that I made him feel bad about himself." His voice cracks. "We were the only ones left, Tess. We loved each other like brothers."

"So you looked for him?"

"Of course I did."

"What do you think happened to him, then?"

Greg takes another long breath in, as if he is bracing himself for the memories that this turn in the conversation will necessitate. "The night he vanished, he took fifty dollars out of the bank, but he left everything else—his ID, his wallet, everything he owned. My guess is he got on a Greyhound and went somewhere anonymously, then killed himself."

"But then there'd be a body."

"Not necessarily. Maybe a John Doe somewhere. Listen, I know he's dead, Tess. I can't explain how, but I know it. It took me a few years to accept it, and then when I moved to London, I decided that I couldn't think about him anymore—about any of them."

"I'm sorry." She reaches out and rests her fingers on his arm. "I'm so sorry you've had to live with this. And I'm sorry you didn't feel you could tell me."

Then she remembers Carlo's alcoholic mother. "What about your aunt Julianna? Is she still alive?"

"She died a year after he vanished."

"What of?"

"Alcoholism—a GI bleed. She wasn't much older than I am now." He clenches his jaw again.

"What's a GI bleed?"

"Esophageal bleeding. Not nice."

"Did you know she was dying? Or was it a shock?"

"I knew."

"So you got to say good-bye, at least?"

"No." His voice is so quiet that she can barely hear him over the car engine. "I didn't go back to see her."

No wonder he packaged all this away. His family really was an unfathomable mess. He did what he was trained to do. He shut every-thing down in order to focus on the thing that mattered most: the career that would redeem him and allow him to put everything else in the past. Or at least contain it in some way.

She should feel relieved to have this out in the open at last, but the heaviness has not lifted. In fact, the atmosphere in the car feels even more tense and claustrophobic now, as if all the things that he has kept hidden are pressing in on them, sucking up the oxygen.

He turns off the freeway, and they come to a halt in a line of cars waiting to get through the busy junction onto the quiet and civilized streets beyond. Perhaps for the first time since they arrived in Boston, she feels almost relieved to be reentering the suburbs.

"Is there anything else I should know about your family?" she asks. "Are there any other relatives? Did Carlo have brothers and sisters? Do you have grandparents in Pennsylvania? Any more aunts? Uncles?"

He shakes his head. "He was an only child, and I think I told you before, our grandparents didn't come to the States. The Novak grandparents died young—that's why the sisters emigrated—and the rest of the Gallos, as far as I know, never left Italy."

"That's right—you did tell me—they came from a tiny town near Rome, didn't they?" He had mentioned its name once, early on, when she asked him about his Italian side.

He nods.

"Then you must have relatives in Italy still?"

He moves off through a green light. "I probably have a hundred of them over there in Italy, and in Poland, too, but I have never felt the slightest need to track any of them down. One tragic and messed-up family is quite enough."

They are driving along the familiar street. They pass the bakery, the yoga studio, the bank. There are Happy Holidays signs in the windows, and Christmas lights, and dirty snow banked up along the sidewalks.

"I still don't get," she says, "why you didn't feel you could tell me any of this. You managed to tell me about the fire. Why not Carlo? Even just the bare bones?"

His jaw slackens. "I'm so sorry." He signals and pulls into their street. "You have no idea how sorry I am, Tess. I love you—I love you so much. I wanted it to just be me and you, just our little family. I thought it could be that simple."

"Well, it can't." She balls her fists in her lap. "A little family is always going to be part of a bigger one. You have to promise that you'll talk to me from now on, even about the bad stuff—especially about the bad stuff. I know all this must have been unbearable for you. I know the accusations and Carlo vanishing must have been hideous. But it's part of who you are, just like my own experiences dealing with my mother—the sadness, the worry, the guilt—are part of who I am. This is only going to work if we talk to each other. I have to be able to trust you to be honest. The alternative is just too damaging."

He reaches out and folds his hand over one of her fists, enclosing and squeezing her fingers so that she can't see her own hand anymore because it is completely covered by his. Then he lets go and turns down their drive.

She knows she should feel closer to him now, relieved, softened—purged, perhaps. She has the explanation that she's been looking for. It all hangs together; it all makes sense. But she doesn't feel relieved. She feels as if she has dug down to the foundations of their home, only to find that they are cracked, flawed, and in need of major repair.

CHAPTER TWENTY-TWO

It is past midnight, they are in bed, and she is feeding Lily again. She is supposed to keep her to regular, every-four-hour feeds, but she has conclusively failed, and Lily seems to feed almost constantly. Since it is more exhausting to resist than to give in and feed her, breast-feeding feels like Tess's main activity these days. Greg is lying next to them with his eyes half closed. She is not sure if he is asleep. Things between them still feel off-kilter. In the four weeks since they brought Lily home, she has tried to put it all behind her, but she can't get past Greg's ability to keep things from her.

When they got home with Lily on Christmas Eve, Joe was waiting for them. They had asked the Schechters' nanny, Delia, to stay with him, and as they drew up, his face was at his upstairs window. He ran out onto the porch as they walked up the path, and Delia took pictures of the four of them as they carried Lily across the threshold.

A broad Christmas tree, laden with lights and decorations, sat in the living room, its peak brushing the ceiling. Joe was excited as he led her to it. "Greg and me wanted to surprise you!" She handed Lily to Greg and exclaimed over it, hugging Joe tightly. Greg came up behind them and put his free arm around her, and Delia took a picture of them all, smiling by the tree with Lily sleeping through it all, in Greg's arms.

Christmas day passed in a blur of colicky yelling, diapers, feeds, and Joe's over-excitement. He ripped into LEGO boxes, a Nerf gun, puzzles, and football annuals, and they sat around the towering tree, ate turkey cooked by Greg, played games, and watched parts of several movies. Everything ought to be perfect, but beneath the loving exhaustion of their first Christmas, questions about Greg's past rose up, one after another. What were his childhood Christmases like? Did he decorate the tree with his parents? Did they eat turkey or goose? Were there Italian or Polish customs they followed, or was Thanksgiving the big celebration and Christmas an afterthought? And did Carlo spend Christmas with them? What about Aunt Julianna? Was she included? Was she an alcoholic when the boys were very young? Was she abusive, disruptive, or simply a sad absence? How did the family deal with her? And how did her cousin deal with his mother?

But, of course, she couldn't ask Greg any of this, because she couldn't risk spoiling Christmas for Joe with the inevitable heightening of tension as Greg's pain resurfaced. And most of the time she was too dazed to face anything that difficult, and so the questions rose and fell, rose and fell.

And since then, for the past few weeks, the stresses of Lily's feeding schedule, her colicky cries, and the constant, anxious monitoring, changing, and comforting seemed to preclude any real discussion. So they cleared away the decorations, then moved through the New Year and into the dark, cold January days.

They are tiptoeing around each other now, caring for the children, caring for each other, discussing Lily's progress, her erratic feeding, her gradual weight gain, the latest checkup, but beneath these practicalities everything between them feels fraught, as if they are picking their way through rooms scattered with glass.

One thing has been put to rest, though: Helena. That morning, when Tess was picking her way up the icy pavement after dropping Joe at school, she saw Helena coming from the other direction, walking toward her own front yard in snow boots and the down coat.

They could not avoid each other, so they teetered across the packed snow, meeting by the border between the houses. This was the first time Helena had encountered Lily, but she did not even glance into the sling. After the birth, Josh had brought over a fruit basket, Sandra arrived with a baby blanket and a casserole, and even Muriel from the house on the corner dropped by with a basket of apple muffins, but so far Helena has behaved as if Lily does not exist.

"So, Tess," she'd said, without preamble, "I hear my husband felt the need to share our marital issues with you." Her green eyes were hostile beneath flicks of black eyeliner, her chin lifted.

"What do you mean?" Tess tucked Lily's hat down. She hadn't spoken to Josh in weeks. Then she recalled the discussion they'd had before Lily's birth, before all of this—but it felt like years ago. It was irrelevant now.

"I gather he told you we've been seeking marriage counseling."

"He might have said something . . ."

"Well, in yesterday's session, Tess, he admitted that he misinterpreted some things and that he told you I was interested in your husband."

It was time to tackle this head-on. She did not have the energy for these games anymore. "And *are* you interested in Greg?"

Helena's face flushed. "That's ridiculous."

"Then why did you lie to me about knowing Greg at Harvard?"

"I didn't lie to you, Tess." She made a pitying face. "I knew who he was. Everyone did."

"Well, he didn't know you. He had no idea you were there around the same time."

"Ha!" Helena gave a high, artificial laugh. "Well, then!"

"Well, what? You made it sound as if you two were friends, but you weren't."

"None of this is relevant."

Tess readjusted Lily's hat. Her feet, on thick ice, were beginning to feel numb. She tucked the blanket more tightly around the sling.

Helena offered a patronizing smile. "It sounds to me, Tess, as if you're the one who's feeling insecure about her marriage."

"Greg isn't interested in you, Helena."

"Really? Then why are you so threatened by me?"

"I don't think I am."

"Now who's being dishonest?"

"OK, fine—I probably was, at the start, when I just moved here, and I didn't know anyone, and you were quite unfriendly, and you seemed to be everywhere, but, really, Helena, I'm definitely not threatened by you now."

"Oh, really?" Helena gave a sharp laugh. "Then why did you try to run me over?"

She opened her mouth to say that it was not deliberate, and then she realized that any more discussion would be pointless. Helena was never going to be honest. She was all about winning, about being the best: the most beautiful, the smartest, the most successful, the most desired. She might or might not believe herself to be in love with Greg, but what she craved, above all, was glamour, recognition, admiration—things that were not available to her in the suburbs. There was a void inside Helena, and she was struggling to fill it. Tess almost felt sorry for her.

And so she said nothing. She turned and walked away, treading carefully so as not to slip on the ice that was layered over packed snow, through the gate and onto the more solid ground of the sanded path, up to the big front porch of the mock Tudor house. She did not turn to see whether Helena was watching her. She did not care.

Lily squirms, and Tess puts her onto her shoulder, patting her back gently. She is so tired that she feels slightly sick. She prays that Lily will sleep, even for half an hour, and not need to be walked around the house most of the night again. Greg doesn't open his eyes or move. He has been meeting with lawyers again today, going through depositions and legal strategies. He is determined not to settle, and so the case could, he says, drag on for a very long time. Now is not the time to make him talk about his family, but there is never a good time. She is going to be tired for months, and he is going to be juggling lawyers and research and patients for the foreseeable future.

And, meanwhile, his past is eating away at them like a parasite. They have to find a way to talk about it.

"Greg," she says quietly, "are you awake?"

"Yeah," he says. "Mostly."

There is silence.

"What's up?" He turns his head and looks up at her, his brown eyes concerned.

"I don't know. I was just thinking . . . I still feel as if there's a lot I don't know about your family. I still feel a bit disturbed, you know, by finding out about Carlo like that—and the way we've been, you know, like nothing happened . . . Do you know what I mean?"

He takes a breath through his nostrils. She waits for him to say it has been an exhausting day, he has to sleep, he has an early start in the morning, there is too much on his mind right now, lawyers and negotiations and recriminations and depositions, not to mention his own research, the sick children he is treating, tomorrow's list—but he does not. He nods.

"I do. So, what do you want to know about my family?"

"Well, I don't know, really. Maybe I just want to know what your parents were actually like, as people."

He closes his eyes again. "They were good people." His voice is flat. "Hardworking people."

"I know, but how about Natalia? Was she a good mother? Was she kind or strict? What was she like?" It is like edging along a precarious, splintering floor, waiting for a plank to break, but she has to do it.

"She was strong, self-contained, kind of stoic. She knew her own mind, but she was nice, too."

"Nice?" It is a banal word to use about your mother.

"I think she was driven a little crazy by small-town life."

"Did she work outside the home?"

"Yes, of course. She worked part-time in a shop, and she did all the books and paperwork for the family business." His voice trails off, sadly. He covers his eyes with one hand.

It is costing him so much to remember his mother, but perhaps it will turn out to be helpful; it might release something for him, too.

"Why was small-town life difficult for her?"

He shrugs. "You know—there was a lot of gossip and sniping. People had a lot to say about Julianna, particularly. I think she was a little ashamed of her sister."

"Was Julianna that bad?"

He drops his hand and stares up at the ceiling again, and, to her surprise, he carries on. "Not always, no. When she was younger, she was kind of wonderful. When I picture her in those days, she's stirring a pot with a book in her hand, her hair a mess. She loved to read, more than anything. She read all the time. She organized her bookshelves according to the friendships between the authors." He looks up at her and gives a tortured smile. "You know—Truman Capote next to Harper Lee, Edith Wharton beside Henry James, J. D. Salinger out on his own by the yucca plant."

She smiles back at him encouragingly. It is the most he has ever said about any family member, and for the first time she feels a sense of loss, not just for Greg or Lily, but for herself: she would have liked to know this difficult, bookish aunt whose life went so badly wrong.

"She'd have liked you," he says, as if reading her mind. "She'd have been interested in your work. She had one friend, possibly her only friend, who was an artist. They were very close. She had a shack in the woods, she kept goats, but she'd studied in New York and Europe. Julianna was just too smart for the life she led; that was part of her problem. She had this fearsome, complicated, restless mind."

"She sounds slightly intimidating."

"She was, a little, I guess. But she could be funny, too. She used to sing goofy Polish songs; she was a terrible singer."

"How bad was her drinking?"

"It came in bouts. But over time, as things got . . . things got worse, I guess her drinking got more consistent."

"What 'things'?"

He says nothing and drops his forearm across his eyes again. She sees his Adam's apple roll as he swallows. "Could we talk about her more another time maybe? She makes me very sad."

"OK. OK, that's fine." She reaches out and squeezes his arm. He doesn't move. "Would you be able to tell me just a little bit about your father before we stop? Can you face that?"

"Sure." Greg drops his arm, looks at her. "He was distant, old-fashioned, a workaholic, strict. He wasn't around much."

"That must be where you get it from."

Greg shrugs but doesn't smile. His jaw is clamped shut again.

"Was he frustrated by small-town life, too?"

"Oh, God, no, he loved it. He loved being the big fish in the small pond. He was into public service, he was on the borough council, the school board—you know, a pillar of the community."

"Were your parents happy together?"

"They were OK, I think. I don't really know." His voice flattens. "You don't think about that sort of thing when you're a kid."

She reaches for his hand with her free one and squeezes it tightly. Lily's squirms on her shoulder but mercifully doesn't wake up. She daren't move her into the Moses basket in case she starts yelling again and Greg stops talking.

"How did they meet?"

He rubs his hand over his face, as if pushing away other, unwelcome thoughts.

"They met in New York, not long after they all arrived in the States. All four of them were working in a garment factory. Natalia and Julianna were seamstresses, and Giovanni and Giacopo worked on the factory floor. I think they spotted these beautiful Polish sisters, and that was that."

She imagines the sisters weighing up life with these dynamic Italian brothers, the four of them deciding to head off to start a business. "How on earth did the four of them end up in Pennsylvania?"

"Giacopo saw the opportunity for a trucking business. He persuaded them all to move. I think he was the real entrepreneur, the one with the vision."

"Giacopo's the one who died first? Carlo's father?"

Greg nods again, almost a wince.

This is beginning to feel cruel. She leans over and kisses his cheek. "OK. I love you. Thank you for telling me about them. I know it's really hard for you to remember them like this, but thank you. I think I just needed to know a bit more about who they were, because, I mean, one day Lily will want to know about them, too, won't she?"

"I know she will." He takes his arm away from his face and looks at her again. His expression is complicated: tense, troubled, and unhappy. She'd wanted to believe that remembering and talking about his relatives would release him from some of this pain, but he doesn't look liberated. If anything, he looks more burdened than before.

Lily's limbs jerk, her eyes open, and, startled by a dream or a vision—some inchoate threat—she opens her bud mouth, and her face crumples like tissue paper around it. Tess shifts her onto the other shoulder and begins to pat her back, but her cries escalate.

"Here." Greg sits up, holding out his hands. "She's all mine tonight. You get some sleep."

"But you need sleep, too."

"No, I don't. What I need is to hang out with my beautiful baby girl." He gets out of bed, takes Lily from Tess, and folds her over his broad shoulder, patting and making "shh" sounds as he walks across the bedroom and out onto the landing. As he turns to close the door behind him, he pauses, and they look at each other. In the shadows she can't make out his expression, but she can feel the anguish of these memories running through his veins like an infection that he cannot cure.

Lily's cries recede as he carries her off down the stairs. Beneath the shrill wails, she hears him singing a low and unfamiliar song in a language she has never heard from him before.

She lies back on the pillows. She was right about one thing: Greg only needed to see Lily, to hold her in his arms and look into her face, in order to love and want her. He is such a tender and protective father, it is inconceivable that he ever could have wanted to abort their child.

Then the memory resurfaces of the question she asked herself out in the snow, when she realized that she was in labor. She had forgotten it—and it feels like a temporary insanity now. She cannot fathom how—even for a single, deranged second—she could have wondered if Greg would save their baby.

CHAPTER TWENTY-THREE

They are on Skype, and Nell's face is lit by a table lamp, so that when she smiles, the dimples on either side of her mouth become deep black commas.

"The weird thing is, when you search for Carlo, you get nothing, absolutely no mention of him anywhere online after the trial. He just vanishes."

"Well, yes, exactly; he did vanish." Tess keeps her voice down because Lily is sleeping in the Moses basket by the bed, a massive relief after four hours straight of colicky howling this morning.

She is folding onesies, her head thick from five weeks of profound sleep-deprivation. Her ears are, very gently, ringing. It is possible that this is a permanent problem. She cannot imagine what she would do if she had to go on photographic assignments now. She is wrung out. She can barely think, let alone organize a shoot, make decisions about angles, lighting, or settings. The galleys of *Hand in Hand* arrived yesterday, and she has hardly even looked at them.

"He has no online presence," Nell is saying, "but guess what I did find."

She sighs. "What?"

"A Facebook reunion page for people who were at Penn Medical School in Carlo's year. The actual reunion's been and gone, but alumni are still posting about it—mostly photos of their beautiful children on Costa Rican holidays or themselves collecting awards, but you should take a look."

"Why? Why would I do that?" She cannot keep the frustration out of her voice.

"Well, I don't know. I was just thinking that if Carlo is, by any chance, still alive, then maybe someone will know where he is."

Tess puts the pink onesie she is folding onto the pile and picks up a soft blanket.

"Nell," she says, "why are you doing this?"

Nell's face vanishes briefly behind her mug of tea. Then she lowers it and leans closer to the screen, tucking a curl behind her ear. Her eyes are wide and clear. "I just think," she says, "that if Carlo is out there, it might be good to find him."

Tess stops folding the blanket.

"I mean, people don't just vanish." Nell puts the mug down. "Do they?"

"Of course they do! Missing-persons websites are full of them—people vanish every single day."

"But what if he's still alive?"

"Jesus, Nell."

"Come on, don't be like that."

"Like what? You're basically suggesting that Greg's still hiding something, and that's . . ."

"Hey, that's not what I'm saying, not at all. Why would you think that?" Nell pauses. "Wait. Do *you* think he's hiding something?"

"No! I just don't know why you're opening this whole thing up again."

"I didn't realize it was closed." Nell's face, close-up and slightly distorted by the camera, is serious.

"It isn't!" Tess hears herself—querulous and defensive and irrational.

"OK, we won't talk about it."

"Talk about what?!"

"Well, all I was thinking was, if Greg could see that Carlo was vulnerable and possibly even suicidal, then why didn't he do something to stop him? Why didn't Greg help him?"

"But that's so unfair! If a person wants to kill themselves, they're going to do it; you can't blame it on the people who love them. We feel guilty enough already without that . . ."

Nell pushes back her hair. "Shit, I'm sorry—your mum. You're right. I'm so sorry. Forget I said it—I'm an idiot. I didn't mean it like that. You know I didn't."

"No, I know, but . . ." Tess tucks her hair back and shuts her eyes. The room actually spins. "Listen. I can't really do this . . . Lily has colic, I've had roughly two hours sleep a night for the past five weeks, I'm breast-feeding her about every twenty minutes, Joe is still unhappy at school, and Greg is working all the time. I honestly haven't got the energy for this."

Nell straightens her shoulders. "Of course you haven't. I wish I could come over there and help you. You look totally shattered, you poor thing—and I really want to meet my goddaughter."

"Well, unless you can breast-feed her, you'd be no use to me right now."

Nell laughs, and the tension eases. Neither of them wants to bicker, least of all over Skype.

"I do wish I could come and see you, though." Nell's features briefly pixelate, then right themselves again. "Every morning I wake up worrying about you over there, and I don't know why. I want to see you."

"I know. I want to see you, too, but you've got the twins and a catering business to run, and you definitely can't turn down two weddings in order to come here. I won't let you."

"We might need the money, actually—four of Ken's colleagues just got made redundant, and he told me last night that he's worried he might be next."

"But you said things were going better for him lately."

"He thought they were, but this latest round of redundancies has really rattled him. If he did lose his job, there's no cushion at all—we've got almost nothing in the bank. I daren't even buy a Boston flight in advance."

"Listen, it costs a fortune to fly to Boston, and at the moment all your goddaughter does is yell, eat, and poo. Don't even think about coming to visit us. Lily and I will both be a lot more fun when she's through this. Come in the spring, when you know what's happening with Ken's job. Greg says Boston's lovely in the spring. Or, even better, I'll bring Lily home to see you."

A thin wail rises from the Moses basket; the Skype call has to finish.

After she has fed and changed a screaming Lily, Tess paces around the front room, patting her daughter's back until she burps, then perks up. For a while they sit on the sofa. Lily gazes up at her, alert and beautiful. Her eyes are big and deep brown like Greg's. Her hair is definitely dark, and it is beginning to curl at the edges. Her face is pink-cheeked and symmetrical. Tess talks to her, sings songs, blows raspberries on her neck, and for a while everything is perfect.

Then the colic pains come back. It begins with a plaintive hiccupping, and then all Lily wants is to be held and walked up and down and patted and soothed—she stops being a beautiful baby and turns into something tortured, almost animalistic, tormented by pain.

As she paces the house with Lily's cries jangling against the high ceilings, Nell's suggestion that Greg could have done something to stop Carlo from committing suicide replays in her mind. And then suddenly it makes sense. She can't believe she hasn't seen it before. This is the guilt she has always felt in Greg—his constant companion. It is not just survivor's guilt. It is more complicated even than that—it is a guilt that she herself is all too familiar with. It is the legacy of suicide. She should have recognized it the moment he told her about Carlo's disappearance. She, of all people, should have known immediately what it was.

The evening her mother died, Tess was going out to a party. She was in her bedroom playing music, doing her hair, redoing her hair, trying on different outfits, and even though she knew that her mother was not in good shape—sitting downstairs in the living room, immobile, with the white masklike face that always signaled a crisis—she didn't go downstairs. She shut it out, and she sang louder.

She did not want to be responsible for her mother that night. She didn't want to wait for her father to come home from his meeting at school. He said he'd be home by eight. She should have waited for him, been sure that her mother was supervised, but she didn't. She didn't want the responsibility of the pale-faced woman in the chair anymore. She just wanted to be sixteen years old and going to a party.

Soon after she left the house, overly made-up, overdressed, her mother left the house, too—and walked straight to the tube station.

When her father got back from the staff meeting, just twenty minutes later, the police were already on the doorstep.

The guilt ate away at both of them in the years that followed. She is sure that it was guilt that caused her father's heart attack nine years later. Guilt had stretched the fibers of his broken heart too far, and they gave out. It almost undid her, too. For years she felt it was her fault. If she had waited those extra twenty minutes, until her father walked through the door and took over, then her mother would not have gone to the tube station—she would be alive. It wasn't until she was in her twenties, when she finally saw a grief counselor, that she realized she was not to blame for her mother's actions. If it hadn't been that night, that tube train, it would have been another. But even now the guilt will sometimes fold over her like a crippling fog, and she has to make a real effort to lift her head above it and move on.

She stands by the kitchen window, swaying and patting Lily's back as Lily's cries echo off the steel appliances. The last snowfall is turning to slush and ice, but there is more on the way; she can feel it gathering. The bare branches of the trees poke at the murky sky.

It is possible that Carlo did not take himself off on a Greyhound bus to commit suicide. Carlo Novak could be alive. And if he is, then Nell is right that one of the people from medical school might still be in touch with him. If Greg and Carlo could be reunited, then it would release Greg from the guilt he has been carrying all these years about his cousin.

Lily's cries subside, and she drifts into an exhausted, limp, sweaty sleep. Tess knows that if she puts her down, the cries will start again, so she keeps her draped on her shoulder as she gets the laptop from the bedroom and carries it into the kitchen.

If Carlo is alive, it is possible that he eventually returned to Robesville. Home seems like a good place to start. She googles his name and Robesville, but nothing comes up. She is about to give up when she remembers Greg mentioning the Pennsylvania artist, Aunt Julianna's friend. Perhaps she is still there and would remember the family. She might know if Carlo had ever showed up again in town.

She searches for local landscape artists and finds numerous references to a Sally MacManus.

She finds a website dedicated to Sally's paintings, and she skims through the woman's biography. She is clearly well established in the art world—one of her paintings is in the Smithsonian. She has lived in a shack in the woods for almost fifty years. Tess clicks through to the images of the paintings.

They are extraordinary—haunting, realist landscapes in washed-out colors, tawny grays and browns, dreamlike and powerful. There is one of a Pennsylvania farm with snow drifting on the ridges of the hills, another of a river bursting through glistening rocks, one of a closely observed raven with blue-black feathers and an accusing eye. And then there are portraits: a black dog sitting in front of a wooden house, perhaps the artist's cabin, an old woman sewing in a blue chair. But it is the one of a young, dark-haired woman, in profile, uncomfortably close, that makes Tess pause and look again.

Her tangled hair is darker than the blue-black background, and her skin looms out of the frame, the palest shell pink with raw, reddened patches on her Slavic cheekbones. She looks as if she has just stepped in from the freezing night. Her jaw is strong, her troubled eyes hooded, her nose straight and fine above a full mouth. It is a striking, powerful face, and there is an unmistakable family resemblance in the bone structure, those dark, hooded eyes. The portrait is called *Lost* and was painted almost forty years ago. It can only be Greg's aunt, Julianna.

She types an email to "Contact Sally MacManus."

Dear Sir or Madam,

I would like to get in touch with Ms. MacManus and wondered if you could possibly pass on this email to her.

Dear Ms. MacManus,

My name is Tess Harding Gallo. I am married to Greg Gallo, who grew up in Robesville—he left years ago. I am trying to locate his cousin, Carlo Novak, who also grew up there. I think it's possible that you were once friends with my husband's aunt, Julianna. (In fact, I wondered if your portrait *Lost* might be she.) I hope you don't mind me contacting you like this; I was not sure where else to try. Carlo disappeared almost thirty years ago, and my husband has not heard from him since. We would very much like to find him, if he is still alive.

Yours truly,
Tess

Almost as soon as she has pressed Send, she realizes that she is going to have to tell Greg about this or it will be yet another secret between them. Suddenly she feels annoyed that she has allowed herself to get sucked back in. Even if Carlo is alive—which he almost certainly is not—he clearly does not want to be in touch with Greg. Greg is easy to find. It would take one click of a mouse to locate him at Children's.

Telling Greg that she has emailed Sally MacManus is only going to cause more problems. She probably won't get a reply anyway. The best thing to do is forget this. Emailing a stranger was a mistake.

She shuts down her laptop, but even later, as she feeds Lily, burps her, changes her, straps her, squalling, into the sling, and heads out into the cold afternoon to collect Joe, Julianna's beautiful face hovers in her head, as persistent as a ghost.

★ ★ ★

The next day, as she is walking home after dropping Joe at school, Tess gets out her phone and checks her emails. Peering at the screen over the top of Lily's head, her fingers numb and raw, she sees the name *Sally MacManus* in her in-box. Her heart speeds up.

It is probably just a form reply, saying that the message for the artist will be processed, but she opens it right there, standing on the packed snow and ice.

Tess, thank you for getting in touch. I was certainly surprised to hear that Grzegor married. I remember him well, the poor boy. I've often wondered what became of him. I am not well now, can't paint anymore, so I have too much time to think—and I do think about that family more and more these days, though I can't fathom why. Perhaps it's frailty—my mind going back to the past because sometimes it is harder to remember what I did yesterday, or even an hour ago, than it is to remember Julianna in my yard on a summer's day browning her legs in the sun. So it was extraordinary to get your email, like you'd come right out of my mind. To answer your question: no, I have neither seen nor heard from Carlo in decades and don't expect I ever will.

Julianna was my dear friend, but she was not a good mother. You probably know that she drank. Sometimes she'd take off, and nobody would know if she was even alive. I understand why Carlo left and didn't come back, even when she was dying and loved him so. But she was not a bad woman. She could be a great friend, and she was the smartest person I've ever known. We had such great talks! What others saw as selfishness, I understood as unmanageable pain. That family did her awful injustices. So I loved her despite her obvious flaws, but of course I didn't have to live with her.

I hope you find Carlo. Say hi from me if you do. He was a good kid.

Yours,
Sally

P.S. Yes, Lost is Julianna. Wasn't she something?

As Tess turns into Walnut Street, trying to absorb Sally MacManus's words, she looks up, and there is Helena. She is standing on the grassy verge—*curb,* she reminds herself—in front of her house, her fur-lined boots planted deep in gray snow, her long, puffy coat zipped to her chin.

Tess's heart sinks. She slips her phone into her pocket, wondering if she can somehow slide past the woman unnoticed.

But Helena raises a hand, waving her over. "Hey, Tess." She is standing next to a FOR SALE sign.

"Oh, goodness, you're moving?" Tess asks.

"We are." Helena gives a brief smile.

"Where are you going?"

"I've been offered a professorship at Berkeley," Helena says. "Starting in the spring."

"In California? Oh, well, that's great."

They look at each other. Helena's green eyes are cool.

"What will Josh do out there?"

"Oh, he's looking into some academic options right now."

"And can you move your business?"

"Businesses. But it won't affect Dr. Vaus too much. And my partner's taking over the Cambridge clinic."

"So you're really going?"

"Oh, yes." Helena lifts her chin and gives an icy smile. "Relieved?"

She doesn't deny it as she looks back into Helena's eyes. It is hard to believe that not long ago this woman dominated her thoughts, alarmed and disturbed her, seemed to threaten her marriage, her home, her sanity. Helena's actions are simply the by-products of an unhappy marriage and the discovery that career success is not the same as fulfillment.

"Well, good luck." She straightens her shoulders and adjusts Lily's hat. "I hope it works out for you in California—for both of you."

"Oh, it will." Helena shrugs and turns away. "It always does."

As she walks away from Helena, it occurs to her that the immediate, physical threats of the first few months in this house—from Helena, from Sarah Banister—have been replaced by something that is much harder to pin down. Greg's ghosts—Julianna and Carlo—feel more dangerous than Helena ever did.

She gets inside, and without removing her coat or undoing the sling, she types a reply to Sally.

Dear Sally,

Thank you so much for replying to my email. I was fascinated to hear about Julianna. My husband has told me very little about his aunt, as he finds these memories quite painful. I know that Julianna lost her husband when they were both very young, and of course there was the fire, which must have been terrible for her. But it is good to hear that she had a friend like you. If there's anything else you can tell me about her, or the family, I would love to know more. I have just had a baby, a little girl named Lily, and I'd really like to find out more about her relatives, but Greg finds it very difficult talk about them, for obvious reasons.

Many thanks again for your response.

All the best,
Tess

Later that day, as she is cooking pasta while Joe watches the Disney Channel in the front room and Lily, briefly content post feeding, is asleep in her bouncy chair, she checks her emails again. Another message from Sally is waiting for her. She feels a rush of excitement as she opens it.

Yes, I did love her, Tess. I don't know if you know what she suffered at the hands of Giacopo, but let's just say he was a vicious man. The only tragedy is that she married him in the first place. Thank God he died young. But that marriage left her with demons. She got rid of his name—that's why they are Novaks, not Gallos (you knew that, I guess?)—but she could never shake off the things he did to her. Natalia was kind enough, on the surface, but she never wanted to hear the truth about her brother-in-law—too close to home (though I don't think Giovanni ever did anything to her, at least). Oh, Julianna fought them both; she did what she could to stand up to them, but she was never going to win.

I miss her still, you know. She had an extraordinary mind—complicated people often do, don't they? When I first met her, she dreamed of going to college, and I always felt that she could have been some-thing remarkable, under different circumstances—an astrophysicist, an astronaut, a brain surgeon. On a good day she was breathtakingly beautiful, too. But beauty isn't always helpful, is it? Lust and hatred go hand in hand—at least for some men.

She had so much love in her heart, but she could be hell, too—mercurial, complicated, self-destructive. Today, maybe there'd be help for her—therapy, support of some kind—but in those days, in our neck of the woods, all she got was disapproval, small-town gossip, and people taking things from her that they had no right to take.

She was my dear friend, but I failed to help her, and I'll feel bad about that till the day I die.

Yours,
Sally

She rereads the email, several times, trying to make sense of the gaps. The bitterness toward the Gallos suggests a story untold, but she cannot squeeze any more of it from Sally's words. She needs more. She types a reply.

Dear Sally,

Thank you so much for sharing these memories with me. They are so interesting and fill in so many details for me about Julianna. It sounds as if she suffered a lot in her marriage and afterward. This explains why she was so troubled.

But I wonder if you could tell me what you mean when you say that people took things from her that they had no right to take. Are you talking about Natalia and Giovanni, perhaps, taking Carlo away from Julianna? Is that what you mean? Did she fight them for her son? It also sounds as if you are saying that Greg's father, Giovanni, was not a very nice man. Is that what you mean? You say you think he never hurt his wife—but was he perhaps violent toward Julianna?

I hope all my questions don't feel too intrusive. I suppose I want to know more because Giovanni and Natalia are my husband's parents, my child's grandparents. It seems important to me, now, to know what I can about them.

I also wanted to tell you that I am delighted to have discovered your paintings. They really are wonderful. I would love to see them in real life one day.

All the best,
Tess

She clicks Send. Then she forwards both of Sally's emails to Nell, with a brief message explaining what she has done.

After she has drained the pasta, she hears a new message come into her in-box. Leaving the pasta to cool in the colander, she opens a reply from Nell.

God, Tess, this is amazing. Poor Julianna! Stuck in that tiny town, having survived an abusive marriage, and now being controlled by her perfect sister and the brother of her abuser. I am sure she was a terrible mother to poor Carlo, but you've got to feel for her, haven't you? I'd actually been wondering why Carlo was a Novak and not a Gallo (his dad and Greg's dad were brothers, right? The Italians?). So this explains that. I love it that Julianna wasn't going to let him keep the name of her abusive husband. Good for her! Underneath all the destructive behavior, it sounds as if Julianna had a real streak of determination. I mean, in small-town America in the seventies it would have been quite radical to go back to your birth name for yourself and your child, wouldn't it? I doubt if feminism had made it to Robesville. So, good for Julianna.

And Sally sounds fantastic, doesn't she? Thank God Julianna had her, at least. (Do you think they were more than friends?) Don't you want to meet Sally? I do.

Tess logs off. A headache ticks behind her eyes like a grenade. Her left breast is hot and painful: the start of mastitis—she recognizes the feverish sensation, the sharp, swollen pain, from breast-feeding Joe, when she had it several times. Lily twitches again. At any moment the screaming is going to start, and she needs to get pasta into Joe before it does.

But she can't get Julianna out of her head. She feels as if she has pressed on a tender, burning spot in Greg's past—she has found the deep-down place where the inflammation lurks. Sally MacManus has given her another perspective on the family legacy. If Julianna was battling with Greg's parents, then how did Carlo feel about the Gallos? Did he, too, resent them? If something exploded between Greg and Carlo in that fraught period after the trial, when Greg was on the verge of starting Harvard and Carlo felt his life was over, it might have been catastrophic.

Leaving the pasta to get cold, she opens her laptop again and googles Harvard Medical School alumni, adding Greg's matriculation date. She is not really sure why. Perhaps it is just the urge to connect to the person he was then, just starting out, in the immediate aftermath of the trauma. She crouches over the computer and clicks her way to the relevant alumni page. Just one month before they moved to Boston, Greg's Harvard Medical School class had a reunion. Greg would have been too swept up with the new job to even consider going, even if the event crossed his radar.

She tries to log in to the group, but you have to be a Harvard alumnus. She is about to shut the computer when she notices that the reunion has a Twitter feed. She goes to Twitter, finds the account, and scrolls through the alumni tweets. Some are from the group administrator, and they paint a mixed picture of its driven cohort.

43% of us now take prescription meds, 15% have had a midlife crisis.

Half the class has been published, half has had psychiatric help.

Others are from individuals, giving little updates on their career triumphs or attaching nostalgic pictures of themselves and fellow medical students. She has no idea what she is looking for, but as she flicks through the tweets, Greg's name leaps out.

Spring Ball with Tim Knight, Andrew O'Connor, and Greg Gallo! Good times!

She opens the photograph. There is Greg in a dinner suit alongside two young men, with two women in ball dresses—puffed sleeves and frills. They make her think of a line in the Harvard song that she found in Greg's files: "the good and the great, in their beautiful prime . . ."

She looks more closely at Greg's young face. He is thinner, tense and uneasy. His head is tilted, and he is standing slightly apart from the group, arms crossed. The other four are grinning, relaxed, arms around one another, but Greg looks as if he does not belong in the picture, or perhaps in the life itself. She cannot imagine what he must have been feeling at that point. Still only in his early twenties, he had come through the loss of his parents, followed by that year with aunt Julianna and then an accelerated undergraduate degree. His beloved cousin, his only surviving close relative, had been tried for infanticide and had vanished. No wonder he looks disturbed.

She should probably show him the emails from Sally, but all that would do is bring this awful time back to him. It is unlikely that Sally is saying anything about his family that he doesn't already know—though he has never mentioned his aunt's abusive marriage or his parents' attempt to control her, perhaps by controlling her son. But perhaps he doesn't know any of this. A teenage boy might not notice these things, though he would surely have picked up on the tension with his "difficult" aunt. No, dredging all this up is unlikely to be helpful for him.

As she gazes at the troubled, clean-lined beauty of Greg's youth, she hears his footsteps on the basement stairs.

She shuts down Twitter and slams the laptop lid shut. Lily is, miraculously, still asleep. Tess gets up and goes to the basement door. As Greg steps in, she folds herself into his arms, shutting her eyes tightly. She can feel his heart beating beneath his soft woolen sweater. He smells of soap and coffee and cold night air, the leather seats of his car—of himself. He hugs her and rests his chin on the top of her head, and for a few moments neither of them speaks, and she has the feeling that she is holding him up, that if she stepped away, Greg would fall.

CHAPTER TWENTY-FOUR

"I have an idea for you." Greg perches on the side of the bed. It is just before six in the morning, and he's already been for a run through the icy woods, had his shower, and washed down eggs and toast with a double espresso. Lily is sleeping but only lightly. At six weeks, she is feeding and breathing well, she seems more solid, more awake and of this world, but she is still colicky, and Tess knows that if she tries to ease her off her shoulder and put her into the Moses basket, she will wake up, and conversation will become impossible again.

She closes her eyes and rests a cheek on Lily's head, feeling the feathery hair, breathing in her sweet, milky smell. She feels Greg's fingers on her cheek and opens her eyes again.

Something in his face has changed since they talked about his parents. He looks more vulnerable and raw, as if a door has cracked open inside his head, and, no matter how hard he tries, he cannot force it shut again. This, surely, is a good thing, the beginning of a healing process. Perhaps one day he will be able to forgive himself for surviving, just as she has forgiven herself, not all the time, maybe, but much of it. Perhaps one day Carlo will not be sitting between them every time they look into each other's eyes.

It is a week now since she heard from Sally, and there have been no more emails. Perhaps remembering proved too upsetting for Sally, as well. This is probably helpful, because the last thing she needs is something else to conceal from Greg.

"You want to hear my idea, then?" He strokes her hair back off her face. "Or are you too sleepy?"

"Yes, sorry, what is it?"

"OK, so I know Joe was upset that David can't make it to see him this weekend. Well, a colleague of mine has a ski lodge in New Hampshire, up in the White Mountains, and he's offered to let me use it. I know you're tired, and you probably aren't up to going anywhere much right now, but how about I take Joe, just me and him? The snow's good, I can teach him to ski, and I think it would be a great idea for the two of us to have some time together away from all this baby stuff. I know I've been very tied up with Lily, and I don't want him to think I only care about her. Some time together will do us good, I think."

Her first reaction is no—she does not want Greg to take Joe off to a stranger's house in New Hampshire. But then she remembers Joe's face when she told him that David had been called out to an emergency situation in the Middle East and would be gone for at least two weeks, so would not, after all, be coming to Boston this weekend. Joe needs to see his dad, of course, but maybe time with Greg will compensate a little for not having David. And he loves the snow—he'd surely be thrilled to learn how to ski.

"I could drive him up there Friday night—it's only a couple of hours. I can take him skiing and tubing while you have some time here just with Lily."

"What's tubing?"

"You know, it's where you slide down a snowy slope in an inner tube."

She nods. Joe would love that, too.

"Don't you think it'd be a good idea for me and Joe to spend some time together, without you and Lily, so he knows he's important to me, too?"

She tries to smile. He is right. Since Lily was born, he has been focused on her; they both have, for obvious reasons. But Greg, particularly, has been concentrating on Lily to the exclusion of all else. He makes straight for her every night when he comes in. She sees him scanning her breathing, temperature, skin tone. And then he carries her around with him, paces the house with her between feeds, changes diapers. She knows that this intensity comes from his lack of time with Lily. He has so few hours at home, and he is determined to make the most of them. But a couple of times he has been irritable with Joe, snapping at him that it's surely time for bed, or to pick up his backpack, or move his snow boots off the rug. It is not surprising—they are both ragged; caring for Lily has been incredibly demanding—but a couple of times she has seen Joe looking a little lost as Greg walks past him to pick up Lily.

So Greg has realized this and is doing something to rectify it. He has taken a step back and thought through what he has to do to make this family work. The plan is a good one, a solid one.

She is not sure, then, why the thought of the two of them going off to New Hampshire makes her so uneasy. It isn't just the separation from Joe. She was anxious a few weeks ago when David took him to New York for the weekend, but it didn't feel quite like this.

There is probably an element of maternal guilt in her hesitation. The last thing she wants is for Joe to feel as if she has sent him away. She feels constantly as if she is not giving Joe enough attention as it is. It is hard to hug him on the sofa when Lily is screaming in their ears. And she is painfully aware that when he comes home from school, he is still exhausted, much too quiet and withdrawn, even though she has had several meetings with the teachers, and the friendship situation seems to have improved.

Still, she has to step aside so that Joe and Greg can bond. And in some ways it might be a relief to have a weekend when she doesn't have to worry about Joe feeling excluded as Lily cries or needs another feed or diaper change. She is probably worrying too much about everything. The truth is that Lily has been good for Joe in many ways. He doesn't seem to resent her demands. In fact, he has been incredibly sweet with his baby sister, wanting to carry her around, fetch diapers, help with bath time, worrying when she cries. When David came to take him to New York, he insisted on holding Lily when he heard the knock on the door. He showed her to his dad like a little pink trophy.

And David handled the moment wonderfully. He had brought a huge and expensive box of LEGO City for Joe, and he took pictures of them together, but he didn't ask to hold the baby. Instead, he asked Joe if she farted a lot, what color her poo was, how often she ate, whether she yelled all night, and how grumpy she, Tess, was these days.

Before they left for New York, David kissed her on the cheek. "Lily's a firecracker," he said. "Just like her mother." There was sadness in his voice, a note of regret that made them both step apart and become brusque, looking for Joe's coat and boots.

Sometimes she hears Joe chatting to Lily in another room, singing made-up songs, and she waits outside the door with a bursting feeling in her chest. It is as if having someone so much smaller and more fragile in the house has made Joe feel stronger. The protective urge might not banish fear, but it can certainly override it.

"So?" Greg says. "Good plan?"

She nods, stroking Lily's solid little back through the baby blanket that Nell knitted and sent at Christmas, wrapped in tissue paper and ribbons. "As long as Joe wants to . . ."

"Oh, sure, yes, let's ask him, see what he says." Greg gets up and goes over to the mirror. "Only if he wants to." He combs his damp hair back off his forehead. She can see that he is a little bit offended, perhaps even irritated that she has not leaped on this plan. With his hair swept back, his widow's peak revealed, he looks forbidding.

"No, really, it's a great idea." She makes herself sound more positive. "Joe's going to be beside himself at the idea of sliding down a mountain in an inner tube."

Greg looks at her over his shoulder, and, perhaps because of the angle of his chin, she glimpses the young man on the steps of the Philadelphia courthouse, looking down at the camera—and for that second she feels as if she's staring into the eyes of that too-familiar stranger. She looks away and tucks Lily's blanket tighter.

Her intuition has been telling her that something is missing from the story, because, of course, it is. By vanishing, Carlo has become the unanswered question. He is perpetually present, the shadowy figure that has just vacated the room. He is always nearby: slotted between them in bed at night, flitting in their wake, a tall and handsome intruder in the home. Greg must feel it, too. Perhaps this is why he is so uneasy.

She watches him do up his shirt buttons.

"Greg, is there anything I still don't know about your cousin? Anything at all?"

He is fixing a cuff link onto his blue shirt, and he looks up sharply, frowning, his eyes meeting hers in the mirror. "What's brought this on?"

"I don't know."

He reaches for the second cuff link.

"It's just, Nell said something, and . . ."

He tugs down his shirtsleeves, one by one, and turns to face her. "When's she coming to visit?"

"I'm not sure; she's worried about Ken's job, it's a bit uncertain, and I've told her to wait and come when things are less crazy here. Maybe April, when the weather's better."

A look briefly crosses his face—he is relieved.

Lily starts and begins to whimper. Tess pats her back, whispering into her ear, feeling her damp, small face pressing into the crook of her neck, nuzzling, and her love for Lily spreads into a tangible, physical warmth, encircling them both.

"OK, then." Greg shrugs on a well-cut gray jacket. "I need to get moving. So, do you want to ask Joe about New Hampshire when he wakes up?"

"OK—unless you want to ask him yourself when you get home?"

"No, I'm not sure when I'll be back—might be after his bedtime. You ask him."

He comes over to the bed and presses his mouth onto hers, kisses Lily on the head, tenderly. Then he leaves.

Her phone is by the bed. She picks it up, idly, and opens her emails. Two leap out at her: one from Sally MacManus, one from Alex Kingman. She opens Sally's first.

I have had a small stroke— can't sit up too well, not so good, but—your question:

it was not a pot on the stove

she thought he was the only one in the house, she didn't know C was there

he raped her, then he took her child away, that's why she did it, but she didn't know the others were there

S

She rereads it several times. It makes little sense. She has no idea what the "pot on the stove" means, but it is probably a reference to how the fire started. *C* must be Carlo. But that makes no sense, because Carlo wasn't in the house at the time of the fire. Her instinct is that the "she" is Julianna. But who raped Julianna and took Carlo away? It is all confused and brutal. A stroke, of course, can damage more than motor skills. Sally's memory, logic, recall could all be skewed now.

She needs to find a number and call to see if Sally is all right. But she does not actually know this woman. She can't just phone. Sally is a semi-famous artist; she'll have people rallying around her to help.

She replies, though, right away.

Dear Sally,

I am so very sorry to hear about your stroke. Do you have people helping you there? I hope you are OK. Do please let me know if I can do anything at all to help you.

I am intrigued by your comments—I am not sure I understand about the pot on the stove. I assume you are talking about the house fire? Are you saying that it wasn't an accident? Is the "she" you refer to

Julianna? Are you saying, even, that Julianna burned the Gallos' house? Or am I misunderstanding your words?

I also don't quite understand your reference to a rape. Was Julianna raped? If you could explain a little bit more, when you're well enough, that'd be great. But please don't answer any of this if it is difficult for you; I do understand. The most important thing is that you get better.

Wishing you all the best—and please don't hesitate to ask if you need anything at all,

Tess

She reads Sally's email again. She is about to forward it to Nell, when she stops. It does not feel right to send this to Nell. This is between her and Sally. She saves it in a separate folder.

Then she opens the email from Alex Kingman.

Dear Tess,

I am hoping we can meet. I did leave you a detailed message about this some weeks ago now, but you didn't reply, so I thought I should wait till you'd had your baby. I am sure you must have by now? I have information that you must hear if you are up to it. Please, could you call me? Or email me back, as I would very much like us to meet? (I have something to show you.)

Alex Kingman

She remembers then that the night Lily was born, she'd ignored a voice mail from Alex—she'd deleted it. She has been skirting around him in her mind for weeks now. It would surely help him to know that he'd made a mistake and that there is no chance of bumping into his nemesis on the local beach—that whatever he thinks he has found or knows, he is wrong.

Perhaps it is the warmth of the bed, the feel of Lily against her chest, or the oxytocin coursing through her system, but she feels a moment of altruism, almost responsibility, toward Alex Kingman and his troubled circumstances. What she knows will release him, too, in a way.

She types a reply with one thumb.

Hi, Alex,

I did have my baby (Lily, five weeks early). I'd be happy to meet you. I also have information that might be helpful for you.

When would suit you?

Tess

Alex is sitting at a corner table, hunched over a smartphone. He looks up as she walks through the crowded Cambridge café toward his table, and she hesitates, thinking that she has the wrong man. But he sees her and gets up, smiling. He has changed enormously. His cheekbones are gaunt, vanishing into a beard that has grown bushy and unkempt. His eyes are puffy, with livid violet shadows beneath them.

"Tess. Hey!" He leans over Lily in the sling, kissing her on both cheeks as if they are old friends. "You look terrific." He nods. "Really terrific."

"You're very kind." She unwinds her scarf, pulling off her hat. "But I doubt I look terrific."

He peers into the sling at Lily, curled against her chest. "And this beautiful baby . . ."

"This is Lily. I'm hoping she's going to stay asleep while we talk, but she might not. She's been quite colicky."

"Don't worry. I did twins, remember? No single infant could possibly rival that. So, what can I get you, Tess?" He hangs a smile on his thin face. "Coffee? English breakfast tea? Cake? Cookies?"

"An Earl Gray would be lovely if they have it—any tea if not."

Alex walks over to the counter. His clothes drape from his shoulders. He looks diminished in all dimensions. Perhaps he is ill. She pushes this thought aside and sits down, sliding off Lily's woolly hat and easing herself out of her coat sleeves, one by one, keeping her movements smooth. Lily shifts but doesn't wake. At six o'clock it is dark outside, and the street is busy with people going home from shopping or meeting for early drinks.

The café is packed with Harvard students, many sitting alone with headphones, staring at their MacBooks. She pulls her phone out. There are still no messages. She spoke to Greg and Joe after they arrived in New Hampshire last night. Joe sounded breathless and hyper, telling her about the hot tub on a deck and all the snow—how the house was high up in the mountains, down a long, long road. "We're in the middle of nowhere! There's nobody here at all! It's like Narnia!" She heard the anxiety as well as the excitement in his voice.

"Greg will look after you," she said. "And you're going to have such a good time tomorrow—are you going tubing first or skiing?"

"We bought a snowsuit—it's red and black. And then tomorrow we have to get ski boots and skis fitted," he said. "We're not buying those; we're renting them. Then Greg's going to take me up really high in a ski lift."

She'd googled Greg's colleague's house. It looks extremely remote. It is down a mile-long track high in the White Mountains, and the nearest town is four miles away. There are hardly any other houses nearby. But it is five miles from a ski area, and on an autumnal Street View the colors looked stunning. It must be magical up there in the snow. She can see why Joe felt he'd arrived in Narnia.

She called them again this morning at breakfast, but there was no reply. Greg said they were going to head out early, and there is, she assumes, no cell phone reception on the ski slopes.

They will be fine. This will be good for the two of them. She has to get out of their way and allow them to bond. Nothing bad is going to happen.

Alex comes back with a pot of Earl Gray, a chocolate brownie, and a slice of carrot cake.

"They do great cakes here," he says. "My wife and I lived in Vienna for a year when we were first married, and we became pastry aficionados. When we moved back to Boston, we lived right here in Cambridge—she was doing her Master's in education at Harvard—and this was the only place that could equal the Viennese . . ." He trails off. His mouth sags as he pours the tea.

"How are things . . . with your wife?"

"Oh," he says, "you know, hell. We're in a custody battle right now. I've—well, I've taken a . . . well . . . I've taken a leave of absence from the firm to deal with it. I may have to sell my place in Marblehead to cover legal costs—thankfully, it's in my name, I inherited it from my mother—but, well, hey, we really don't need to talk about all that, do we?" He glances at the sling. "Six weeks already! Wow."

"Yes. She was born five weeks early, though; that's why she's still so small."

"Sure, and you have a son, too, right? How's he taking to his little sister?"

"Actually, Joe's been really good about her so far, fingers crossed. I was expecting jealousy, but I suppose with her being so much younger than he, she's not so much of a direct threat. But it's early days."

She realizes that Alex's hand, holding the teapot, is trembling. She straightens; there is no point in small talk when they are only here to discuss one thing. "OK," she says. "So, I wanted to let you know that I spoke to Greg, and he told me everything. Carlo Novak is Greg's cousin. I thought you'd want to know . . ."

Alex listens, intently, not touching his tea or cake, as she tells him the whole story. When she has finished, she waits for him to express surprise, perhaps throw back his head and laugh and tell her how relieved he is to have it all cleared up, but he does not. He picks up his cup and takes a sip, his eyes fixed on nothing.

"It's all there," she says, as if it is up to her to provide Alex with evidence. "I've even exchanged letters with a woman who knew Greg's Aunt Julianna, Carlo's mother. That's a very sad story. But, really, that's all I wanted to tell you: it all checks out."

"I know it does."

"Oh?" She puts down her cup. "You do? Right. OK. Well—sorry, are you saying you know everything I've just told you already?" It is not clear why he didn't interrupt her. "Did you know about the Philadelphia trial?"

He nods.

The straps of the BabyBjörn carrier are digging into her shoulders, but she can't undo them because she can't risk Lily waking up and yelling or needing to be fed. She suddenly feels sweaty, with Lily pressed against her like a hot-water bottle and the overheated, noisy café closing in.

"After we met, I did some research," Alex says. "A lot of research. I tried to contact you. I left you a voice mail, but you didn't call back, so I figured you didn't want to hear from me, and I left you alone."

"Yes, well, now I know everything, too." She bites into the carrot cake. The icing is sharp and gritty, and the cake tastes overwhelmingly of cinnamon. It forms a sticky, sweet lump in her throat. She takes a gulp of her tea, leaning forward and sideways so that she is not holding hot liquid over Lily's head.

"Tess," he says, "you aren't going to want to hear what I have to say."

She swallows hard, but the fistula of cake will not shift. She feels her breasts begin to tighten. The burning patch on one of them is a warning—she needs to latch Lily on really properly to head off a bout of mastitis, and she does not want to have to do that here, in front of Alex Kingman—all the grappling and maneuvering. Suddenly she regrets coming here to meet this man. She should have refused his invitation. They could just as easily have done this on email. The urge she briefly felt to get out of the house and do something different was a mistake.

"After we met, I remembered something very important." Alex's eyes are fixed on her face, his cheekbones sucked into the vortex of his waxy, overgrown beard. "The memory came at me out of the blue late one night when I was going through legal stuff—out of my subconscious, I guess. I met Carlo once, before the Florida spring break. Just one time, but I remember it quite clearly now."

"Oh, really?"

"It was at a college party, in a student house—it would be thirty years ago, but it's clear in my mind now. My brother and his friends were drunk, and they were kidding around about seeing double, because Carlo had showed up with this guy who looked almost identical to him, only younger, still in high school. Of course, now I know exactly who it was."

"Greg! You met Greg. Well, there you go. How funny." She feels relief, and then surprise at the relief. She had no idea that she harbored any residual doubts about Greg's story.

But Alex isn't smiling back.

"So you believe me now that Greg is Carlo's cousin," she says. "That's good."

Alex presses a hand flat on the tabletop and shakes his head. "I'm sorry, Tess, but I don't."

"But you just said—"

"The cousin Carlo brought to the party was not the man you're married to."

She is exhausted, lactating, hormonal, mildly feverish, and suddenly she feels an intense, almost physical irritation sweep across her skin. She is not going to be led to yet another crossroad in Alex's meandering mind. "Why are you saying this?"

"Carlo's identikit cousin was gay, Tess. He was definitely gay. I remembered that, because there was some trouble about it that night. Someone knew someone else from their hometown. He told everyone about this incident where Carlo's cousin and another local boy were caught together by a waterfall. It was a small-town scandal. There was hostility from some of the guys at the party after that. They were a bunch of unreconstructed Midwesterners, you know, and there was some nasty talk about AIDS and faggots, and it spilled quickly into physical aggression. I remember Carlo got very angry, very fast. I don't really remember what happened in the end, but the one thing I do recall, quite clearly, is that Carlo's cousin was gay."

"Oh, for God's sake!" She hears herself give a brittle, high laugh. "Are you trying to tell me that Greg is gay now, Alex? Because he really isn't. Carlo must have brought another cousin, or maybe not a cousin at all—a friend, an acquaintance. You said yourself it was thirty years ago. This is completely ridiculous." But as she says this, she remembers Sally's first email, her surprise that Greg had married.

Alex leans closer, shaking his head. She can smell tannin on his breath.

"You aren't hearing me, Tess. That's not what I'm saying." He lays his fingers on her forearm and presses, as if trying to push his message into her skin.

She whisks her arm away. "Then what *are* you saying?" It is possible that Alex is actually having a breakdown. She feels sorry for him, but clearly she never should have agreed to meet. This is the last thing she needs right now.

"Carlo Novak vanished, Tess. There's no trace of him after he left Penn Med."

"I know that. Greg thinks he committed suicide."

"His body was never found."

"Yes, we know that."

"Do you also know about the fire? And about Carlo's mother, Julianna—who drank herself to death?"

"How do you know all this?"

"I told you, I've done a lot of research lately. What do you think that kind of trauma would do to boys at that age? They both would have been pretty unstable by the time the trial was over, don't you think? When Greg was starting Harvard, what kind of a state would he have been in?"

"This isn't any of your business, Alex. I don't know what you're implying, but this is Greg's past, his private stuff, and I really don't think we should be talking about it."

She reaches around for her coat from the back of the chair. Lily wakes, turns her face up, her cheek flushed, nose poking up like a tiny button mushroom. The noises of the café, the folksy music, the voices all around them seem to intensify, as if someone has cranked up the volume.

"Wait—don't go, Tess, please. I checked the facts. Grzegor Gallo started Harvard at almost the exact time Carlo Novak dropped out of medical school."

"I know that! I just told you all this, and before you say anything, I've seen pictures of Greg at Harvard. I've seen his notes, his files, his certificates, so if you're about to try to tell me he wasn't there—"

"I'm not—"

"Good."

"But I don't think Carlo killed himself—"

"Oh, for God's sake. Are you trying to suggest that Greg killed his cousin? If you are, then this is beyond ridiculous. Greg's not a killer." Lily jerks, and her little body stiffens. "He loved his cousin!" She tries to stand up, but the table is pinning her in.

"Your husband is lying to you, Tess." Alex pushes his hair back. For a second she is transfixed by the wasted architecture of his face—the deep eye sockets, the sunken cheekbones. Lily writhes against the sling, opening her eyes wide.

He reaches into his satchel and pulls out a file, shuffling papers, laying them on the table. She looks at them. They are photocopies of old newspaper articles.

"You need to read these."

"What are they?"

"I had them sent to me from a local historical archive in Pennsylvania."

She is about to walk away, but a masthead leaps out: the *Robesville Eagle*. It is a black-and-white pixelated scan of the front page of the morning edition of the local paper, dominated by the image of a blazing building; there are fire trucks in the background, in the foreground a soot-streaked firefighter, pushing back his helmet.

She squints at the blurry print, speed-reading as she jiggles Lily.

Tragedy struck a Robesville family last night when a blaze broke out at the three-story home of local businessman Giovanni Gallo, 48, a highly respected member of our Robesville School Board. Randolph A. Smith Jr., Assistant Chief for the Robesville Fire Department, said someone ran to the station at 3:45 p.m. shouting that a house on Pleasant St. was burning. "I went out to take a look and saw flames lighting up the sky," said Assistant Chief Smith. "The house was fully engulfed by the time we got there."

When firefighters arrived, the fire had entered every room and wall space of 2201 Pleasant St., and smoke was pouring from all the windows. Intense heat made it impossible for any rescuers to enter the building. Firefighters from as far away as Marion Township and West River battled the flames, preventing them from spreading to neighboring houses.

She pushes the paper back to Alex. "I don't want to talk about this with you, Alex."

"Just read the whole thing." Alex pushes it back to her. "Please, Tess. Read it."

Neighbors gathered, and by 5 p.m. firefighters were able to use ladders to access the roof and break out the loft windows using long poles so they could then drag more hoses into the building.

"We could see right away, the family had not survived," said Chief Smith.

Mr. Gallo and his wife, Natalia Gallo, 47, both died. It is believed that the couple's niece, six-year-old Claudia Novak, also perished in the blaze, though this is still to be confirmed.

For a moment her legs feel weak. She rereads the sentence, taking in the words but not the meaning. It makes no sense. There was no little girl in the house that day.

She forces herself to keep reading.

The Gallos' surviving son, Grzegor, 16, a junior at Robesville High, was not home at the time of the blaze. The boy had returned to Pleasant St. at 5 p.m., when the building was all but destroyed. His cousin, Carlo Novak, 19, a college student who was home for the summer, had arrived at the house at 4:00 p.m. Novak attempted get into the burning building, but neighbors pulled him out and restrained him.

"I smelled smoke and came right out," said Evelyn King, 78, whose next-door residence was undamaged. "There were flames pouring out the downstairs windows. I called to my son, and he ran to the fire station. Then we saw Carlo trying to get in to help his relatives—the sight of him screaming as the menfolk pulled him back will stay with me forever. His face was black with ash. I've never heard a noise like that come from a man before. God help them all."

Grzegor Gallo is currently being cared for by Julianna Novak, 44, at her apartment on Falls Rd.

Pleasant St. is still closed, and all traffic is being diverted via Damson and Pine.

She pushes the paper back at Alex. She is suddenly very cold and shaky.

Alex slides another page toward her.

It is another article, written a week after the fire. There is a family portrait, in grainy black-and-white. She recognizes Giovanni and Natalia and a boy who looks like Greg but, also, somehow, not. He has an innocent smile, hair that is lighter, brushed into a side parting, and his face is thin and pale. Beneath this is a photo of a beautiful little girl with dark curls and huge dark eyes. She reads the caption.

Claudia Novak, 6, perished in the Pleasant St. fire.

The page is shaking in her hand, and she can feel Alex's eyes on her face as she turns to the next article.

Robesville Fire Chief calls for "Vigilance in the Home"

The cause of the tragic Pleasant St. fire that claimed the lives of Mr. and Mrs. Giovanni Gallo and their six-year-old niece, Claudia Novak, last Saturday was a pot of food left on a kitchen stove, said Fire Chief Michael Dooley.

"This tragic fire is a lesson to us all. An untended pot on the stove caught fire, and the flames quickly spread through the residence. We must all be vigilant in our homes," said Chief Dooley. "It is matter of life and death."

"Mr. Gallo was a pillar of our community," said Mayor Randall Gerber. "He and his wife and that little child they took under their wing will be greatly missed. This is a terrible loss."

A neighbor, Doncilla Henderson, 23, had kind words to say about the family. "My mother worked with Mrs. Gallo at Woolco," Henderson said. "She was a great lady; she'd do anything for anyone. She and the baby shouldn't even have been there—usually at that time Mrs. Gallo would be fetching her from day care. But I guess she didn't go that day."

The little girl's mother, Julianna Novak, and brother, Carlo Novak, 19, were too distraught to comment.

The Gallos' only son, Grzegor, 16, is a junior at Robesville High. "Grzegor is a quiet, studious, straight-A student. He is one of the best academics we've ever had here at Robesville High," said Principal Jim Swain. "He's had some social challenges lately, and he's a very sensitive boy, but he has his whole life ahead of him still. We are all praying for him."

"Our prayers are with the family," said Mayor Gerber. "This is a tragedy for our whole town."

A memorial service will be held at St. Savior Catholic Church, 10:00 a.m., Saturday, June 28.

There is another photograph below the piece, a formal school portrait of a boy seated sideways, looking into the camera. At first she sees only Greg's young face again, chubbier, softer around the jaw. But something is not quite right about it. She looks more closely. The features are like Greg's, but the eyes, the expression, the feel of him, aren't right. The caption says his name, but this boy is not Greg.

She feels as if a cold hand is squeezing her chest, stopping her from breathing. She shoves the papers back across the table. She has to get out of this café, away from the photographs of the boy with Greg's name, and the other child, Claudia, the lost, dark-eyed girl. She has to get away from them and from Alex. She grabs her bag and coat, knocking the cup of tea so that it sloshes into the saucer.

Alex watches her, dully, as if exhausted.

She pushes out of the café, bumping hard against a woman who is coming through the door, making her spin like a bowling pin and cry out angrily—and then she is standing in the street, sucking in gulps of freezing air. Lily, pinned to her chest, straightens her limbs and lets out a thin, high cry of alarm.

She pushes her way along the crowded street, away from the café, away from Alex and his papers. She can't make sense of anything. The sky is murky, the night smothering the city like a dirty, coarse blanket. She feels as if she has dreamed this encounter with Alex Kingman—as if she is sick, unhinged, feverish. She starts to run then, pushing her way through a group of shrieking teenagers, past a woman carrying several paper bags of groceries—faces turn, curious, irritated, as she shoves her way into the side street where she has parked the car.

With one arm she protects Lily as she fumbles in her pocket for her keys and beeps the locks. Lily's face is like a small, crumpled flower. She opens her mouth wide and lets out a long, plaintive cry.

Tess pulls out her phone and calls Greg's number. It goes straight to voice mail. She dials it again as she struggles to undo the sling and maneuver Lily into the car seat, strap her in. She dials again as she gets herself into the driver's seat, starts the engine.

Greg is not picking up.

Panic begins to spread through her chest. She sees the teenage boy's face again, his brushed hair, his gentle expression. That one photograph told her what Alex might never have made her believe. And she understands, at last, what this is.

She is not married to Greg. She is married to Carlo.

She could call the police, but what could she say to them? That she believes her husband stole his cousin's identity? That he is an impostor? They would think she was insane. They would keep her in a room for hours and hours asking her questions, checking facts, while all the time Joe is a hundred and fifty miles away in the mountains with a man she does not really know.

It will be faster to go up there and bring Joe home herself. Once she has him safely home, she will deal with everything else. All that matters now is getting to Joe.

She scrolls through emails, finds the White Mountains address, jabs it into the GPS. The car has snow tires; it can cope with the mountains. There are blankets in the back—she always has some in the car—and a snow kit, a shovel, a first-aid box. She has enough diapers and wipes, a couple of spare outfits for Lily, her phone. She can get to New Hampshire. She has to, right now.

The roads are crowded with people returning from shopping expeditions and Saturdays out, heading off for dinner, for cocktails, to concerts, movies, and the theater. The GPS says she should make it to the White Mountains by 9:30 p.m. but in this traffic, who knows how long it will take even to get out to the freeway?

The face of the dead little girl looms in her mind again, those half-moon Novak eyes and dark curls. Claudia is Julianna's other child. The child that Natalia and Giovanni took in. Or—if Sally MacManus is to be believed—just took.

Claudia was Carlo's baby sister, and Carlo is . . . Carlo is Greg. She braces her arms on the steering wheel, feeling as if it might come off in her hands, leaving the car to careen into the street. He had a sister. Julianna wasn't his aunt; she was his mother. No wonder he had to stop when he remembered her songs, her bookishness. She feels as if she is on a mountain, watching this avalanche of lies boom down toward her, knowing that in a moment they will shatter her bones and suffocate her.

He didn't lose his parents in the fire; he lost his baby sister, his uncle, and his aunt. Could she have gotten this wrong? Maybe she is interpreting this the wrong way—there are so many stories and half stories: Alex's, Greg's, Sally's. It is impossible to know what is true anymore.

But, no. Alex was clear that years ago he met Grzegor, the gay cousin—the boy in the photo with the neat hair. And he recognized Carlo on the beach. Greg, her Greg, is Carlo Novak.

The garbled references in Sally's last email begin to make sense. Raped by Giovanni, Julianna became pregnant with Claudia, and then the Gallos took her away. No wonder Julianna was going out of her mind. A widow, a nonconformist, damaged by an abusive marriage; a drinker, possibly in a lesbian relationship with Sally MacManus—she would have been powerless against the Gallos, who had a whole disapproving community behind them. She would have been ostracized and overruled. Perhaps setting fire to the Gallos' house was not an act of madness but of despair and fury, a protest aimed at the man who raped her, then took her child. Sally said "she" didn't know "the others" were in there. The neighbor in the news article confirmed that Natalia should have been collecting Claudia from day care. Maybe Julianna thought only Giovanni was home. If Giovanni was Claudia's father, then Claudia was the biological sister of both boys. It is too confusing—there is too much to take in or sort out, too many half-answered questions.

The only thing she knows for sure is that Greg has lied. About everything. And right now he is over a hundred miles away up a mountain, with Joe.

Lily's cries are hoarse now, hicuppy, desperate. She is going to have to stop and feed her before they carry on. The traffic isn't moving anyway; in ten minutes she has only traveled three blocks. The soreness in her breast is becoming acute. She probes the area with her fingers, and the pain makes her dizzy, as if a hot blade has slid into her flesh. She is going to have to pull over and breast-feed before they go any farther.

She must stay calm. She must not panic. None of this will get any easier if she panics.

She thinks about Joe in the wilderness with a man who—but she can't think about that. She is not sure how she could have allowed this to happen.

She pulls into a side street, gets out in the freezing air, and undoes Lily's straps with shaking hands, bringing her into the front seat. Lily is so distraught now that for a moment they simply wrestle. Lily's tiny arms and legs flail; she jerks her head away from the breast, too deranged to know that what she needs is right in front of her.

Tess feels the tears burning behind her eyes. "Just eat!" she barks. Lily opens her mouth, shocked, and Tess shoves her breast deep into it. For a second Lily's eyes bulge, her limbs go completely rigid, but then her jaw clamps down, and she gives a suck—just one—a huge and painful, burning bite, and then again, a faster suckling, and suddenly she is gulping and pulling, almost choking to feed.

Tess feels her milk drop. It burns through the inflamed duct, and after a minute or two of sickening pain she feels a creeping relief as Lily's frantic sucking lengthens into smoother, deeper movements, milk washing over the inflammation, pushing it aside, soothing it.

Her ears ring; her mouth is dry. She feels feverish and odd. She looks down at the tiny, red, panicky face, Lily's big brown eyes bulging over the mouthful of breast.

"I'm so sorry, my poor little darling, I'm so sorry." She strokes the damp hair off Lily's forehead. She tries to breathe slowly. She looks at her phone. She has called Greg seven times in the last half hour.

She calls Nell's number and listens to it ring. It is midnight in England. Nell will be asleep. But what could she do anyway? It would be impossible to explain what she now knows. She is on her own. Nobody is going to sort this out for her.

He must have kept up the lie until he believed it himself. That is the only way it could have worked. Somehow, over the years, he has turned himself into Greg—his own version of Greg. This is why he hid Sarah Banister's true identity. This is why he didn't want a baby. A baby would only complicate this terrible deceit. He would have to lie to his own child about who she was.

But he loves Lily. She knows it. She has witnessed his love, has felt it. And he loves her, too. That is real. Or is it? She has no idea what is real anymore. How much longer would he have lied? She has no idea what he is capable of.

And he has Joe.

The key to the next two hours on a busy northbound freeway is not to think. She just has to get herself and Lily safely to New Hampshire and get Joe back.

* * *

The I-95 north is bumper to bumper. She keeps to the slower lanes, pressing on across the state line. A sign flashes past.

New Hampshire: Live Free or Die

She can't stop thinking about the little girl trapped in the house when she should have been at day care. Then she realizes that Natalia is not Lily's grandmother; she is Lily's great-aunt. Julianna is the grandmother. A woman who might have lit the fire that killed her brother-in-law, her sister, and her own baby girl.

It is too much, too awful. She pushes them all into the back of her brain. If she keeps thinking about them, she will lose it. She just has to focus on getting Joe back. She turns on the radio—a report of a car crash somewhere in Massachusetts; a family of four has been run off the road by a truck and killed. She switches it off again and glances back at Lily. She is sleeping, chin on her chest, hat skewed over one eye.

The traffic has thinned, and snow is falling now, rapid, thin flakes that melt on the windshield. There is snow on the trees and piled up alongside the freeway. She obeys the GPS directions, coming off the freeway when it tells her to, passing through small towns with spangled lights and lit-up storefronts, then pushing onward, higher into dark, deserted, densely forested roads.

All she can see now is the patch of road ahead of the car, illuminated by the headlights. The snow is coming down more heavily, and although the roads have been cleared and gritted—sanded, dammit—earlier in the day, the snow is beginning to accumulate, muffling the tires and giving a strange, unreliable feel to the car's steering mechanism. She is glad of the snow tires and the knowledge that she has a shovel, blankets. The windshield wipers clunk as they push the flakes aside. The tires thud beneath the wheeze of the Volvo's heating system.

The headlights catch the occasional flash of a snow-capped mailbox, reflective numbers looming from the darkness and vanishing again. Skeletal trees crowd the roadside, tall, patient figures stepping out of a dream, punctuated only by the occasional vast evergreen, taller than the cypress at home, dense and solid and black at its core.

She turns off this road onto a single track that is has no signposts. The trees press closer, and as she rounds a bend, her headlights catch yellow eyes—a deer? a fox?—that pop, then vanish into the darkness. The Volvo tires thrum against the packed snow, and she prays that nothing will leap out, forcing her to brake, because she knows she cannot control the car, and they are high in the mountains now; this road could be clinging to a sheer drop. But she keeps going, hunched over the wheel, thinking of nothing but driving—squinting through the snow, which is falling so earnestly, so determinedly, coating the windshield, piling up as the wipers shove it aside.

The mechanical voice of the GPS breaks the silence, and she turns again, off this track: blackness.

You have reached your destination.

But there is nothing here.

She creeps along the track. All she can see are snow-laden branches, but then her headlights round a corner, and she is in a circular driveway— and there is Greg's car in front of a tall wooden house. Its windows are lit up, and snowy steps lead to a garlanded front door. She comes to a halt and turns off the engine, and for a second she just sits there, dazed, in the silence as the heater clicks off and her heart thumps against her breastbone. It is almost ten-thirty. But she is here. She has made it.

She fumbles out of the car and crunches around to the backseat, bundling the sleeping Lily into a blanket. Somewhere, an animal shrieks. The air is bitterly cold, and the smell of fresh snow explodes in her head. Snowflakes patter down onto her hair and face as she tucks the blanket tightly around Lily and climbs the slippery steps to the front door.

Before she can raise a hand to knock, it opens, and he is there, peering over his reading glasses, wearing a black polo sweater, jogging shoes, thick wool socks. For a second she feels relief at the sight of him—she wants to sink into his arms. Then, of course, she doesn't.

His eyes are wide. "Tess? What the—what on earth are you doing here? How did you—oh, my God—here, come in, come inside!" He opens the door wider, spreads his arms, glancing behind her as if checking to be sure that nobody else is with her. She pushes past him, clutching Lily tightly against her chest.

"Where's Joe?"

"Joe?" He stands very still. "He's upstairs, asleep."

"Where? Where is he? Which room? I need to see him."

"Tess—"

"Take me to Joe," she growls.

"What is this?" He sounds less confident.

She shakes his hand off her arm and looks around the high-ceilinged, cedar-paneled living room. It smells of woodsmoke. Warmth pulses from a wood-burning stove. There are leather sofas, thick neutral rugs, and tartan blankets draped on armchairs. His laptop is open on a coffee table, a glass of whiskey beside it. Jazz filters from speakers. The windows are black.

"Where is he?" Her voice rises.

"Tess, honey, give me Lily."

She ignores him and makes for the wooden stairs. Her boots slap as she runs up the steps. He is behind her.

"Where is he?" She feels panic fizzing through her veins as she gets to the landing. He puts his hands on her shoulders, but she jerks away.

There are several doors leading off the long corridor. She lurches through one: a wood-paneled room with a luxurious bed covered in a rich blue quilt. There is a painting on one wall of a lake, and a Native American rug across the polished floor.

"Wrong one," he says smoothly. There is a chill to his voice now. "He's here, look, down here." He walks ahead and pushes another door open.

There is a nightlight, Joe's backpack is on the floor by a single bed, and his shape is there, under a striped quilt. She throws herself onto her knees by the bed, pinning Lily to her with one arm. Joe's eyes are closed. He is on his side, hair mussed. He looks pallid. She touches his shoulder, but he doesn't move. He doesn't even twitch, and she feels a moment of terror as she reaches out her fingers for his cheek.

It is warm.

"Joey?" she whispers. "Joey? It's me."

His eyelids flicker.

"Sweetheart. It's me. It's Mum. Are you OK?"

He blinks and frowns, trying to focus on her face.

"Love, Joey, are you OK?"

He squints at her, as if he thinks he is dreaming. "Mum?"

"It's me. I'm here now."

He struggles to sit up, then folds his arms around her neck, squashing Lily between them, burying his face in her hair. She wraps her one free arm around him, wanting to squeeze him tighter than she ever has in his life, breathing in his sleeping-boy smell.

"Are you OK?" Her voice wobbles. Lily wriggles her limbs but doesn't cry.

Joe nods, his face still in her neck.

"I'm here." She forces herself to sound far, far calmer than she feels. "Lily and I missed you so much, we decided to come and get you."

"Hello, Lily," he mutters.

Lily squirms between them. Tess pulls back, gently, and Joe lies down again, putting his head on his pillow, eyelids drooping. She tucks the duvet over his shoulder, pressing it with her hand and feeling sudden, hot tears of relief fill her eyes.

Then she turns. Greg is leaning against the doorframe. With the light behind him she can't see his face, but when he speaks, his voice is flat, emotionless, and somehow mechanical.

"What is this, Tess?" he asks. "What are you doing?"

CHAPTER TWENTY-FIVE

She has to get out of Joe's room if she is going to confront her husband, but he is blocking the door. For a moment she is at a loss. She has been so focused on getting here that she has not thought beyond her arrival. There is no mental map that will get her out of this situation.

She presses Lily against her chest, folding both arms over her, swaying softly—her daughter mustn't wake up. With Greg blocking the doorway, Lily in her arms, and Joe asleep behind her, she realizes that she'll only be able to leave this house if Greg lets her.

She steps forward. "I'm taking Joe home."

His face is neutral. "Why?"

"You know," she says. "You know why."

"Do I?"

She steps, as assertively as possible, toward him, but he doesn't move. She stops. "We can't talk here."

He glances at Joe's bed, then back at her. Then he turns. She follows him out of the room and into the corridor.

There is a floor-to-ceiling window at the end, and she can see Greg's broad back reflected in it. He has taken off his reading glasses, and his eyes are fixed on her face. He is unshaven. His shoulders are powerful in the black sweater. Her arms tighten around Lily, whose nose is nestled into her neck.

"What's going on?" he asks in that same oddly detached voice.

"Downstairs." She nods at the stairs behind him. "Not here."

He hesitates, then turns and walks slowly away from her, along the corridor. She follows him down the stairs.

The wood-burning stove glows a deep, fleshy red behind him.

"I can't believe you drove all the way up here."

"You weren't answering your phone."

"But I've emailed you a few times this evening about it; I knew you'd be worried. I dropped my cell on the mountain today; it's somewhere out there on a ski slope."

She shakes her head. Everything he says feels like a lie. But she hasn't checked her emails all day.

"I can see why you panicked." His voice is mechanical. She remembers him telling her once that the biggest compliment a colleague could pay him after surgery was: "You're a machine, Gallo." He sounds like one now. "Why don't you give Lily to me?" he says. "Sit down, and I'll make you something to eat. Did you eat yet?"

She steps away from him. "I don't want anything to eat. I just want to take Joe home."

"OK." He nods. "But it's a long drive, and it's late. At least have a coffee before you go."

He turns, stiffly, and goes across the room to the galley kitchen. She watches him fill the kettle and put it on a stove, then reach for a whiskey bottle and pour a large measure into a crystal glass. He comes back, holding the whiskey out to her. She shakes her head.

He takes a swig from it himself, then walks across the living room to stand with his back to the stove. She wonders whether she could get upstairs, grab Joe, and get back down and into the car without him trying to stop her. She has no idea, because she cannot fathom what is going on behind his impassive face.

It strikes her, then, how isolated they are in this wooden house, hemmed in by miles of New England forest, muffled by snow. She does not know what he might do if she tries to take the children away in the middle of the night. He cradles the glass, watching her, waiting.

Her arms are weak from holding Lily so tightly. She looks down at her baby. Lily's cheeks are pink, her mouth slightly open, her dark hair in waves around her cherubic face. She thinks again of Claudia— the sweet little child with dark curls and brown eyes, just like Lily. She feels herself harden.

Greg asks, "How did you find this place? It's hard enough to find in daylight."

"GPS."

He shakes his head.

She says nothing.

"Are you angry at me?" he asks. "I just assumed you'd check your emails. You always check your emails."

On the bookshelf next to him she sees a silver-framed photo of a family: a handsome, gray-haired man about Greg's age, with a blond wife holding a baby, and two small blond children grinning photogenically. The man looks older than his wife—a second family, perhaps. Greg follows her gaze. "That's Ben. This is his house."

Lily squirms against her neck and then settles again. It is three hours—more—since she last fed. Her diaper is heavy.

"She must need a change," Greg says, as if he is listening to her thoughts. "Did you bring a diaper bag? Is it in the car? Give me the keys, and I'll go get it."

No way is she giving Greg the car key.

"She's fine."

She needs to get the children out of here. She wills Lily not to wake up. She is in her favorite position—nose in the crook of Tess's neck, belly pressed against her shoulder.

She looks up and realizes that Greg has moved closer. Her legs suddenly feel odd. She is breathing too fast.

"Actually," she says, "I would like something to eat. What have you got?"

"Bread? Brie? Soup?"

"Yes, please. And a coffee."

He puts his whiskey glass down and walks steadily back toward the kitchen.

But the kitchen is not far enough away that she can run upstairs for Joe and get out without Greg stopping her.

The only way to do this is to be direct and calm.

He is getting out bread, unwrapping the cheese, reaching for a knife in the knife block.

"I'm going to go upstairs to get Joe now," she says, loudly. "I'm going to take him back to Boston. We can't do this in front of Lily and Joe."

He stops what he's doing and turns to face her, knife in hand. "Do what?"

"You know."

"Do I?" He puts down the knife and steps toward the kitchen doorway. "What's this about, Tess?"

"You know what this is about."

"Tell me anyway." He stops.

"OK." She looks him in the eye. "You've lied to me. You aren't Greg Gallo. I know who you are."

He looks back at her, intensely. And then something happens that she wasn't expecting. The whole structure of his face collapses. It is as if the muscles and tendons and bones have all been severed. He turns and goes back to the sink; he bends over, gags, and she hears the contents of his stomach splatter against the ceramic. She smells bile. He throws up twice more.

Then, still not looking at her, he turns on the tap and opens the back door. She feels a blast of cold air as he steps outside. She sees him take a huge breath, his shoulders rising.

Grabbing Lily with both arms, she runs for the stairs. She takes them two at a time, pressing Lily's head into her neck, and hurtles along the corridor to Joe's open door.

"Joey." She shakes him. "Wake up. Wake up. We're going to go back home tonight. Right now. We're going. Get up, love."

Lily whimpers and wriggles.

"Joey!"

He sits up, his hair sticking up. His eyes are startled.

"Sweetie, you need to get into the car, right now." She tugs at his arm. "Come on." Lily begins a thin, high, panicky cry.

"Lily's crying." Joe blinks.

"Joey, get up, love."

Lily takes a rasping breath in, and, in the pause, Tess hears footsteps coming up the stairs.

"Get up, Joe! Now!"

He gets out of bed. His feet are bone white and bare. She grabs a blanket from the bottom of the bed and wraps it around his shoulders. There is no time for clothes. "Come on. The blanket will keep you warm. You can sleep in the car, you and Lily, but we have to go now. OK? Right now."

Joe's mouth wobbles, and he looks up at her. "Why?"

"It's OK, love, don't worry, don't worry—we just need to go get in the car, OK? I'll explain everything when we're in the car, OK?"

Then she feels his shape behind her, blocking the light from the hall.

She puts an arm around Joe and pins Lily to her body.

Greg is watching her. His face is whiter even than Joe's feet.

She lifts her chin. "Get out of my way."

Very slowly, he steps aside.

She sweeps the children past him and down the corridor.

"It's OK," she says to Joe. "Just come with me, and I'll tell you all about it a minute, but for now we just need to go to the car."

"Tess!" He is coming behind them. "Stop. Please—"

Lily starts to cry properly then, her mouth opening, her lungs stretching.

Tess whisks Joe to the bottom of the stairs without looking back and wrenches the front door open. She can't think about his bare feet on the snow—she beeps the locks and gets him down the steps and into the car first, then presses his screaming baby sister into her seat next to him. Her hands are shaking as she does up Lily's straps and grabs Joe's seat belt.

"Everything's OK, sweetie. Do your belt up—I'm just going to say good-bye to . . . to Greg . . . then we'll be on our way."

Joe turns to his sister. She hears him say, "It's all right, Lily. I'll look after you. Don't be scared."

"Good boy." She touches his head, then slams the door and clicks the locks, securing them both in the car. She is breathing fast.

Greg is standing on the snowy steps. He has not made any attempt to follow her to the car. In the yellowish light his face looks sickly, his eyes hollow. For a moment she almost feels worried about leaving him, but then, of course, she doesn't.

As she opens the driver's door, she feels a sudden anger roar through her body. "How could you do this?" she bellows. "How could you lie to me like this? Who the hell are you? What sort of a monster are you?"

He covers his face with his hands. She can see his fingers pressing into his eyeballs. She glances down at the car. Joe's face is at the window. The forest around the house is completely still. Beyond Lily's cries, she can hear the patter of snow on the Volvo roof and on the branches and mountain slopes that stretch out for miles around them. Greg drops his hands then and takes a step down.

She beeps the locks, gets into the car, locks the doors again, and turns the engine on, feeling the tires grip as she moves forward. As she passes the house, her headlights briefly illuminate Greg's stricken face. He is hollowed out; he looks half-dead.

CHAPTER TWENTY-SIX

It is two in the morning by the time she gets off the freeway. She had to stop at a gas station to feed Lily, and she gave Joe hot chocolate and held him close against her with her one free arm as Lily fed. His eyes were dazed, and he didn't ask what they were doing, and that seemed far worse than if he'd cried or thrown a tantrum or simply demanded to know what was going on.

Both Lily and Joe are asleep in the back of the car as she pulls up outside the house. She leaves the car in the street and runs up the icy path. In the dim light the house looks wearily welcoming. The skewed brickwork seems like a touching quirk, the porch a solid shelter from the freezing January wind. She unlocks the door and runs through the rooms, grabbing a carryall and throwing toiletries into it—diapers, wipes, onesies, a few of Joe's clothes, his teddy, the iPad, some of her own underwear, a sweater, jeans, her laptop, a phone charger, her passport, Joe's. But Lily, of course, does not have a passport. She can't think about that.

At three in the morning, with Joe asleep in the hotel double bed and Lily fed, cleaned, and tucked up in a travel basinet, she calls Nell.

"We're downtown now," she says, when she has explained everything that has happened. "We're in the Marriott."

"Oh, Tess." Nell's voice wavers. "My God, I'm so sorry—this is horrific. This is so much worse than anything I ever imagined could be going on. I'm so sorry." She can hear the twins bickering in the background, getting ready for school.

"It's OK."

"Of course it isn't OK."

"I know, you're right. It's not OK at all." She feels her throat tighten. But she isn't going to cry again. She won't allow herself to do that. She glances at Joe and Lily. She cannot fall apart. It is just not an option.

"So you didn't talk to him?"

"I had Joe and Lily, and I had to get out of that house."

"No, you were absolutely right. You did the right thing."

"I don't know how to do this, Nell. I feel like calling the police, having him locked up."

"Just don't do anything in the condition you're in, OK? What he's done is unforgivable, but you don't know the whole story yet. You're the strongest, bravest person I know, and there's something in him that you fell in love with, and that's what you have to cling to right now."

"He's a liar—he's monstrous."

"He's lied on a grand scale—my God, he has—but I don't think you could have fallen in love with him if he was truly monstrous."

She tries to consider this—just how duped could she have been?—but she can't straighten it out in her mind; she can't even work out what she feels. Shock, mainly. Disbelief. It is a vertiginous sensation, as if she is standing on a precipice staring into nothingness, knowing she is about to fall but not knowing how far the fall will be, or how hard.

"I don't know what to do."

"You have to somehow have faith that, while he's obviously made some catastrophic mistakes, he isn't an evil person."

"I don't know who he is."

"Listen, I'm going to come to Boston. I can cancel things. I can get a flight tomorrow."

"No! Don't. You haven't got any money."

"I don't care about that. You can't be on your own there."

"I'm not on my own. I'm with Joe and Lily." She realizes that, in fact, the last thing she wants is Nell flying over here. She cannot handle the extra responsibility of Nell's concern, her horror, her protectiveness. If Nell came, she then might, actually, just fall apart. "I don't want you to come. I need to do this on my own."

"But—"

"I mean it, Nell."

"OK. But if you change your mind, I'll get on a plane."

"I won't."

"Fine. So, I think what you have to do, when you're ready, is hear what he has to say."

After they have talked some more and agreed to talk again later, she hangs up. But there is no way she can sleep. She paces the room, then gets back on the bed and opens her emails. There are four from him. Even the sight of his name—the lie of it—makes her feel sick again. She forces herself to open the emails anyway.

The first three are explanations—increasingly apologetic—for the lost phone and lack of communication. There is an attachment on one, a picture of Joe, beaming, on skis. She feels a flash of pain—for Joe. He has done this to Joe, too.

The fourth is longer, written this evening while she was on the road.

She gets up, finds a bottle of red wine in the minibar, pours it into a glass, and takes it, along with her laptop, back to the bed. She props herself up with pillows, takes a swig of the wine, and starts to read.

Tonight everything fell apart, as I think I always knew it had to. I cannot tell you how many times I've wanted to tell you the truth about myself, my background, what led me to this situation. I've begun to tell you countless times, and I've always had a good reason to stop, but the bottom line is cowardice: I was afraid I'd lose you. And now I think I have. If you will let me, I'd like to tell you the full truth, so you can at least understand why I did what I did. I'll drive back to Boston tomorrow. You must stay in the house with the children; I can stay in a hospital apartment for now. If you could get Sandra's nanny to look after Lily and Joe just for a couple of hours tomorrow, then we could meet. I don't want to do this over the phone or email. I know you won't want to meet in the house, so I will wait for you by the ice rink at Boston Common tomorrow at noon. If you'd rather meet somewhere else, or at another time, just let me know, and I will be there.

I love you so much, Tess, and I am so sorry for hurting you and Joe and Lily like this. I love the three of you more than you can possibly know.

She rereads the email, then deletes it. As she stares at her in-box, a message sent before Greg's catches her eye. It is from Sally MacManus. She opens it, hoping that it might contain something that will illuminate this mess.

But it is just a few lines.

Dear Ms. Harding,

I regret to inform you that Sally MacManus passed away peacefully late Friday night. I am going through her emails, informing those with whom she has corresponded. The funeral will be close family and friends only, but details of memorial arrangements are on Sally's website.

I am very sorry to give you this sad news.

Yours truly,
Edna Santiago (assistant to Ms. MacManus)

CHAPTER TWENTY-SEVEN

He is standing by the ice-rink fence. She spots his dark ski jacket first, and his gray scarf, his tall, straight, shoulders-back posture, and she has the urge to run to him and feel his arms fold around her again. But then the feeling drains away. She walks up the frosted path across the Common toward the rink, digging her hands into her pockets and hunching against the raw wind that sweeps across the snow-scattered grass.

The rink is full on this busy, clear-skied Sunday. Couples skate hand in hand, parents hold on to their wobbling children, friends jostle and laugh, while a few confident skaters weave effortlessly through the pack, their bodies still and graceful, as if they are moving in a different time dimension.

She reaches him, taps his arm, and stands back.

"Oh, thank God you came." His face floods with relief. "I wasn't sure you would."

They look at each other, dazed by what has happened to them. She can see that he hasn't slept, and she knows that he will see the same in her.

"Where are Lily and Joe?"

"Delia has them. I'm parked under the Common. I have less than an hour." She looks at her watch but doesn't see the hands.

"Are they OK?"

"Yes, they're fine."

"What have you told Joe?"

"Nothing, really. I have no idea what to tell him."

"Tess—" He reaches out to her, but she flinches, and he lets his hand drop to his side. "I'm so sorry."

"Just tell me what I need to know."

"I'm not sure how much you've worked out already . . ."

"Then start at the beginning."

"You know who I am?"

"I know your real name is Carlo Novak."

He nods. "Well, the things you already know about Carlo—me—are true."

"Everything?"

"Yes. My father died in a car accident when I was four years old, and my mother was . . . unstable. She grew gradually worse over time. Growing up, I spent a lot of time with my aunt and uncle and cousin, Grzegor." He swallows.

"You had a sister. Don't leave that out."

"I was about to . . . I had a sister. Yes, I had a sister named Claudia." His mouth spasms, and he grips the fence. "I was thirteen years old when she was born. I don't know who her father was—my mother would never tell anyone. But Claudia was, like, this angel for me. She was . . . I loved her more than I can possibly describe to you." His voice wavers again, and for a terrible moment she thinks that he might break down. She knows she won't be able to handle that. If he does, then she will have to walk away.

But he gathers himself, staring for a moment at the skaters. Then he looks back at her again. His voice is flatter, as if he has managed to distance himself, just slightly, from what he has to tell her.

"I did my best to take care of Claudia when my mother couldn't, but I was just a kid, really, and I had to go to school every day. My aunt and uncle couldn't have any more children after Grzegor. They took Claudia to live with them when she was two."

"And your mother just let them?"

"No. God, no. She fought them, but ultimately she was powerless. My uncle threatened to involve the authorities and have her declared an unfit mother, and it wasn't an idle threat. She knew if he did that, she'd lose what access she did have to Claudia, and she might lose me, too."

He stops talking. His eyes search hers. "I wanted to tell you this, Tess. I almost told you, so many times. You have no idea . . ."

"But you didn't."

The sound of skates biting into the ice, the voices, the smell of hot dogs, and the dull hubbub of the city seem to recede for a moment, and it is just the two of them, looking at each other.

She feels the knot in her chest harden, and she looks back at the skaters. "Tell me about your cousin," she says. She can't bear to say the name. She can't bear to look at him.

"OK." She hears him suck in air. "Grzegor was three years younger than me. We were really close; I spent a lot of time at their house. I guess I wanted to be with Claudia. My cousin was gay, and, growing up in that town, I was the only person he could talk to about it. Being openly gay at our high school was basically unthinkable. And then, when he was sixteen, something very bad happened. It was my fault. I did something, and it had . . . it had unspeakable repercussions."

She turns and makes herself look at him again. "What did you do?" She is not sure that she can bear to hear any more confessions, but she knows she has to.

He folds both hands tightly over the fence as if it is the only thing that will keep him upright. "OK. It was the summer after my first year of college. I'd gone back to Robesville because of Claudia—by that time my mother was a mess; she was broken, really, drinking pretty heavily. I was nineteen, and I got a summer job, but I was mostly staying with the Gallos, spending as much time as I could with my sister, who was the most gorgeous six-year-old by then. Natalia was always welcoming, but I knew Giovanni didn't want me in the house. I probably wasn't the easiest person to be around."

"What did you do?" she asks grimly.

"Grzegor and I had a big fight. I honestly don't know how it started—it was about Giovanni and me, I think—but it escalated. He said some things that I now know weren't true, but at the time they triggered something pretty dark in me—"

"What things?" She is not going to let him gloss over any details.

"He said that I was harming Claudia by coming back. He said Claudia didn't want me there; she thought of him as her brother, not me. It hurt me deeply, and I did something I'm very, very ashamed of. Grzegor had told me about a boy he'd been secretly seeing—the two of them had been going up to one of the waterfalls. After our fight, I went storming out of the house, and I bumped into some guys I'd known back in high school. We got drunk, and I told them about my cousin. They went up to the falls the next day."

She dimly remembers Alex Kingman saying something about a small-town scandal. She can see the agony on Greg's face as he continues, but she feels nothing for him, no compassion, just numbness.

"It had devastating effect on the family. Giovanni couldn't handle it. He was angry, openly disgusted, ashamed, mortified—it was nasty. Natalia, I think, already knew about Grzegor's sexuality, but she was furious with me for what I'd done, really bitter about it. Claudia didn't understand what was happening, but I'm sure she knew everyone was mad at me, and I wasn't able to see her to explain, because I wasn't allowed in the house. Grzegor was in a terrible state. He was in a gifted-student summer program at the high school, and things were unbearable for him."

"This was the summer of the fire, wasn't it?"

Greg nods. "It was just a few days later. Giovanni was home sick for the first time ever, in my memory. I can only guess that they were both so upset, they kept Claudia home, too, that day, and they were so distracted, they left a pot on the stove, and it caught fire. I was effectively responsible. My actions led them being home, in that state, that day." He stops and shuts his eyes. He is fighting to stay in control of the memories, his emotions.

She remembers Sally MacManus's statement that it was not a pot on the stove but Julianna who set the fire. But telling him this will involve a level of intimacy that she can't manage right now. So she says nothing.

"When someone ran into the bar to say the house was on fire, the first thing I did was look at the time," he continues. "And I remember thinking, it's OK, at least nobody's home, because Claudia should have been at day care, and Natalia would be picking her up. I knew Grzegor was at the high school, because I'd seen him heading down there on his bike that day, and Giovanni would be where he always was, at work. I ran over there, but when I turned into the street, one of the neighbors was yelling that my aunt, uncle, and Claudia were inside. I tried to get into the burning house, but I couldn't . . ." He covers his face with a hand and turns his head away.

She stares at the skaters without seeing them. She thinks of the neighbor's description, in the newspaper report, of him, soot-faced, dragged back, pinned down as he bellowed for his family. The inside of her mouth feels sandpapery.

"So, that fall, I went back to Philly, Grzegor moved in with my mother, and you know the rest. We were all broken, in different ways."

She feels the pain radiating from him, and for a moment the numbness goes, and she feels a rush of pity, and her impulse is to comfort him, but then she reminds herself what he has done—all the lies he has told her, the sheer, brazen lie of him. A gust of wind blows up across the Common, slicing through her wool coat, right to her skin. Her body gives a sudden, violent shiver.

"You're cold."

She ignores him. "So in Philadelphia you met Sarah Banister."

He nods.

"Did you give her drugs to make her miscarry your baby?"

"You know I didn't, Tess."

"I don't know anything about you!" Her teeth are chattering now.

"You do. You know that much," he says gently. Then he adds, "You're freezing. Shall we go get a cup of coffee?"

She cannot be inside a café with him; she cannot sit across a table from him. He seems to understand this, too. "There's a stand, right there—look." He points to a hatch by the skate rental. "A hot drink will warm you up."

She hugs herself, and they walk, side by side, toward the counter. All around them people in woolen hats and gloves are queuing for skates—some sit and fumble with laces, calling out to one another, laughing. A woman with long blond hair teeters across the rubber matting on blades, making Tess think of the mermaid in the fairy tale, walking on knives to be with her love.

Greg comes back with a couple of coffees. As he hands one to her, she looks at his familiar fingers around the cup and realizes they will never touch her body again; he is no longer her love. He is separate now, moving away from her, sliding out of reach. The realization is like a fist hitting her sternum—for a moment she struggles even to take a breath.

They carry the steaming cups back to the same spot by the railing.

"So Sarah made up the accusations?"

"It's exactly how I told you."

"No, it's not—not exactly—because it was you on trial, not your cousin." She spits the words out.

He nods. "I know. If I ever let myself think about the lie I was living, even for a second, I feel as if I'm drowning. I can't explain to you how I was able to do this—I guess I just shut off so completely from my old self that it didn't feel like a lie anymore. I certainly don't feel like that person. I feel like he's gone. I just feel like me."

She watches a tiny child zip between the adults, smaller, faster, and more fearless than anyone else on the ice.

"What happened to Grzegor? Where did he go?" She isn't sure she wants to know the answer to this, but she has to hear it anyway.

He takes a sip of his coffee. His face is set, the tip of his nose is red, but his skin is as pale and gray as the ice.

"He was meant to start Harvard that fall. He'd rented a studio in South Boston for the summer and found himself a summer job in a gay nightclub. After the trial, when I dropped out of med school, I went there to see him. I hadn't seen him in a year, and I was shocked at the sight of him. He'd lost a lot of weight, and he looked really unwell. His place was squalid; there were empty bottles everywhere. I tried to clean it up, and I put him to bed. There was no food in the place, so I went out to the store, and when I got back, about an hour later, he was gone." He is staring straight ahead, but even without looking into his eyes she can feel that this is the truth.

"So he just never came back?"

He gives a brief nod. "He took fifty dollars. I saw, later, when I got his bank statements, that he'd been to the ATM earlier that day. I think maybe he planned to see me one last time, then go. I looked for him everywhere, I asked anyone I could find, but no one had seen him."

"Didn't you report him missing?"

"No, I didn't. I did go to the police, but when I was waiting to file the missing-persons report, I realized that the second they typed my name into their computer, it would all get complicated. I can't begin to describe to you the level of mistrust I had for the police at that point in my life." He turns to look at her, and his eyes are haunted. "During the trial they treated me with . . . there's no such thing as innocent until proven guilty, Tess, that's for sure. So I walked out of there. I didn't report him missing."

"OK, but how—how the hell—did you get from that . . . to this?"

He takes another sip of the coffee. He looks older, suddenly, grayer—the lines around his eyes and mouth deeper, his eyes shrunken in their sockets. She realizes then that he is, in fact, three years older than he told her he was. He is fifty already. She does not even know his birthday.

She feels a wave of dizziness, the vertigo again, but he is talking. "The day he was due to register at Harvard," he says, "I still believed he was coming back, and I decided I couldn't just sit there and let him throw the scholarship away. It occurred to me that nobody at Harvard really knew him, and I looked enough like him that anyone who saw him at an interview would recognize me as him. All his photos looked like me, too. So I went along and matriculated for him. I thought I'd get all the information, so when he came back, he'd slot right in. I know it sounds crazy, but at the time I honestly thought I was doing the right thing."

"How could that possibly be the right thing?" Her hand is shaking so much that she has to bend down and put the coffee on the ground.

"I think my rationale was that I couldn't let his life be ruined, too. I felt responsible for everything bad that had happened to him. I *was* responsible for it. I couldn't save my mother. I couldn't save Claudia or Giovanni or Natalia. But maybe I could save him."

"Even if it meant doing something criminal?"

"I didn't think about it like that, not at that point. I just packed up his studio, moved into his dorm, got a haircut, wrote his signature on everything. I was basically holding his life open for him, and I had to work senselessly hard to get it right. He got a perfect MCAT score—he was already famous for that—and the pressure to live up to him was huge. But by pushing myself to my absolute limits, I realized, for the first time in my life, what I was capable of."

"You liked being him."

"No, I didn't like anything. I just worked. I called myself Greg, and I worked harder than I'd ever worked at anything, ever."

"And at what point did you realize he wasn't coming back?"

"I don't know. After a year, maybe? On a gut level, I probably knew far sooner, but it took me a while to accept it, and even then, for years after he went, I'd see his face in the street, you know—I'd catch a glimpse of him in the market or going down the escalator into the subway, and I'd run after him and tap him on the shoulder, and he'd turn and . . ." His face grows even more sunken-looking.

"So you think he did kill himself?"

He nods. "I'm sure of it. It was an act of kindness to do it that way. I think he wanted to die, but he knew what I'd been through already and didn't want me to have to deal with that, on top of everything. He wanted to protect me from having to find his body and hold a funeral and mourn and bury him. He was the kindest, sweetest person, Tess. You'd have loved him. I loved him."

"Do you think he knew what you'd do?"

He shrugs. "I've asked myself that a lot, and I'll never know, but sometimes I think he knew me better than I knew myself."

"So you just stayed? You just carried on the lie?"

"I graduated top of the class," he says. "They were throwing money at me. For the first time in my life I felt I had a future."

She looks at the rink again. Some people waddle, toeing the ice cautiously; some cling to the fence, afraid to let go, while others push out, alone, too fast, then crash down.

"But you could have turned yourself in."

"I could have, but I didn't want to go to jail. It was that simple. So I shut down my old self, and I focused on being the best doctor I could possibly be. It might sound inflated, but I also wanted to do some good in the world."

"But then you met me. You weren't 'doing good' to me or to Joe—and to Lily? Would you have lied to Lily forever about who she is? Because this isn't just your identity anymore—it's hers, too. Your daughter might not ever have known her real name. How could you do that to her?"

He rubs a hand through his hair. "This is the reason I was so afraid of being a father. I came so close to telling you, that time when you were pressing me about not wanting to have a baby. I almost just told you, but it seemed like such a terrible thing to do to you—you were pregnant, you'd abandoned a whole life to be with me, you'd trusted me. And I was too much of a coward. I knew you'd walk away if you knew the truth; my God, who wouldn't? I kept telling myself I'd find a way to tell you when the time was right."

"My God." She closes her eyes, needing to shut him out.

"I love you. I never wanted to lie to you. If you hadn't gotten pregnant, I would have told you. I was fully intending to. I was trying to work out how to do it—I mean, it's not the sort of thing you can blurt out on a first date—but then out of the blue you were pregnant, and that changed everything. I felt like it would ruin your life if I told you."

"Do you have any idea how warped that is?"

"I know it is. But I couldn't imagine living my life without you. I couldn't lose you."

"Well, you have. You've lost me. We can't be together now. How could this possibly work? It can't—it can't ever work." Her voice shakes, and she feels a physical pain spreading through her chest, as if her ribs are cracking open.

He turns to face her.

"All I can tell you is, I've lived this way for so long now, it doesn't feel like a lie anymore. It feels like the truth. This is who I am now." He rests his hand flat on his chest. "This is just me."

"But it's not just you! It's you and me and Lily and Joe—and it's all built on a monumental lie."

"But the important bit is true—I love you. When I met you, that very first time, when you came to take my picture, I knew right away that this was going to be bigger than anything I'd felt for anyone. My first impulse was to walk away. But, instead, I got into my car, and I drove down to see you in your studio. I couldn't walk away from you then, and I can't now."

She shakes her head. "But I can." She steps back. "I can walk away from you. I have to."

She turns, hunches her body against the bitter air, and walks, head down, fast, away from him, back across Boston Common, that frozen, windswept patch of land hemmed in by skyscrapers. And with every step her harsh breaths echo around her head, and she understands that something inside her has ruptured and will never heal.

EPILOGUE

The French doors are open to the overgrown back garden. It has been a fine June day, and the sun is easing behind the Downs, bathing the slopes in deep golden light, making the trees glow as if they have been dipped in honey.

Joe and the twins are wrestling on the trampoline, yelping, and Lily is on a rug at their feet. She is wearing striped tights and a knitted sweater, surrounded by cushions, gnawing on a rice cake. Her dark hair curls around her face, and her eyes are huge, wide and curious, a deep Italian brown, like her father's. She has just learned to sit up, and her solid body wobbles as she turns her head, as if the weight of it might be prove too much for her tender spine.

Tess pours them both a glass of wine, and they stretch out their legs.

"God, I'm glad you're back," Nell says. "I used to go 'round the long way, so I wouldn't see the Dutch people coming out of this house."

"I felt bad turning them out; they were expecting at least two years here."

"I know, but it's your house. You bought it; you earned every brick in this place. They're fine, anyway. Apparently they're buying a place just up the road, so you'll be neighbors. You can all be friends."

"I think I've had enough friendly neighbors to last me a lifetime."

They both gulp their wine, and Tess glances behind her, into the kitchen. Joe's pictures are back on the fridge, the cupboard door still needs fixing, a Dutch child has crayoned on the side of one cabinet, there are the remains of fish sticks and beans all over the counter, and the smell of a baking chocolate cake wafts through the air. The floor needs a good cleaning. It has never felt more like home.

"So, when are you going to see him again?" Nell puts her glass down.

"He's coming to London for a conference next month."

There is a pause. They look at each other, both struck, yet again, by the awfulness of what has happened.

"How can you bear it, Tess? You must be so angry all the time."

She looks down at Lily and then out at the hills. "I was, at first," she says. "In those horrible weeks after I found out, I felt so much rage—I almost turned him in."

"I know you did."

"I actually stood on the doorstep of the local police department, with Lily in the sling, but I couldn't do it."

"That was the right decision. I mean, what would it have achieved?"

They have had this conversation many times before, but they keep on having it, in different forms, because neither of them can quite get a grip on the implications, the enormity of his deceit.

"Well, I didn't hold back to protect him. I did it for Lily and Joe—and probably for myself, too. It could only harm us all if he went to jail."

"But do you feel like he's a criminal, really?"

"I know he must be, because he's stolen an identity, he's broken the law, but it's hard to really feel it, because, at the same time, he's Greg, and he hasn't harmed anyone; in fact, quite the opposite—he's saving children's lives all the time."

"He harmed you."

She looks up at the spreading pinks of the sky. "I think probably the good he does in the world outweighs that, in the grand scheme of things."

Nell shakes her head and picks up her wine again. "Well, I couldn't be that magnanimous if it was me he'd done this to."

Lily squawks. They both look down at her, and she looks back at them and gives a messy grin. Tess slides off the chair and bends to pick her up, feeling the solid, reassuring weight of her. Lily's small hands cling around her neck, and her sticky face presses against her cheek. Tess kisses the stickiness and settles Lily on her lap, wiping her face with one shirt cuff. This is Greg's punishment. This is what he is missing out on—the daily closeness with Lily and Joe, these small moments of pure, physical love. He must remember Claudia every time he holds Lily, not least because Lily looks so much like her aunt. He knows what he is missing. It must be torture for him.

She thinks about him as a teenage boy, desperately trying to hold his precarious little family together, waking in the night to feed and change his baby sister, trying to protect her and his mother, struggling to keep them all together but ultimately failing. When she thinks about Greg's past this way, she aches for the boy he was. It explains why, later, he did what he did. It also explains the connection she felt to the hurt part of him and why she recognized it, instantly and intuitively: they both know what it is like to be raised by a mother who could not be saved.

"I get why you didn't turn him in." Nell interrupts her thoughts. "But it's quite odd that Alex Kingman didn't go to the police, isn't it?"

She stiffens. She still does not like thinking about Alex. "Oh, I expect he did."

"Do you? Why?"

"Well, he would, wouldn't he? I mean, he needed to feel he wasn't simply a victim. He needed validation for all those memories, and he needed to feel he was pinning something down, making someone pay. But I'd imagine the police were faced with a man in a midlife crisis, making wild and ancient accusations about an eminent Harvard pediatric heart surgeon, and even if they got as far as checking up on Greg, they'd find this godlike being, with glowing references and a solid paper trail. I mean, on paper, Greg's exactly who he says he is. They'd believe him, every time."

"Who wouldn't?"

They look at each other and exchange a weak smile.

"What he did"—Tess strokes Lily's hair back off her forehead—"was catastrophically misguided, but I don't actually want him to suffer anymore. I think he's suffered enough."

"Has he?" Nell says, smiling at Lily. She pulls out a tissue and reaches across the table to wipe Lily's mouth again. "Has he, really?"

"I think he's been suffering his whole life. His career has been an attempt to make amends. He might have eventually coped with losing his aunt and uncle, but he could never get over Claudia being in the house."

"Did you ever tell him about Sally MacManus's email? I mean, does he even know that Julianna probably started the fire, so it wasn't his fault?"

Tess nods.

"How did he react? It must have been huge for him. He's blamed himself for Claudia's death for over thirty years."

"I don't know what he felt. I wasn't going to talk to him about it. I just forwarded all Sally's emails to him. But, to be honest, I don't know how helpful that will be. I'm not sure if it's any better to know that your own mother was to blame."

The boys are running up the lawn toward them. She sees Joe's bright face between the twins, relaxed and happy again, back where he belongs. He was never going to settle in Boston, because their home there was built on cracked foundations; it was all wrong. And perhaps he was picking up on that, though, of course, he could never have articulated it that way.

"We're going to do Xbox," he yells as the boys run past, shoving each other to get through the French doors, their feet slapping on the kitchen floor and down the hall. Lily watches them go, eyes popping, then shouts, "Dah! Dah!" She waves her arms, lurching to follow.

There is birdsong and the distant hollering of the boys. Lily wobbles and wriggles, desperate to join them. To distract her, Tess blows into her neck, making her chuckle crazily.

"Do you think you'll ever be able to forgive him?" Nell asks.

"Oh, God, I don't know." She reaches out for her wine, takes another mouthful, and closes her eyes. "But Lily needs him. We've agreed that when she's old enough, he'll tell her the truth, so she can make up her own mind about what he did. I just hope it won't shake her sense of who she is. That's why I went through all that business of changing her name. Lily needs to be a Harding."

As she says this, she suddenly understands why Julianna replaced her children's birth surname with her own. There is a power in naming, something men have always known. Giovanni could take Claudia physically, but she was still a Novak, still Julianna's child. She might never know the truth about Julianna; that probably died with Sally. She might never know whether Julianna was the victim of a terrible injustice or whether she really was unable to mother her children. All she knows for sure is that Julianna was a woman who married the wrong man and lived in the wrong place but had a friend who loved her and cared.

She and Nell sit in silence, watching shadows lengthen and deepen over the Downs as the sun sinks.

"You'll meet someone else one day," Nell says eventually.

"I don't want to meet anyone else. I only wanted Greg. I don't want anyone else."

"Then maybe there's a chance that you two will somehow get past this . . . I mean, maybe you'll find some way to move on, one day, and make it work?"

"We could never do that."

"But—"

"I'll always love him, but I'll never trust him again."

"Oh, God, I wish I could make this better for you."

"It's better already. Waiting for Lily's passport was the worst bit, but I already feel stronger just being back in my own house again. We're doing OK, the three of us. David's being nice, and I'll pick up work again, and Greg at least is good about money. I mean, I know it's not going to be easy, but I want it this way. My plan is to keep my life extremely simple from now on."

"You'll be OK."

"I'll be more than OK. This is *me*. I actually like being on my own. I always have."

Their eyes meet over Lily's head, and in the kitchen behind them the timer begins to ping, a high, frantic, urgent sound.

"It's a sign!" Nell says.

"Of what?"

"I don't know. That it's time for chocolate cake?"

They stand up. Nell goes in to deal with the cake, and Tess rests her face on Lily's fat cheek for a second. She is deep-down tired; a part of her is wrecked and maybe always will be, but she can feel her own resilience forming itself around this new, damaged area, containing it, sealing it off. She closes her eyes and breathes in Lily's sweet baby smell. Then she steps back into her house.

ACKNOWLEDGMENTS

I am so grateful to my inspired editor Stef Bierwerth, to Kathryn Taussig, Hannah Robinson and all the fantastic Quercus team, and to Judith Murray who made this possible in the first place—I know how lucky I am. I am also enormously grateful to Dr. Nick Haining, my dear friend, whose patience, time and expertise on transatlantic pediatrics improved this book enormously (the remaining errors are all mine). A huge thank you to Dr. Brenda Kelly for gynecological and neonatal expertise, Professor Robin Choudhury and Dr. Audrey Marshall for cardiology specifics; Dr. Michael Dilorio and Dr. Hadine Joffe for Harvard insider tips; Robert 'Birdy' Ellison for your brilliant legal eye and Carolyn Djanogly for a wonderful insight into the photographer's life—all of you have far more pressing things to do, and I so appreciate the time you took to help me out. Likewise, thank you Anita Vadgama Roberts, Dr. Louise Hoult, Lori Knowles and Chris Kjellson for answering far too many of my questions, and Leanne Kelly for being such helpful early reader. Thank you to my family: Sue and Peter Atkins, Paul Atkins, Claire Jones, Jenny Atkins and my Izzie, Sam and Ted Shaw, for all your enthusiasm and support. And as always, best of all, thank you John.

ABOUT THE TYPE

Typeset in Dante MT at 11.5 / 15 pt.

The result of collaboration between typeface artist Giovanni Mardersteig and punch-cutter Charles Malin, the Dante fonts were originally developed as hand-set punches in 1955. The fact that Dante was so easily recreated in machine-set and then digital versions is a testament to its designers' skill.

Typeset by Scribe Inc., Philadelphia, Pennsylvania.